Cracked Sapphire

JANE BLYTHE

Acknowledgments

I'd like to thank everyone who played a part in bringing this story to life. Particularly my mom who is always there to share her thoughts and opinions with me. My wonderful cover designer Amy who did an amazing job with this stunning cover. My fabulous editor Lisa for all the hard work she puts into polishing my work. My awesome team, Sophie, Robyn, and Clayr, without your help I'd never be able to run my street team. And my fantastic street team members who help share my books with every share, comment, and like!

And of course a big thank you to all of you, my readers! Without you I wouldn't be living my dreams of sharing the stories in my head with the world!

CHAPTER One

July 28th
2:10 A.M.

She was cold.

Shivering.

Eventually, it pulled her from sleep, and sixteen-year-old Sapphire Hatcher, blinked her eyes open. Stifling a yawn, she turned to glance at the glowing clock radio on the small nightstand beside her bed. It was a little after two; that meant she had another four hours left of sleep before she had to get up and get ready for school.

No.

Wait.

It was summer vacation; that meant she got to sleep as late as she wanted.

With a smile she reached over the side of the bed to grab her quilt. It was a hot night, but she was a cold sleeper. That worked for her favor in summer, but not so much on those freezing cold winter nights.

"Saph?" a sleepy voice asked, and her little sister lifted a head from her pillow in the bed on the other side of the nightstand.

"Just grabbing my quilt," she whispered. "Go back to sleep, Emmy."

"You're always cold," her sister murmured, already rolling over and kicking her sheet down to the bottom of her bed.

Too tired to argue, Sapphire spread the quilt over her bed, and snuggled down into her mattress. She was glad that her parents couldn't afford AC for the whole house, or she would be too cold and never be able to sleep in the summer.

She was just drifting back to sleep when she heard footsteps and muffled voices in the hall. Sapphire didn't pay it much attention. Besides her little sister, she had three older sisters, as well as her parents, who all lived here. More often than not, someone was up and about and doing something.

Pulling the blankets up to her chin, she sighed contentedly, then her head snapped up as the bedroom door was flung open hard enough to send it crashing into the wall.

"Dad?" Sapphire asked as she sat up, expecting to see her father standing there, probably in a rage after losing big playing poker or blackjack or whatever game he and his gambling buddies had been playing tonight.

But it wasn't her father standing in the doorway.

It was a man.

No, two men.

There were two men storming into her bedroom.

With guns. Sapphire had never seen a gun before. She hated them; she knew how dangerous they were.

Like they were on a mission, the men stalked across the carpet toward the beds.

Her little sister had also sat up at the sound of the door bursting open and slamming into the wall. Emerald sat frozen in place, staring at the men, her green eyes wide with horror, her mouth hanging open and releasing a quiet keening sound.

Without thinking, Sapphire threw back her covers and jumped out of her bed, running to her little sister's and putting herself between Emerald and the men.

She had no idea how that would help, but she didn't want these men touching her sister.

Screams sounded from another room.

Followed promptly by the sounds of a struggle.

What was going on?

Were there more men here?

Who were they?

What did they want?

Where were her parents?

What was happening to her older sisters?

"Come here, kid," one of the men said, making a grab for her.

Sapphire wrapped a hand around Emerald's shoulder and dragged her along as she darted toward the window. From the screams, she knew that something was going on in another room. Getting out through the bedroom door was probably pointless, but maybe they could jump out the window before the men got to them. Her sister was a hot sleeper and insisted their bedroom window remain open from April through October, so all they'd have to do was jump. They'd most likely survive the fall from the second floor without any broken bones, then they could run and hopefully get help before these men hurt her sisters and parents.

Unfortunately, things never got that far.

The men were quicker than she was, especially since she had to drag Emerald along with her, and they intercepted her at the window as she was shoving the curtains out of the way.

"Don't make me angry, kid," the same man who'd spoken before said as he reached for her. "You won't like the consequences."

The other man ripped Emerald from her arms. Her sister was clearly in shock as she did nothing but hang limply in his grip.

She, on the other hand, was more angry than scared right now.

That probably wouldn't last, but she had to take advantage of it while it did.

When the man reached for her, she swung a fist, connecting with his shoulder, inflicting little damage, but it distracted the man enough that he wasn't ready for her ramming her knee into his groin.

A satisfied smirk curled her lips up as the man grunted in pain. He might be bigger and stronger than her, but that didn't mean that he automatically got to win.

Aiming her next attack at his neck, she slammed her palm into it, and was again rewarded with a sharp gasp.

She won again.

Not wanting to push her luck, she lunged for the window. She hated leaving her sisters and parents behind, but she couldn't stop these men. They needed help. She'd jump, run to one of the neighbors, and ask them to call the cops.

"I don't think so," the man said as he grabbed her and yanked her back inside just as she had swung one leg over the windowsill. "What did I say about making me angry?"

Right now, she didn't care about making him angry.

All she cared about was getting out of here alive.

As she was dragged farther into the bedroom, she fought with everything she had. She alternated between swinging her fists and clawing with her nails at the arm that restrained her. She kicked her feet and threw her head back, hoping she could get him in the nose, get him to let go of her so she could take another go at getting out the window. She'd be faster this time; she just needed one more try.

"You gonna help me or what?"

"I got my girl under control," the other man said with a laugh.

Sapphire watched as the other man threw Emerald to the floor then came toward them. She fought as hard as she could, but the two men were too strong, and between them, they were able to yank her arms behind her back and tie her wrists together. Then she was shoved down onto Emerald's bed and held in place with a knee on her stomach and large hands on her shoulders.

The man she'd attacked was breathing hard, but now that he knew he had her under his control, a slow smile lit his face. "You're going to regret that little stunt, kid."

Although her mind screamed at her not to say anything, to not antagonize him further, her mouth didn't seem to get the message. "You won't get away with this. I'll never stop trying to get away, and I will. Then I'm going to call the police, and they're going to throw you in prison."

The man just laughed. "Open wide," he said as he held up a balled-up piece of material and duct tape.

Again, she knew it would anger him, but she couldn't stop herself from clamping her lips together. Sapphire knew she was making things worse for herself, but she couldn't seem to help it.

Undeterred by her refusal to open her mouth, the man simply put his thumb on one of her cheeks, his fingers on the other and squeezed until he forced her mouth open. Then he shoved the material in her mouth and wrapped duct tape around her head, holding it in place.

Gagged and restrained, Sapphire felt her bravado begin to waver. The anger that had consumed her just moments ago was fading, and in its place was fear. A kind of fear she'd never felt before. It burrowed down deep inside her, took hold, and then grew, spreading its tentacles throughout her body. She knew that soon it would consume her and she would be unable to do anything but whimper and cower as Emerald was doing.

The man hoisted her over his shoulder, while the other man grabbed Emerald and brought them both downstairs, lining them up beside Diamond, their oldest sister, and twins, Ruby and Amethyst. They were all gagged, with their hands tied behind their backs just like she was. All of them looked as terrified as she felt, and all but Amethyst were crying.

Her parents were there, too. But unlike her sisters, they weren't restrained.

Confused, she looked from the men—there were another three in addition to the two who had been in her and Emerald's room—to her parents who were sitting side by side on one of the sofas in the living room.

"See, just like we told you, they're all beautiful girls," her father said to another man, one she hadn't noticed who was sitting on the other sofa.

"They are," the man agreed. "Very beautiful. And they are all teenagers, yes?"

"Yes," her father nodded eagerly. "The oldest is eighteen, the youngest fifteen."

"They are all virgins?"

"Yes," her father answered, a little less confidently this time.

"You don't sound sure," the man on the sofa said. He turned to the other men who were standing around. "Check."

Check?

What did that mean?

She was still a virgin. She had a boyfriend, and they kissed and made out; he liked to touch her breasts, and sometimes she would give him hand jobs, but that was it. He'd never even touched her down there. She was only sixteen, and while other girls her age might be ready for sex, she wasn't.

"Start with her," the man from her room said with a nod of his head in her direction.

Two men grabbed her by the shoulders and she was dragged to her feet. The man pushed her nightgown up around her hips, then her panties down around her knees. Roughly, he spread her legs and shoved a finger inside her. She flinched at the intrusion and the shaft of pain and tied to pull away.

Her sisters were all crying out, but her parents were doing nothing.

Nothing.

Not a thing to stop these men from touching her.

What was happening?

She didn't understand.

"This one is definitely a virgin," the man said, pulling his finger out of her. Then he leaned in and whispered in her ear, "Although I'd be happy to change that."

She was released and dropped to her knees, shivering and crying, while the men proceeded to check each of her sisters in the same manner.

"This one is a little loose," the man announced when he got to Ruby.

That was ridiculous; she knew none of her sisters were having sex. Why did any of this even matter? Sapphire wished she knew what was going on, and yet, at the same time, she dreaded finding out.

"She's a virgin, I swear," her father said.

"Since we can't be positive, you only get half of the money for that one," the man in the chair said.

"But full price for the others?" her father asked.

Full price?

For her?

And her sisters?

It sounded like her parents were selling them to these men.

But that was ridiculous.

People didn't sell other people. They weren't property to be sold.

And yet ...

She'd heard of human trafficking.

That wasn't what was happening here though.

It couldn't be.

Why would her parents sell her and her sisters?

They would have no reason to.

Except ...

Her dad gambled a lot, and her mom was addicted to shopping. They argued about money all the time. She was sixteen, not six; she knew that they were in debt. *Deep* in debt. But not deep enough to do this.

"Fifty thousand for the four girls we believe to be virgins, twenty-five for the other. We'll transfer the money into your account now, and as soon as you verify that it's there, the girls become our property. If you want them back, you'll have to pay a lot more than what you got for them. You have no say over what we do with them or who we sell them to. They cease to belong to you and become the sole property of me, until I sell them on. You won't be updated on what happens to them, and you will not attempt to make any further contact with me or anyone else from my enterprise."

Property.

They were talking about her and her sisters like they were property instead of people.

Her parents were selling them.

For a little under a quarter of a million dollars.

Selling her.

They were selling her.

Their own daughter.

To these monsters who were going to do who knew what to her and then sell her to someone else who would no doubt do worse.

This had to be a nightmare.

A horrible, terrifying nightmare.

But the dull throb between her legs said it wasn't.

This was her new reality.

∾

3:03 A.M.

"The money is in the account."

The glee in her father's voice as he said those words really hit home to Sapphire.

This was happening.

Really happening.

It wasn't a nightmare; it wasn't a hallucination; it wasn't a joke; it was reality. Her parents hadn't done this on a whim. They'd managed to track down people who dealt in human trafficking, make a deal with them, discussed money, told the people where they lived, and brought them here in the middle of the night. They'd sat by and watched while their daughters were dragged out of their beds and assaulted, doing nothing to stop it.

Maybe she didn't have the most loving parents in the world. They didn't spend much time doing family things, and they didn't go on many family vacations. Her parents didn't monitor her schoolwork or what she was doing when she went out with friends. But she had never, in her wildest dreams, thought they would do something like this.

"Then the deal is complete," the man who appeared to be in charge said as he stood. "The girls are ours now."

How was this even possible?

How could you just buy people?

She might be only sixteen, but that didn't mean she *belonged* to her parents. They had no right to do this.

Indignant anger wasn't going to help her right now. The man from her bedroom wrapped a hand around her neck and dragged her roughly to her feet.

"Careful," the man in charged snapped. "Don't damage the merchandise. I want to move these ones as quickly as we can; I don't want to have to wait for marks and bruises to fade."

The man muttered something under his breath, but removed his hand from her neck, and wrapped it around her right bicep instead.

It was so humiliating to be treated like this.

Merchandise.

That was all these men saw her as.

They didn't care about her; she was only as something that would make them money. Presumably a lot of money if they had just paid her parents fifty thousand dollars for each of them, except Ruby who they believed wasn't going to earn them as much. Sapphire had no idea if that made her sister's fate better or worse.

Part of her expected her parents to come to their senses.

To realize they couldn't sell their own children to sex traffickers.

To realize how wrong this was.

To realize they couldn't go through with it.

To put a stop to this before it was too late.

But they didn't even so much as look over while the men dragged her and her sisters through the house and out the door.

Outside, they were taken to a large van parked in the driveway. The back of the van was opened and she was shoved inside, a metal collar was clamped around her neck, a chain attached to the collar which was then clipped into a metal ring in the wall of the truck. The chain was short and only allowed her to sit with her back against the wall, her bound hands squashed in between.

Each of her sisters was restrained in the same manner. Diamond, Ruby, and Emerald were still crying, Amethyst growled through her gag at the man who restrained her, anger shooting from her blue eyes at all of their captors. The men didn't seem to care: this was just a job to them. They'd probably done this dozens of times before and would do it dozens of times in the future.

Sapphire didn't know what to do.

She just sat there, trying to comprehend the gravity of the situation, but her mind still couldn't get past her parents selling them.

Right now, she couldn't even allow herself to think more than a minute into the future, because never before had the future seemed so terrifying.

She didn't want to think about what was going to happen to them when they got to wherever they were going.

She definitely didn't want to think about what was going to happen to her after that.

Sapphire had to believe that there was a way to escape.

Or that the cops would come and rescue them.

That could happen.

Right?

As the truck door closed, they were plunged into darkness. Somehow, that made things seem so much worse. How could she fight what she couldn't see?

She could hear Ruby crying. Emerald was sitting right beside her, and she could feel her little sister's shaking.

The bottom may have fallen out of her world, and she may be so scared she could barely think straight, but she wasn't alone.

Her sisters were here, and they were going to need each other to survive this.

If they could stay strong, then there were five of them together against these men. While the men may still have the advantage, at least together they stood a chance. And a chance, no matter how slim, was something. Something she wasn't about to give up.

Since her hands weren't an option, Sapphire reached out with her legs and nudged Emerald. Her sister stilled.

"Mmhmmhmm," she mumbled through her gag. She wished she could talk. It would be so much easier for them to console and encourage one another if they could speak. How were they going to come up with a plan like this? Hopefully, when they got to wherever they were going, the men would take the gags off, and they could come up with a way out of here. For now, though, this was the best they could do.

Keeping one foot touching Emerald's leg, she reached out with her other leg until it made contact with whomever was sitting opposite her. She didn't know which of her older sisters it was, but she nudged them.

"Hmm mmm mhmm," she mumbled, trying to tell them that they had to stick together. They had to have hope.

What she was trying to communicate must have worked because within a minute she felt two more legs touch hers.

Together.

They were together in this.

Right now, they were all each other had.

Unable to talk, the five of them just sat there, feet touching, drawing whatever comfort they could from one another.

Sapphire loved her sisters; they were all close in age. Diamond was the oldest, and at eighteen she had already graduated high school and would be going off to college in the fall. Amethyst and Ruby were seventeen and would be seniors in the coming school year. She was sixteen, about to start her junior year, and Emerald was fifteen; she'd be a sophomore. They all fought a lot—like sisters do—arguing over clothes and makeup and time spent in the bathroom. While they all had their separate lives—friends and boyfriends and hobbies—they were family, and they loved each other.

Every time she had bickered with them ran through her mind.

Regrets.

She was only sixteen, and yet, she felt like she had a whole lifetime of regrets.

There were so many things that she would have done differently if she'd known that her life was going to end like this.

No.

Stop it, she reprimanded herself.

Her life wasn't over. She was still alive and so were her sisters. As long as they were breathing, she wasn't going to give up hope.

She couldn't.

She wouldn't allow herself to.

The truck stopped moving, the engine turned off, and any courage she'd been mustering, vanished.

This was it.

She was about to find out what the rest of her life looked like.

Her eyes squinted when the truck was opened and bright light flooded inside. Part of her wanted to close them, block it all out, pretend she was three years old again, and the scary things in the world could disappear if you just closed your eyes.

We're together.

Sapphire just had to keep reminding herself of that; she wasn't alone in this. Her sisters were right here with her, and while she was a little embarrassed to admit it, she was glad they were here. Being alone would have made this so much worse.

Without preamble, the men climbed into the back of the van, unclipped the chains from the hooks in the wall and dragged them out. Sapphire stumbled as she was climbing down, thudding painfully onto her knees. The man from her bedroom yanked her right back up—hard —and she knew that if he hadn't been ordered not to leave a mark on her, the man would have beaten her already. She knew he wanted to. She could feel it. He wanted to punish her for hitting him.

As she was pulled forward, she saw the huge house before them. She didn't know what she had been expecting, but it wasn't this. The house was gorgeous, made of stone, with vines spread out across at least half of the front. It looked like some fancy hotel, and for a moment, she wondered if this was all just some big joke. Like, at any second now, her parents were going to come running outside laughing, and telling them that their dad had won big, and they were going to be staying here at this gorgeous hotel for summer vacation.

But that wasn't what happened.

"Put the blonde ones in the east wing, and the brunettes in the west," the man in charge ordered. "The oldest goes up to the north end with the other eighteen and overs; put the other two in separate rooms. I want that one ..." He pointed at her. "... prepped immediately. I have a buyer I think will be interested in her."

His word was obviously law around here because the men followed his directions without hesitation.

Just like that, no discussion, no chance for them to say goodbye, they were split up.

Sapphire struggled against the grip of the man dragging her away from her sisters. She didn't want to leave them; she didn't want to be on her own.

Alone, she wouldn't survive this ordeal.

Alone, she was going to crumble under the weight of the terror that was living inside her.

Alone, she was going to die.

CHAPTER *Two*

July 29th
4:38 P.M.

She felt groggy.

Confused.

Not altogether sure where she was, what was going on, or to be honest, who she was.

Instinct told her that she should stay buried deep inside this little cocoon of oblivion, but even though darkness lapped at the edges of her mind, anxious to pull her under once again, now that she was conscious, she couldn't go back.

The events of the last couple of days played through her mind like a movie. The men in her bedroom, finding out her parents were selling her, being gagged and restrained and thrown in the back of a truck, driven to a huge mansion, ripped away from her sisters without the chance to even say goodbye.

Sapphire didn't know if she was ever going to see them again.

She didn't know if she was ever going to go back to her old life.

She didn't even know how long she would *have* a life.

After being split up, she'd been taken inside the mansion and put inside a room that had been sparsely, but nicely, furnished. The gag had been removed, as had the tape binding her wrists together behind her back. The metal collar was left on, but the chain had been replaced with a longer one that had been hooked into a ring embedded in the wall farthest from the door. The chain had allowed her to roam the whole room, including the attached bathroom.

At first, she had stubbornly refused to use the bathroom, as though by doing so she was accepting her fate. But, in the end, the need to pee had overridden her pride, and she had used the toilet and taken a shower. Then since the only other furniture in the room was a chest of drawers, two nightstands, and a bed, she had taken refuge on the bed. Sapphire hadn't expected to sleep—she was too scared, too angry, in too much shock, but her exhausted body and mind had had other plans.

She had only woken when someone had jabbed a needle into her arm.

Then she'd promptly passed back out.

Until now.

Heart thundering in her chest, Sapphire drew in a deep breath and then counted backward from ten. On one she made herself open her eyes.

What she found was not what she'd been expecting.

She was lying on a bed of straw. There were chest-high wooden walls on either side of her, and a waist-high door about ten feet from where she lay.

She was in a barn.

Specifically, in a stall in a barn.

Like an animal.

Immediately, she scampered up onto her backside and shuffled backward until her back hit the fourth wall.

Her hands went to the metal collar on her neck. She yanked at it as hard as she could, trying to dislodge it. Her mind told her that it was pointless; the thing wasn't coming off, but she wanted out of here.

Now.

She wanted to go home.

No.

Not home.

She never wanted to go back to that place again.

But she did want to get as far away from this barn as it was humanly possible to get.

"The collar doesn't come off."

Sapphire started at the sound, shifting to her knees, ready to bolt away from this newest danger.

"It's okay; it's just me. I'm not one of them."

She looked at the girl who stood in the stall beside hers. The girl looked about her age, with shoulder length blonde hair and brown eyes. Just like herself, the girl had a metal collar around her neck with a chain running from it to a ring in the wall. Sapphire's hands found the chain attached to her own metal collar and ran it along them until she touched the metal ring in the wall. The men who had her were clearly taking no chances. They weren't going to let her just escape and get away. No doubt they had a large sum of money riding on selling her to just the right perverted but wealthy monster.

"I'm Tasha. Who are you?" the girl asked.

She opened her mouth to answer but no sound came out. The fog that had covered her when she first woke up was mostly cleared away now, and the starkness of her new reality was quickly sinking in. Swallowing hard, she whispered, "Sapphire. What is this place?"

"A holding pen," Tasha answered.

"For who?"

"For us." Tasha waved her arm, and Sapphire staggered to her feet, took a tentative step forward, and finally took in the rest of her surroundings.

The barn was large. There were eight stalls to her left, and another six to her right. A long walkway ran from one end to the other, and on the other side, there were fifteen more stalls.

Every single stall had a girl around her age in it.

Every.

Single.

Stall.

Twenty-nine other girls were here too.

What had happened to them? Had they been sold like she had?

"Tasha?"

"Yeah?"

"How did you get here?"

"I was a runaway. Dad was an alcoholic, beat my mom when he was drunk, then turned his attentions on me. I ran, was on the streets for a couple of weeks, then I met someone who I thought was a youth pastor at a local church. He offered to help me find a safe place to stay. I believed him. He lied. He wasn't a pastor; he worked for a human trafficking ring. He tied me up, took me to this shipping container, left me inside there for days. And then he brought me here."

"How long have you been here?"

Tasha shrugged. "A couple of days."

"Why are we here?" She didn't understand the point of this. She had thought the men who took her were going to sell her to someone else. Was that person the one who'd brought her here? If it was, why was he keeping them in a barn? Did he have some kind of weird fetish?

"For the hunt," Tasha replied.

"The hunt?"

Tasha just nodded.

"What is *the hunt*?"

Tasha didn't answer.

She looked around at the other girls. They'd all been here longer than she had and obviously knew what was going on, but she had no idea. They had to tell her. She had to know how bad this was. Obviously it was bad, but she wanted details. Knowing what to expect was the only thing that was going to ease the pressure in her chest enough that she could breathe normally.

No one answered her.

Several of the girls were crying; a couple were curled up in balls in their stalls. The feeling of fear and despair was heavy in the room. It was like a presence all of its own. It seeped inside her, infecting her like a virus. The symptoms were immediate: her breathing accelerated, her hands were sweaty, tears began to trickle down her cheeks, and she began to shake like she had just been shoved inside a freezer.

Why was this happening to her?

Okay, so she wasn't perfect. She didn't always listen to her parents; she fought with her sisters; she didn't always do her best in school because talking with her friends was so much more fun than listening to teachers drone on and on about things that didn't interest her. Sometimes she was mean to her boyfriend, not because she didn't love him, because she did, but because sometimes her emotions just got the best of her. Sometimes she wasn't even that nice to her friends, again not because she didn't adore them, but because she was a sixteen-year-old girl, and sometimes teenagers weren't the most rational people on the planet.

But none of the things she had done—not even kissing one of her best friend's ex-boyfriends just hours after they broke up—meant she deserved this.

She had been sold and brought here against her will; she was supposedly going to be forced to participate in some sort of hunt, and none of it was fair.

Sapphire wanted to scream and sob and stomp her feet and shout about the unfairness of it all, but that was pointless. It wasn't going to achieve her goal. And right now, her only goal was getting out of here before this hunt thing.

"Why haven't you tried to escape?" she asked Tasha.

Tasha nodded down to the end of the barn, and Sapphire looked through the partially open doors to see two men with machine guns standing guard. She looked down the other end and saw it was similarly manned.

Like a yo-yo, once again, the tiny bit of hope that had been blooming inside her, disappeared.

"So, there's no way out of here," she whispered, dejectedly, sinking down to sit on the straw.

"There's no way out," Tasha said, her voice just as hopeless.

Then this was it.

If she couldn't find a way to escape, then somehow, she had to find the strength she needed to survive. She had to do whatever it took to keep herself alive for as long as she could. Her sisters were gone; it was just her, on her own.

Sapphire curled herself into a ball, her arms wrapped tight around her churning stomach. There was no one to help her, no one to turn to, no one to tell her everything was going to be okay even if they both knew it was a lie.

It was just her.

Just her.

The loneliness was almost as crushing as the terror.

Part of her wanted to go to sleep, block this out for as long as she could. The other part never wanted to sleep again because every time she slept, she woke up in a worse situation than she'd been in before.

She didn't want to know what was coming next.

CHAPTER *Three*

July 31st
7:02 P.M.

Sapphire was bored.

She hadn't thought it would be possible to be bored when she was this scared out of her mind, but she was.

For two days she had sat in her stall in the barn. She and the other girls were fed three times a day. "Fed" was a little misleading. She didn't receive a regular meal; she was fed some sort of vegetable slop served to her in a trough.

A trough.

As if anything could be more demeaning.

One of the men with the guns would come in and pour some of the slop into the trough inside each of their stalls. She didn't have cutlery, so she had to either scoop it up with her hands or stick her face in and eat it that way.

It was so humiliating that if she wasn't so hungry, she wouldn't have touched it at all.

Her water situation wasn't any better. She had a bucket that was filled with a hose once a day. That had to last her until the following day, so she had to ration what she drank and what she used to clean herself after she did her business—which she had to do in a corner of the stall.

There was nothing else to do but sit.

And sit.

And wait.

For what, she still wasn't quite sure.

Sometimes she talked to Tasha or one of the other girls nearby, but most of the time they all just sat in their stalls, aimlessly staring at the ceiling or trying to nap. She had even used some of the straw to braid into a string that was as long as her stall.

Now she was just sitting.

It was exhausting waiting to enter hell.

She hadn't really slept—maybe dozed for a few minutes off and on —and at this point, she felt like a zombie. Sapphire wondered if she was ever going to feel normal again.

What would the rest of her life look like?

Was she going to be kept here indefinitely?

What would happen when the hunt started?

Where would she end up after the hunt?

Would it be better or worse than here?

When her parents had first sold her to the traffickers—which was only three days ago, but felt like a lifetime—being kept in a barn wasn't what she had been expecting.

So far, no one had laid a hand on her, other than drugging her and bringing her here. But she hadn't been raped. What was with that? She didn't want to be. The ball of dread in her stomach grew every time she thought about it, but isn't that why human traffickers sold people? For sex?

Is that why she was here?

Was this like a holding pen for girls before they were sold?

Just then, an icy sense of dread filled the barn.

Sapphire got to her feet, took a step forward, then froze in place.

A man was walking down the center of the barn. She hadn't seen him before. He wasn't one of the guards or one of the men who fed them. She didn't need to be told that he was the one in charge, but he wasn't the man who had been in charge back at her house.

Had she already been sold?

Is this where she was going to spend the rest of her life?

Sapphire's head was spinning from all the questions tumbling around inside it.

"The hunt is about to begin," the man announced, a huge smile on his face. He was kind of good-looking for an older guy, his eyes were a bright piercing blue, his skin was tanned, his dark hair was sprinkled with gray, and he was dressed in what looked like a very expensive suit.

She still wasn't entirely sure she understood what the hunt was. None of the other girls had been able to properly explain it to her beyond it being the reason they'd all been brought here.

"The rules of the hunt are simple." The man walked up and down the barn as he spoke. "You will remove your clothes. Your chain will be removed, and you will be taken outside where you'll be released into the woods with a ten-minute head start. When you hear the horn sound, the hunt has begun. There are thirty men waiting; each of them has paid a hundred thousand to be here tonight. Whoever catches you is your new owner. You will be brought back here to wait until the hunt is over, and after all of you have been found and caught, you will be taken to your new homes."

Sapphire just stared at the man.

What he just said was ludicrous.

She wasn't going to go running through the woods as prey for some sick, perverted monster to hunt.

As though anticipating that might be their response, the barn filled with the men holding machine guns.

Two options.

That was all she had.

She could do as the man had said—take off her clothes, be taken outside, and run until someone caught her. Or she could die right here and now.

Sapphire couldn't deny that she was tempted.

At least, if she was dead, it would be over.

She wouldn't have to be afraid, she would never be hurt again, and she would be at peace.

But ...

She couldn't do it.

It wasn't in her nature to just give up.

So, with shaking hands, Sapphire took off the nightgown she'd been wearing when she went to bed seventy-two hours ago, along with her panties, and dropped them on the straw. The other girls were doing the same. Some were sobbing; some were wailing; some were just staring vacantly into space, already sunk so far into shock, they could no longer function.

The men started moving from stall to stall, pointing a gun at the girl inside as another man walked in, unsnapped the chain from her collar, and led her outside.

Sapphire shifted her weight from one foot to the other as she waited her turn. There was so much nervous anticipation inside her as she wondered whether it was actually possible to outrun the men.

What if she could find a way out of the woods before she was caught?

That had to be possible, right?

Like, woods had edges. They didn't go on forever; she just had to find a road or a house and tell someone she needed help. Then the cops could come, and all of these girls could go home. She could tell them about her sisters, and they would rescue them, and they could just go back to their lives, and it would be like none of this had ever happened.

"Move to the back wall," a voice ordered her.

She complied without complaint, already preparing her body for the journey ahead. It wasn't going to be easy, but she liked to run, had even done cross-country for a while when she was in middle school.

A gun was trained on her head as the door to her stall opened and a man came in, undoing her chain then shoving her toward the door. Sapphire stumbled but started moving. They needn't have bothered with the gun; she wasn't going to cause them any trouble. She wanted her chance at escape and being shot didn't accomplish that.

Outside, the girls were hovering about, surrounded by the men with guns. She couldn't see the men who had supposedly paid big to be here tonight, but she didn't want to. She had to focus on her goal, not worry herself about those men and what would happen if one of them found her before she got to help.

Sapphire lost track of time, her entire focus was on what she was about to do.

She didn't notice anything else happening around her as she surveyed the woods. They looked dense. It would be hard to run through them, but if the men were going to hunt them, then there had to be space for them to ride horses or motorcycles or whatever they were going to use to give themselves the upper hand.

All of a sudden, a shrill whistle sounded. Taking it as her cue, Sapphire ran.

And ran.

And ran.

Twigs and branches tore at her bare skin and tried to ensnare themselves in her hair. Rocks and tree roots littered the ground; her bare feet soon grew numb from kicking into them and stomping over them.

Nothing was going to stop her.

The occasional scream pierced the night, but she did her best to ignore them. She couldn't think of those girls and their fate at the moment. She couldn't think of anything that would distract her.

Most of the girls looked like they'd headed straight when they'd entered the woods, but she had veered to the right because she'd noticed a slight slope and had hoped it might lead to a river. If it did and she could get into the water, then she thought she might be home free. The men were probably expecting them to stay on land, and while there might be men manning the perimeter on the other side of the river—assuming one was there—she wasn't going to cross it, she was going to swim down it until she was far enough away from the barn.

For once, luck was on her side and she caught sight of water through the trees.

Despite the tightness in her chest, Sapphire pushed on, and within minutes, she was bursting through the tree line to find herself standing in front of a river.

"Thank you," she murmured aloud to no one in particular.

It was hot out and the cold water against her naked skin refreshed her as she clambered down the bank and into the water.

She wasn't a great swimmer, but she was good enough to swim out to the middle of the river and head in the same direction as the current. There was no use fighting against it because it could be her friend, carrying her along with it and helping her move faster.

As she kicked her legs and swung her arms, Sapphire felt herself start to relax. She was doing this. She really was. It was going to work. She just had to keep going and sooner or later she was going to find someone who could help her.

The knot in her stomach began to undo.

Then she swam headlong into a net.

~

8:50 P.M.

Something tangled around her.

At first, Sapphire thought it was reeds or grasses or maybe even eels or some other sort of river creature.

She wasn't really much of an animal lover and definitely not wild animals, so panic surged through her as she fought off what she thought was some fish trying to attack her.

Her panic quickly turned to full-blown terror when she realized that it wasn't reeds or some animal trying to hurt her, but the thin strands of a net.

Frantically, she tried to free herself from it.

She swung her arms and kicked her legs and twisted and turned in circles.

It didn't do any good.

A whirring sound joined the sounds of her splashing, and then she was lifted up out of the water.

It was growing dark, but there was still enough light to see that there was a boat just beneath her and to her left.

A single man sat on the boat.

He was smiling up at her.

She didn't smile back.

The net she was in swung sideways, and then she was lowered back down until she was sitting on the floor of the boat. Water streamed down her, puddling underneath her, but she didn't bother to wipe it away. The net didn't lower, and she was too tired to fight it this time.

She was too tired to fight, period.

She was done.

What was the point in continuing to try to find ways to escape when it was never going to happen?

She had to accept her fate.

The longer it took her to accept, the more she was going to keep getting hurt. She wasn't going to escape. She wasn't going to have a normal life. She was going to be sold, presumably to this man in the boat, and then she would be his to do with as he pleased. He would rape her, maybe beat her. If she was lucky, she might be blessed with a quick death.

The man stepped closer and crouched beside her. Although she didn't want to, her gaze was drawn to his. He looked much younger than she had expected, probably in his mid-twenties, he had green eyes that didn't look evil even though she knew that he was, and messy reddish blond hair.

"I like you," he drawled. "I like the strong ones; they always have a better chance of surviving."

So, he wanted to keep her alive for as long as he could.

As if her life wasn't already bad enough.

He stood and reached above her, fiddled with something and the net came tumbling down.

She could try to run.

Jump back into the water and swim like her life depended on it—because it did.

But she didn't.

What was the point?

Instead, she just curled her knees up to her chest, wrapped her arms around them, and waited to see what he was going to do.

Once again, he crouched before her. He examined her, and Sapphire wondered whether she should do a better job of covering her naked body, but decided in the end, it didn't really matter. She belonged to this man now, and he was going to do a whole lot more to her than just look at her body.

He reached out a hand as though he were going to stroke her cheek but stopped just inches from her skin. His eyes met hers again and she saw something flash through them. If she wasn't so exhausted, she might have figured out what it was.

The man sighed, then he stood and reached over, picking up a metal chain that he snapped onto the collar around her neck.

That was it.

She was claimed.

Never again would she be her own person.

Now she was his.

If he didn't intend to do anything to let her die too quickly, then she prayed that he wasn't going to hurt her too badly.

Sapphire zoned out. Maybe that was the way to survive this. Just let her mind go blank—no thinking, no feeling, just emptiness. Perhaps, if she did that long enough, her mind would just stay empty.

That was probably the best she could hope for.

Time blurred into nothingness, and she was only vaguely aware of the fact that they were no longer on a boat. She was being walked across the very same woods that only an hour or so ago she had run through, fueled mostly by hope.

Now she was hopeless.

She had heard that word so many times before, but she'd never truly grasped just what it meant. She'd always thought that hope was something you always had. At the very least, a little bit of it.

But now she knew.

Hopelessness was like the rest of the world going on and no one noticing the gaping hole inside you. That hole grew and consumed every single molecule of your being until all that was left was a shell of a person.

That's all she was now.

Just a shell.

Not a person.

"Trust me."

The words ripped her out of her thoughts—not so much the sound of the voice, but the words themselves.

Trust.

What place did that have in the world she had been thrown into?

None.

And yet those were the words that the man who had paid a hundred thousand dollars to come here tonight to hunt and buy another person had said.

Why would she trust him?

He was leading her through the woods by a chain attached to a collar around her neck like she was some sort of animal. He was taking her back to the barn where he would presumably show that he had hunted his girl and got his money's worth, and then he would take her back to his house or wherever it was he intended to keep her.

He was the last person on the planet that she'd trust.

They came out into the clearing; the barn was just up ahead. She could see there were several men standing about with chains in their hands, the girls she'd spent the last couple of days with attached to them.

"Trust me," the man whispered again, leaning in so close his mouth was right on her ear.

It was like he didn't want anyone to accidentally overhear him, but why would he care? And why did he want her to trust him? Was that his perversion? Convincing himself that she wanted this as much as he did, and that she wasn't just his prisoner?

"When it goes down, just drop to the ground and stay there. I have to walk you back into the barn to be processed. I'll have to leave you for a moment, so remember what I said. Okay? Okay?" he repeated when she didn't respond.

Sapphire had no idea what he was talking about, but she didn't want to make him angry, so she nodded.

The hustle and bustle of the barn was barely noticed as she allowed the man to lead her inside and back into the stall that she'd spent the last forty-eight hours in. She wondered absently how it would differ from her new home, but mostly she just shivered. She was still wet from the river and walking through the woods as the sun set and the heat dropped had made her cold.

The man from the boat left her in the stall and moved away as two other men—one with a gun—took his place. They were saying something to her, but she couldn't really hear them. She could just see their mouths moving.

Then the barn erupted into gunfire.

Remembering the boat man's words, she dropped to the ground, just like he'd told her to do.

Screaming filled the air.

There was so much shooting.

She started as something dropped to the ground just outside her stall, the door of which was still open.

It was Tasha.

The girl was covered in blood, her eyes were open, and they locked on hers. Tasha opened her mouth, closed it, and then her eyes went blank.

She was dead.

She had died right in front of her.

Sapphire had never seen anyone die before. She'd never even seen a dead body before. Now people were dying all around her. She could tell by the screams. They were horrible screams filled with pain and terror.

Then abruptly, everything went silent.

For some reason, that seemed scarier than the shooting and screaming.

Footsteps thundered toward her and then someone was kneeling at her side. A hand rested on her shoulder and she was eased over onto her back.

The boat man knelt beside her.

"Are you hurt?" he asked as he covered her with a blanket.

Sapphire shook her head.

"I wasn't sure you heard me outside, but you remembered. You did good, kid." He smiled down at her, then very gently picked her up, cradling her carefully in his arms.

Who was he?

He didn't look evil and he didn't feel evil. He felt different than the rest of the men here, but he *was* here.

He had to be a bad guy.

Maybe he ran his own human trafficking ring and he wanted to eliminate his competition.

"We'll get that metal collar off you as soon as we can," the man told her as he carried her outside.

"Who are you?" she whispered.

"Detective Rowan Brown. I'm an undercover cop who was working to bring down the group of human traffickers who run the hunts. You're safe now, kid."

Safe.

She didn't think she would ever feel safe again, no matter how long she lived.

Exhaustion took over, and Sapphire let her head rest against the cop's shoulder and closed her eyes.

Seconds later, she was asleep.

CHAPTER *Four*

Ten Years Later

January 2nd
9:22 P.M.

She couldn't wait to get out of here.

This had to have been the worst Christmas and New Year holidays of her life.

And she was only nineteen.

Amelia Lexis sighed to herself. She had hoped that her parents would be more receptive to hearing that she wanted to drop out of college. She had tried to explain to them that it was a waste of time and money for her to keep going when she had no idea what she wanted to do with her life.

What was the point of going to school when you didn't know what you wanted to study?

So, she had decided to drop out. She was in her sophomore year, and so far, she hated every single class that she was taking. Amelia didn't want to be tied down, sitting in a room all day, studying, writing papers, studying for exams. That wasn't her.

She wanted to be outside in the fresh air and sunshine, enjoying her life.

Amelia wasn't quite sure yet exactly what she wanted to do, but she knew it was going to be something outdoors. Maybe she'd get a job at the local zoo. She liked animals, and she'd loved going there as a kid. Or she could be an adventure guide. She liked to kayak and ski and hike; she could definitely do something like that. She also liked sports. Maybe she could teach swimming lessons or coach sports. That could be fun.

What she did know was that she didn't want to go through life going to a job every day that she hated like her parents had. Growing up, both her mom and dad had worked long hours—her dad in real estate and her mom in catering. They worked hard, and while they made good money and she always had the material things she wanted, what she'd wanted most was them and time together, and that she'd never had.

That wasn't how she wanted her life to play out.

She didn't want to spend every day doing something that her heart wasn't in. She wanted to be excited to get up each day and go to a job she loved. She didn't want to dread the end of the weekend; she wanted to long for it. Until she could figure out just which direction her life was heading in, she didn't see the point of remaining in college. She was going to keep bartending and spending time with her friends, and then when she knew what she wanted to do, she would figure out what she needed to do to get there, and if necessary, go back to school.

It all seemed to make perfect sense.

But her parents didn't see it that way.

When she'd sat down the day after Christmas to tell them that she wouldn't be going back to college, they had gone ballistic. They'd lectured and ranted and raved and complained and carried on and on, refusing to listen to her side of things.

Why were parents always like that?

Why did they think they always knew better?

Sure, she was only nineteen, but that didn't mean her views on life were in any way wrong. Why was it better to go to college, wasting her parents' money and her time, while she tried to figure out what she wanted to do with her life, than to work full time and figure it out?

Amelia had tried to tell her parents that, but they just didn't get it.

As much as she had wanted to leave immediately, she had stayed through New Year since her parents were having a huge party New Year's Eve that all of their extended family would be attending, and she'd wanted to catch up with her cousins whom she hadn't seen in years. That week had been tense. She'd tried to avoid her parents as best as she could, sleeping late so she wasn't out of her room until after they had gone to work, then going to a friend's house in the evening so that by the time she got home, they had already gone to bed. It hadn't been the way she'd wanted to spend the holidays, but it was what it was.

She hoped it wasn't always going to be that way. Amelia loved her parents, and as crazy as they drove her sometimes, she knew they wanted the best for her. Right now, they just disagreed on what that was. Maybe once they saw that she wasn't throwing her future away—which had been their way of describing what she was doing—then they would realize that there was more than one way to get to the same place.

That day wouldn't be today, and it wouldn't be tomorrow, but hopefully, it wouldn't be too far away.

Amelia yawned as she turned onto the empty road that would eventually lead her back to the apartment she shared with her two best friends. She loved Toby and Grif; they'd known each other since kindergarten, and although both guys were super sexy, they were her friends, and she would never do anything to risk that friendship. Living with them had been a blast, and she hoped that they would continue to be roommates until they all fell in love and got married.

Speaking of falling in love, she really needed a boyfriend.

It had been four months since she'd broken up with her high school boyfriend. They'd gone to different colleges on opposite sides of the country, and although they had vowed they would find a way to make it work, they'd broken up over the summer when they both realized it was never going to happen.

She was lonely. Sure, she loved Grif and Toby, and they hung out together a lot, but they both had girlfriends, and whenever they did couple things, she always felt like the third wheel. There was a cute guy who came into the bar she worked in almost every night. He had an English accent and the dreamiest blue eyes she'd ever seen. Maybe she should ask him out. Sometimes they flirted, and he seemed to like her, but she wasn't very good when it came to asking guys out.

Amelia stifled another yawn. She was tired. That kind of drained tired that emotional turmoil always left you with. It was going to be a relief to get home where she didn't have to talk to her parents for a few days at least, maybe even a couple of weeks if she texted a few times.

A flash of red and blue caught her attention.

A police cruiser was behind her.

She was the only car on the road. It was a quiet one at the busiest of times, let alone at nine at night in the middle of winter with icy sleet swirling around outside.

Hoping it just wanted to pass her on its way to wherever it was going, Amelia pulled her car over to the side of the road, but the police cruiser followed her.

Had she been speeding?

She didn't think so, but she'd been distracted thinking about the falling-out with her parents, so there was a possibility that she had been going a little over the limit.

Amelia chewed on her nails as she waited for the cop to get out of his car and walk to hers. She'd never gotten a ticket before. She didn't usually drive much. College had only been a fifteen-minute bike ride away, and work was only a five-minute walk. The only time she ever drove was when she went home to see her parents.

She jumped when the cop tapped on her window, and then she rolled it down.

"Night, ma'am. License and proof of insurance, please," the cop said.

She nodded and reached over into the glove compartment to fish out her proof of insurance, then pulled out her purse and opened it to get her license, then handed both to the cop. "Here you go, officer."

"Wait here, please," he said as he headed back to his car.

She rolled up her window and resumed chewing her nails; it was what she always did when she was nervous or scared.

The wait seemed like an eternity, but eventually she saw the silhouette of the cop in his headlights as he came back toward her car.

Good.

Now she could get back on the road. She still had another hour before she reached home, and she just wanted to get back, climb into bed, and go to sleep.

"Ma'am, I'm going to need you to step out of your vehicle," the cop said when she rolled her window down.

"What? Why?" she asked, confused. Maybe she had been speeding a little, but you didn't get arrested for that, did you? She didn't want to have to call her parents to come and bail her out on the heels of telling them she was dropping out of college.

"Ma'am, step out of the vehicle, please," the cop repeated, his hand moving to rest on the butt of his gun.

Scared, but more scared to do nothing, Amelia unclipped her seat belt, opened her door, and climbed out into the cold.

"Turn around, hands on the roof," the cop ordered.

She did as she was told—anything not to get in more trouble, and once he put her in his car, she'd ask what he thought she had done wrong.

"Sir, please, I didn't—" Amelia started, but never finished her sentence. Something was slammed into the back of her head. and she dropped unconscious to the ground.

CHAPTER
Five

January 3rd
2:44 A.M.

"Why do I let you talk me into these things?"

Detective Sapphire Hatcher didn't bother to take her eyes off the scene outside her window to look at her partner, but she did roll her eyes. "Because I'm always right."

"And very humble," Elijah Newton laughed.

The laugh grated on her nerves.

Not because she thought he was mocking her. She knew that her partner was a good guy and a good cop and that he trusted her instincts, but she didn't like people laughing at her.

Especially when it came to her job.

Which was pretty much her entire life.

And the only thing keeping her sane.

"He's had her for three weeks. He had the first girl for six weeks, the second for five, the third for four; that means that he should have already killed number four and be ready to dump her body," Sapphire said, although it just about killed her. She hated to admit defeat, and the facts were that she hadn't been able to save this woman. Nor the one before her, nor the one before that. Or so many others in the four years since she'd become a cop. "He left all three previous victims in dumpsters behind movie theatres. He's used a different theatre each time, and he hasn't used this one yet. There's a good chance that he'll be here tonight. This could be our chance to finally get him."

"You don't need to convince me, Saph," Elijah said quietly. "If I thought you were wrong about this, I wouldn't be here."

She hated when he called her Saph. There was only one person who had ever called her that and that person was gone now. But she couldn't very well go around talking about that. While her boss knew about her past, she'd been a minor and a victim so her identity wasn't publicly known as one of the victims saved when the human trafficking ring had been closed down, but that didn't stop the rumors or the whispers. She was sure that many of her colleagues knew who she was, but none of them had enough gall to mention it to her face.

So, she kept her mouth shut, endured the whispers, and did her best to ignore them and focus on her job. Sapphire knew she was obsessive about her work, a workaholic. She also knew that some of her colleagues didn't like her. Even though she was good at her job, she sometimes had trouble working with others—she had major trust issues —and she was stubborn, brisk, and liked to work alone whenever she could.

But she had an excellent close rate for her cases, and she worked well with Elijah because she respected him, so the department tolerated her quirks.

"Want something to eat?" Elijah asked.

"No, thank you."

"Something to drink?"

"Nope."

"We've been sitting here for five hours already, and you haven't had anything."

"Not hungry or thirsty," she said shortly. When she got into this zone, she regularly forgot to eat. If she drank, she'd have to go to the bathroom, and she didn't want to miss this. Her entire focus was on the dumpsters behind the movie theatre, scanning back and forth for any signs of movement. This guy wasn't getting away again.

If they didn't get him tonight, another girl would die.

He probably already had his next victim. So far, it looked like as he took another girl, a day or two later he dumped the body of the last one. From what they could tell, he killed them a couple of days before he dumped the bodies. She wasn't sure if there was any significance to that. Maybe he wanted to scare the next victim into submission by showing her what would happen to her if she disobeyed, or maybe just to terrify her by showing her what he was capable of.

There was so much they didn't know about him yet.

She had worked this case around the clock for the last four months, in between her heavy case load, staying up until all hours of the night. She was determined to find this man and stop him. She felt some sort of affinity with these girls. Maybe it was because they were only a little older than she had been when she was sold to human traffickers. It wasn't a new experience for her; she often got overly invested in cases. Some days Sapphire wondered how she had ever passed the psych exam to become a cop, but every day she was grateful that she had. She didn't know what she would do without her job.

"Elijah," she said suddenly as something caught her attention. "Look, there." She pointed to a corner of the theatre. "Do you see that?"

"I do," he responded, already grabbing his gun and climbing out of the car.

She followed suit, adrenaline buzzing through her system. Not only did her job give her some peace of mind after what she had lived through, but the adrenaline rush that she got every time she chased a bad guy pushed away the fear she still felt on a daily basis.

They crossed the street and ran down the alley. "Freeze! Hands where we can see them," Elijah yelled as they got closer and saw that there was indeed someone here.

The person started and spun to face them.

It was a young man, younger than she'd expected; he looked to be in his early twenties, if that. He looked terrified. Again, he wasn't what she'd expected of the man who'd so methodically abducted and murdered three women so far.

"Down on the ground," she ordered when the man made no attempt to put his hands where they could see them like her partner had told him to.

Shaking, the man did as she told him. He lowered himself down to the dirty concrete and put his hands up in the air.

While her partner kept a gun trained on him, Sapphire put hers away and pulled out her handcuffs, cuffing the man before dragging him to his feet and shoving him up against the brick wall of the theatre. "Where's the body?" she demanded.

"What body?" the man asked.

"There's another one here," Elijah said, reaching around the corner of one of the dumpsters and pulling out a girl who looked around eighteen or nineteen. Had the man brought his next victim with him?

"Please," the girl begged, "we didn't do anything. We just came out here to make out. We work here."

Sapphire gave both the girl and the guy a once-over and found that they were indeed dressed in uniforms from the theatre complex. A little of the wind went out of her sails. She didn't think this was who they were looking for. She didn't *feel* any evil inside either of the young people, and she always trusted her gut.

"It's not them," Elijah said.

"I agree." She was disappointed this wasn't the serial killer that she and her partner were hunting, and she didn't want to waste any time on them. "Give us your names then go back inside. We'll speak with you later today," she added briskly.

The two complied, and Elijah jotted the information down. They would speak with them later just to make sure they didn't know anything, but she already knew it wouldn't yield anything. They were just two kids making out in an alley—nothing more, nothing less.

"I think we should call it a night," Elijah said when the two young people headed back down the alley. "It's nearly three thirty. I don't think he's coming here. We should go home, get some sleep."

She wasn't ready to give up yet. "There's still time for him to come," she protested.

"I know you don't like letting things go, but maybe this time—" He broke off as a shot rang out.

Both of them turned in the direction the gunshot had come from in time to see a man dressed all in black, with what looked like a body slung over his shoulder, shoot the young man they had nearly arrested. Sapphire grabbed her gun, but the man in black had already dropped the body and grabbed the girl, dragging her up against his body and blocking any shot they might have had, especially in the dark.

"Put your weapon down," Sapphire ordered.

The man in black ignored her.

"Stop now," Elijah said.

Again, the man in black ignored the command.

Everything that happened next transpired in rapid-fire succession.

The man in black fired a shot at Elijah.

Her partner dropped.

The man fired a shot at her.

Pain sliced through her arm.

The force of the shot knocked her backward, and she hit her head.

The man in black moved the gun to the head of the teenage girl he was using as a human shield.

He fired.

The girl dropped.

Their eyes met.

Sapphire could see the exact second that the other woman's life ended.

Then the pain washed her into unconsciousness.

10:13 A.M.

"How much longer?" Sapphire asked, shifting restlessly on the uncomfortable hospital bed. She was more than ready to be out of here.

"As long as it takes for the doctor to discharge you," Detective Gray Yul told her. He and his partner had shown up at the hospital not long after an ambulance had brought her here.

"I'm ready to go *now*," she said. She was getting annoyed, and, as much as she hated to admit it, anxious. That was why she was always moving—always busy, always occupied. When she wasn't, the fear and anxiety she'd been living with for the last ten years crept back in. If she had to stay here much longer, she was afraid she was going to lose her mind.

"Well you can't go now," Zeb Tuck told her with a smile. "You know the rules. You were injured—shot. You need to stay here until a doctor discharges you."

She *did* know the rules.

She just hated them.

"We can take your statement now, while we wait," Gray suggested.

At least that was something to do even if it wasn't something that she particularly wanted to do. "Okay," she agreed with as much enthusiasm as she could muster.

Sapphire still remembered giving her statement a decade ago. Detective Rowan Brown had tried to make things as easy for her as possible. Going slow, giving her plenty of breaks when she was starting to get too overwhelmed, making sure that she was coping as best as she could after what she had been through.

Even worse than giving her statement was testifying.

Having to stand up in court and tell what had happened to her was one of the most horrific moments of her life. Especially having to tell the court that it was her own parents who had done it to her.

Apparently, after the men had thrown her and her sisters into a van, her parents had trashed the house and inflicted wounds on one another, then dialed 911 and told the cops who arrived that six men had broken in, assaulted them, kidnapped their children, then left them for dead.

With no evidence contrary to that, the cops had believed them.

Until she had been found three days later and the truth had come out.

Her parents were both serving life sentences in prison.

"Sapphire?" Zeb asked, sitting beside her on the bed. "You okay? You need a doctor?"

"What?" She blinked, unaware that she had just zoned out. She used to zone out a lot when she was first rescued, but over time she had learned to control it. She had learned to control a lot of things. "No, I don't need a doctor." She shook her head, partially to emphasize her point and partially to clear her mind.

"We can wait a while before we do this," Gray said, but they both knew they couldn't. They needed her statement if they were even going to stand a chance at finding the man who had now killed six people.

Four young women, and the couple from last night.

But not her partner.

Elijah was still alive.

She didn't know how he had managed to survive a bullet to the chest, but she was so glad that he had.

"How's Elijah doing?" she asked. It had been a while since she'd gotten an update from his doctors. She knew he had made it through surgery and was now in the ICU. His doctors were giving him an eighty percent chance at living, but whether he would ever recover enough to return to his job remained to be seen.

"I'm sure he's doing the same, but I can go and check for you," Gray offered.

"If you don't mind," she said. She couldn't focus on giving her statement until she was reassured that her partner was still alive.

"Sure thing." Gray nodded.

He headed out the door, and she and Zeb sat in silence while they waited for his return. Sapphire wondered whether they were going to be assigned to work this case with her now that Elijah was in the hospital for the foreseeable future. She didn't really want to work with anyone else; she did her best work when she was on her own and didn't have to devote time to playing nice with others.

But if she *had* to work with other detectives, then she supposed she couldn't ask for anyone better than Gray Yul and Zeb Tuck. Gray was in his early forties and had been a cop for twenty years. He was married with two little girls, and he had a reputation for being great with victims. Zeb Tuck was younger, only two years older than her. He was single, smart, dedicated, and he had a great sense of humor. If she hadn't had the sense of humor ripped out of her by what happened in that barn all those years ago, she probably would have found him a lot of fun.

"Elijah is still hanging in there," Gray announced as he joined them in her hospital room again.

Relief flooded through her. Elijah was probably as close to a friend as she was ever going to have, and she didn't want to think about the possibility of losing him.

Then she drew in one deep, long, slow breath and refocused herself.

Her partner was going to live. She was sure of it. Now she had to do her job to make sure this monster of a man never took the life of another human being.

"We were watching the movie theater in case the killer chose it to dump the body of his latest victim. We assumed that if he stuck to his routine, he would be leaving the body last night, and he hadn't gone to that theater before. I saw something move, and then Elijah did, too, so we went to check it out. There was a young couple there. They worked at the theater, must have snuck out the back door to make out after the last movie finished and before they cleaned up. We told them to leave, and then Elijah said we should call it a night. I was telling him there was still time, and he was saying that sometimes I find it hard to let things go." She didn't want to add that detail in, but she had to be as accurate as possible. "Then we heard the shot."

"Only one?" Zeb asked.

Sapphire nodded. "When we turned around, the guy was on the ground. There was a man standing there, dressed all in black. It looked like he had a body draped over his shoulder. Both Elijah and I pulled out our weapons, but he dropped the body and grabbed the girl who was standing there screaming, using her as a human shield. We told him to stop, but he started walking toward us. He kept coming." She had to pause to control the emotion in her voice. "He shot Elijah, then me, and then the girl he was using as a human shield. She dropped to the ground." Sapphire couldn't stop the shudder that rippled through her as she remembered watching the life extinguish in the woman's eyes. It reminded her of the last time she had watched someone die.

"What happened next?" Gray asked gently.

The gentleness had the opposite effect on her. It didn't calm her. It angered her. She didn't want to be handled, and she didn't want to be coddled. She wasn't a helpless, terrified teenager anymore. She was an adult. A cop. She didn't need anyone treating her with kid gloves. "I must have passed out. I think I bumped my head when I fell down after

I was shot." She absently touched the small lump on the back of her head and the bandage that was wrapped around her arm. The bullet lodged in her bicep had been removed in the ER and the wound stitched closed. She'd been lucky that was all that had happened to her; she could have been killed.

"I know it was dark, but were you able to see anything before you passed out?" Zeb asked.

"He was wearing a mask. I couldn't see his face."

"Did he say anything?" Zeb asked.

"No," she said, but then paused. "Wait, I think he did say something." She scrunched up her brow and closed her eyes, putting herself back in the alley, concentrating on each thing that happened one at a time. "After I passed out, I was only out for a moment, then I woke up, but I didn't want him to know. He was dragging the body he'd brought with him and the one of the young man he killed down to join me, Elijah, and the teenage girl. Then before he left, he said, 'Not today. You're not going to catch me today.'"

"It sounds like he knows the end is coming at some point," Zeb said thoughtfully.

"Is there anything else you remember?" Gray asked.

"Fish," she said immediately. "I remember smelling fish." She had no idea what that meant but it had to mean something.

The room to her door swung open, and a nurse came in. "I have your discharge papers, Detective Hatcher."

Perfect.

That was exactly what she wanted to hear.

Sapphire was pumped and ready to get back to work.

"You're not going anywhere but home to bed," Gray told her, correctly interpreting the look on her face. "Boss's orders. You take the rest of the day off work, then tomorrow you can be back to working this case."

She wanted to argue.

She wanted to stubbornly head back to work.

But she had a headache, and her arm throbbed. Maybe a few hours of rest would do her good. As much as she wanted to work, she didn't want to miss something because she was tired and in pain.

She was going to catch the man who had almost killed her and her partner if it was the last case she ever worked.

2:13 P.M.

"Do you need anything?"

Sapphire shook her head. The last thing she wanted after the day she'd had was to be fussed over. "I'm fine."

"Why don't you go lie down for a while?"

"Not tired."

"How can you not be tired? You haven't slept in over thirty-six hours."

"What else is new?" she muttered. She didn't sleep a lot. Sleep made you too vulnerable; you couldn't protect yourself; you didn't know what was happening around you, not to mention the nightmares. For the last decade, Sapphire had gotten by on the bare minimum of sleep, and by now, she had trained her body to survive that way.

"You think you can keep this up indefinitely?"

"Do you?" she shot back and then immediately regretted it when she saw the look on her sister's face. "I'm sorry, Diamond. I know you're only trying to help. I'm not sleepy, but I'll go lie down in a bit. Right now, I just want to sit here. Maybe I will have a cup of tea." She didn't really want one, but her oldest sister liked to take care of them. It was how she coped, and she knew Diamond would be shaken up by her being shot, so the best thing she could do right now was at least make sure that her sister was all right.

"Okay, I'll be right back." Diamond smiled, then hurried to the kitchen.

Having made her sister feel better, Sapphire felt a little better herself. She was so much more comfortable when it came to other people and their emotions than she was when it came to her own.

"You really okay?" Amethyst asked. Of all her sisters, Amethyst was the most like her. In a way, they had recovered the best from what they'd been through, and, in a way, they had recovered the worst. Diamond and Ruby had accepted that their past was what it was and that the effects would last for the rest of their lives, while she and Amethyst lived more in a state of denial.

"Of course." She nodded vigorously. Hell would freeze over before she ever admitted to another living soul that she wasn't okay.

"Liar," Amethyst muttered.

Sapphire didn't disagree. It was one thing for her sisters to know that she was lying and another for her to admit it out loud. Besides, family was different from everyone else, and she would forever be grateful that she hadn't lost all of hers.

Her parents were in prison, and even if they weren't, she wouldn't want anything to do with them after what they had done. Her little sister Emmy had never been found. But she had her three older sisters, and for now, that had to be enough.

Not just for now.

Forever.

This was her family.

No more, no less.

She wasn't unhappy about it. She loved her sisters. The four of them lived together in a house they had built five years ago. The downstairs had a library for Ruby, an art studio for Diamond, a study for her, and a gym for Amethyst. There was also the main room that had a kitchen at one end, a sitting area, and a dining room table. Upstairs there were five en suite bedrooms—one for each of them and one for Emerald for when she was finally found and brought home.

Sapphire had to believe that would happen.

She couldn't allow herself to think that her little sister was already dead. It was bad enough believing that her sister was out there somewhere being raped and tortured, but dead was worse, because dead was final.

One day she would get the last piece of her family back.

"Here you go," Diamond said, handing her a cup of steaming tea.

She wrapped her hands around it and the warmth went a little way to warming the cold inside her. No matter how much she tried to deny it—even to herself—she was shaken by what had happened. Seeing her partner shot and being shot herself, but even more than that was seeing that girl die. It reminded her so much of watching Tasha die in the barn. The girl had come so close to being saved only to get caught up in the cross fire when the human traffickers returned fire at the cops.

Watching Tasha die had haunted her for a decade.

She wished she could erase the memory from her mind, just like she wished she could wipe away the memory of watching that girl die last night.

"Elijah is okay, right?" Diamond asked.

Sapphire arched a brow. That wasn't the first time her sister had asked her that since she'd gotten home from the hospital. It wasn't even the second or the third. Why was she so worried about Elijah? He was her partner and she wanted him to make a full recovery, but what difference did it make to Diamond? It was probably just her sweet sister caring about anyone and everyone. Sapphire was so glad that what Diamond had been through hadn't taken that part of her away. Her oldest sister had always been so kind, so generous, always thinking of others and never of herself, and it would have been such a loss to the world if that had been ripped out of her because of the injustice of what their parents did to them.

"Last I heard, he's doing fine," she assured Diamond. "I asked Gray and Zeb to text me if anything changes with Elijah. If I hear anything, I'll let you know, okay?"

"Thank you." Diamond smiled and then sat down beside her, hesitantly reaching out an arm to wrap around her shoulders.

Although she didn't like to be touched—something that annoyed her more than it probably should because it seemed so textbook post-traumatic stress disorder—today, she leaned into her sister's embrace. It was exhausting being strong all the time, and every now and then, she allowed herself just a moment or two to absorb the strength of the people she loved.

This was one of those moments.

She was eternally grateful that her parents hadn't robbed her of her sisters.

"Who wants a straight-out-of-the-oven chocolate chip cookie?"

Ruby asked, carrying a plate over to the sofas where the rest of them were sitting.

That was something she could never resist. Sapphire reached over and took the biggest cookie on the plate. That first bite was heaven, and she sank down into the oversized couch cushions. When it had come time to furnish this house, these couches were the first thing she had picked out—the softest, coziest ones the store had.

"Why don't we all sleep down here tonight?" Ruby suggested. "We'll bring down our pillows and quilts, spread them out on the floor. We can order pizza, make s'mores, drink cola, watch movies all night, and just talk. You know, like we used to when we were kids."

They didn't talk much about their childhoods. By unspoken agreement, it was off limits; it was too hard to talk about that time because it was a reminder of what they had lost.

But tonight, it felt different.

For the first time, she didn't get that knifing pain in her chest thinking about some of the good times she had shared with her sisters growing up.

The others were all looking at her, awaiting her reaction. Since she was the one who had just been shot, she supposed they were waiting for her to make the final decision.

"That sounds like fun." She smiled and felt the collective unuttered sigh of relief. A rare laugh burst out and she shook her head at all of them. "We're an anxious group, aren't we? Just for tonight, let's pretend that the last ten years never happened. Let's just be four sisters. We'll talk, do facials and paint our nails, then we can order pizza, make brownies, and watch movies just like normal people do." It felt good to just do something normal. She didn't even really like facials, and she never painted her nails because she couldn't stand it once it got chips in it, and she usually had to remove the nail polish just hours after putting it on.

"Brownies!" Amethyst squealed with uncharacteristic enthusiasm. Chocolate chip cookies might be her weakness, but brownies were Amethyst's.

Her smile widened at her sister's joy. Diamond, too, had relaxed and had started chattering away about the dozens of bottles of nail polish she had in her bathroom, and Ruby was mentioning her favorite facial.

This was all so normal, and it wasn't as hard as she'd thought it would be. She loved her sisters so much, and together they had made it this far. She didn't know what the future held for them, but in their own way, they were as happy as was possible—given their pasts.

Time didn't heal all wounds, but it certainly did dull them a little.

CHAPTER *Six*

January 4th
8:51 A.M.

She had actually gotten a reasonably good night's sleep last night.

And she'd gotten more than her usual four to five hours.

After hanging out with her sisters, she had fallen asleep on the couch and managed to get a full eight hours. She felt rested and refreshed. Her head didn't hurt anymore, and there was only a small jab of pain when she moved her arm as it tugged on the stitches. She was ready to get back to work and find the man who had tried to kill her. Sapphire knew she would find him; she wouldn't stop until she did, and once that happened, she would make sure that he spent the rest of his life in prison.

Her mind was already ticking over, trying to figure out what the smell of fish meant. There were a few small lakes near here, and they were only a few miles from the ocean, a lot of places for people to go fishing. There were cabins around the lake, and some properties had their own fishing lake. Maybe the man owned or worked at a fish market. Those were a lot of places to check out, and checking all of them wasn't feasible, especially since they were on the clock. The killer no doubt already had his next victim and if he stuck with his MO, they only had two weeks to find her.

At least they had something to go on, and that was more than they'd had yesterday. You didn't smell that strongly of fish if you hadn't been around them. It was almost like he'd come straight from catching and cleaning fish.

As soon as she got to her desk, she was going to add that to the profile. After three deaths—six now—they had quite a detailed profile on this serial killer. She just wished that profile included a name and address, as well as some forensics that would nail this man to the wall when they finally got him in custody.

Even though it had only been around thirty-six hours since she'd last been here, it felt good to park her car in the department's underground parking lot and take the elevator up to the homicide floor.

Sapphire paused as she stepped off the elevator. *This* was her purpose in life. This was why she had been spared, why she'd been rescued instead of sent off to live with some pervert who would use her and then kill her. It was to do this, to help save the lives of others. To find the evil in the world and extinguish it before it could claim another soul.

If she couldn't do this, she'd rather be dead.

Without her job, she was nothing.

When she got older and had to retire, she hoped that death would catch her soon afterward.

But not today.

Death hadn't gotten to her yet. She'd managed to escape it twice now—once, ten years ago, and again, yesterday. That meant that she hadn't yet done all that she had to do on life's journey.

Striding over to her desk, Sapphire paused once again as she passed Elijah's. It was odd not having him here. They had been partners ever since she got her detective's shield and was assigned to homicide. Some of the other people in the department had thought it was unfair that she had been put here while she was still so young, but she'd worked hard to achieve this dream. She'd graduated high school early, then taken an accelerated college degree so she could graduate from university early as well. She had immediately joined the police force and worked uniform for a couple of years before getting this job.

Elijah wasn't like that, though. He had been supportive of her from the beginning, and she had learned a lot from him. Although they weren't really what one would call friends, she hoped that he would make a full recovery and be back to work soon.

She missed him.

She hadn't thought that she would ever be attached enough to anyone besides her sisters to miss them, but apparently, she was wrong.

Sapphire was just sitting down at her desk when she heard a door open behind her. Her boss, Sergeant Debra Langsworth poked her head out of the door of her office.

"Oh, Sapphire, you're here. Good. Can you join me in my office for a moment, please?" she called.

Her boss no doubt wanted to check in with her after yesterday's events, probably to ask whether she needed to speak with the department's shrink. The answer to that question would be a definitive no. Sapphire didn't do shrinks. Not since the one she had been sent to after she was rescued a decade ago. That woman had been the most useless doctor on the planet. All she had done in their sessions was try to make excuses for her parents and what they had done.

Sapphire hadn't wanted to hear that.

They had sold her and her sisters to human traffickers, knowing full well what would happen to them, then lied about it to the cops, just so they could pay off their debts and take an around-the-world cruise.

She wasn't ever forgiving them for that.

Her steps slowed as she entered the office. Her boss wasn't alone in there. Gray and Zeb were here, along with another man. The stranger was attractive—very attractive. He was a few years older than she, with messy brown hair, and inquisitive brown eyes, he was tall and even though he was dressed in blue chinos and a light gray sweater she could tell that his body was chiseled to perfection. What she noticed most about the man was that nothing about him screamed cop.

Turning suspicious eyes on her boss, she asked, "Who's the new guy?"

"I'm Gideon," he answered, standing and holding out a hand.

Sapphire ignored him, her gaze fixed firmly on the sergeant.

Sergeant Langsworth squirmed under the scrutiny. "This is Gideon. Dr. Barlow. He's a criminal psychiatrist. He's here to work the movie theater dumpster serial killer case with you. You, Zeb, and Gray."

That she would be working with Gray and Zeb, she had already assumed. That she would be working with some shrink, had never even entered her mind.

Because she didn't always think through her actions or the things she said, Sapphire glared at the doctor and then her boss. "We don't need some criminal psychiatrist to help us with this case. I don't need *anyone* to help me with this case. I can work it on my own until Elijah comes back."

"No," Sergeant Langsworth said with a finality that conveyed any argument was not going to result in her getting what she wanted.

Still, Sapphire had to argue.

It wasn't in her nature to just give in.

"It'll take too long to get everyone caught up. Besides, we have the fish angle to pursue. We don't need him." She jerked her head in the doctor's direction.

"We've been working this case for months now without any real progress. You were shot by the man we're looking for, and you're lucky that I'm letting you remain on this case. The fish angle is something to consider, but we don't know that it's going to lead anywhere. Having Dr. Barlow consulting with us might get this man off the streets before anyone else dies. That's what we all want, isn't it?" Sergeant Langsworth arched a brow at her, clearly saying she had pushed her luck as far as her boss's tolerance would go.

Glowering, Sapphire snapped her lips together, lightly biting her tongue to keep from arguing further. The only reason she was restraining herself was because she *did* want this man off the streets more than anything else, and if she was forced to work with the sexy doctor to do that, then she would. She wouldn't like it, but she'd do it. Because this was bigger than her, and she would never endanger anyone else's life because of her hatred of shrinks.

"I want you to take Dr. Barlow, Gray, and Zeb into conference room

A and run through the case for them, getting them up to speed as quickly as possible," Sergeant Langsworth ordered.

She didn't move, still partly hoping there was a way to convince her boss that she didn't need any help on this case, that she was perfectly capable of handling it on her own.

"Sapphire," her boss said, a warning in her tone.

"Fine," she snapped. If she had to do this, then she may as well just get it over and done with.

Without waiting to see if the others were following her, Sapphire stalked off to her desk, grabbed the stack of case files that pertained to this serial killer and headed for the conference room.

If she had to work with a shrink, why did it have to be a hot one?

~

9:18 A.M.

The first thing Gideon noticed about her was her eyes.

They were a stunning shade of green, unlike anything he'd ever seen before. They were the shade of the fresh new leaves that uncurled on the branches of all the deciduous trees in the springtime.

It wasn't the color that had spoken to him, though. It was what was hidden inside them.

Pain, anger, distrust—such a medley of emotions he hadn't seen in a very long time. Her pain spoke to him; it drew him to her; it filled him with a need to find a way to wipe it all away. It filled him with a protectiveness that wasn't new to him. It was the very thing that had led him into psychiatry. He wanted to save people. He wanted to fix their problems. He wanted to help them have a better life.

She, on the other hand, didn't seem to feel the same way about him.

Detective Sapphire Hatcher stalked out of Sergeant Langsworth's office like a petulant child.

"Don't take offense," Sergeant Langsworth told him. "She had a rough day yesterday, and she's worried about her partner. She's just angry with herself that she hasn't solved this case already because she knows that means other teenage girls are going to die."

"No offense taken," he assured the sergeant. And it was true. He understood Sapphire Hatcher probably better than she understood herself.

Because he noticed everything, he caught the look that passed between the other two cops in the room. A look that suggested that part of Detective Hatcher's attitude was that she didn't always play well with others. Gideon wondered how that would affect the case. He was here whether Detective Hatcher liked it or not, and as much as he wanted to help her, he wouldn't let that interfere with what he had come here to do. From what her boss had said, Detective Hatcher was a dedicated cop who had an excellent close rate who respected and was respected by her partner, and who managed to focus on her job despite the rumors that circulated about her in the department.

Intrigued as he was by the detective, he set that aside to focus on this case. As much as Detective Hatcher couldn't live knowing that man was out there and would continue to abduct and kill young women until he was dead or arrested, he couldn't either.

"After you, detectives," he said, standing and waiting for them to lead him to the conference room.

Gideon followed Detective Yul and Detective Tuck through the squad room filled with detectives, and into a small room where Detective Hatcher had already taken a seat at the large table and was arranging her files. She didn't look up as they entered the room, but that didn't seem to bother either of the male detectives, nor did it bother him. She was territorial about her case. He understood that, but he also sensed that her primary goal was finding this serial killer, and that she would swallow her pride and suck it up and do what she had to do to make it happen. She just wouldn't like it. Nor was she going to make it easy on him.

"Detective Hatcher, you flew out of the sergeant's office so quickly, we didn't get to properly meet. I'm Dr. Barlow. Gideon," he added, walking over to the table and holding out his hand for her to shake.

She stared at his hand like it was a snake, then glared up at him. "I know. You told me your name in the sergeant's office. You're Gideon

Barlow. I'm Sapphire Hatcher. That's Gray Yul and Zeb Tuck. We all know our own names; now, can we just get to work?"

Biting back a smile, he took the seat beside her. He liked a challenge, and he thought Sapphire Hatcher just might be the biggest challenge he had faced in his career so far. "Absolutely." He nodded vigorously. "Since it's your case, and you're the lead detective, why don't you run everything through for us. I'm sure the other detectives know some of the details, but I only got a brief outline from your sergeant."

Detective Hatcher looked at him suspiciously, like she thought he was trying to trick her, and she wasn't completely wrong. He wanted to get to her. He wanted to gain her trust, and then he wanted to use that to help her however he could.

"We didn't know we had a serial killer at first," Detective Hatcher began. "The first victim was eighteen-year-old Fiona Madison. She had just graduated high school, was excited to go off to college in the fall according to all of her family and friends. And then one night she never came home after a party at a friend's house. It was deemed a missing person's case, until her body was found six weeks later, wrapped in a tarp and lying in a dumpster. Other than marks on her right ankle, indicative of a restraint—probably a metal ring—and marks on her neck, indicative of being strangled, there were no other injuries."

"Why did you determine he kept her alive for six weeks?" Gideon asked, although he already knew the answer. Even aside from being a criminal psychiatrist, it was pretty obvious. Eighteen-year-old girl kept prisoner for six weeks, there was only one thing that sprang to mind.

"He raped her," Detective Hatcher said simply. Her eyes were empty as she said the word, and her tone neutral, but it was exactly that that told him what he needed to know.

"Badly?"

"Extensive internal damage," Detective Hatcher confirmed. "Just a day before Fiona's body was found, another girl went missing. Zoe Fawkner was only sixteen. She had taken the family car out for her first long drive on her own—not just to and from school picking up and dropping off her sibling. She never came home. Despite the fact that she was a minor, it was still marked as a missing persons case because she had run away before. But that was two years ago. She'd been doing good since then." Detective Hatcher sounded upset about this, like they all should have known better. But that was the thing with hindsight—looking back, you could always see the path you should have taken.

"How long did he keep her?" he asked.

"Five weeks. She was found the same way as Fiona was, only at a different movie theatre complex. Next was seventeen-year-old Misha Heart, he had her for four weeks. By the time we found Zoe's body we knew that we were looking for a killer and not just missing girls, but he kidnaps his next victim before he dumps the girl he already has, so it's hard to get ahead of him."

"He's methodical, though," Detective Tuck said.

Gideon nodded. That was odd. The man was so meticulous about how long he kept each victim, and yet, he was also so forensically conscious. At first glance, those two things seemed to point to the same goal, the more methodical and careful you were, the less the chance you'd be caught. But in this case, being so obsessive about how long he kept each victim, gave the cops a chance to get a read on him and predict his behavior. Which was exactly what had happened, only it hadn't worked out the way Detective Hatcher and her partner had hoped.

"You don't have any forensics yet, is that correct?" he asked.

"Correct," Detective Hatcher said with a sigh. She wore her long brown hair loose and it hung around her face like a protective shield, but she couldn't hide from him. Sapphire Hatcher felt the pain of the victims suffering as though it were her own. He could see why she was such a good cop. The empathy with the victims in the cases she worked, meant she worked each and every case she was given with every single ounce of her being. He wondered what kind of toll it had taken on her.

"If he stuck to his plan, then he already has his next victim," he said thoughtfully. "He'll keep her for two weeks, and then the next for a week."

"And then what?" Detective Hatcher finally met his gaze squarely. There was desperation in those beautiful green eyes as she sought answers from him, as though without the answers she didn't know what to do next.

"I don't know," he said simply. There was no way to know what the man's endgame was, or when he intended to end things. He could restart his cycle or kill himself; he could turn himself into the police or start a new cycle or any one of hundreds of other possibilities. "For now, I think we should focus on trying to figure out who his current victim is. Perhaps if we can figure that out, then we can find a way to get ahead of him."

"Yeah," Detective Hatcher said, but her tone was listless.

As strong as her desire was to save every victim she came across, there was a piece of her that was missing.

Hope.

Sapphire Hatcher was hopeless.

~

2:23 P.M.

It hadn't even been two days yet, Amelia Lexis thought as she stared out the window.

She suspected that the man who had kidnapped her had deliberately put a window in her room to torment her. There was nothing else to do in here but stare out of it. Watching as the world carried on without her.

Did anyone even know that she was gone?

Had they found her car?

Did they know that she had been kidnapped and not just left, or had car troubles and walked off, getting lost in the woods and freezing to death?

Or maybe he had taken her car, hidden it so no one would ever know what became of her.

Amelia brushed at the tears that trickled slowly down her cheeks. She knew that crying wasn't going to help her. It certainly wasn't going to undo the metal chain around her ankle.

Still, she had been kidnapped, knocked unconscious, brought here, chained up, and, well ... she wasn't quite ready to acknowledge what else had happened to her yet. But if anyone deserved to shed some tears, it was her.

For the next few minutes, Amelia gave herself permission to sob her heart out as she thought of everything that she might never get to do if she never made it out of this room alive. She would never get to figure out what she wanted to do with her life and go and do it. She would never get to make amends with her parents and have the relationship with them that she wanted. She would never get to fall in love, get married, and raise children of her own.

Her life could end at any moment.

Right here in this horrible room. It was more of a studio apartment. There was a kitchenette in one corner, with a small table that sat two, as well as a sofa and a TV. There was a bed in another corner, and a door in a third that she assumed led to a bathroom.

The fourth corner was where she was restrained.

He had made it into a padded cell of sorts. Padding covered the wall from floor to ceiling about ten feet along each of the adjacent walls. The chain, that the metal ring around her ankle was attached to, only allowed her to move a foot or so in either direction, not far enough to get past the padding on the walls. There was also padding on the floor, making a triangle.

Amelia had to assume that the padding was there to prevent her from hurting herself. Isn't that what they did with mentally ill people who were a threat to themselves? They put them in a padded cell?

If he'd tried to make sure that she couldn't hurt herself, that meant he intended to keep her here for a while, right?

She couldn't think of any other reason to do it. It must have taken him a while to put the padding up, and you definitely didn't go through all that trouble just to keep someone here for a day and a half.

Had he done this before?

It was reasonable to believe that he had. Everything about the abduction and where he had kept her was so premeditated and perfectly executed. He had to have experience. Was he some kind of serial killer?

So far, he hadn't told her what he wanted from her; he hadn't told her much of anything. Whenever he was here, he just issued orders and made her do what he wanted, and then he always had a meal, watched some TV, and left.

Resolutely, she dried her wet cheeks.

Thinking about what he'd done and how bad her predicament

might be wasn't going to change anything. If she wanted to change her circumstances, she had to figure out a plan.

It was obvious she was in an apartment, since when she looked out the nearest window, she could see other buildings, cars, and people on the streets below. Knowing she was in a populated area and not in the middle of nowhere, she'd tried screaming for help.

It hadn't worked.

No one had come.

She assumed that meant that no one could hear her. Whether that was because he had soundproofed this apartment or because there was no one else in this building and everyone else was too far away to hear, she didn't know.

Not that it really mattered.

Amelia knew that she couldn't rely on anyone else to get her out of here. If she wanted to escape, it was up to her and her alone.

Ideas.

She needed some ideas.

She was a movie buff; she watched everything from action, kid's movies, comedies, romances, science fiction, fantasies, and horror. She had watched all the cult classics, and the obscure films that hardly anyone had ever heard of.

Right now, one movie in particular was springing to mind.

Amelia knew that a lot of people didn't like the Saw movies, but she had enjoyed the way they all fit together, highlighting one man's experiment to infuse others with the same love and respect for life that he himself had learned.

There was a scene in the first movie where one of the characters had cut off his own foot to get out of a metal ring much like the one that now restrained her. There was also a scene in the beginning of the third movie where a different character broke his own foot to pull it out of a metal ring.

Would she try either of those if she could get her hands on the tools that she needed?

Yes. She was positive that she would.

All she needed was a chance to get her hands on something that she could use. The chain didn't let her reach any of the things in the apartment, but when the man came, he always unhooked the chain from the wall so he could make her do ...

Well, he undid the chain from the wall.

She didn't think that he was ever going to be stupid enough to give her a chance to escape, but he might not notice her taking something and hiding it to use later. Right now, he watched her like a hawk. But she'd only been here for a day and a half; over time, he might grow complacent. Then she would make her move.

Amelia could wait.

She was patient.

She would play along and do whatever he asked of her, but she would always be looking for her chance.

Feeling a little better now that she had a plan, Amelia rested her head back against the padded wall and curled her legs up, trying to warm up a little. It was cold in here. She was still wearing the same clothes she'd had on when she had left her parents' house two days ago, but since she'd anticipated being in the car until she got home, she hadn't been wearing a coat, and her leggings and sweater didn't offer much warmth.

If she wasn't so afraid of him, she would have asked him to leave the heat on next time he dropped by. That probably would have been pointless though, since he had kidnapped her and was keeping her chained up. It wasn't like he cared about her comfort levels. All he was interested in was doing what he had to, to keep her alive until he was done playing with her.

She wondered when that would be.

How long would she have to try to get her hands on something that would help her get out of here?

Could she last that long? Physically and psychologically?

For the moment, she had her plan, and that gave her something to feel grounded to, but if no opportunities presented themselves for her to put it into action, then she would start to lose hope. And once you lost hope, you were already as good as dead.

She had always thought of herself as strong, but she had never been in a situation like this before, so she didn't know if she was as strong as she believed herself to be.

Once, when she was eight and she'd been away on a girl scouts camp, one of the leaders had a heart attack. They'd been out there alone all night in the dark until the other group had come to meet up with them. She had kept all the other girls calm and done what she could to help the leader, and in the end, everything had worked out. She'd felt so grown up that day—almost invincible. She'd been in control and had been able to take care of others.

She wanted that sense of control back.

She wanted to feel invincible.

She wanted everything to work out okay, so she could go home to her family.

～

4:51 P.M.

Sapphire shivered as they stood on the side of the road. Why did it have to be so cold? She couldn't take the constant shivering as well as having to deal with possibly the most obnoxious human being on the planet.

Dr. Gideon Barlow.

She had only known him for a few hours, and he was already driving her crazy. Now she had an additional reason for wanting to close this case as quickly as was humanly possible.

Although getting Dr. Barlow out of her life wasn't the main reason she wanted this killer in custody. Getting Amelia Lexis back alive was.

The young woman had been with the killer for almost two days now, and if he stuck to his usual MO, she had only twelve days to go before she would be found wrapped in tarp in a dumpster at the back of a movie theatre.

Sapphire hated that she couldn't rescue this girl.

What was the point of being a cop if you couldn't save everyone?

"How do we know that Amelia Lexis is the killer's next victim?" Dr. Barlow asked as the two of them and Gray and Zeb stood around a car parked on the side of a quiet highway.

"What? You think she just pulled over, got out, and decided to walk off into the woods and just vanished?" Sapphire demanded.

The smile Dr. Barlow gave her bordered on patronizing. "That is a possibility. The car could have broken down; her phone could have been dead; she might have walked off trying to find help, gotten lost and froze to death somewhere out there." He waved his hands at the woods that bordered the road on both sides.

"Could have. Might have. That's all just supposition. We don't have any proof of that," Sapphire reminded him.

"Nor do we have any proof that this girl was abducted," he shot back with an irritating calm.

Why couldn't he get emotional? Annoyed, frustrated—anything but this annoying overly calm and rational tone that he seemed to use no matter how much she tried to get some reaction out of him.

It wasn't just because she wanted to. He had started it. He'd tried to provoke her by introducing himself to her again when he and Gray and Zeb entered the conference room. He knew that she already knew what his name was. She might not have been happy to be forced into working with a shrink, but she wasn't stupid. She had heard his name. He'd just being trying to get a rise out of her, and it had worked.

No one infuriated her this much in such a short amount of time.

"Proof?" she asked incredulously. "Three other girls also disappeared while driving alone on remote roads. All of their cars were found parked at the side of the road. There were no signs that they had been run off the road and stumbled off—injured and disoriented. It was like they had deliberately pulled over, parked, and then they just disappeared. Three other times. Exactly like this. Identical circumstances. That's my proof."

Dr. Barlow just smiled.

That *shrink* smile.

The one that made her blood boil.

"That is pretty compelling proof," he drawled.

She took a long, deep breath so she didn't say something she would regret later. "Amelia Lexis disappeared in the same way as the previous three victims. She fits the age demographic that the killer has been targeting. We need to talk with her family and friends to confirm that they don't believe she would simply have walked off of her own free will, then we can officially work this as an abduction."

"It is interesting that all of the girls pulled their cars over to the side of the road," Dr. Barlow said, thoughtful now.

"There were no signs of a crash, no marks on the back of the car to indicate someone deliberately ran them off the road. The cars of the other victims were all inspected; there were no mechanical reasons for the cars to be stopped. These are all young girls, only in their teens, they all went missing at night, and all on deserted roads. It doesn't seem like the kind of place that they would feel comfortable stopping on, especially alone," Zeb said.

"Why do you think they stopped their cars here?" Gray asked Dr. Barlow, clearly interested in the shrink's opinion, unlike herself. She didn't need some criminal psychiatrist to tell her how to do her job.

"Because they felt safe," she answered before Dr. Barlow could say a word. "Whoever abducted them used a ruse that got the girls to stop their cars of their own free will. Whatever it was had to be something that wasn't threatening. Maybe he faked a breakdown of his own car. Maybe he staged a crash. Maybe he lay at the side of the road and pretended to be injured. Whatever it was, it was compelling enough that three young teenage girls, alone at night on a deserted road, felt safe enough to get out of their cars."

Dr. Barlow nodded. "The abductions were seamless. He didn't leave behind any witnesses. He didn't leave behind any evidence of what he did to get them to pull over. He didn't leave *any* evidence behind at all."

"It wasn't just the abductions that were done seamlessly," Zeb added. "The body dumps were seamless too. No witnesses, no hair or fibers left behind on the bodies. No DNA either, which, considering the extent of the internal damage from him raping them, means he spent a lot of time being careful while he held them prisoner, and then cleaning the bodies when he was done with them."

Sapphire hated that.

She hated when killers just threw away their victims like they were trash.

Yes, it was probably partly because of her own history, but it was also because it was just plain wrong. You didn't treat other people like that.

They were *people—not garbage*—and she couldn't stand when she saw bodies left in dumpsters or thrown in shallow graves or discarded like they didn't mean anything.

It was wrong.

Because they did mean something.

They meant a lot.

They were people.

People.

And that meant they deserved better.

They deserved justice.

And she was determined to get it for them.

"Sapphire?" A hand lightly touched her shoulder, and she automatically jolted away from it. No one touched her without her permission. No one.

"What?" she asked, taking a step sideways. "And since when are we on a first name basis, *Dr. Barlow?*"

"I thought since we're going to be working so closely together there was really no need for formalities," the shrink replied, undaunted by her attitude.

What was wrong with him?

He was supposedly some top criminal psychiatrist. Couldn't he see that she didn't want to be chummy with him? If they had to work together, then so be it, but that was it. She didn't want to be friends with this man. She didn't want to be friends with anyone. She just wanted to do her job, save as many people as she could, bring as many criminals to justice as she could, spend time with her sisters, then die.

"We were discussing more theories about the case. It looked like you zoned out," Dr. Barlow continued, only now his eyes had gone all doctor-like and were trying to pry inside her mind and figure out what was going on there.

Sapphire curtained her gaze, and fixed him with a fake smile of her own. No one got inside her head. It wasn't a pretty place to be. She was stuck with it, but that was no reason to let anyone else in. "And what theories were you discussing?"

"Gideon was just saying that he thought the man we're looking for is probably involved somehow in law enforcement," Gray replied.

So, it seemed they were all on a first name basis now—all except for her. "*Dr. Barlow*," she said, deliberately emphasizing the formal name, "isn't the first to come to that conclusion. That is what Elijah and I had in our profile. The abductions, the lack of evidence, the way he left the bodies, the fact that there was no connection to the victims besides the fact that they had all been driving alone on deserted roads at night—it was an obvious conclusion to come to."

If this was the best that the criminal psychiatrist could do, then what was the point of having him here?

She would have been better off on her own. At least then, she wouldn't have to waste mental effort on dealing with this man.

"We aren't going to find anything else here," she said, turning and heading for the car. She was ready to be out of the cold and she was ready to be away from Dr. Barlow for a while. "We may as well head back to the precinct. Start looking for anyone in law enforcement who has any connection to fish."

Sapphire was sure that was the key.

If they could figure out the connection to fish, they would have their killer.

~

8:40 P.M.

"You would not believe my day," Sapphire said as she dropped down into a couch in her living room.

"I thought you were going to be home early tonight," Diamond said. "You know, because you were shot yesterday."

Oh, right.

She'd forgotten about that.

She'd been way too busy to worry about it.

If it hadn't been for her boss forcing her to leave, she would still have been at work, trying to find who was involved in law enforcement and also had a connection to fish. So far, she hadn't been able to find anything, and she hated that she had been forced to stop just because someone else decided she should go home and rest. The next person she investigated could have been the one she was looking for. Now she would have to wait for tomorrow to continue her search. What would happen to Amelia in that time?

Whatever it was, it would be horrific.

And that thought tortured her.

How could she go home to her beautiful, comfortable house, eat a nice dinner, go to sleep—even if it was only for a few hours—while Amelia was suffering?

While millions of people around the globe were suffering.

That thought consumed her most days. There was so much suffering in the world, and she wanted to stop it, but she couldn't. That was her own personal hell. Knowing that people suffered, and there was nothing she could do to stop it.

"Sapphire."

She jumped as someone poked her shoulder. "What?"

"I asked you how your arm was feeling today," Diamond said.

"It's fine. Not bothering me at all," she answered honestly.

"Then what has you in a mood?" Amethyst asked, passing her a bowl of plain pasta—her favorite meal—and sitting beside her.

"I'm not in a *mood*," she protested, although she knew that was a lie. She *was* in a mood and she knew exactly who was to blame for said mood.

"Liar." Ruby called her out on her fib.

Sapphire couldn't help but smile—the first one since she had found out she was being forced to work with a shrink on a case that was probably way more personal to her than it should be. That was what family did. They called you out when you were doing the wrong thing or when you lied or when you made bad choices. They did it because they loved you, and even though it might annoy you in the moment, knowing that you meant enough to someone that they wouldn't let any bad behavior slide, was kind of nice.

"So, what's up?" Ruby asked, joining the rest of them in the living area.

"It's not Elijah, is it?" Diamond asked, sounding stricken.

Again, Sapphire had to wonder what her oldest sister's sudden interest in her partner was all about. "No, nothing to do with Elijah. He's doing better. He's doing well. He's going to be in the hospital for a while, but he's out of danger now. I even spoke to him at lunchtime today. He sounded weak, but like his usual self—he complained about being holed up in bed and not able to help with the case."

"Oh, good," Diamond said, dropping her gaze to her hands in her lap that she had scrunched tightly together.

"So, if it's not Elijah, and it's not your arm bothering you, then why are you complaining about your day?" Amethyst asked.

"Since Elijah is in the hospital, I expected to have to work with another detective on all my current cases. I assumed it would be Gray and Zeb since they were the ones who interviewed me in the hospital after the shooting."

"But it wasn't them?" Amethyst asked.

"No, it was, but Sergeant Langsworth assigned someone else to work the serial killer case with us."

"Who?" Ruby asked.

"Dr. Gideon Barlow," she replied. She didn't even like to utter the man's name. It felt like some urban legend, if she said his name so many times in a row, he would appear behind her to babble smugly about his theories, which were conclusions she had already come to herself.

"A psychiatrist?" Diamond asked. Given their history and what had happened to them when they were all teenagers, she wasn't the only one with experience with shrinks. They all had spent time in a psychiatrist's office.

"The most obnoxious one I've ever met." She pouted, probably looking very much like a petulant toddler instead of the twenty-six-year-old homicide detective that she was.

"Why? What did he do?" Ruby asked.

"He thought he was going to come riding in and solve this case, but all he did was give theories that Elijah and I had already come up with."

"And?" Amethyst asked.

"And what?"

"And what specifically did he do that's got your panties all in a knot?"

"It was his attitude," she said, defensive now. "He kept trying to provoke me by being all polite and smiling and making a big deal about how he wanted us all to work together for the common good."

"So, let me get this straight," Amethyst snickered. "The psychiatrist your boss brought in to help find a man who has killed six people now, as well as trying to kill two cops, was friendly, wanted to work with you to get this serial killer off the streets, and that has you all in a tizzy."

"Not a tizzy," she said, scrunching her forehead into a frown.

"Sounds like a tizzy." Ruby giggled.

"He sounds like a nice man. Why are you being so hard on him?" Diamond asked.

"I'm not being hard on him," she growled. These were her sisters. They were supposed to be on her side, not the side of some shrink they had never even met. "And he isn't a nice man. He spent the whole day deliberately trying to provoke me. Like when the sergeant dropped it on me that I'd be working with him, he introduced himself, then when I was getting things ready to brief Gray and Zeb and him in the conference room, he came in and introduced himself again."

"So, he wanted to make sure you knew his name since you'd be working with him, and now you hate him?" Diamond asked, her eyes wide in confusion.

"It wasn't what he said; it was how he said it," she harrumphed. "He's pompous. He thinks he's better than us because he's a psychiatrist and we're just cops. He thinks he's going to come in and solve this case, just like that, and take the credit for it even though Elijah and I spent hours and hours working on this."

"You're worried about not getting credit for solving a case?" Diamond asked. "That doesn't sound like you."

Sapphire shook her head. That wasn't it. She didn't know how to explain to her sisters that Gideon Barlow got under her skin and drove her crazy.

"You know what I think?" Amethyst asked.

"No, and I don't want to either," she said sullenly, taking a mouthful of the pasta, that had now gone cold.

"I think," Amethyst continued, undaunted, "that you like him."

"Like him?" she repeated, horrified. The very notion was absurd.

"That's what it sounds like. Was he an attractive psychiatrist?"

Amethyst goaded, ignoring the swat on the shoulder her twin sister gave her.

"He ... he was ... I suppose ..." she stuttered.

"So, he was pretty hot, huh?" Amethyst laughed smugly.

"I suppose he was physically attractive," she said haughtily. "But that has nothing to do with things. He was smug and pompous and annoying and smug—"

"You said that one already," Amethyst said.

"Whatever," she said, grabbing her bowl and standing up. "I don't like that man. I don't care that he's attractive. He's is a pompous, arrogant man who I am only working with because I've been forced to. As soon as this case is over, he'll be gone and I'll be relieved to see the last of him."

"Methinks thou dost protest too much," Amethyst singsonged.

"Give her a break." Ruby nudged her twin. "You can see that she likes him but doesn't want to admit it."

"I don't like him," she said. "And I'm not going to waste my night sitting around talking about him. I'm going to eat my dinner and do a little more work before I go to bed. And I don't want to hear another word about Dr. Gideon Barlow. It's bad enough I have to work with him. I don't want to think about him or hear about him or talk about him at home."

With that, she turned and stalked off upstairs to her bedroom.

As well as calling you out when you were doing the wrong thing, family also loved to tease you mercilessly.

Her sisters were wrong.

She didn't like Gideon Barlow.

What was there about him to like? So he had warm brown eyes, and no doubt a body that would have most women drooling.

But not her.

She didn't care about those things.

All she cared about was saving as many people as she could.

She did not like Dr. Gideon Barlow.

She did not.

~

10:33 P.M.

With a yawn, Gideon pushed back from the table.

It was time to call it a night.

He'd been working this case nonstop all day, and he needed a break. He needed to turn off his mind for a while—relax, take a shower, get some sleep. Often, once he stopped trying so hard to find the answers, he finally found them.

The mind was funny that way.

It was a mystery that he didn't think anyone was ever going to fully solve, and truth be told, he kind of liked it that way. Although he had spent his entire adult life studying the mind—how it worked and the things that influenced it—he was still surprised by things that people said and did.

Immediately, his thoughts turned to Detective Sapphire Hatcher.

Not that they had strayed far from her since the time they'd met this morning. There was something about her that screamed out to him. No matter how hard he tried, he couldn't shut it out.

She needed help; he just had to figure out how best to help her. Dealing with her was going to be like walking a tightrope. If he didn't push her hard enough, he was never going to gain her trust, but if he pushed her too hard, he'd push her away forever.

And that didn't sit well with him.

It was more than just wanting to help her fight her demons so she could finally find a way to be free of them. It went deeper than that. He was attracted to her. That made sense; she was a gorgeous woman. She obviously worked out, probably partially because of her job and partially because she needed to know she was strong enough to fight off anyone who came after her, or at least to give herself the illusion that she could. She had long brown hair with natural red and blonde highlights, and those eyes of hers were just amazing.

Physical attraction was natural, but this inability to stop thinking about her was something else.

Gideon was never one to fight his feelings; he'd seen how doing that turned out. He knew the damage that denying oneself the necessity of emotion did to a person. His paternal grandparents had had two children—two boys. The younger was his father; the older one had disappeared from a park when he was nine, never to be seen again.

No ransom.

No body.

Nothing.

His young uncle had simply vanished.

The effects that had on his grandparents and his father lasted even until today, some fifty years later. His grandfather had become cold and hard, pushing away his wife and remaining son in an effort to protect himself from getting hurt again. His grandmother had refused to believe that her son was dead, insisting to this day, that one day he would return to her. They still lived in the same house. Their oldest son's room remained a shrine to him, untouched from the day that he had disappeared.

His father, too, had been touched by what happened to his big brother.

Growing up, Gideon and his younger brother were nearly stifled with love. Overprotective was an understatement. His parents didn't let them go anywhere alone. They were homeschooled; they had few friends. They were never allowed to go to sleepovers at the homes of friends they *did* have, and all play dates had to be at his house.

Having been made to feel unworthy by his parents, his father had made sure that he showered his own children with love. Every time they got a good grade on a paper, won a soccer game, or any other achievement—no matter how small—there was a celebration with cake, balloons, streamers, gifts, and trophies. Their father wanted them to know that he loved them because grief and trauma had denied him that show of love from his parents.

It was his own family's tragedy—and the way it had affected them—that had led him to criminal psychiatry, and thus to Sapphire Hatcher.

Her boss had told him a little about Sapphire's past, and being curious, he'd dug a little deeper, learning all there was to know about how she and her sisters had been sold to human traffickers by their own parents.

Gideon couldn't imagine that damage that would do to a person.

He knew what it was like to feel smothered, to wish for a moment alone so you could just do your own thing without being constantly monitored. But he had always known that he was loved. Always.

Sapphire hadn't had that.

The very people who were supposed to be there to nurture her and support her—no matter what she did—were the very people who had betrayed her.

Just knowing what she had been through made him want to simultaneously track down her parents in prison and personally show them what he thought of their despicable behavior, and then he'd go to Sapphire's house, drag her into his arms and just hold her and tell her that she deserved better.

In his career, he had never dealt with a human trafficking victim. He had dealt with rapists, serial killers, child abductors, pedophiles, gang members, and drug dealers. He'd also dealt with human traffickers but never one of their victims. In a way, that made Sapphire a challenge. He wanted to learn; he wanted to figure out how to help her; he wanted to find if there was a way to help her get past what she had lived through.

"You're so egotistical," he muttered to himself as he stood and stretched, then strode to the hotel room's window, looking down at the sprawling city beneath him. "She doesn't need you to save her. She seems to be doing pretty okay on her own."

And she really did.

Yes, she struggled to work with others sometimes, no doubt because of major trust issues, and a desire to save people that was all consuming to her to the point where she would struggle to let go of work and take time off to do things for herself just for fun. Despite that, he saw a kind-hearted woman who was filled with a true desire to help others. She worked hard; she was smart; and there was just something about her edginess that made him like her even more.

She was coping the best way she knew how.

Just like his grandparents had, just like his father, and in a way, just like him. Learning how the mind worked, specifically about how trauma affected it, was his way of coping with his overbearing parents.

Gideon knew that it didn't make sense to be this infatuated with Sapphire so quickly. Despite his interest in human emotion and the workings of the mind, he didn't believe in love at first sight. But lust at first sight mixed with a desire to figure out a way to help her—that he absolutely believed in.

Taking a bite of the now cold pizza he had bought on his way back to the hotel he was staying in while he worked this case, he took a drink from the bottle of Coke. Then, despite the fact that he knew he needed rest, he returned to the desk and opened his laptop back up.

As soon as he sat back down, his border collie jumped off the bed where she'd been curled up napping and went right to the last of the pizza.

"Leave it, Luna," he warned. "I fed you already, no pizza for you."

Luna just looked up at him with those big brown eyes.

Gideon sighed, then laughed. "Fine, eat the pizza."

The dog responded by immediately grabbing the last slice of pizza and running off to the corner of the room, as though she had to protect her prize in case he changed his mind.

Returning his attention to his laptop, if Gideon knew Sapphire— and in the twelve hours or so that he had, he thought he had her pretty well figured out—she would be sitting in her house, probably in her bedroom dressed in pajamas, curled up on her bed, with her computer on her lap, working to find the serial killer she so desperately sought.

She wouldn't stop working for sleep.

She couldn't.

That need inside her to save others wouldn't let her do anything that wasn't work.

If he achieved only one thing during his time here—in addition to helping the cops solve this case—it would be to help Sapphire realize that she wasn't doing anything wrong by taking a little time for herself. He wanted her to learn how to have fun, how to let go, how to relax. If she would let him, he'd take her out for the day. They would go wade in a creek or ride on a Ferris wheel. They'd eat cotton candy and go to the circus. They would laugh and talk and have fun.

Fun.

He wasn't sure she knew the meaning of the word.

He wanted to teach her.

Perhaps he even *needed* to teach her.

All he had to do was find a way to convince her to give him a chance.

But for now, he had a case to solve. Sapphire was convinced that the fact that she had smelled fish on the man who had shot her meant something important, and he trusted her instincts.

So, he would work until he couldn't hold his eyes open any longer.

If Sapphire was giving up sleep to find this killer, then so would he.

CHAPTER Seven

January 5th
9:04 A.M.

For some reason, this was the part of her job that she hated the most.

It wasn't dealing with victims or coming face-to-face with the vilest of criminals. It also wasn't seeing the mangled bodies of those who had met an unfortunate end. It was this. Standing outside the house of a victim's family about to go in and ask them about the person they had loved and yet lost.

Sapphire wasn't sure exactly why this bothered her so much.

It wasn't like her own family had cared when she and her sisters were gone. When the cops had gone to interview them, all they'd done was lie and make up a story that made them look like poor, grieving parents who had been beaten up trying to save their children from the bad men.

But, whatever the reason, she hated doing these family interviews.

Today, she and Gray and Zeb would be speaking with Amelia Lexis's family. She wanted to get confirmation from the family that they didn't believe that their daughter would voluntarily make herself disappear.

Although it was cold out, she didn't want to wait in her car for the others to turn up, so she was standing on the sidewalk outside the Lexis family home, hovering from foot to foot and rubbing her hands together trying to keep warm.

Last night, she'd been back to her usual four hours of sleep, but she actually felt more energized than she had yesterday morning when she had gotten a full night's sleep. It was probably because for once her dreams had been pleasant. Most nights she slept dreamlessly, occasionally—perhaps once or twice a month—she would have nightmares. But last night she had dreamed about a man. The two of them had been laughing, then they were kissing, and the next thing she knew, they were making love.

Sapphire laughed.

She never had sex dreams, and she had no idea what had brought this one on.

The face of the man in the dream had been fuzzy. She didn't think it was anyone specific; it was probably just her silly sisters and all their talk about how they thought she liked Dr. Barlow.

That couldn't be more untrue.

In fact, it was the exact opposite of truth.

"Finally," she muttered as a car pulled up on the curb. Zeb and Gray were supposed to meet her here at nine, and it was already nearly quarter past. It wasn't that she minded waiting. She knew traffic could be bad on these cold, icy winter mornings, but she was glad they were here. She just wanted to get this interview over with so she could go back to trying to find this killer.

The car door opened, and her mouth fell open when she saw who it was.

It wasn't Gray or Zeb.

It was Dr. Barlow.

What was *he* doing here?

He wasn't supposed to be here; he was supposed to be back at the precinct doing whatever it was he had come here to do.

Sapphire thought she'd have at least another hour or two before she had to deal with him again.

Apparently, she wasn't that lucky.

"Why are you here?" she asked when he walked over to her.

"Good morning to you, too, Sapphire," he said. His brown eyes crinkled as he smiled at her, undaunted by her lack of enthusiasm at seeing him.

"I was expecting Zeb and Gray," she said.

"We decided I would be of better use here, with you, interviewing the parents, and they would be better off going through files," he told her.

"*We* decided?" she shot back. "I don't remember my opinion being sought."

"Don't worry, Sapphire, I don't bite." He chuckled. "Now let's get inside; you look cold. You should have waited in your car."

She was about to tell him that she should have done whatever suited her, but he touched his hand to the small of her back to turn her and guide her up the garden path.

At his touch, her skin broke out in a mass of goose pimples.

The face from her dream suddenly became clear.

It was Dr. Barlow's face.

She had spent the night dreaming about making love to a shrink.

A shrink she didn't even like.

Sapphire gasped.

"What's wrong?" Dr. Barlow asked, immediately attentive.

"Nothing," she muttered, yanking herself away from him and hurrying up the path. Why was she dreaming about this man? *Her sisters.* It had to be because of her sisters. They had put this idea in her head right before she went to bed. It was simply the power of suggestion.

"Are you sure you're okay?" the shrink asked as he came up behind her as she pressed the bell and waited for the door to be answered.

"Yes, of course," she replied haughtily. She just wanted this case to be over and this man to be gone. She didn't like him. She didn't.

"Hello?" Matt Lexis said as he opened the door.

Pleased to let her mind focus solely on work, Sapphire relaxed a little. "Mr. Lexis, I'm Detective Hatcher, and this is Dr. Barlow. I called last night to set up this time to talk to you about your daughter."

"Ah, yes." He nodded and held the door open wider so they could enter. "Please come in. My wife is in the kitchen; we've been waiting for you. I thought you said there would be three of you, though. Three cops," he added.

"There was a change in plans," she said, trying to resist the urge to toss a frown in Dr. Barlow's direction.

"I don't know what we can tell you," Mr. Lexis said as he led them through a lounge room, down a short hallway and into a bright, airy kitchen. "Amelia just left here the other night. Nothing seemed unusual."

It was normal for victims' families to think that they didn't know anything relevant to their loved one's case. Often, it was true, but sometimes, it wasn't. Sometimes they did know something helpful; they just didn't know they knew it.

"That's fine, Mr. Lexis," she said. "We'll just ask you a couple of questions, and if you don't know the answers, we'll just continue working the case. And if you do know something, we'll add that to what we already know."

The man nodded and pointed to the table where his wife was sitting. Trish Lexis was like an older version of her daughter. Both Amelia and her mother had the same brown eyes, the same red hair, the same freckles, the same broad shoulders and long limbs.

The woman looked up at them and nodded her greeting. "Do you want something to drink?"

"No, thank you," Sapphire replied, taking a seat.

"I'll have a coffee, please," Dr. Barlow said.

Mrs. Lexis nodded and stood, poured a cup of coffee, brought it to Dr. Barlow, and returned to her seat.

"What can you tell us about the last time you saw Amelia?" Sapphire asked.

The couple exchanged glances, then Mr. Lexis was the one who spoke. "It didn't go well. Amelia told us that she was going to drop out of college. She didn't have a plan of what she wanted to do with her life; she had just decided that it wouldn't be college. We were disappointed in her. We worked so hard all her life to give her the very best of everything, and then she just wanted to throw it all away to wander aimlessly through life."

From the look on their faces, both Mr. and Mrs. Lexis now realized what a mistake that had been.

Everyone had to find their own path in life, and it had to be their own.

You couldn't always be what someone else wanted you to be.

She would know.

She had tried for the last decade to be what other people wanted her to be because she wasn't even sure who she wanted herself to be.

"Did you argue with her about her decision?" Sapphire asked.

"Not argue, exactly. We expressed our displeasure, and it put a dampener on the Christmas and New Year celebrations. Amelia left a couple days early, but I think she was more upset we weren't supportive of her idea than angry with us," Mr. Lexis replied.

"Do you think that Amelia was upset enough with you that she would hurt herself? Or that she would want to leave her old life and start a new one?" Sapphire asked. She didn't like having to ask already grieving parents such questions, but it was her job. She had to know if there was any chance that Amelia wasn't the serial killer's next victim because if they were wrong, they would waste valuable hours looking into her life. Hours that could be better spent either finding the killer's real next victim or trying to find the killer himself.

"No," Mrs. Lexis said firmly. "She might have been upset with us, but she was excited about trying to find her purpose in life. She wouldn't have hurt herself, and she wouldn't have just disappeared."

Sapphire believed her. "When Amelia left, did you notice anything unusual? Maybe a car in the street that took off the same time she left? Or maybe a car hanging around during the time she was here?"

"There was nothing unusual," Mr. Lexis said. "She just said goodbye, grabbed her suitcase, and drove off."

"I thought we had time," Mrs. Lexis said, her eyes going vacant. "I thought that she would come to her senses, go back to college, and everything would go back to normal. Or if she was insistent that she wanted something else, she would find out what it was, and we would realize that she knew what she was doing. Wherever she is, do you think she knows we're proud of her?" The woman looked up now, her gaze begging them to reassure her.

She wanted to, but she didn't know what to say.

Turned out she didn't have to.

"I'm sure she knows," Dr. Barlow spoke up. "Family is like that. Even when other things cloud it, deep down we know that the love is always there."

"Thank you." Mrs. Lexis smiled gratefully.

There was only one last thing she needed to ask before they could leave. "Mr. and Mrs. Lexis, did Amelia mention anything to you about any fears that someone had been following her or done anything to scare or upset her either in real life or on social media?"

"No, nothing," Mrs. Lexis said softly.

"Thank you for your time," Sapphire said, pushing back her chair and standing.

"We can show ourselves out," Dr. Barlow said as he stood as well. "We're doing everything we can to find your daughter."

He thought he was so smart.

He thought he had it all figured out.

He thought he knew how all families worked.

But he didn't.

Sometimes family just hurt your feelings, sometimes—like with the Lexises—they loved each other, but they made mistakes because they were only human. But sometimes family was your worst enemy and their only goal was to destroy you for their own personal gain.

10:21 A.M.

"Where are we going?"

Gideon looked over to Sapphire. She was sitting in the passenger seat of his car, staring at him suspiciously. Although he knew it was probably a bad idea and was likely only going to wind up making her more irritated with him, he couldn't help but smile at her. She was always so wary about everything, always expecting the worst-case scenario. Which he supposed made sense, given her past and what her own parents had done to her.

"I want to run a theory by you," he told her.

"What theory?" she asked.

"I want to wait until we're there before I ask your opinion."

"When we're where?" she asked again, clearly frustrated.

For the life of him, he couldn't quite figure out why it was that she disliked him so intently. At first, he'd thought it was because he was encroaching on her territory, and she felt like she was going to be shafted out of her own case. While that made sense and he suspected that was a part of it, he thought that there was more to it. Gideon had hoped that this car ride, when it was just the two of them alone and she couldn't outright ignore him by working, would be a good time for them to talk, to get to know each other a little better, and maybe he could figure out where she was coming from.

Risking her wrath, he ignored her repeated attempts to find out where they were going and instead decided to take a leap of faith. He had long ago learned that sometimes the best way to work as a psychiatrist was just to trust what your gut was telling you, and right now, his gut was telling him that beating around the bush with Sapphire was only going to make her feel like she was being played. That—more than anything—was what would make her shut down.

"When Sergeant Langsworth asked me to consult with your department and help with this case, she gave me a little bit of background on the cops that I would be working with."

Sapphire's mouth fell open and for a brief second he caught a glimpse of vulnerability in her green eyes that were always so carefully clothed in a mixture of dedication to her job and mild irritation at the people around her.

It was gone almost as soon as it was there, and she was back to her usual frustration. "What does *that* mean?"

"Exactly what you think it does," he said, watching the road and then glancing back at her. He wasn't afraid of her. Gideon suspected that part of the reason that Sapphire was always so brisk with people was because she wanted to continue to perpetuate this air of dislike of everyone around her to keep them away. If people were afraid of her, they wouldn't try to get close to her, and she wouldn't have to worry about letting anyone in.

"So, what?" she replied, resting her head back against the headrest and crossing her arms across her chest, aiming for nonchalance but failing. "So, you know about my past. Good for you."

"You know it doesn't change how I see your ability to do your job, right?" he asked. He wondered whether she doubted herself and that was part of the reason that she didn't want him here. Was she afraid that if he found a critical piece of information pertaining to this case that people were going to think less of her?

"Why would it?" she snapped. "I studied hard in college, graduated at the top of my class. I passed my psych exam, and I've been a good cop for the last several years."

So maybe it wasn't lack of confidence in her abilities to do her job that had her resenting his presence here.

Or she was just trying to confuse him.

She was definitely a tricky one. It wasn't going to be easy deciphering her secrets.

"I don't doubt that you're a good cop. No one does. That isn't why your boss asked me to come. This man we're hunting tried to kill you. Have you given any thought to what you're going to do if he comes back to try to finish off what he started?"

He didn't like the idea of the killer learning that he was unsuccessful in his attempts to kill Sapphire and her partner. The killer had been meticulous in everything he had done so far, and Gideon was sure he wouldn't like loose ends. As long as this killer remained at large, Sapphire was in danger, which was all the more reason to find this man as quickly as they could.

Sapphire waved a hand disinterestedly at his suggestion that she might be in danger. "I hope he does come after me. At least then this would be over."

Well, she certainly didn't suffer from a lack of ego.

"Still, I think you should be careful. You live with your sisters, right? I'd hate for them to get caught in the cross fire."

"Leave my sisters out of this," she said fiercely.

Noted.

Bringing up her sisters was going to have the opposite effect than what he wanted to achieve. Pushing her was one thing, but he had to remember that he was walking a tightrope; one wrong move and he would lose any chance he had at helping Sapphire.

They were approaching their destination. It was time to make his offer. Who knows, maybe coming right out and offering would be enough to get her to open up. "Sapphire, if you ever need someone to talk to, then I'm here. Any time, day or night. I'm a good listener, and anything that you say to me will be kept completely in confidence."

"I'm not in the market for a shrink," she said, disdain dripping from her voice, so there was definitely a reason she didn't like psychiatrists. Maybe that meant her dislike of him wasn't personal. She just didn't like him because of his job. That was definitely something he could work with. He just needed to find a way to show her that he was different than the shrink she had been a patient of in the past. If he could convince her that she could trust him, he could get her to share her pain with him, and he could help her.

"If you change your mind—"

"I won't," she interrupted. Then she growled when she saw where they were going. "Why are we coming back here?"

"I told you. I have a theory on the killer," he said as he drove down the road where Amelia Lexis's abandoned car had been found.

"And you have to bring me here to tell me?" Sapphire asked. "Why can't you just tell me your theory when we get back to the station and Gray and Zeb are there so they can hear it too?"

Because he had wanted a little time alone with her.

Not that he was going to say that out loud.

He'd dreamed about Sapphire last night. She'd been naked and in his bed, her hands roaming his body, touching him everywhere, kissing him, making love to him. By the time he woke up, he'd been so hot and bothered he'd had to have a cold shower before driving to the Lexis house.

"I guess I could have told you at the precinct," he agreed as he pulled the car to a stop. "But I wanted you to see."

With a groan, she got out of the car and then looked at him expectantly. "So?"

"I figured out why all four of the women pulled over even though they were alone on a deserted road at night." The realization had come to him in the early hours of the morning, and once he'd figured it out, he'd finally felt like he had earned a couple of hours sleep.

"Oh?" She arched a brow but looked skeptical.

"Amelia and the others weren't targeted. There was no one stalking her or following her. She was simply a victim of circumstance by being in the wrong place at the wrong time."

Sapphire made a *hurry up* motion with her hand.

"They pulled over because they thought that they had no choice. That they had to do it. We discussed the possibility that we were looking for someone who was involved in some form of law enforcement. I think they pulled over because they saw the flashing lights and heard the sirens of a cop car."

Sapphire gasped, and the color drained from her already pale face. "You think that we're looking for a cop?"

"I think it's the only thing that makes sense. What else would make a young teenage girl, who had no doubt been schooled to keep herself safe and avoid dangerous situations since she was just a child, pull over and get out of her car alone at night?"

The look on her face said that she agreed with him. Her devastated green eyes met his. "We're looking for a cop. We're looking for one of my colleagues."

Unfortunately, Gideon agreed with her.

12:09 P.M.

He snuck away here whenever he could.

This was his happy place.

It definitely wasn't the happy place of anyone else who came here.

He chuckled at his own joke. That was quite the understatement. Not many people came here, but the ones who did never left.

Well ... they left, but not alive.

This was his kill room.

It wasn't much, just a small shack out by a lake where he came and stayed when he went fishing. He'd been lucky to find this place. It was secluded, and when you were sitting by the lake, a fishing pole in your hand, the birds chirping, the wind in the trees, you felt like you were in the middle of nowhere. But he was a busy guy, and he didn't have hours to spend driving out to the country to go fishing, so being only twenty minutes from his house meant he could come out here any time he wanted.

Most days he made at least one trip out here. Not because he had to. He didn't keep his victims here. He just liked it out here. He liked the quiet; he liked being surrounded by nature; he liked not having to be bothered by people for a while.

He was *not* a people person.

His job required him to pretend that he was, and he hated it. Half the time, all he did was fantasize about slitting their throats or grabbing the nearest heavy object and slamming it into their skulls. He liked the sound a skull made as it shattered. He remembered the first time he'd done it. It hadn't been anything planned. It was completely sponta-neous, and he'd even been a little surprised that he'd done it. It wasn't until the mug connected with the woman's head that he realized what he'd done. Of course, the blow hadn't been hard enough to kill her, and since he didn't want a mess left behind, he struck her several more times until he finally finished her off. Then he'd had to find a way to dump the body so that it wouldn't point back to him, but that was a different story.

He picked up a jar he had on the small table in the corner. He used it to hold fish hooks, but it could be used as weapon. Perhaps he could kill the next one by beating her head in ...

No.

Stay strong.

Stick with the plan.

That was the way to make sure he didn't get caught.

Although ...

He'd have to change how he dumped the bodies. Now that the cops knew for sure that he was leaving them at movie theater dumpsters, they would no doubt stick cops at every single theater when they knew it was time for him to dump the next body.

Damn his obsessive-compulsive disorder that forced him to dispose of the next girl in exactly two weeks.

He had known that starting down this road was a bad idea because he knew himself well enough to know that he wouldn't be able to break out of the pattern once he'd started it. Well, there was nothing he could do about it now; he was just going to have to work with what he had. Changing the way he threw away the girls when he got done with them was bad enough, but making that change was a necessity. It was survival, so he would find a way to cope with it.

Changing anything else was out of the question.

As much as he wanted to bash Amelia Lexis's head in, he wouldn't.

He couldn't cope with any more changes, no matter how much he wanted to.

And he did want to.

Setting the jar back down, he took the two steps from the table where he stored his fishing equipment to the large bench in the middle of the room. When their weeks were up, this was where he brought the girls. He laid them out on this bench, then he climbed on top of them, wrapped his hands around their necks and squeezed.

As much fun as it was bashing someone's head in, there was nothing like watching the life drain slowly out of a person.

It was a rush like nothing else.

He liked eyes. People said they were the windows to the soul, but he had a different opinion. To him they were the windows to the afterlife.

What lay beyond this life?

He didn't know.

Every time he climbed onto a victim and started squeezing the life out of them, he watched carefully for clues. He could see the changes, the life slowing ebbing away was evident, as clear as day. He could even tell the exact second when their life was over. He didn't need to check for a pulse or put an ear to their chests to see if they were still breathing. He just knew.

He *knew*.

So why couldn't he figure out how to read what they were seeing after they passed from this life to the next?

Frustrated, he thumped a fist on the bench.

He wanted answers.

He needed them.

Maybe this time, he would finally see something. He had tried different positions, leaning in close, keeping a bit of distance, looking in both eyes, focusing on one at a time, but so far, nothing had worked.

Next time, he was going to try going slower. That could be the problem. He went too fast; he put his hands around their necks and squeezed until they died. It happened too quickly, they didn't get a chance to see what was waiting for them until they were already walking through death's door, and by then, they couldn't show him. It was too late.

But this time, he would change his method. He would squeeze for a while until she blacked out, and then he would wait for her to regain consciousness. Surely, that would make sure there were some signs in her eyes about what she had seen. Then once she was awake, he'd start the process all over again. If he did it enough times, he should get the answers he was seeking.

He was starting to get excited. He wished he didn't have to wait another eleven days to get his next chance.

What if it didn't work the way he had planned?

What would he try next?

Amelia Lexis would be kept alive for two weeks, then he had one more chance after that. It had originally been part of his plan—set himself a deadline to get the information he wanted so he was motivated to actually do what he had to, to get it.

If it didn't work, he didn't have a backup plan.

His anxiety levels were rising.

He struggled to cope when things didn't go according to his plan. He liked the world to be orderly, organized. He liked to know what was going to happen and when. He lived according to his routines, and when something happened to mess them up, he had been known to flip out.

But that wasn't going to happen this time because there wasn't going to be anything to flip out about. He would get the answers he needed, either from Amelia Lexis or whoever he chose next. He had plenty of opportunities to get his information. It would happen. It had to because he honestly didn't know where he would go after this.

It was time to leave.

Time to set the peace and tranquility of nature aside for now and return to the concrete jungle of the city. If he didn't have this place to come to, he probably would have lost his mind long before now. This place was his medication; it was what he needed to survive, and without it, he wouldn't need anyone else to tell him what lay beyond death because he would be experiencing it for himself.

With a sigh, he walked outside, closing the shack door behind him. Before he got in his car, he took a moment just to look at the way the weak sunlight glittered on the lake. It was gorgeous. All the happiest moments of his life focused around the outdoors—hiking, camping, fishing, boating, rock climbing, skiing. It didn't matter what he was doing. As long as he could feel the sun on his face and the wind in his hair, he was happy.

It was getting harder and harder to leave here.

To go back to his real life that was really more his fake life. This was what was real to him, this right here. Maybe once he had his answers, he would just disappear and live out here. There were plenty of fish in the lake, and he could probably grow a few things in a garden.

Soon.

Soon he could make that dream a reality, but for now, he had to play the part, do his job, pretend he was who everyone else thought he was.

Play the game.

It was what most people did on a daily basis, only the mask he wore covered secrets that were a little more macabre than others.

3:45 P.M.

. . .

Her mood was at an all-time low.

They were looking for a cop.

That still hadn't really sunk in.

Sapphire was in shock; she felt like she was walking around in a daze, and she couldn't concentrate. She kept running through all of her colleagues and wondering if any of them were capable of doing this.

It should have occurred to her before now.

Of course, they were looking for a cop.

Who else could it be?

The way the bodies were dumped, the way they were cleaned so carefully, and the way all the women pulled over without being run off the road.

It was all so obvious.

Obvious, but horrifying.

Cops were supposed to be the good guys. It wasn't like she was some naïve little girl who thought that all police officers were superheroes who could do no wrong. She knew that there were bad apples in any bunch, and the police force was certainly no exception. She even knew that there had been a cop amongst the men who were arrested in the woods that day ten years ago.

But this was different.

These were her colleagues.

They were people that she saw every single day.

For months—or years—she had been coming to work and been in the same building as the very killer she was hunting.

It was unsettling, to say the least.

What if it was someone she worked closely with? What if it was someone she spoke to on a daily basis? What if it was someone she sat beside? What if it was someone working this case?

She knew it wasn't Elijah, he had been with her the night they'd been shot. They knew the man who shot them was the killer they were looking for because he had one of the bodies with him. That excluded both her and Elijah from being the killer, but everyone else was still a suspect.

How could she look at anyone she came into contact with and not think that it could be them?

They needed to find this man—now, more than ever.

If the killer really was someone who was close to this case, he was able to keep track of their progress. He knew what they were doing; he knew their theories; he knew every single thing they were doing and could adjust his plans accordingly.

Feeling like there were a million pairs of eyes watching her every move, Sapphire walked down the hall to the vending machine. She needed sugar. A lot of it. Slipping some money into the slot, she punched in the code for her favorite candy bar, a Snickers, and watched as the little arm holding it in place moved sideways and the candy bar dropped down. She stooped to get it, wincing slightly at the pull on her arm. She kept forgetting that she had been shot because she had much bigger things to worry about.

It'd only been forty-eight hours since the shooting, and she didn't think she had taken any painkillers besides what the doctor at the hospital had given her. She didn't usually like to take medication because at the back of her mind she was suspicious that someone was going to use them to dope her up so they could do whatever they wanted with her.

It was stupid. She knew that, but it was hard to shake.

Slipping in another dollar, she pressed the buttons and waited for the can of Diet Coke to drop. She was about to reach for it when someone stopped her.

"I got it."

She blinked and looked over to see Dr. Barlow beside her. Without waiting for her permission, he nudged her sideways, leaned down and scooped up the can and opened it before holding it out to her.

"There you go." He smiled. That smile that she hated so much. He thought that he was so smart just because he had come to the conclusion that they were looking for a cop. She should have figured that out on her own. She already knew they were looking for someone in law enforcement, and she would have come to the conclusion it was a cop eventually.

"I could have done that myself." She frowned.

"I know you could," he agreed, his smile never faltering.

Why did this guy smile so much? And why wasn't he put off by her attitude like everyone else was? She never really worried about her snarkiness pushing people away because she didn't want them to be close to her anyway.

"Your arm looked like it was hurting you," Dr. Barlow continued, still grinning at her like an idiot. "I brought some painkillers for you."

"I don't need any," she snapped, ignoring both the bottle in his hand and the can that she no longer felt like drinking.

He cocked his head, looking at her inquisitively like she was an alien he was trying to figure out. Was that why he wouldn't leave her alone? Why he had cornered her in his car earlier? He had admitted he knew about her past, maybe the fact that she had been a victim of a horrendous crime appealed to the shrink in him. He probably wanted to try to fix her. Well, if that was what he was after, he was going to find himself sorely disappointed. She didn't need any fixing, and even if she did, she certainly wouldn't want this stranger fixing her.

Right now, she had too much work to do to be wasting time with this man. Turning on her heel, she headed back to her desk.

"Sapphire," Dr. Barlow said, running around her so he was in front of her. "Why are you always so stubborn? I was just trying to help. You were shot and came back to work the very next day. You were wincing; I wasn't trying to upset you. Honestly."

"I'm not stubborn, Dr. Barlow, just busy," she said, her tone dismissive.

He rolled his eyes at her, which she supposed was an improvement. At least it was an emotion besides the cheery, upbeat persona he was constantly wearing. She held back a smug smile. She hadn't lost her touch.

"I think we've moved past the formal phase," he said. "You call Gray and Zeb by their first names, so I know you're not opposed to it. Just with me."

That seemed like a statement, not a question, so she didn't bother to respond, she just sidestepped around the shrink.

He was a persistent one and dodged around her again, blocking her path. "You're always stubborn with new people, aren't you? It takes a while to earn your trust. I get it. That makes sense, given what you've been through. But I'm not the enemy here. I'm here to work with you; we have the same goal; we both want to find this killer before anyone else dies. Since we're going to be working together, don't you think it makes sense for us to just get along, be friends?"

Friends?

She almost laughed in his face.

She didn't do friends.

"No, I don't think that makes sense, Dr. Barlow," she added purposefully. She didn't know how much clearer she could make it. "You don't really want to be my friend. You want to get inside my head because you think I'm some sort of interesting project for you. You think just because I was sold and very nearly sent off to live with some pervert that gives you the right to stick your nose into my business. I didn't ask for you to help me, and I don't need help. Just stay away from me, Dr. Barlow."

With that, she edged around him, careful not to touch, and headed straight for her boss's office. She'd had enough of this. Surely she shouldn't have to work with someone who just wanted to profile her and then try to insinuate himself into her life so he could try to play with her mind. He probably wanted to write a paper on her or something.

Well, that wasn't happening.

"Sergeant?" she called out as she knocked on the office door.

Sergeant Langsworth looked up. "Sapphire, what can I do for you?"

"We need to talk."

Her boss nodded and then indicated the chair on the other side of the desk. "Take a seat."

"Thank you." She sat down and then said, "Does Dr. Barlow really need to keep consulting with us? Wasn't he just here to see if he could point us in a different direction? He's done that now, although we would have gotten to the same conclusion on our own, but now that we know we're looking for another cop, he doesn't really still need to be here. We know the people here the best. We're the ones who know what we should be looking for. Gray, Zeb, and I can take things from here."

For a long moment, the sergeant just looked at her. Her eyes seemed to pierce right through the shutters she always kept carefully in place to see right inside her mind. She hated when people thought they could figure her out.

"I'm sorry, Sapphire, but Gideon is staying until we have the killer in custody, so you're going to have to find a way to work with him."

"But he thinks that I'm some sort of project that he can work on as a side act while he's here, because you told him about my past," she said, a slight accusatory hint to her tone.

"I told him what I thought he needed to know," Sergeant Langsworth said calmly. "I'll talk to him about making sure that he sticks to this case while you're here at the station. I didn't ask him to come here and be your doctor, and he shouldn't be pressuring you if you're not interested, but he will be staying here until this case is closed."

"But—"

"No. No buts," her boss said firmly. "Find a way to make this work."

Sapphire wanted to keep arguing, but it was pointless.

She didn't want to be forced to keep working with Dr. Barlow, but it seemed the only other option she had was to take herself off this case.

That was not happening.

So, she was going to have to suck it up and find a way to work with Dr. Barlow. She just hoped this case was over sooner rather than later because she couldn't get rid of the feel of his fingers touching her arm.

As much as she wanted it to, his touch didn't repulse her.

She liked it.

She didn't know why, but she did.

∾

7:50 P.M.

She felt on edge.

Unsettled.

The shock of finding out that they were looking for a cop had worn off, but it had left her in a sort of wrung out state that she didn't know how to find her way out of.

Sapphire had considered going for a run. That usually helped her work off any pent-up energy, but right now, it was blowing snow outside, and if she tried to go jogging, knowing her luck, she would slip and break a leg and be shoved out of her own case while she recovered.

She could go to the gym, run on a treadmill, ride an exercise bike, do a weights session, but there would be too many people there, and she often felt too nervous in large groups of people to properly concentrate.

She could always go home, of course, but that would mean she either had to hang out with her sisters or go to bed. Hanging out with her sisters was about the last thing she wanted to do because she knew they were going to continue to needle her about Dr. Barlow. And if she went to bed, she was never going to fall asleep; it wasn't even eight o'clock.

Since the sergeant had kicked her out of the office, she had decided she should come to the hospital to check up on her partner. She would have stopped by at some point anyway, but probably not until later. She knew from experience that Elijah was just as much of a night owl as she was.

"Hey, partner," she said as she opened his hospital door and he turned his head from the TV to smile at her. She had never really realized how lucky she had been to have Elijah as a partner. If he knew about her past, he never brought it up. He always valued her thoughts and insights, and he never got upset with her when she was brisk or became all obsessive about a case.

"Hey, yourself," he said. "You come by to update me on the case?"

"And to see how you're doing," she replied, taking the seat beside his bed.

"Doing better. My doctors think another day or so and I can go home. Since I'm going to need some help getting up and around for a while, I'm going to stay with my sister and her family for a couple of weeks before I go home."

From the look on his face that bothered him a little. They never really talked about their lives outside their jobs much, so she didn't know what his relationship was like with his family or why having to stay with them would be upsetting. Maybe he just didn't like the idea of not being able to take care of himself.

That, she totally understood.

When she'd first been rescued from the woods ten years ago, she had been placed in foster care until an aunt and uncle had taken her in. Back then, she hadn't been able to do much for herself. It wasn't that she'd been physically incapable of it, but those first few months, she had been in shock, barely able to breathe let alone function like a person. She had needed help with even the most basic of things like getting dressed, taking a shower, eating. Slowly, she'd started to feel again, the numbness and shock wearing away, and that had presented a whole new bevy of problems, but she'd gotten her independence back and that helped a lot.

"Those weeks will fly by," she encouraged. "You'll be back at work before you know it." She was sure that she was every bit as anxious for that to happen as Elijah was.

"Your sister stopped by today with muffins," he said, pointing to a basket of raspberry and white chocolate chip muffins sitting on the table under the window.

"Diamond?" she asked. Those were her sister's favorites, but why would Diamond make them for Elijah and then come all the way down here to drop them off when she knew that she would be coming here at some point today?

"Yes." He nodded, but suddenly averted his gaze. "So, what's new with our case? You made any progress finding the man who shot us?"

Narrowing her eyes at the abrupt topic change, especially since Elijah was the one who had brought up her sister and the muffins, she acquiesced and went back to the reason for her visit here. "We are making some progress," she said somberly. "We think that we're looking for a cop."

Elijah's eyes widened, and then he swore—something he rarely did. "We knew we were looking for someone in law enforcement. We should have already narrowed it down to cop."

She felt his frustration because she felt the same way. "We hadn't discounted it. We knew it was a possibility, and we were just still keeping our options open, including anyone who had anything to do with any type of law enforcement, including support roles. But we also had to take into consideration that anyone with any basic knowledge of how to perform a successful murder was still a suspect. There are so many crime shows and books and movies, too. It's not like you need any training to know to be smart about how you commit your abduction and to make sure you don't leave any physical evidence behind. Anyone with a brain knows how to do that. So it was just too early to narrow things down to a cop specifically."

"You trying to convince me or yourself?" Elijah asked.

Sapphire glared at him. "I'm not trying to convince anyone of anything. I'm just saying that it was only natural that we hadn't narrowed things down to a police officer."

"I agree with you. We did everything we could and worked this case as hard as was humanly possible. We both nearly died trying to stop this man, and we successfully figured out where he was going to be. *You* successfully figured out where he would be. You don't need to beat yourself up."

"I'm not," she huffed.

The look he gave her said he didn't believe her. Which annoyed her, mostly because he was right. She was beating herself up over not having come to the cop conclusion on her own.

"So, what tipped you off about the cop angle?" Elijah asked.

"Not what ... who. It was Dr. Barlow, the criminal psychiatrist that Sergeant Langsworth had brought in to work the case with us. He was the one who said he thought it was a cop car that got all the girls to pull over on those deserted roads."

"I take it you don't like Dr. Barlow."

"I never said that," she snapped, a little too readily.

"You didn't have to. It's written all over your face. Has he done anything inappropriate to you?" he asked sharply.

That coaxed a smile out of her. It was sweet of him to worry about her. "No, nothing like that. It's just his attitude. He acts all pompous and arrogant all the time. It's like he just came here to add another notch to his belt and show us up, try to prove that he's smarter and better than the cops. He's always smiling, and no one who's in this line of work should be smiling all the time. He acts like he knows everything, even things that are none of his business, and he won't take no for an answer. He just pushes and pushes until ..." She trailed off, not wanting to verbalize the way her mind had been going to finish that sentence.

"Until what?" her partner asked.

Until he got himself under her skin and she couldn't stop thinking about him or the way her skin had tingled when he'd touched her. Until she couldn't think about anything but what his fingers would feel like touching her bare skin. Until she actually hoped that when she went to sleep tonight, she might dream about him again.

"Until he drives me crazy," she muttered.

Elijah barked a laugh. "Sounds like you like him and that's why he's driving you crazy."

If one more person said that to her, she was going to lose her mind.

She did not like Dr. Barlow.

Okay, she would concede that she found him physically attractive, but that was it.

Nothing more.

Maybe she needed to just take him up on his offer to talk, sleep with him, get it out of her system so she could just forget about him and move on.

"I don't like him. I just want him gone. We don't need him, but Sergeant Langsworth seems to think differently, so I'm stuck with him until this case is over. But after that, he'll go back to his job, we'll continue with ours, and that will be that. All that's important is finding this killer before Amelia Lexis dies."

That was what mattered.

Not herself and any crazy thoughts and feelings she might be having.

Amelia was alive out there somewhere and she wanted to bring the girl home alive. She would sacrifice anything—most certainly her own fleeting happiness—to make that happen.

9:09 P.M.

This was possibly the worst idea he'd ever had.

Gideon knew he shouldn't be here.

Sapphire had made herself very clear, as had Sergeant Langsworth. So long as he was here working this case, he had to keep his focus on the case and not on Sapphire Hatcher.

So, why couldn't he leave this alone?

Why couldn't he leave *her* alone?

Right now, he honestly didn't know the answer to that. All he did know was that no matter how hard he resisted, there was something pulling him closer and closer to Sapphire.

He couldn't get her out of his head. He thought about her constantly. Even when he was working this case, she was always there, hovering at the back of his mind, never giving him even a moment's peace. And he wasn't sure he wanted her to. There was something about Sapphire that intrigued him, that called out to him. It went deeper than just wanting to help her. He wanted ...

Well, he wasn't one hundred percent positive yet exactly what he wanted, but he knew he couldn't just let her walk away. He couldn't just pretend that he was only here to work this case and then he would walk away.

Which was why he was here.

He'd waited for her to leave the station, hoping to catch her as she did and just ask her to talk, but she must have snuck out. He didn't think that she would go home just yet, and since there was a snowstorm outside, he had deduced that this was the only place she would logically go.

So, he was sitting in the hospital waiting room, waiting for Sapphire to finish visiting with her partner.

Gideon felt nervous.

That was extremely out of character for him. He didn't get nervous. He dealt with serial killers and human traffickers, gang leaders and rapists, and none of that made him nervous. He could look them in the eye without blinking.

But sitting here waiting to talk to Sapphire had him a quivering mess.

His hands were sweaty, his stomach was spinning in a million somersaults, and he couldn't sit still. His knee was bobbing up and down, his hands were constantly fiddling with something, and every few minutes he got up and paced the room, checking the hallway to see if Sapphire was there yet even though he could see it perfectly well from his seat.

There she was.

Striding purposefully out the door, shrugging into a sensible black woolen coat, and heading for the elevator.

Gideon actually had to draw in a deep breath before he stood and walked toward her. "Sapphire."

She stopped and turned, displeasure filling her face when she saw it was him. Did she really dislike him that much? Sure, he had been egging her on a little, smiling at her because he knew it unsettled her, but that was just because he wanted to break through her barriers. He wanted to see the real Sapphire, not just this façade that she wore for the world. He knew that she was beating herself up for not realizing she was looking for a cop until he told her, but he didn't think she could hate him for that, because deep down she knew that they were on the same side. Gideon was sure that if he could just figure out the source of her dislike for him, then he would know everything he needed to.

"Why are you here?" she snapped.

"To see you." Okay, that was a lame answer, but it was like a part of his brain left him whenever he was around her.

"Well, it's late and I'm tired. Besides, you'll see me tomorrow at work." She deliberately turned her back on him and resumed walking toward the elevator.

He followed.

Because, again, he couldn't stay away from her.

"Didn't I make myself clear at the station?"

"No, you did. You told me to stay away from you, and I heard you loud and clear."

"You being here suggests otherwise." She shot him a disapproving frown.

"I guess it does." He chuckled. For some reason, he found her attitude cutely amusing despite the fact that he knew that was not her intention.

"Sergeant Langsworth said she was going to talk to you, tell you to focus on the case and stop trying to get me to talk about my past."

"She did," he told her.

Sapphire finally stopped walking. "I don't know how else to say this. I don't want a shrink. I don't want to talk about my past. I don't want a new friend. All I want, Dr. Barlow, is for you to leave me alone."

He should honor her wishes.

He should apologize for being here and leave.

He should tell her that he was going to do as she asked and back off.

But he didn't.

Because he couldn't.

The universe was telling him that if he walked away, both he and Sapphire would regret it for the rest of their lives.

So, he stayed.

And because he was a glutton for punishment, he made another attempt at trying to convince her that she could trust him.

"I just want to talk. Nothing bad can happen from a little chat, right?"

Sapphire rolled her eyes and started walking again. "Okay, maybe I'm not saying it right, maybe I need to make a comprehensive list of everything that I do not want to do with you. I don't want to chat. We have nothing to chat about." She punched the button for the elevator harder than was necessary, then frowned at him again. "How did you know I would be here?"

"Deduction."

"What?"

"Simple deduction," he said with a grin. "Since you were shot, the sergeant won't let you work late. It's snowing so you can't go running, and I can't imagine you being much of a gym person. You could go home, but I'm guessing you don't sleep much, so it's too early for bed. I suppose you could have gone home and spent the evening with your sisters, but I figured you wouldn't do that, you'd come here, to update your partner on the case."

"I don't like you, but I have to admit that you're good at what you do."

He couldn't help but smile at that. It was odd, but he appreciated the compliment just as much as he liked her telling him that she didn't like him. It was because of the look in her eyes. It didn't look like she didn't like him. There was no anger or resentment in there, and no heat in her tone. It was almost like for some reason she thought she should dislike him, so she was acting on that.

"I knew I could get a compliment out of you if I tried hard enough," he teased.

She smiled.

A small one, but it was definitely a smile.

"Is that a smile?" he asked with mock shocked horror.

"No, it isn't," she said, but once again, the corners of her mouth quirked up.

The elevator doors opened and they both stepped inside. "Are you parked in the hospital's underground parking garage or the one across the road?" He was sure he already knew the answer, but he hoped it was a good lead-in to what he wanted to ask next.

"The one across the road," she answered suspiciously. "Why?"

"I'm parked there, too. We could walk together. Not as friends," he added quickly. "Just as two people who happen to be walking in the same direction."

"I suppose," she huffed.

For the next minute they rode the elevator in silence. Gideon couldn't be more pleased with the progress he was making. He was sure she would have been angrier with him turning up here at the hospital, but maybe she was too tired to put up much of a fight tonight.

"I know you don't want to be friends—"

"That's correct," Sapphire inserted.

"But I do want you to know that I respect you. I respect you as a cop. You're smart and you trust your gut, and that makes you really good at what you do."

"Thank you," she said, casting him a shy glance. A nice one, no anger, no frustration, no annoyance, and her voice was sincere. He guessed she didn't get a lot of compliments—or at least not a lot of compliments that she believed. That she believed him when he told her she was good at her job touched him. It was nice to know that she trusted his opinions, if not himself, in general.

"And I respect you from coming back after what you lived through, for taking control of your life, and for dedicating it to helping other victims."

He felt the switch flip in her before she even said a word.

"I knew it," she sighed. He'd expected anger, but it seemed she was disappointed in him instead. "You want to make me a project. You shrinks are all the same. You think that you can take what happened to me and use it to make yourself famous. Well, get that notion out of your head. I don't need help with anything. My life is fine, and it would be even better if you stayed out of it."

The elevator doors opened and Sapphire practically ran out of it.

This time, he didn't bother following.

Despite the bad ending, he actually felt like he had made progress with her tonight.

Now he finally knew what she had against him. It wasn't personal. She had obviously had a bad experience with the shrink she had seen after her rescue. A shrink who had wanted to use her trauma to further his or her own career. If he could track down the psychiatrist, he'd make sure they lost their license if they were still working. No one in a position of power should treat a patient that way, especially one who had been through something so awful.

The reason for her dislike of him seemed like a reasonably easy obstacle to overcome. All he had to do was show her that he wasn't like the psychiatrist who was supposed to help her, but who'd hurt her instead.

"You're not getting away from me that easily, Sapphire Hatcher," he whispered under his breath. "I like you, and I think that we could help each other find some happiness. You're a stubborn one, but so am I."

CHAPTER
Eight

January 6th
3:27 A.M.

Amelia looked at the cast iron kettle in her hands.

This was all she had been able to get her hands on, and she wasn't sure that it was enough.

Or she was afraid it was.

Now it was time to decide if this was something she could actually do.

It was one thing to contemplate how, if she could only get her hands on something sharp, she could cut off her own foot, or something heavy enough to break it so that she could pull it through the metal ring clamped around her ankle. It was a whole other thing to actually do it.

The thought of hurting herself made her stomach churn. She thought if she actually tried to do it, she would probably be sick, throw up all over herself, and she hated the sight and the smell of vomit. It was why she thought she might never have kids, or perhaps adopt an older one. She just couldn't stand throwing up and babies, and little children threw up a lot.

But if she wimped out, she would die here.

She knew that was this man's endgame.

For now, he was having fun, stopping by and raping her, playing his crazy games of make believe. He liked hurting her—got off on her screams. No matter how hard she tried to hold her screams inside, he had a way of coaxing them out. Sooner or later, he was going to get bored, lose interest in her, and then he would kill her.

This could be her only chance.

Was she really going to let it slip through her fingers?

There was only one answer to that question.

No.

She was not.

It was a simple plan, not easy to commit, but simple nonetheless. She'd use the kettle to break her foot, hitting it as many times as it took. Once she pulled her ankle through, she'd run. Or drag herself along the floor if she had to. All she had to do was get to the door, open it, and find help.

"You got this," she whispered to herself.

Amelia drew in a long, slow breath, preparing herself for what she was about to do. Then she lifted the kettle and held it above her foot. Her hands were shaking, and she wondered if she was even going to be able to hit herself hard enough to fracture the bones and slip through the metal ring. This wasn't going to be a one and done situation.

"You don't have a choice," she reminded herself. "This is your only option. Just do it already, and get it over with. Just think about your end goal. The sooner you do this, the sooner you'll be home."

Without giving herself another second to dwell on what she was going to do and how badly it was going to hurt, she swung the kettle down and slammed it into her foot.

As expected, the resulting pain shot right up her leg and straight to her stomach. She gagged, desperately trying to keep down the bowl of plain rice she'd eaten a couple of hours ago.

Amelia knew if she stopped now, she might never start up again. She managed to keep her dinner down, and with a scream of determination,

Amelia lifted the kettle and brought it down once again on her foot. More pain shot through her body, but she shoved it away and didn't stop—up and down, over and over. She blocked out anything that wasn't going to help her achieve her goal.

She didn't notice that she'd thrown up several times; she didn't notice the blood; she didn't even feel the pain anymore.

All that mattered was getting out of here alive.

She had so much to live for, so much she wanted to do with her life, and she wasn't going to let this monster take it away from her.

She was stronger than him.

She was stronger than she had thought.

She was strong enough to survive.

Breathless, she sank back against the padded wall, panting and shaking and dripping with sweat. Although she didn't want to, she looked down at her foot; it was a mangled mess. She hoped it was broken enough to get it through the metal ring because she didn't think she had it in her to hit herself again.

Watching something like this play out in the movies and doing it in real life were completely different things, and it took her longer than she would have liked to force her shattered foot and ankle through the chain. But she did it.

She was free.

For the time being, adrenaline was coursing through her system, dulling the pain and giving her strength that she shouldn't have, given what she'd just done. Amelia took advantage of that and began to drag herself toward the door. It would be faster to walk, but since that was out of the question, she didn't want to waste time looking for something to use as a crutch.

Considering all she had to use was her arms and one good leg, it didn't take her too long to reach the door. Standing was not negotiable. She had to reach the door handle and prayed that when she did, she found it unlocked. For all she knew, the man had put padlocks or something on the outside of the door, making sure that, even if she did escape the chain, she would never escape this room.

She pushed herself up so she was sitting, half leaning against the door. Amelia got her good foot beneath her, and with her hands planted on the wooden door, she somehow managed to lever herself into a standing position.

The change in position from being on her stomach on the floor to standing sent her stomach lurching, and she threw up again. Her phobia of vomit forgotten, she reached for the door handle, turned it, and was pleasantly surprised when the door opened.

Scared to change her position once again, Amelia used the wall for leverage and began to stumble down the hall.

It was long and seemingly endless, and if, at the end of it, she found a staircase, she had no idea how she was going to get down it, but worrying about it wasn't going to change anything. The hard part was over. All she had to do now was get outside. It was night, but surely, there would be someone about. A passing car at least that she could flag down and ask them to take her to the police station.

Or the hospital.

The pain in her ankle was starting to make itself known, and she wasn't sure how much longer she was going to be able to keep going before she passed out from the pain.

Amelia turned the corner and started down another hallway. Up ahead was an elevator.

Hope surged inside her.

All she had to do now was get to it. It would take her downstairs, and then she would just have to get out the front door.

So close.

She was so close.

"Don't give up now," she urged herself aloud.

Her hands were shaking so badly she could hardly use them to pull herself along.

But she wasn't going to stop.

Not for anything.

She was about halfway down the hall to the elevator when the doors suddenly opened.

A man stepped out.

Him.

Her captor.

The hope that had been keeping her going vanished. She had been so close, but it wasn't close enough.

His eyes widened when he saw her, shock quickly passing through his face before a smile settled on his lips. "Seems it was good I came back for a second round tonight," he said as he strode toward her.

The fight gone out of her, she just stood, her back pressed to the wall and waited.

It was over.

He had won.

He would get to kill her after all.

He stood in front of her and stared into her eyes for a long moment. There was something in his eyes—not anger or fear that she had almost escaped; it was almost like he respected her attempts to free herself.

Maybe he would spare her after all.

That thought vanished as quickly as it appeared when the man wrapped his hands around her shoulders and slammed her head backward into the wall.

The first blow stunned her.

The second made her dizzy.

The third tossed her into unconsciousness.

∽

7:24 A.M.

"This is all wrong," Sapphire said as she crouched beside the body. "We were supposed to have another ten days to find her."

Her heart was breaking.

She might put on a tough girl attitude, but that was more for her benefit than anyone else's. After what she'd been through, how could she do her job if she didn't make sure everyone else saw her as strong? How could she do her job if she didn't believe that she was strong?

But deep down, her heart bled for every single victim in every single case she worked. Sapphire wished so badly that she could save them all, and while for the sake of her own sanity, she had to accept the fact that was never going to be possible, it didn't mean she didn't do everything within her power to save those who were put in her path.

She had failed to save Amelia Lexis.

For four months she'd been working this case with her partner, and what little they knew, hadn't been enough to save the first three victims. It hadn't been enough to save Amelia either.

The guilt she felt over that wouldn't go away for a long time.

Although she knew she wasn't personally responsible for the evil that bad people inflicted on their victims, it didn't mean that she didn't feel like some tiny part of it was her fault.

As though reading her mind, Dr. Barlow said, "None of this is our fault. We did everything we could to find her. You worked this case harder than anyone I know would have. That he killed Amelia early is not because of anything you did or didn't do. Okay?"

His words reassured her a little, and she gave a shaky nod, just able to keep back the tears that had been building up and threatening to spill out.

After that little stunt he'd pulled last night at the hospital, nothing Dr. Barlow had said should offer her any measure of comfort. He was good, she'd give him that. He'd almost had her believing that she was wrong, and that all he had wanted was just to be her friend while they worked this case.

But he'd been lying.

He had just wanted to lull her into a false sense of security before convincing her to talk to him. She wasn't sure what fame or notoriety he thought he was going to get. Her case was ten years old. It had been big news back then and dozens of journalists had been desperate to get a story from her. They'd hit up her shrink, offering her good money to tell all about her and what she'd lived through.

That had been just another blow that had come one after another at that time in her life. Not only was she battling to process what her parents had done to her, and the fact that she had almost been sold to someone who would have done unspeakable things to her, but her four sisters had still been missing.

Dr. Barlow was just like that psychiatrist had been. He didn't really care about her. That silly smile, the laid-back easygoing attitude, the lame jokes, the pretense at innocent friendship—it was all just a con so he could get what he wanted from her. It was about him, not her.

She'd been annoyed when Dr. Barlow approached her at the hospital last night, but his act was so charming, so disarming, that she had actually been about to concede that perhaps he wasn't quite as obnoxious as she'd thought he was. He had coaxed a smile out of her; he'd gotten her to agree to walk to the parking garage together. Saying nice things about her had gotten her to lower her defenses. Something she never did.

Well, lesson learned.

She wasn't going to let anyone take advantage of her ever again.

Sapphire just wished that the physical attraction she felt for him would go away. Having to see him every day and work with him, she couldn't deny it revved up her libido. She'd even dreamed about him last night despite the fact that she'd been hurt by his games.

"He must have killed her because she got free," Dr. Barlow was saying.

She was glad he was focusing on the case. If both of them just worked this case, kept thing professional, then maybe she could stop lusting after him and just get through this. "She broke her own ankle and foot to do it," she said, her gaze fixed on the mess that had once been Amelia Lexis's foot. She knew the girl had done it herself instead of the killer because the girl was covered in vomit. The pain of breaking her own bones had made her throw up.

"A brave girl," he said quietly, obviously as disturbed as she was thinking about the determination Amelia must have had to do that to herself.

"But it wasn't enough," she said sadly. "She went through all of that to get free, and then he killed her anyway."

"Probably found her as she tried to escape, bashed her head in, and then dumped her body because she was of no use to him anymore."

He said it so matter-of-factly that it made her angry.

No one had the right to just throw someone away like this.

"Why did he have to kill her?" She jerked to her feet and paced restlessly around the alley. "He didn't have to do that. He could have just restrained her again, made sure that she couldn't get free this time.

There were still ten days to go before she was supposed to die. He could have given us that time to find her. If he had, we might have found her alive. But now she's dead, and he's going to be looking for another victim. Who knows how long we'll have to find the new victim. Is he going to keep her for the full two weeks he would have spent with Amelia? Is he going to keep her ten days to finish off the two weeks between killing the last victim and taking the next? Is he completely off script now? If he is, then that means that anything could happen. We don't have any physical evidence. If we can't predict his behavior, how are we ever going to find him?"

"Sapphire ..." Dr. Barlow stood before her, his hands on her shoulders, stilling her pacing. "Calm down. It will be okay. We'll find this man."

"How can you know that?" It had been a long time since she had allowed anyone else to console her with their promises, but right now, she needed someone to reassure her, even if that someone was Gideon Barlow.

"Because neither of us will stop until we get him."

The answer was so simple, yet it *did* give her the reassurance she needed.

He was right.

She would never stop until they had this killer in custody, and she sensed that whatever shortcomings Dr. Barlow had, leaving while a serial killer was still out there stalking new victims, wasn't one of them.

Sapphire lifted her gaze so it met the psychiatrist's. He was watching her, his dark eyes staring into hers like he could actually see into her brain.

Could he?

She wasn't used to be around people who were this perceptive. Most people bought the act she put on, but he didn't. He didn't seem to be afraid to push her. He didn't worry about upsetting her, and he'd brought up her past twice now. In all these years, she and her sisters hadn't even talked about it that many times.

Despite her belief that he wanted to use her to further his career, when she looked into his eyes, she didn't get that vibe.

The vibe she got was different.

She saw desire in his eyes.

He was attracted to her just like she was attracted to him.

Sapphire gasped. Shock passed over her face, and she didn't even bother to try to hide it.

Despite the freezing cold morning, heat seemed to develop between them, and she realized that she wanted him to kiss her.

Dr. Barlow felt it, too, because his head dipped, and automatically she tilted her face up toward his.

"We got a witness."

They leapt apart like teenagers caught by their parents, as Gray and Zeb came to join them.

"A witness?" she asked, trying to school her features back into her usual calm, unflappable look.

"Someone saw a man dump the body," Zeb told them, shooting both her and Dr. Barlow a strange look.

"Enough to get a proper sketch?" she asked, starting to get that buzz of excitement that accompanied a break in a case.

"Maybe ... we'll get him to work with someone. But there was one thing he remembers noticing. The man who dumped the body was wearing a uniform. A police uniform," Zeb informed them.

Confirmation that Dr. Barlow was correct in his assumptions they were looking for a cop. And if this witness had seen enough to give a detailed description to a sketch artist, they may be able to finally ID the man they were looking for. Maybe even by the time she went home tonight he would be in custody.

Then, who knows, maybe she and Gideon Barlow could be friends.

Or even spend one, hot, passionate night together before he left.

8:31 A.M.

Uh, her head hurt so bad.

She hated being sick, and the flu was the worst. It just made you feel so miserable. Her stomach was all flip-floppy, and her head pounded. She was achy all over and was coughing and sneezing up a storm.

The worst part about being sick was having to miss a day of school.

Seventeen-year-old Thea Brody knew that she wasn't like most kids her age. Most kids her age would love a day off school; plenty faked being sick all the time to be able to stay home and skip tests and papers. But she loved school, she loved learning, and she wanted to get good grades.

She had to if she wanted out of this life.

Not that her life was bad exactly.

It was pretty typical stuff. She had three younger brothers, and her father had walked out on them and her mom. That left them struggling financially, and her mom having to work three jobs just to make ends meet. She had a job, too, so she could help contribute, and so did her fifteen-year-old brother. The thirteen year old was counting down the years until he could help out, and the eleven year old was already talking about ways he could help out—lemonade stands and bake sales. The kid was a little business tycoon in the making, he was going to go far in life. They all were, because they all had drive. They all had a desire to make something of themselves and be the best they could be.

When you had a loser dad the temptation was always to become bitter and angry, to resent what his leaving had done to you and to spend your time complaining about how unfair it was. But Thea wasn't like that. She didn't want to dwell on the past. She wanted to focus on the future, because she knew it was going to be a bright one.

So, unlike a lot of her friends, being at school meant something to her. It meant working toward a job where she would bring home a steady paycheck and not have to worry each month about the gas or electricity or water being turned off. And it meant being able to take care of her mom so she didn't have to work so hard.

That was why she worked hard every day. That was why she took every class, every paper, every test, so seriously. She had to get good grades because the only way she was going to college was with a scholarship, and those were hard to get. So, besides school and work and chores at home, and the very occasional special treat day with her friends, she studied as hard as she could. And it was paying off. She had a 5.0 GPA and had already been offered early acceptance into a great college, providing she finished off her senior year like she had started it.

And she would.

Because she had big dreams and she was determined to make those dreams a reality.

That was it.

She was going into school no matter how sick she was. Thea really didn't want to miss the test that she was supposed to take in biology today. Her mom had ordered her to stay home and had driven the boys to school before she would head off to her first job. If she hurried to school, she could take her test, go to the rest of her classes and be home long before her mom came home in between her first and second job. She'd even be home before her brothers so none of them could use it against her, like siblings were inclined to do.

Ignoring the pounding headache that pulsed between her temples, Thea pushed back the covers and staggered out of her bed. She grabbed the same pair of jeans she'd worn the day before and the sweater she'd left out yesterday when she had optimistically hoped she would make it to the second day of school after Christmas break.

Thea was just shoving her feet into a pair of boots and debating whether she could be bothered doing anything with her hair when she heard the doorbell.

Who could that be?

She grabbed her backpack and her toothbrush—she wasn't making another trip up the stairs to brush her teeth after she dealt with whoever was at the door—and headed downstairs. Their house was small: one living area, an old kitchen with appliances so out of date they didn't work most of the time, and three small bedrooms upstairs. Her three brothers shared the master bedroom because it was the biggest, and she and her mom had one of the small bedrooms each. There was only one bathroom and sharing it with four other people sucked. The first thing she was doing when she bought her own house was renovate it to make sure every bedroom had its own bathroom.

Dropping her bag on the table, she set her toothbrush next to the kitchen sink and went to the door. She'd taken so long, whoever was there had probably left already. If it was a package, hopefully, the delivery guy had left it. She didn't want to have to squeeze in a trip to the post office between everything else she had to do.

Half expecting to find no one there, Thea was surprised to see a cop standing on the front doorstep.

Her heart dropped.

Cops only came to your door when something was wrong.

Had something happened to her mom?

To one of her brothers?

All sorts of scenarios—none of them pleasant—started spinning through her head. Car accidents, guns, fires were all featured prominently in her panicked mind.

Tears were already brimming in her eyes as she prepared herself to take the bad news. Her flu symptoms forgotten, she would gladly suffer through a million flus if it meant that her family was okay.

Then she blinked, and all her worries faded somewhat. She knew the man who was standing on her doorstep. Maybe this wasn't an official call. Maybe it was a social one.

"Uh, hi," she said.

"Hi, Thea," he smiled. "I saw your car in the driveway. You not in school today?"

"Sick," she replied.

"Oh, no." His brow crinkled in concern. "Sorry to have got you out of bed."

"You didn't," she assured him. "I was supposed to stay home, but I have a test, and I'm feeling a little better," she lied, just in case he ended up talking to her mom about his visit.

"Happy to hear you're feeling better." He shot her a smile. "I won't hold you up long. I just wanted to check in and make sure you were okay. I was heading off to work ..." He gestured at his uniform. "... and I heard a report of a break and enter just next door. The guy ran when he heard the sirens, but I just thought since I saw your car and knew you were home, I would make sure that you were okay."

That was nice of him.

Not many people in today's world took the time to worry about someone else. Her dad certainly hadn't. He'd walked off leaving his wife to raise four kids under six all on her own. She wished her mom could find a great guy to share her life with, someone like the cop standing on the doorstep. Not him exactly, but someone who cared about people, someone who'd treat her right, take care of her like she deserved.

"I'm okay," she assured him. "There's no one in here but me, but thank you so much for taking the time to check."

"Do you mind if I just pop in and check really quick? Just to be safe," he added, flashing her another smile.

She wasn't supposed to let men into the house when she was home alone. She wasn't supposed to let anyone into the house when she was home alone. But this was a cop, and she knew him. Her mom and brothers knew him too.

"Sure." She smiled back, holding the door open wider to let him in. "When exactly was this break and enter?" she asked. She'd been home since four o'clock yesterday afternoon, and she didn't remember hearing any sirens. She had taken a quick nap after her mom and brothers left. Maybe she'd missed the sirens while she'd been asleep.

"Oh, it was about an hour ago," he said, walking around the ground floor of the house, giving it a quick once-over.

An hour ago would have made it around seven thirty, right around the time her family had left.

There hadn't been any sirens.

Uneasy now, Thea picked up her bag. "I really have to get going. I have a test at school. Thank you again for stopping by to check that everything was okay here." She took a step toward the door, intending to open it in an effort to hurry him along.

Before she could reach it, she was slammed into from behind.

For a split second, she thought that the cop had been right, and that the burglar really had hidden out in here and had taken him out and was coming for her next.

But then she realized she was wrong.

It wasn't the burglar shoving a sweet-smelling rag to her face, covering her nose and mouth, and shoving her up against the wall.

It was the cop.

Thea tried to fight back.

She tried to get out of his grip, but all she achieved was knocking over the family photo from Christmas Day that her mom had printed and put in an old frame. It was the only framed photo in the house. The rest were all on their cell phones and the old laptop her mom had to save up for a year to get her, and she heard the glass shatter as it hit the scuffed floorboards.

That was the last sound she heard before whatever he drugged her with knocked her out.

~

10:47 A.M.

This was about as bad as things could get.

Not only were they looking for a cop, but the killer they were hunting changed his MO by bashing Amelia Lexis's head in instead of strangling her ten days before he was supposed to kill her. And now he'd also changed up how he kidnapped his victims.

Sapphire felt like this case was quickly spinning out of control, and if they didn't get a handle on it soon, it would be too late. This killer would just keep on doing what he was doing indefinitely until he died.

She couldn't let that happen.

Her life was spinning out of control, too, and she needed her job to be the stable thing it had always been for her.

She had been going to kiss Dr. Barlow.

What was wrong with her?

She didn't even like him.

What had she been thinking?

Despite her shock, Sapphire couldn't even say that if the opportunity to kiss him again presented itself that she would say no.

She groaned. She must be losing her mind.

"Everything okay?" Gray asked her.

"What?" she asked, looking up at him.

"You groaned. You okay?"

"Oh, yeah, just frustrated by the way the case is going," she covered. By the look in his eyes, he didn't buy it, but he didn't say anything.

"He's going totally off script," he agreed.

"Right now, the only thing we had going for us was that he was predictable. We knew when he was going to take another victim; we knew where he was going to take them; we knew how long he was going to keep them alive; and then, where he was going to dump the bodies. Now we don't know anything," she finished, annoyed. How could they solve this case if they were now flying blind? Since the MO had now changed, everything else was up in the air. They needed some forensics or they needed a sketch from the witness who had seen the killer dump Amelia's body. Without either, she didn't know what their next move would be.

"We know that he's a cop, and we know that whatever he's trying to achieve, he hasn't yet," Dr. Barlow said.

That was true.

But it wasn't helpful.

There were hundreds of cops in this city. They couldn't go through them all one by one; there wasn't time.

She had been working the fish angle for days now, and so far, it hadn't turned up anything useful.

Sapphire was starting to feel helpless, and when she felt helpless, all those feelings from the past that she had learned to keep tucked away out of sight, started to push their way back into the forefront of her mind. She didn't want to go back to that place. She wanted her equilibrium back, but this case and spending all this time around Dr. Barlow were messing with that.

"What *is* he trying to achieve?" she asked. Wasn't that why Dr. Barlow was here? To give them his insight into this killer to help them find him? If he couldn't do that, then he may as well just leave. At least that would sort out one of her problems.

"I think it's a combination of reliving a traumatic event from his past and trying to understand something specific about that event," Dr. Barlow replied.

Well, that wasn't helpful.

A million different things could be deemed a traumatic event. That wasn't anything that was going to help them narrow down a suspect, and that was really all she wanted right now.

"Given that he's abducting the girls on a deserted road—this last victim obviously excluded—and he's dumping them in back alleys behind movie theaters, I'd guess that one or both of those things are related to the trauma," Dr. Barlow continued.

That was at least a little more specific. "So, we should start looking into cops with any link to a traumatic past related to an accident or something on a road or anything at a movie theater," she said.

"No guarantees we could find either," Zeb said. "An accident we can maybe find, but if he was a victim of a crime, or a family member was, then his name could have been kept out of things for his protection."

Sapphire couldn't help but think of her own past. She wasn't sure how much Gray or Zeb knew about it, but she was sure they knew something. Just like she was sure that knowing what she had lived through influenced what they thought of her ability to do her job. Sapphire knew that she had to prove herself every single day. There would always be doubt in people's minds about how long she could hold it together, fear that she would lose it at some point, have a breakdown or do something crazy.

But she wasn't going to do any of that.

She was in control of herself and her emotions.

Yes, occasionally they got the best of her, but it was only temporary. In the end, she always managed to put them back in place.

As long as she believed that she wasn't going to fall apart, she wouldn't.

"Since he's targeting teenage girls, can we assume that he was a teenager himself when this traumatic event occurred?" she asked Dr. Barlow. She already knew that was how she would profile it, but she wanted to do something to take the focus off herself since all three guys were staring at her.

"That's what I would assume," Dr. Barlow replied.

"Well, that at least narrows it down. We're looking for a cop who had something traumatic happen when he was a teenager, either on a secluded road or at a movie theater. We should start by looking into the specific roads that the victims were abducted from and the movie theaters he has dumped bodies at."

"Will do." Gray nodded.

"I think we can learn a lot from this abduction scene as well." Dr. Barlow looked thoughtfully around the room they were standing in.

Just as she and Dr. Barlow got back to the station after leaving the scene where Amelia Lexis's body had been dumped, then doing the notification to her family, they'd gotten a call that a delivery man had called in a potential crime scene. He'd come to the front porch, found the front door open and signs of a potential scuffle, and dialed 911.

Although there was nothing substantial yet to prove that this case was related to the others, a neighbor across the street had seen a cop knock on the door about twenty minutes before the delivery man had called it in.

The missing girl was Thea Brody, she was a seventeen-year-old senior, who, according to her mother, had been home sick. By the time cops showed up on the scene, there was no sign of the girl. Her car was still in the driveway, her bag on the floor, and cell phone and keys in her bag. The school said she hadn't showed up there, and none of her friends had heard from her.

"She knew him," Sapphire said, scanning the room. "She was home sick, but from the looks of things, she had decided to go to school anyway. Her bag is down here by the door, and she had already put her keys and cell phone in it. According to her mom, she took her studies seriously and had been upset she was going to miss a test today. Thea heard the knock at the door while she was upstairs—"

"Could have already been down here," Zeb inserted.

"No, she brought her toothbrush with her." She pointed to where the toothbrush lay beside the kitchen sink. "She was upstairs; she was sick; she didn't want to go back up to brush her teeth after she dealt with whoever was at the door, so she brought it with her."

"Good catch." Dr. Barlow smiled.

His admiration shouldn't make her feel good, but it did. "She answered the door," Sapphire continued. "She sees a cop at the door, and she wouldn't have been threatened by that. She had no reason to be."

"I think she knew him," Dr. Barlow said. "Teenage girl, home alone. I think if he was a stranger, she wouldn't have let him in, even if he was a cop."

"I agree," she said. "He was in here. He got her from behind. She was near the door, he came at her, there was a scuffle. That's how the picture got knocked over and broken. He overpowered her since there were people about, unlike with his previous abductions where they were alone in the middle of nowhere, he would have had to do things differently. He either drugged her or knocked her out. No signs of blood, so I think we can assume he drugged her."

"We know we're looking for a cop. If she knew him, then we should look into any incidents here that the cops were called to, or any incidents on the street where the Brody family were interviewed as witnesses," Dr. Barlow said.

"Or he lives on the street," Sapphire added. "If he's a neighbor, then she'd know him and wouldn't feel threatened or scared letting him in."

That was the kind of thing she'd been looking for.

This was the kind of thing that could actually lead them right to the person they were looking for.

This was the kind of thing that could solve this case, bring the killer into custody, and send Dr. Barlow out of her life and back to where he came from.

So why didn't she feel happy?

~

12:00 P.M.

Gideon watched Sapphire as she entered the room with four coffees balanced in her hands. She set three on the table then circled right around to the side farthest from where he was sitting and took a seat at the other end of the conference table where they were working.

Despite her penchant for masking her emotions, she was pretty obvious with her actions.

She was avoiding him.

He knew the reason. It was because they had almost kissed back at the scene where Amelia Lexis's body had been dumped.

Was it the smartest move, making out at a crime scene?

Absolutely not.

If they hadn't been interrupted by Gray and Zeb, would they have kissed?

Absolutely.

If another opportunity to kiss her presented itself, would he grab it with both hands and kiss her like he'd been wanting to ever since they met?

You bet he would.

If he didn't know that Gray and Zeb would be walking in at any moment, he would grab her right now. Pull her out of the chair she was stiffly perched in, shove her up against the wall, thread his fingers through that soft brown hair, press his lips to her plump ones, and kiss her until they both forget where they were.

As though somehow sensing what he was thinking, Sapphire lifted her head from the file in front of her, her green gaze darting to his.

The vulnerability in her eyes stalled his libido.

She looked scared.

That definitely took the wind out of his sails. Was he wrong in thinking that the two of them could make out while he was in town, then he could just walk away and both of them could go back to their lives like nothing had happened?

Sapphire was strong—tough—but how much of that was an act and how much of it was real?

He knew what she had gone through, and he knew that the trauma still impacted her a decade later, but he also knew that whether she admitted it or not, she was attracted to him. She wanted to kiss him. She might not like him, but she would still make out with him given half an opportunity.

But if he was going to cause her more long-term damage, then any making out was off the table.

She might not like him, but he liked her, and he didn't want to hurt her. She didn't believe it, but he truly did want to help her, and it wasn't to get anything out of it for himself.

"Where are Gray and Zeb?" he asked, deciding to let the issue of their near kiss stand to the side for the time being.

Sapphire cleared her throat, her normally steady gaze suddenly couldn't find anything to settle on, instead darting around the room at a near frantic pace. "They, uh, they were just finishing up a couple of things. They'll be here soon."

From the sound of her voice, she hoped the sooner, the better. For no other reason than to put her at ease, he hoped they'd be here soon too. "Do you want to wait or start without them, catch them up when they arrive?"

She picked up her coffee and took a long drink. It seemed like she was debating her answer. "We should start."

"Okay, so we know we're looking for a cop, and we suspect that it's a cop that Thea Brody and her family knew."

"I spoke with Thea's mother and her brothers, and none of them said there had been any incidents at their house that required police intervention. I checked 911 call logs and they support what the Brody family said—dispatch has never sent officers to their house before today."

"What about the dad?" he asked. None of the family had mentioned him, and although they suspected that Thea's case was related to the others—particularly since Amelia was dead and they knew he would be replacing her with another teenage girl—they didn't have any definitive proof. The change in MO could be the devolving of the same serial killer, or it could be the father making an attempt to get his kids back.

"According to Mrs. Brody, her husband walked out on her when Thea was six. She has raised her four kids on her own ever since. All four kids appear to be good kids, they work hard at school, they don't get into trouble, they make good grades, they have friends who like them. There are no problems with teachers, other students, or the law. Despite their financial struggles, they seem to be a regular and happy family. If you're suggesting that you believe the father came back and abducted his daughter, I would think that to be highly improbable."

His gut said Sapphire was right. If the father were back, he was unlikely to just come in and kidnap his daughter; he was more likely to come back and go after the whole family. Maybe turn up at the house one evening, maybe go after his ex-wife, threaten her that he wanted back in the kids' lives, maybe go after all four kids at one time. But that he would just go after his daughter and abduct her didn't seem like the actions of a deadbeat dad eleven years after he split.

"So sticking with the theory that Thea's abduction is related to the others, and we're looking for a cop, since none have ever had to respond to an incident at the Brody house, were you able to find any cops who live close by? Preferably someone in the same block, close neighbors rather than people she might only be on a nodding basis with would be more likely to get Thea to let them into the house when she was home alone."

Sapphire nodded. "I did find one."

"Who is he?"

"His name is Mason Wharf," she replied.

Something about the look on her face piqued his interest. They were onto something. He was sure of it. "What do you know about him?"

"Well, he's thirty-four years old, married with one kid."

"Boy or girl?" he asked.

"A girl. Rumor has it—and I'm only repeating what I heard, I have no first-hand knowledge of this—he wasn't happy when he found out he and his wife were having a girl. I think she'd be about one and a half now."

Interesting. So, the man had something against women, could be why he was targeting teenage girls. "What else do you know about him?"

"He has a problem with taking orders. There are a few reprimands in his file for him ignoring direct orders from his superiors and going off to do his own thing. His neighbors dialed 911 a couple of times to report loud arguing coming from the Wharf house. Cops would respond, but there were never any marks on the wife or the baby, and because Mason was a cop, nothing was ever taken any further. But then, there was an incident, about six months ago."

"An incident?"

"A suspect—I think she was a drug addict caught with just enough ecstasy to put her into the dealer category—accused him of sexually assaulting her. According to the woman, he was driving her to the precinct to book her, when he took a detour, stopped under a railway bridge, raped her, then drove her to the station. She was on ecstasy at the time she reported it, and Mason denied it. So it was a he said, she said situation. Cop versus drug addict. I'm sure you can figure out how that played out."

He could.

The woman's testimony would be written off as the drugged imaginations of an angry dealer trying to work the system to get herself out of charges, and a potentially dangerous cop was left on the streets.

"Do you know him personally?"

"Not really. I've met him a couple of times. I think we both worked a case the year before last where someone was kidnapping little girls, sexually assaulting them, and then dropping them off at hospitals. Everyone worked that case," she added. The rush of emotion mixed with guilt that flared in her eyes was one he had already seen several times in the few days they'd known each other.

"What was he like?" Gideon asked, wanting to keep her focused on this case.

"Angry. He was always angry. I mean, we were all angry that someone was hurting those innocent children, but his anger was different."

"Given what you've just told me, this guy certainly fits with our profile. He likes raping young girls. The rape accusation six months ago could have been what set this whole thing in motion. When Gray and Zeb get here, they should look into Mason Wharf's past, see if they can find anything traumatic either at a movie theater or on one of the roads the victims were abducted on. I think you and I should go and have a talk with Mason."

This could be the break in the case they needed.

This could be it.

If Mason Wharf was the killer, then he would be in custody, and hopefully he would tell them where he had Thea Brody, then this case would be over.

Gideon had to decide what came next with Sapphire.

Either the two of them spent one night together before he went home, or he admitted it was more than she could cope with, and he would leave before he could hurt her.

He didn't like either of those options.

～

12:24 P.M.

"All right, I'll go and see if he's here in the precinct," Sapphire said, pushing to her feet. If they were right about Mason Wharf, this case could be over today. As glad as she would be to get this man off the streets, knowing that Dr. Barlow would be leaving filled her with a weird kind of emptiness she had never felt before.

She really had to get a grip.

Why was she getting all bent out of shape about some shrink she'd only known for three days?

It wasn't as if she even liked him, and yet, his words, his admiration, his slightly goofy personality, they all did something to her.

They made her feel real.

And it had been ten years since she had last felt like a real person.

She had mostly forgotten what that was like. Yes, she functioned every single day. She went to work. She got along with her colleagues, even if she was a bit prickly. She was doing good in the world by putting dangerous men and women in prison. She hung out with her sisters. She did most of the things that normal people did, but there was something inside her that was missing.

A piece of her, that had been taken by her parents and the men they sold her to, that she couldn't get back.

It was the piece that made her human.

She didn't feel things the way most people did. It was usually a balancing act keeping her emotions carefully tucked away in their respective boxes so she didn't have a breakdown. As much as that worked, and allowed her to work the job she adored, it also meant giving up a lot of things. Friends, and definitely a boyfriend, were out of the question when you wouldn't allow yourself to feel all the good things that still existed in the world.

For some ridiculously strange reason, Dr. Barlow made her want to feel those things. He made her want to just go out and have fun without worrying constantly about her responsibilities and her cases and doing everything she could to arrest as many criminals as she could before she died. In the last ten years she hadn't really done anything for fun. Even when she spent time with her sisters, she was usually thinking about a case—or several—and would pull out her phone or laptop to check something out.

What would it be like to go out with Dr. Barlow? Just the two of them—laughing and talking and having fun. That seemed so far removed from her life that she could barely imagine it.

"Sapphire."

Somehow, while she had been lost in thought, Dr. Barlow had stood and circled the table to come and stand before her.

"Yes?" she asked, refusing to let her gaze meet his because when she stared into his eyes all she wanted was for him to kiss her. She couldn't stop thinking about their near kiss this morning, and she knew that he had been thinking about it too. His thoughts had practically reverberated around the room, screaming what was going on inside his head.

He reached out and very gently took her chin between his thumb and forefinger and nudged until she reluctantly lifted her eyes to meet his. "Earlier, at the crime scene, I was going to kiss you," he acknowledged, making every nerve in her body tingle. "But—"

"Did you guys ... oh, sorry, we're interrupting," Zeb said as he and Gray came bustling into the room.

Sapphire jerked away from Dr. Barlow's grip, his touch no longer making her feel good inside. Now, it just made her cold.

He had been going to kiss her, but he had obviously changed his mind.

"You're not interrupting," she said, her cop face and attitude firmly back in place.

The look she shot her colleagues clearly conveyed they better not mention what they thought they had just seen, because Gray asked, "Were you able to find any cops who've been called out to the Brody house or who live in the same block?"

"We have. Mason Wharf."

Both their eyes lit up at the name, obviously recalling the same things about the man that she had.

"I'm going to go and talk with him. Why don't you two look into his past and see if you can find any of the potential traumatic events we spoke about earlier," she said.

"Sure thing," Zeb agreed. "Meet us back in here when you're done."

"I will." Without looking back, Sapphire breezed out of the room and beelined for the stairs. She took them three at a time, and while she didn't care if Dr. Barlow followed her or not, she heard the unmistakable sound of his footsteps behind her.

This was exactly why she didn't bother dating. She would rather spend her entire life alone, doing her part in keeping people safe and focusing on her job, than the emotional roller coaster of navigating a relationship with someone who could crush her in just one simple word.

But.

She hated that word.

Even considering kissing Gideon Barlow was a mistake, and although she hadn't realized it until he said he'd been going to kiss her *but*, she had actually wanted him to do a whole lot more than kiss her. And she didn't mean sex. She had wanted him to ask her out on a date; she'd wanted them to fall in love; she'd wanted a husband and kids and normal life like everyone else had.

She was an idiot.

That wasn't in the cards for her, and she would have to do a better job of reminding herself of that.

When she reached the floor where Mason Wharf worked, she opened the door and headed in. This was where her focus needed to be, on stopping a man who abducted, raped, and murdered teenage girls. Having a husband and children would only distract her from her job. She had been saved. It was her duty—her responsibility—to save as many other people as she could.

"Mason?" she called out as she approached his desk.

He looked up at the sound of his name. "Detective Sapphire Hatcher, right?"

"Right," she replied. "Would you mind giving me a minute of your time?"

"Uh, no, I guess not," he said, but his expression said he would rather do anything but.

"Thanks, we can go up to homicide if you want, or we can just talk in one of the rooms down here."

"Down here is fine," he said, leading her over to an interview room.

Dr. Barlow followed, but she blocked him out of her mind just like she wished she could erase him from her life.

"This won't take long," she said as they took seats at the table. "Do you know a Thea Brody?"

"Yes. The Brody family lives a couple of houses down from my wife and me. Sometimes I'll clear their driveway for them in the winter, and Thea has babysat Lily a couple of times."

"Have you seen them today?"

"No. Why would I have? I came straight to work this morning."

"Your shift started at nine, you didn't pop by there on your way here?"

"I said *no*," he repeated, anger vibrating off him. If he got this angry this quickly, she could picture him raping those girls so badly he tore them up inside.

"Thea Brody is missing," she announced.

"And you think *I* did something to her?" He tried to look incredulous but just looked plain furious.

"Did you?"

"Of course not."

Sapphire nodded slowly. "But you do like young girls, right?"

"I'm married." He spat the words out between clenched teeth.

"And yet, you took a little rendezvous with a girl only two years older than Thea under a railway bridge," she said, hoping if she made him angry enough, she would get a confession.

"She was lying. She was so high she didn't know what was going on. No charges were filed," he growled.

"She was high. Doesn't mean she was lying. Maybe after that, you thought it was best not to leave your victims alive so they could turn you in. Maybe you thought keeping them for a few weeks, having your fun with them, then killing them to keep them quiet was a better idea."

"You're accusing me of being the serial killer that shot you and Elijah?" Mason Wharf demanded.

"Are you?"

"I never killed anyone in my life. I've never even laid a hand on anyone. If you want to talk to me again, you better speak to my union rep first." With that, he shoved his chair backward, making the legs screech across the floor and stalked to the door.

"I'll do just that, Detective Wharf," she said before the door swung closed behind him.

So, she hadn't gotten the confession she wanted, but that didn't mean that Mason Wharf was out as a suspect. On the contrary. Given his behavior and his anger, he had very much secured his place at the top of her list.

~

5:58 P.M.

She had successfully avoided talking to Dr. Barlow for the last few hours.

Sapphire counted that as a win.

Now if she could only do that several dozen more times, he would finally be out of her life.

All they needed was some definitive proof that Mason Wharf was the serial killer they were looking for. He was still denying it, and now he had legal representation, so she couldn't speak with him again. What they needed was physical evidence of some sort or a witness who could identify him. The witness who had seen someone dumping Amelia Lexis's body couldn't say if it was Mason Wharf or not because it had been dark out.

First thing in the morning, she was going to stop by the morgue and the crime scene labs and see if they had anything for her. And she would take—*literally*—anything at this point. Didn't matter how small it was. Anything that would help them, she could work with it and make it go some way to getting Mason Wharf in custody.

Thea Brody's time was running out.

The thought of the girl alone out there ate away at her.

What she had been through had changed her. She barely remembered the teenager she had been before that night, and as much as that upset her, how many people would be dead now if she hadn't been changed and become a cop?

Sapphire leaned back against the wall of the elevator. She was exhausted. Despite the fact she didn't sleep much and worked virtually around the clock, she didn't usually feel like this. This exhaustion could be laid squarely at the feet of Dr. Barlow.

He had done this to her.

With his *but*.

"You're not supposed to be thinking about that anymore," she told herself aloud.

There really was no need to think about it. The kiss had never actually happened. She had never really been going to fall in love with Gideon Barlow and marry him and have kids; that had been a daydream that would never have been actualized. He didn't even live in the same city as her, so realistically, what could ever have happened between them? At best, she had missed out on one great night—and she knew it would have been a great night—of sex.

That was it.

Nothing to lose sleep over.

So why did it feel like there was now a huge, gaping hole in her heart?

Because she was lying to herself. That was why.

The doors beeped as they slid open, and she pushed herself upright. Feeling like her limbs had been filled with concrete, she dragged herself out of the elevator and into the parking garage. She hadn't parked in here today. Her car was in the alley behind the police precinct.

Some days she couldn't face parking in the dark underground lot. It was just too dark, too claustrophobic, and it made her think of her past.

That was the thing about your past.

It was part of you forever.

It was inescapable.

As much as you wished you could take out an eraser and rub it all away, you couldn't. It was there, lurking in the dark recesses of your mind, ready to pop out and make itself known whenever it felt like it.

Crossing the parking lot, Sapphire headed to the back emergency-exit door. It would have been easier to just walk out the front door, but she had a feeling that Dr. Barlow was going to make another attempt at talking to her, and she wanted to avoid that at all costs.

Never be alone with him; that was her goal for the next few days. She wasn't sure it was an achievable goal, but she was going to do her best to make it happen. She got it. He didn't want to kiss her anymore and was glad they had been interrupted. What was there to talk about?

She reached the door and pushed it open, drawing in a sharp breath as the icy cold wind hit her. There were flurries of snow in the air, and all she wanted to do was get home, have a hot shower, put on her pajamas, and climb into bed. She wouldn't sleep. She'd probably work until around one or two in the morning, but at least she could do it from the warmth and comfort of her bed.

She was going to have to avoid her sisters too. She had been ever since they had told her it sounded like she had a crush on Dr. Barlow. She didn't want to get caught up in another conversation about that because then she was going to have to admit that they were right.

Well, they *had* been right, but they weren't anymore. Having Dr. Barlow tell her he was glad they hadn't kissed kind of took the wind out of her sails.

Life could be so complicated sometimes.

All she wanted was to do her job and forget about her past. Was that really too much to ask?

Sapphire wrapped her coat tighter around herself as she left the parking lot and started for her car. She didn't get more than a couple of steps down the alley when something slammed into the back of her head.

The blow wasn't enough to knock her out, but it was enough to stun her and cause her to lose her balance. She hit the pavement hard, and pain shot up from her knees and hands, which had taken the brunt of the fall.

She reached for her gun, but another blow had her sprawling down onto her stomach. The cold of the concrete, which was lightly dusted with snow, seeped quickly into her, making her feel clumsy and sluggish even despite the two blows to her head.

Whoever had attacked her came closer, stopping at her side and roughly grabbing her wrists and duct taping them together. Then he wrapped a strip of material around her eyes, blindfolding her.

Just like that, she was thrown back in time ten years.

She was sitting in the back of the van, her wrists bound behind her, the metal collar around her neck, gagged, and unable to see in the pitch black.

Her breathing began to quicken.

Panic started to flow through her.

She felt dizzy, and she was pretty sure it had nothing to do with the head injuries.

Why did he have to blindfold her?

If he hadn't, she wouldn't be losing it like she was.

If she couldn't pull it together—and quickly—he was going to kill her or rape her or do whatever it was that had him lying in wait for her out here.

"Drop this case," a voice growled. She couldn't place the voice. It didn't sound familiar, but it also seemed like he was deliberately disguising it.

"What case?" she asked, her voice a lot weaker than she liked. Her panic, aching head, and the cold were getting to her. This guy obviously assumed she would automatically know what he was talking about, but she had several open cases she was working right now.

"If you don't back off and leave me alone, you won't like the consequences."

Was this Mason Wharf?

Was he trying to threaten and scare her into backing off and taking his name off her suspect list?

If that was what he was trying to do, he was going to be sorely disappointed.

She would never back off.

All she had in her life was her job, she had nothing to lose and she would work every case with everything she had.

"I can't do that, Mason. The best thing you can do for yourself right now is untie me, let me take you inside, and tell us where you've stashed Thea Brody. If you turn yourself in, then we might be able to make a deal." Sapphire hated not being able to see because she couldn't tell if Mason was likely to do as she said or not.

"I told you I didn't kidnap her," he growled. So, she'd been right. This was Mason.

She was starting to shiver in earnest now, and her head was hurting so badly that she just wanted to zone out and forget about everything. But she couldn't do that. It was just her and Mason out here, and he definitely had the advantage. She had to do whatever she could to talk him into turning himself in.

"This isn't a good idea, Mason. It isn't going to help you. You know I'm a detective. We're right outside the precinct. Anyone could come out here at any moment." She knew that wasn't true. It was why she parked her car out here because it was quiet and she didn't have to see anyone, but she hoped he didn't know that. "Hurting me is only going to hurt you in the long run. Do the right thing. Let's go inside together and confess everything. Don't let Thea die."

"How many times do I have to tell you?" he screamed. She felt the whoosh of air before the blow came, his foot connecting with her side with every word he spoke. "I did not kidnap Thea. I did not kill anyone."

There was no way she was going to convince him to do the right thing.

He was stuck in some delusion, or he was too arrogant to admit what he'd done. Whatever the reason, Mason wasn't going to turn himself in.

The fear and panic she'd been trying to stamp down was rising.

She was going to die out here in a cold, dark alley.

Her body would no doubt be thrown away like garbage.

After everything she'd been through, this was how it was all going to end.

≈

6:09 P.M.

. . .

Where was she?

Sapphire had snuck away while he'd been in the bathroom. She must have been waiting for an opportunity to slip away without him noticing because she never left work this early.

She was avoiding him.

And it did *not* take a genius to figure out why.

It was his stupid *but*.

'*Earlier, at the crime scene, I was going to kiss you. But ...*'

That was what he had said.

So *very* stupidly said.

It hadn't come out the way he intended, and then Gray and Zeb walked in and interrupted, and he hadn't had a chance to explain what he meant. Every time he'd tried to approach her today, she was always conveniently in the middle of a conversation with someone else, and she made sure that they were never alone in a room together.

Gideon hated that he'd hurt her; it was the last thing he wanted to do. It was, in fact, the very thing he'd been trying to avoid. He could see that Sapphire wanted more than just a one-night stand. She wanted more than perhaps she even realized, and one night of sex—no matter how good it would have been—was only going to cause her more pain in the long run.

He was sure that if the two of them could just talk, he could explain why he thought them kissing was not a good idea. Sapphire was a logical woman. She would no doubt understand and agree.

But to do that, he was going to have to pin her down, which he knew wouldn't be easy.

Maybe he would go to her house, talk to her there. He knew she wasn't afraid of him, and her sisters would be there, so she shouldn't be too upset. And since they were supposed to be working a case together, and he was here until it was solved, the quicker they cleared the air the better.

He scanned the parking garage, but he couldn't see her anywhere. He knew she hadn't gone out the precinct's front doors because he had asked, and no one had seen her leave. That meant she was down here somewhere. He hadn't been long in the bathroom, so he knew that she hadn't gotten too far. If he was quick enough, he would catch her down here.

Perhaps he should go wait by the exit; that way, she would be forced to go past him. But it was just like her to refuse to stop and put her window down, and he'd have to come all the way back and get his car. He knew what her car looked like, so maybe he should try to find it. If he could get to her before she got into her car, he would probably have a better chance at getting her to listen to him.

That was probably wishful thinking.

Gideon wasn't sure he was going to be able to get her to listen to him. Not that he would give up trying. Sapphire had gotten under his skin in a way no one else ever had. He liked her. Like, he *really* liked her, and if he didn't live in a different city, he would have been prepared to put in the work it would take to gain her trust. It wouldn't be easy. Someone who had been hurt so badly would find it near impossible to trust anyone ever again, but he would have worked as hard as it took to prove to her that he was someone she could depend on.

He paused in the back corner of the garage. He could hear something—an argument or a fight of some sort.

While he should probably just ignore it and continue searching for Sapphire, something stopped him from passing on by. Instead, he opened the door and headed up the flight of stairs.

As soon as he reached the top, his heart stopped.

Sapphire lay on the ground. She was restrained and blindfolded. Mason Wharf was crouched beside her. Her coat was unbuttoned, and his hand was up inside her sweater.

"You think you're so much better than everyone else, don't you? You know what you need, Detective Hatcher? You need someone to do you so hard that stick comes out your—"

Gideon didn't remember moving.

All he knew was that one second he was standing at the top of the steps, and the next, he was hurling himself at Mason Wharf.

He collided with the other man and both of them fell sideways, hitting the concrete hard.

A deep-seated protective rage, unlike anything he had ever felt before, took over his body and he swung his fists at the man—over and over again. It didn't even register that Mason had stopped fighting back after about the fourth blow and now lay limply beneath him.

Eventually, he stopped, panting hard as he looked down at Mason's bloody face. The blood did little to ease his anger. All he wanted to do was beat the man until he was dead, but Sapphire needed him.

Staggering to his feet, he crossed the couple of feet between them in one stride and knelt at her side. She wasn't moving, but when he reached to grab her handcuffs, she flinched.

Wanting nothing more than to gather her up in his arms and reassure her, he had to first make sure that Mason no longer presented any threat to her. Grabbing hold of one of the man's wrists, he dragged him over to the wall and handcuffed him to a pipe.

Then he went back to Sapphire. Very gently, he reached out and touched her neck. He knew she was alive, but there was blood on the grubby snow beneath her head, so he needed to know what he was dealing with medically before he could begin to deal with the psychological trauma she had just endured.

Her pulse was weak, and her skin was icy cold to the touch. She obviously had a head injury, most likely from being knocked to the ground when Mason attacked her, and knowing how angry Mason was, he had no doubt inflicted other injuries as well.

"Sapphire," he said softly. "It's Gideon. You're okay now," he assured her.

Reaching up, he slid the blindfold off. Her eyes underneath were scrunched closed and she didn't bother to open them. Since she hadn't flinched away from him, he assumed that she had heard him and knew that it was him and that she was safe now.

"I'm just going to sit you up so I can free your hands, all right?" he asked, wanting to try to keep her calm by letting her know what he was doing before he did it.

She didn't protest, so he gently took hold of her shoulders and sat her up slowly, mindful that depending on how hard she'd been hit in the head she could have a concussion and any movement could make her nauseous. Her hands were bound with duct tape, so he propped her up against his shoulder and pulled his keys from his pocket so he could use the small pocketknife he kept on a key chain to cut her free.

Sapphire had started to shiver, no doubt a combination of shock and the cold. He had to get her inside. "Sapphire, I'm just going to pick you up and carry you inside out of the cold, okay?"

Again, there was neither a protest nor an acknowledgment of his words, so he scooped her up and carried her down the steps and back into the parking garage, leaving Mason out in the cold. Gideon couldn't care less if the man succumbed to hypothermia. Right now, Sapphire was his priority.

In the parking garage, he heard footsteps. "I need help over here," he screamed out, and felt Sapphire flinch at his loud voice.

The footsteps immediately got louder, and a second later, two female cops appeared. "What happened?" one asked, eyeing Sapphire in his arms.

"This is Detective Hatcher. She was just assaulted by Detective Mason Wharf. He's handcuffed to a pipe out there," he replied, nodding his head at the door to the alley behind him.

One of the women immediately headed off in the direction he indicated; the other pulled out her radio. "Does she need an ambulance?" she asked.

"She does. At the least, she has a head injury. Mason Wharf had her on the ground when I found them. He was sexually assaulting her." His heart burned as he said the words, as if this woman hadn't been through enough, and now she had been attacked once again for simply doing her job. The funny thing was, he hadn't even liked Mason Wharf for the murders before now. But why else would the man attack the lead detective on the case if he wasn't guilty?

The woman called for backup and an ambulance, and Gideon tried to calm the anger that surged through his body and made him see red enough to focus on Sapphire. She was still shaking. There was blood on his coat. From the way she held herself stiffly, he suspected that Mason had hit or kicked her in the ribs or abdomen.

He had to breathe through his anger or he was going to find himself back in the alley pummeling on Mason until they would need fingerprints to identify him.

"I'm going to go put her in my car," he told the female cop. "She's too cold. I don't want her to get hypothermic."

The woman nodded, and as the parking garage began to fill with cops, he noticed one following him to his car. He hoped it was because they were worried about Mason somehow getting free and not because they were unsure whether or not he was a threat to her.

Because he would never do anything to hurt the woman he cradled gently in his arms.

Bundling himself and Sapphire into the passenger seat of his car, he reached over and shoved the keys in the ignition and turned the engine on so he could get the heat blasting. Someone passed him a blanket and he wrapped it around her, hoping between the heater, the blanket, and his own body heat he could get her temperature up a little before the ambulance arrived.

"Sapphire, honey, can you open your eyes and look at me?" he asked. He wanted to assess the damage to her head and getting a look at her pupils would help him to do that.

She shook her head frantically at his suggestion. He had no idea what specifically was scaring her at the moment, but it no doubt had something to do with her past. What just happened had probably triggered a memory she had either repressed or fought on a daily basis to keep buried.

"You're safe now, okay?" He made his voice sound strong and sure despite the fact that as what he had just witnessed sunk in it felt like his entire body had turned to Jell-O. "Mason is in custody. He can't hurt you again. If you just open your eyes, you'll see that we're sitting in my car."

She shook her head again, harder this time, and her trembling was increasing, not decreasing. She was going into shock. Tears began to seep out of her closed eyes, rolling slowly down her pale cheeks.

He wished he knew specifics about her abduction and the few days she had spent with the human traffickers before she had been rescued. If he knew some details, he might be able to figure out what exactly had triggered this reaction. Just a few days ago she'd been shot, and she had managed to hold it together, so it was something different about this assault that had upset her to this point.

The blindfold.

She still had her eyes squeezed closed, like she expected to find something awful if she opened them. If she'd been blindfolded at some point during her captivity, she probably expected to find herself back in that same situation if she opened her eyes now.

"Sapphire, take my hand," he said, reaching inside her little blanket cocoon to take one of her hands and lift it to his face. "It's just me—the guy who drives you crazy. See?" He took her fingers and traced them across his face, then he pressed a light kiss to her wrist. "See? Just me. The man who made a mess of things earlier when he told you he had been going to kiss you ... *but*." He rested her palm against his cheek and continued. It might not seem like the best time to have this conversation, and yet, his heart said it was, in fact, the perfect time. "I want to kiss you so badly, but I'm afraid of hurting you. We don't even live in the same city, and I don't know what your expectations are. I don't know if you want more than just a kiss and a brief affair or if you want something long-term. You're a beautiful, strong, smart, sexy woman, and any guy would be lucky to have you. *I* would be lucky to have you, but I won't do anything to hurt you, and until you open up to me and talk to me, I won't kiss you. That's not a threat, and it's not blackmail. I just can't hurt you, and I will if I don't know what you want from me."

Very slowly, her fingers curled around his.

Her eyelashes fluttered on her cheeks, and a moment later, he was looking into those stunning green eyes.

Only this time, they weren't perfectly guarded, they weren't cool, calm, and collected.

This time, they were swirling with a stormy mass of emotions. Fear and panic, sadness and loneliness.

She had just taken the very first step toward trusting him.

∿

11:52 P.M.

The memories were jumbled inside her head.

Not because she had been drugged or beaten or anything, but because her brain simply didn't want her to remember.

At first, she hadn't. When she'd woken inside that barn ten years ago, she hadn't remembered it, nor had she when she'd been rescued and gone to live with her aunt and uncle. But bit by bit over time, those memories had slowly started resurfacing.

Usually, she shoved them back down, but tonight, she hadn't been able to do that.

Until Gideon had somehow managed to calm her down.

Sapphire had him to thank for the fact that she was still alive. If he hadn't gone looking for her and happened to stumble upon them in the alley, Mason Wharf would have raped and killed her.

She had no doubt about that.

The man had a violent temper, and she had set it off by accusing him of being the killer. At least now, he would be thrown in prison, taken off the streets where he could never hurt another person, and hopefully, he would see that he had nothing to lose by telling them where Thea Brody was and the girl could be rescued and reunited with her terrified family.

That was all thanks to Gideon.

Sapphire wasn't even pretending anymore that she didn't like the man—not to anyone else and definitely not to herself. It wasn't just that he had saved her life. It was that he had been honest with her. Instead of being afraid of upsetting her, he had told her exactly what his thought processes had been when he had rethought his desires to kiss her.

She respected that so much.

Being a victim meant that people often treated you with kid gloves. Her aunt and uncle had done it all the time when she first went to live with them. They never wanted to do anything to upset her because they thought that if they did, she might fall apart. That was why she liked being around her sisters. Since they had all lived through similar experiences, they didn't do that to one another. It was also probably why she acted so tough and standoffish at work, having people not like her was so much easier than having them treat her like a china doll that might crack into a million pieces if they said or did the wrong thing.

But Gideon had just talked to her. Told her what was going on inside his head. He hadn't been afraid that she would break.

"Here's some ice." Amethyst knocked at her bedroom door and came in.

"Thanks." Sapphire shifted slightly against her pillows, wincing at the resulting stab of pain in her chest and stomach.

"Are you sure you shouldn't have spent the night in the hospital?" her sister asked, handing her the ice pack which she gingerly placed against her bruised ribs.

"Positive. This is where I can relax, not there." It was no surprise that being in the hospital made her think of the days immediately following her rescue that she had spent in a hospital. Today, especially with memories shimmering so close to the surface, she just couldn't spend the night there.

"I get that," Ruby said from the doorway. "I hate the hospital."

"We all do," Diamond added, joining them. "That's no surprise, given that we all spent time there following the worst time in our lives."

"You doing okay?" Ruby asked, coming to perch beside her on the bed.

"No broken bones, no concussion, just bruising and a headache," she reminded her sisters.

"You were lucky," Diamond said.

"I was," she agreed. Thanks to Gideon. If he'd been even a little slower finding her, Mason Wharf would have done more than kick her a few times and put his hand up her sweater.

Although she tried to stop it, the memory seeped back in.

She could feel Mason's cold fingers brush the underside of her breast as he shoved her sweater up.

She could feel her fear as she had known what was coming next.

Then her mind flew back in time ten years.

She was in her room at the mansion she and her sisters had been brought to that night they were sold.

Exhaustion had her collapsing onto the bed and falling asleep, voices and hands had roused her.

There had been men there.

A lot of them.

Most she hadn't seen before, but the man from her bedroom whom she'd hit, had been amongst them.

She had been gagged and blindfolded, then held down while the men pulled her panties off and took turns performing oral sex on her. They weren't allowed to have sex with the girls, as it ruined their resale value, but apparently, they had found a way around that.

The blindfold had come up a little and she'd watched as each head dipped between her legs, ripping another piece of her away each time.

The anger, the humiliation, the fear, the heartbreaking pain of being completely helpless and at their mercy was made worse by the fact that, although she hated what they were doing and wanted them to stop, she had come several times.

It wasn't intentional.

She wasn't feeling any pleasure.

But the human body was created a certain way, and it was designed to make you come when someone stimulated that part of you.

Knowing that in her head, and having been told it several times by the shrink she'd been sent to, didn't mean she had yet accepted it.

Even her body betrayed her that day.

And that was why her brain had tried to protect her by burying those memories away. But it hadn't worked. They'd come back, and tonight she had been terrified that if she opened her eyes, she would see the same things she had when her blindfold had slipped that night—a dozen men laughing and joking and trying to make her own body turn against her so they could further traumatize her.

It'd been just a game to them.

Just like attacking her had been just a game to Mason Wharf.

But Gideon wasn't like that.

He didn't play games.

She'd been saved twice now—once by Detective Rowan Brown, whom she still kept in contact with, and once by Gideon Barlow.

As grateful as she was, she hated that she hadn't been able to save herself.

That she hadn't saved herself made her feel so useless.

Tears filled her eyes, and since she had already cried in front of one person today, she didn't want to do it again. "I think I'm just going to turn the light off, try to sleep," she told her sisters.

"You're shaking, let me grab you another blanket from the linen closet," Diamond said, and she didn't have the heart to tell her sister that she wasn't cold—and it wasn't the cause of her trembling.

"Thank you," she replied.

"Do you need any painkillers?" Amethyst asked.

"I'm good," she said through a yawn.

"Here you go." Diamond returned, blanket in her arms.

"Thanks," she said through another yawn. Sapphire picked up the cup of tea Diamond had made her when they'd returned from the hospital thirty minutes ago. As much as she lived on coffee—she needed the caffeine to function—tea was her relaxation drink. There was something about breathing in the smell, and taking sips that almost burned your throat on the way down, that made her feel all cozy and safe.

"Okay, well, we'll let you get some rest," Ruby said, reaching out to brush the hair off her forehead and tuck it behind her ear before standing up. "Call out if you need anything."

"I will," she promised. She wanted to ask her big sisters to stay in here with her tonight so she wouldn't be alone when the nightmares came for her, but something—her pride, her fears, her stubbornness—made her keep her mouth shut.

It had been the same when Gideon had said goodnight at the hospital.

She had wanted to ask him to stay with her, at least a little longer, but she hadn't been able to make the words come out.

"Night, night, sweet dreams," Diamond said as she tucked her in then switched off the bedroom light as she, Amethyst, and Ruby filed out.

Alone, Sapphire took another sip of tea and let the warm liquid soothe her. She was sleepy, not just tired, which surprised her. Given the shock and trauma of what happened tonight, she thought she would be tired, but way too wired for sleep.

Then it hit her.

The tea.

Her sisters must have crushed up some sleeping pills and put them in the tea.

Maybe she should be angry about that, being drugged against her will, but Sapphire wasn't angry in the least. On the contrary, knowing that her sisters had done that because they knew her so well—well enough to know that she would never voluntarily cave and take a sleeping pill because it felt like a weakness, like giving in—and that they loved her enough to do what was in her best interest, just made her feel loved and cared about.

Setting the tea cup down, Sapphire fluffed her pillows and snuggled down onto her mattress, cocooning herself in her blankets and quilt. It wasn't quite as good as being cocooned in Gideon's arms earlier, but it was still nice.

Letting her eyes close, she drifted off to sleep without having to count thousands of sheep like she did most nights.

CHAPTER
Nine

January 7th
4:26 A.M.

Things were working out pretty well.

So far, the cops were totally clueless.

They thought that the man they were looking for was Mason Wharf. The man was a volatile idiot; there was no way he could do this. This required sophistication. It required forethought and planning. It required the ability to remain calm, stick with the plan, but also be able to compromise if you had to.

He thought he had shown he was capable of all those things.

When he had walked into the abandoned apartment building where he'd built his own version of the padded room and found Amelia Lexis hobbling down the hallway with a foot and ankle she had broken herself, he'd been surprised, at first. More than surprised, he'd been shocked. But then he had been a little in awe of her. He wasn't sure he would've had the guts or the fortitude to smash his own bones to get free.

Part of him had wanted to let the girl live. After all, she'd gone to so much trouble to try to escape. But that would have been a mistake. She had seen him; she could identify him, and that was something he couldn't let happen. So, he'd smashed her head into the wall over and over again until she stopped breathing.

Then he'd had to spend the rest of the night cleaning.

Besides having to clean down the body like he always did, he had to make sure that he hadn't left any of himself behind, so he had also scrubbed down the room. There was blood everywhere, and now that Amelia had managed to get free, he was always going to worry that one of his next girls might get free, too, so he had scrubbed away every drop of blood, wiped every surface, removed everything of his that he kept there, and cleaned the place out.

It wasn't safe now, and he was so glad that he had used two locations, because now all he had to do was take his next victim to the fishing shack and keep her there. At least that way, if she managed to get free, she wouldn't be able to get to help. Even though it was close to the city, it would still take her a while to find her way out of the woods and to the road.

Content and confident that he had everything completely under control, he slipped out of the house. It was nice out here in the cold night. While it had been snowing lightly earlier in the evening, now it was still. The clouds had cleared, and the moon was shining brightly.

He liked winter. There was something about the menacing cold, the gloomy gray weather, the spindly half dead looking trees. It appealed to him. Maybe it had something to do with the fact that he was a killer and every bit as menacing, dark, and gloomy as the wintertime was.

He knew he should probably be in bed, getting some sleep, but he just couldn't settle. It had been a busy night, full of hoopla at the precinct. Mason Wharf had apparently gone off the deep end, assaulted the lead detective on the case who had accused him of being the serial killer. His assault had been interrupted, and the cop was going to be fine, but the whole station was buzzing about it.

How stupid could Mason be?

Oh, well. At least for now, the cops wouldn't be looking for him because they thought they already had their man. He wasn't one of those killers who was into grabbing fame and glory. He was fine with the cops thinking his work was really the work of someone else.

He was doing this because he wanted to find out what lay beyond death.

It was something that had haunted him since he was seventeen years old.

A night with his girlfriend at the time had turned into a nightmare, and he had never been able to forget it.

He believed that there was one defining moment in a lifetime, and that was his. It was the day that his life changed. It was like he had been standing at a fork in the road. He could have gone to the left, but instead, that event had happened, and he had been thrown down to the right whether he liked it or not.

And that was how he'd gotten to this place.

Did he regret what had happened?

Yes and no.

He wished that he hadn't lost someone he cared about, but he wasn't unhappy where life had taken him. All in all, he was pretty content with his life, even if he wouldn't be where he was without that one moment in time.

Since he was up and about like the creatures of the night, he thought he may as well drive out to the fishing shack. He felt like a little fun, a little release. Just because he was being as careful as it was humanly possible to be, it didn't mean that he hadn't slipped up some-where. There was *always* a chance that he would make a mistake, and the cops would be on to him.

Remain positive.

That was his life motto.

When life threw you lemons, you took them and smashed them into a million pieces to make yourself feel better. None of this lemonade nonsense. He hated lemonade. Lemonade was for people who were too stupid to take life by the horns. They wanted to sit back and pretend that everything was all sunny and rosy, but it wasn't. The world was a dark place, and the quicker you accepted that, the easier your life was.

He wondered if Thea Brody had already come to that conclusion.

He'd had four girls come through his life now, and he was always interested to see how each one was going to react. None of the four had been the same, so far. One had given up so quickly, he'd barely been able to use her properly for her allotted time. One had screamed abuse at him every single time he stepped into the room. Another had cried incessantly; that had gotten old really quickly. Then there was Amelia Lexis who had somehow managed to find the strength to escape. He wondered how Thea would react.

Well, he would soon find out because he was already in his car driving toward the fishing cabin.

The anticipation had him buzzing as he drove along.

He was so excited his hands were literally shaking. He hadn't really had any time to spend with Thea. The abduction had been tricky, and he'd had to stash her in the car for a while before he'd been able to sneak away long enough to drive her out here and leave her tied her to the table.

Without him even realizing it, he slowed when he reached a certain point in the road and came to a stop.

He always stopped at this point.

It was the point where he had reached the fork in the road of his life.

Every time he crossed this point, he remembered that day. Seventeen years old, scared, confused, unsure of what he should do. He had taken the coward's way out that day, and it had shaped every aspect of his life since.

There was no other traffic this time of night, so he got out of his car and walked to the very spot where the car had crashed. That night there had been glass and bits of metal everywhere. There had been tire marks on the road, and the tree the car had hit had been half bent over.

Now, in the thin light of his headlights, there were no signs that someone had ever died here.

That made sense, of course. It had been many years, so of course, there was no evidence of the crash, but someone had died here. That should be represented in some way. Maybe he would build a memorial of some kind here after he was finished with his plan and he got the answers that he sought because, for now, that had to remain his number one priority.

Especially with the police closing in.

They would learn soon that Mason Wharf wasn't the killer, and they'd start looking into other cops.

Sooner or later, they would have to figure out that it was him that they were hunting. It was inevitable. Unless he was able to get the answers he needed about what lay beyond this life quickly and then stop taking more girls. Then maybe, if the killings stopped, they would eventually have to move on, file this as a cold case as more and more new cases continued to pile up.

For now, though, he wasn't going to worry about that.

He was just going to get back into his car and go visit Thea Brody.

5:15 A.M.

She had been lying here, staring at the ceiling for hours now.

When was he coming back?

Or did she really want to know the answer?

Thea was stuck between wanting him to come back and dreading when he did.

What was he going to do when he got here?

She was terrified to think about that.

Maybe it was a good thing he hadn't come back here after all.

Because there was nothing else to do, Thea tugged on the ropes tying her wrists to the table. They didn't budge. Just like they hadn't budged the last thousand or so times she'd tried to get loose since he'd brought her here.

As well as being tied to the table, she was gagged. Thea wasn't sure if that was because she was in an area where someone might hear her if she screamed for help or just because he had gotten annoyed with her constant talking.

Make a connection with your captor. That was what you were supposed to do if you were kidnapped, right? You were supposed to try to make them see you as a real person and not just an object in their game so that it made it harder for them to hurt you. Or kill you.

That was what she remembered reading in a criminal psychology book. She kind of had a thing for the criminal justice field and had even toyed with the idea of becoming a crime scene tech. She thought that blood spatter was interesting and that it might be something she would like to focus on.

If she ever got out of here.

If she didn't, some blood spatter expert might be examining her blood, splattered all over the place, to try to figure out what had happened to her and who had done it.

She didn't like that option.

She couldn't give up. She fought every day to help her family, to support them as best as she could, to study hard in school, to get good grades so she could have the future she wanted. She wasn't letting some crooked cop steal that away from them.

She didn't want her mom and brothers having police officers turn up on their doorstep, informing them that her body had been found. She didn't want the extra financial burden to fall on her mom or her younger brothers, nor did she want them to have to suffer through losing her and dealing with her murder.

That meant dying in here was not an option.

It was up to her to do whatever she had to, to make sure that it didn't happen.

She couldn't rely on the cops finding her. If they knew that they were working with a killer, they would have already done whatever they had to, to stop him. That meant that they had no idea who this man really was. If they didn't know who he was, then they didn't know where he had stashed her.

This was all on her.

She needed a plan.

Since she couldn't seem to get herself free, the only option that seemed to be available to her was talking—*if* she could convince him to take the gag off.

So that made that her number one goal.

Maybe if she could break things down into tiny little steps then she actually could make it out of here alive. If she let herself get over-whelmed, then she wasn't going to be able to function, but breaking things up so she only dealt with one thing at a time was probably the only way she could hold onto her sanity.

Already, Thea could feel it slipping.

Her grip on it was tenuous.

At any second, it could fall away, and she would be left a shivering, sobbing, useless wreck.

If she didn't have a family at home waiting for her, then she would probably just give up. But she did have a family who loved her. They would be praying for her, and she could feel that strength seeping into her. It was their love that was going to get her through this. Every time she felt like she was losing it, she would think of them. Picture the picnics they sometimes took in the summer, going out to some quiet spot, hiking through the woods, swimming in a lake or a river, laughing and talking and taking a little time out from the busyness of everyday life. Or the snow days when they would all gather in the living room, make homemade lasagna or macaroni and cheese or some other comfort food, then curl up on the couch, eat junk food, and play board games.

Family was what life was about, and she wasn't ready to leave hers yet.

Was that a car?

A flash of light filled the shack where she was being held, followed by the rev of an engine.

It was him.

He was here.

Butterflies swirled in her stomach. She wasn't sure that she could do this. But it wasn't like she had a choice. She had been abducted, thrown in the trunk of a car, brought here, and tied up. If she wanted to get home, she had to be prepared to do whatever it took.

Whatever.

There wasn't anything she wouldn't do to get out of here. All that mattered was going home. Anything else, she could find a way to deal with later.

"Hello," a voice sung out as the door opened. The light from the headlights had gone, but he flicked on a switch near the door and the light above her came on.

Her eyes tracked his every move as he crossed the couple of steps from the door to her side. Her eyes met his, and she found that she couldn't look away. He didn't look evil. He didn't look like the kind of man who kidnapped teenage girls, but she couldn't let looks deceive her. He *was* that kind of man because he *had* done this.

"Mmhmm," she mumbled through her gag.

"You want to say something, Thea?" he asked with a chuckle, brushing the back of his knuckles across her cheek. Although his touch made her cringe inside and her stomach revolt, she kept her face impassive and nodded. "I guess it doesn't hurt, but you start babbling too much, and I'll put this back on."

She nodded again. She would agree to anything right now as long as she got this disgusting tape off her mouth. Her mouth was so dry, and she was tired of the way the tape pinched her lips. She just wanted it off.

He reached over, and in one quick movement, ripped the tape off, taking a layer of skin along with it. Thea winced, but really, even the burning pain on her lips couldn't dampen her relief at being able to open and close her mouth again and breathe through it if she wanted.

"Water?" he asked, holding up a bottle.

Thea nodded eagerly, and he unscrewed the cap and tipped a little into her mouth. She almost choked on it as he poured too quickly. Most of it sloshed down her chin, but some ran into her mouth and she greedily swallowed a couple of mouthfuls. Too soon he stopped, taking the bottle and setting it down on a bench behind him, as though he knew she needed more and deliberately wanted to deprive her of it.

Now that her throat was no longer dry, she met the man's eyes once again. "Why did you kidnap me?" she asked.

"Because I wanted to," he replied with a small smile.

"What are you going to do with me?" She had asked him this earlier, but he hadn't given an answer—just got frustrated with her. Maybe now that he didn't feel the pressure of getting her locked away, he was more inclined to answer her questions.

"Play with you for a bit," he said with a wink.

His words were like a bucket of ice water, chilling her to the bone.

She knew what he meant by playing.

Shoving aside her fears, she didn't break eye contact. "And then what?"

"Then I'm going to kill you."

"How?"

"I'm going to strangle you."

His honesty was both reassuring and terrifying. "Why?"

"Because I want to see what you see when you're dying."

That wasn't the answer she'd been expecting. So, this went deeper than just wanting to abduct, rape, and murder her. He wanted to learn something from her. If she had to guess, it was because he had lost someone close to him, and he wanted to know where they were. She believed in Heaven and Hell, and she believed that to go to Heaven you had to have a personal relationship with God and with His Son Jesus Christ. She didn't believe that people like this man went to Heaven, so she didn't think that he was going to get the answers that he sought from her. Did that mean he was going to get angry at her? Hurt her more before he killed her?

"Did you lose someone?" she asked. "Is that why you want to see what is after death? So you can see where they are now?"

"I did. It was a long time ago. That day was … eventful … to say the least, I let someone down, wasn't there for them, and now they're gone and I can't make that right."

Since she could see the genuine pain in his face, she said, "I'm sorry. I know what it's like to lose someone you care about. He didn't die, but my dad walked out on us when I was six. I can't really remember him very well anymore, but some days I miss him. Not *him* exactly, but what a dad is supposed to be."

"It sucks to lose someone, but you seem to be a nice kid. This isn't personal. You were just a convenient choice. I'm sorry."

He actually looked like he was.

That gave her hope.

She knew he wasn't ready to let her go just yet, but she had just built a foundation.

"All right," he said. The sad look left his face, and now he looked menacing. "I've indulged you long enough. Now, it's play time."

Thea choked back a sob and hoped she wasn't going to let this destroy her when she was making progress getting through to him.

∾

8:02 A.M.

He was two minutes late.

Two minutes.

Why did two minutes make her feel like she was about to lose her mind?

Sapphire sat in a chair at the kitchen table, an untouched mug of coffee clutched tightly in her hands. Her leg bounced up and down in an erratic pattern of nervous anticipation.

The anticipation of seeing Gideon again after last night left her feeling like a teenage girl going out on her first date with her first crush.

Only she wasn't a teenage girl, they weren't going on a date, and she didn't get crushes.

Well ... She hadn't before Gideon, at least.

Now, she wasn't so sure. She didn't know what the future held for them. Gideon was right. He lived in another city, and she had been far from forthcoming about the attraction she had for him. Even if they found a way to make things work, she wasn't sure how she would cope being in a relationship. She was used to being on her own, just having to worry about herself and her job, but if she was in a relationship, she couldn't be a workaholic all the time; she'd have to consider the other person's feelings and needs. And the intimate stuff ... she had no idea how that was going to go. Not just physical intimacy, but the emotional intimacy. She didn't know how to let people in anymore, and Gideon was a psychiatrist. His thing was examining feelings and emotions and making sense of them. Most of the time, she hid hers away because they terrified her.

It was ridiculous to think that any relationship with him could work.

And yet, that was exactly what her mind seemed to be stuck on.

A car horn honked, and she jumped so much coffee sloshed all over the sides of the mug and down her hands, puddling on the table.

"I'll clean that up. You go to work," Diamond said. Her oldest sister had been sitting at the table watching her all morning. The scrutiny had only made her edgier. She didn't like being examined so closely. It made her feel like she now had the pressure of her family on her to try to see if could make things work with Gideon because she knew they wanted to see her happy—just like she wanted to see them happy. None of them had been particularly successful in the relationship department since their parents' betrayal.

"Thank you," she said, going to the kitchen to run her hands under the tap, then without bothering to dry them, she picked up her bag and slung the strap over her shoulder.

"Aren't you going to invite him in?" Ruby asked, emerging from her library.

"No, I'm not," she said. There was no way she was introducing Gideon to her sisters when she was so confused about her growing feelings for him. "He's just here to pick me up for work, so I don't have to drive. That's it. Nothing exciting." Although she was sure she was capable of driving after Mason's assault last night, before he'd left the hospital last night Gideon had offered to pick her up at eight and drive her to work, and she had accepted before her brain had even processed the offer and vetoed it.

Before her sisters could pry into her life anymore, she hurried out the door, closing it firmly behind her.

Gideon's car sat on the street outside her house and the moment her eyes spotted him in it, she felt a sort of peace settle over her. The sleeping pills her sisters had given her last night had helped her sleep, but they hadn't done away with the sense of dread that had hovered over her— even as she slept.

For some reason, Gideon was able to clear it away even though he hadn't done anything but sit in his car and wait for her.

"Morning," she said as she opened the passenger door and got in.

"Good morning." He shot her one of his winning smiles, then held up a cup of coffee. "For you," he said, passing it over. "I know how much you love the stuff."

"This is from my favorite café," she said, touched.

"Yep, I stopped over there on the way here," he told her as he drove off down the street.

"Thank you." It was such a small gesture, and for someone who didn't have anyone in their life who did things like that for them, it was the small gestures that moved your heart the most.

"You're welcome," he replied like it was no big deal. "How are you feeling this morning? Were you able to sleep?"

"I slept," she said, leaving out the fact that it was only because her sisters had crushed sleeping pills and put them in her tea. "And I'm sore, but it's manageable."

"Did you have any nightmares?"

He really wasn't one to respect boundaries. That was not the kind of question one colleague asked another, especially when that colleague had only known you for four days. Despite that, she answered him. "No. I don't have nightmares very often."

"That's good. I'm glad." He said it like he really meant it. Like perhaps he had first-hand experience of how suffering with nightmares affected a person. He knew all about her past, but she hardly knew anything about him. It was time to change that.

"So, what made you decide you wanted to become a criminal psychiatrist?" Sapphire asked.

"My father had an older brother who was abducted. The way it affected my grandparents and my dad, it made me want to do my part in stopping that from happening to another family. Much the way I suspect what happened to you made you want to do your part in stopping that happening to another person."

He really wasn't shy about bringing up her past, no matter how many times she told him she didn't want to talk about it. "Hey," she said when she noticed they had turned left instead of right and were no longer heading toward the precinct. "Where are we going?"

"We just need to make one stop before we go in," he replied, making another turn.

"Where?" she persisted. She didn't like being left in the dark; it made her feel anxious.

"Don't you trust me?" He took his eyes off the road to look at her.

No was on the tip of her tongue, all ready to come barging out, but something held it back. She *did* trust Gideon. She wasn't sure how or when that had happened, but she did.

"Good." He grinned, like her silent acknowledgment that she trusted him really meant something to him.

They sat in silence for the next few minutes as Gideon drove through the gray morning. Until Gideon turned into the street where she and Elijah had sat in their car four days ago in the early hours of the morning, hoping to catch the serial killer in the middle of dumping the next body.

"What are we doing here?" she asked, confused.

"I just want to run something through with you," he replied.

That wasn't enough information. "Gideon, you're keeping something from me." She shot him a pointed frown.

"Hey, you called me by my first name," was the only reply she got. The words were accompanied by another grin. He really smiled too much for someone who had no doubt seen the things that came with a job in law enforcement.

"Don't stall," she warned. "Why are we here?"

"You said you trust me." With that, he got out of the car and had circled it and opened her door for her by the time she undid her seat belt.

"That trust only goes so far," she muttered as she followed him over to the alley behind the movie theater where she'd been shot. Which reminded her that the small wound was itching like crazy, and she couldn't wait to get the stitches out in a few days' time.

"I want you to walk through for me exactly what happened that night."

"Gideon," she sighed, exasperated.

"I'll tell you why we're here as soon as you're done," he promised.

With another sigh, she obliged. "We were sitting in our car over there." She waved a hand to where Gideon had parked his car. "Elijah wanted to go home. He didn't think the killer was going to show up. Then we saw something. We got out, came running over, guns drawn. There was a young guy here. He didn't have a body with him, and although we cuffed him, he didn't seem like our guy. There was a girl with him. We talked to them, realized it wasn't who we were looking for, and let them go. Elijah wanted to call it a night. I wanted to wait a little longer. We were arguing, then there was a shot. We turned and saw a man with what looked like a body slung over his shoulder shoot the guy we nearly arrested. He grabbed the woman, used her as a human shield, and started coming toward us despite our orders to stop."

"Where were you and Elijah standing when this happened?" Gideon interrupted to ask.

Sapphire walked a little farther down the alley. "About here." He nodded for her to continue, so she did. "We both ordered him to stop and to put his weapon down. He kept ignoring us. Neither of us had a clear shot because of how he held the woman. Then he shot Elijah, then me, then the girl. The force of the blow knocked me over, and I fell here." She pointed to the spot. "He dropped the girl as he shot her. Our eyes met, and I watched her die," she finished softly.

"Where exactly did he drop the girl's body when he shot her?"

Not sure why it mattered, Sapphire replied, "Right where you're standing. Now I've played along. I've told you what happened that night even though you already know. Now you tell me why we're here."

"Crime scene found something."

"Well, that's good," she said, although the look on Gideon's face had her doubting that it was.

"Yeah, it's good," he echoed.

"So, what did they find?"

"A pen. They were able to get a print off it."

"And they got a match?"

"They did."

"It wasn't Mason Wharf's, was it?"

"No, it wasn't."

"So, whose was it?"

"Sapphire ..." He looked pained and took a step closer, reaching for her hand. "The print belonged to Zeb."

She gasped, and yanked her hand back, as though it burned. "It couldn't have been."

"It was."

"Well, he was here at the scene after the shooting. He probably just dropped it then."

Gideon shook his head. "The pen was found underneath the woman's body. That's why I brought you here, so you could play through everything that happened, make sure you were one hundred percent certain about the way things played out. According to what you said, the only way that Zeb's pen could have gotten underneath the body was if he was the one holding her before she fell. It must have slipped out of a pocket as he was shooting."

She shook her head wildly—wanting to refute his words, prove that they were wrong. "I don't believe it. I know Zeb. I've known him for years. He's a good guy. He's not a killer. He didn't kidnap and rape those girls then throw them away like garbage. He didn't shoot me and Elijah. He wouldn't. I don't believe it," she said again as though saying it would make it true.

"I'm sorry. I really am, but you don't have a choice. Zeb was here that night—that's what the evidence says. He was the one who shot you," Gideon said softly, reclaiming his grip on her hand. "He had Misha Heart's body with him. That means he is the serial killer you've been looking for."

She still wanted to refute his words, but how could she?

Everything he had said was true.

In shock, she didn't even fight it when Gideon slipped an arm around her shoulders and guided her back to his car.

She had been betrayed once again by someone she trusted.

Zeb had been her friend—or as close to a friend as she had—and she hadn't seen who he really was.

He was a kidnapper, a rapist, and a murderer. He had tried to kill her and her partner and almost succeed with Elijah.

His betrayal cut deep.

This was exactly why she never let people get close to her. You couldn't be betrayed when you didn't let anyone in.

9:21 A.M.

He was worried about her.

Sapphire had been walking around in a fog ever since he'd told her about the evidence the crime scene unit had found.

He hated having to be the one to break the news to her that her friend had been the one who shot her, but he also knew that it would be better coming from him than anyone else. So, he'd done what he had to. But it hadn't been easy.

Gideon still hadn't recovered from finding her being attacked by Mason Wharf last night. He hadn't wanted to leave her. If it had been up to him, he would've taken her from the hospital straight back to his hotel room, but it wasn't his place to do that. So he'd stayed with her until her sisters showed up, and he'd left her with them.

He'd gone back to the hotel and laid awake all night thinking of her.

He hadn't been sure what kind of mood he would find her in when he picked her up in the morning and had been pleasantly surprised to find her in a good one. She had definitely thawed out when it came to him. She'd even stopped calling him Dr. Barlow and used his first name. That was definitely progress.

"How're you doing?" he asked her, probably for the fiftieth time since they left the scene.

"I'm okay," she told him. That was the same answer she'd given him every time he asked, and he supposed it was partially true. She was hanging in there as best as she could after learning that one of her colleagues and a friend of hers had been the one to shoot her.

"You ready to go and find Zeb, bring him into an interview room, and tell him what we found?"

"Yes," she said, standing up and heading for the stairs, then stopping.

Sergeant Langsworth already knew about what had been found. She was the one who had called him and told him this morning, so there was nothing stopping them from going and doing this.

Nothing except Sapphire.

They'd been up to the homicide floor, then back down outside for her to get some fresh air, then back up to homicide, and back outside again.

It was a delay tactic, he knew that, but they couldn't delay any longer. They needed to get Zeb off the streets so no one else died, and they had to get him to give up where he had stashed Thea Brody.

"Are you sure you can do this?" he asked her. "If you're not up to it, no one is going to think badly of you."

"Of course, I can do this."

"You have to treat him like you would any other suspect," he reminded her.

"I know how to do my job. Are you implying I don't?" Sapphire demanded.

"No," he said firmly. "I'm not. You are very good at your job. No one thinks differently. I'm just worried about you."

"Oh." The fire in her green eyes dimmed. "Then, thank you, I guess."

She was very focused on other people saying that she wasn't psychologically competent to do her job. He was going to have to address that issue with her at some point. Not as her psychiatrist, because he wasn't her doctor, but he was her ... Well, he wasn't sure yet what he was. Friend? Boyfriend? Prospective boyfriend?

"Come on." Because he didn't think she could make it on her own, he took her hand and led her inside. He thought she would pull away as soon as they got inside and the prying eyes of her colleagues were on them, but she didn't.

It wasn't until the elevator doors opened on the homicide floor that she took her hand back and went all cop. He could feel the change in her, and any doubts that he'd had that she wasn't up to this, dissipated.

Zeb and Gray were in the conference room where they'd all been working the last few days. Neither of them was aware yet of the evidence that had been discovered because they wanted an honest reaction from Zeb when they presented it to him.

"Morning, Sapphire." Gray beamed at her when they entered the room.

"How are you feeling?" Zeb asked. His face was smooth and calm. He didn't seem concerned at all—so smug, like the possibility of them finding out he was the man they were looking for had never even occurred to him.

"Fine, thank you," Sapphire replied. "Zeb, we need to talk to you."

"About what?" Zeb asked, not a trace of panic in his face or his voice.

"Please come with us to an interview room," Sapphire said. Her tone was controlled and confident. He liked seeing her like this just as much he liked seeing her show a little vulnerability.

"What's going on?" Gray asked, taking a step forward as though to protect his partner.

"Stay back, Gray," Sapphire warned. "Go and talk to the sergeant; she'll explain everything. Zeb, we need you to come with us. Don't make me handcuff you."

"Sapphire ..." Gray frowned and took a step toward her. Without him realizing it, Gideon moved in front of Sapphire. He knew she was the cop and he was the psychiatrist, but his crazy protectiveness when it came to her overrode everything else, including common sense.

"Back up," Sapphire ordered. Her tone clearly said that if he persisted, she would mark him as a threat and act accordingly.

"It's okay, Gray," Zeb said. "I'll go with her. I'm sure this is just some sort of misunderstanding. We'll go sort it out, and then get back to this case."

Sapphire kept her hand on her gun as she led her colleague into an interview room. Gideon followed, watching every single move Zeb made so he could assess if they had the right man this time.

"Okay, I'm trying to play along here, Sapphire, but you have to help me out. You have to tell me what's going on," Zeb said once they were all seated. His face was so earnest, and he seemed so sincere, but Gideon knew never to be fooled by appearances.

"CSU found a pen at the scene where Elijah and I were shot," Sapphire began. She masked the betrayal in her eyes well, but he knew what to look for, and he saw it. He felt it. It was odd, but most of the time, he actually felt what she was feeling as though they were joined together by some invisible thread.

"Yeah? So?" Zeb said.

"There was a fingerprint on it. It was yours." Sapphire paused to let that sink in.

"You're kidding, right?" Zeb asked with a small smile like he was expecting a punch line any time soon.

"We're not kidding."

"Well, I must have dropped it when we were there after you and Elijah were transported to the hospital."

That was exactly the response Gideon had been expecting. Excuses. That was all that was, and a flimsy one at that. The pen was enough to get warrants to check Zeb's house and any other properties he owned, but it wasn't enough to get a conviction. They needed more.

"The pen was found underneath the body of the woman that you used as a human shield," Sapphire told him.

Zeb's eyes grew round as though this was all really starting to sink in. "You really think I did this, don't you? You think that I shot you, that I nearly killed Elijah."

Ignoring his questions, Sapphire continued. "You know Thea Brody, don't you? And yet, you never mentioned that."

"I ... uh ... I wouldn't say I know her," he hedged.

"Oh?" Sapphire arched a dark brow. "That's not what the Brodys said. Mrs. Brody said that your mother lives a few houses down from them, that you're there all the time, that you've even been inside their house before. Why didn't you mention that?"

"I didn't think it was relevant," Zeb said. *Lied.* Gideon could plainly see the panic in his eyes.

"You lied to us. You didn't tell us that you knew a victim in this case, and your pen—with your fingerprint on it—was found at a crime scene. You did this, Zeb. You killed those girls. I don't know why you did it, and right this second, I don't really care. You let us think it was Mason Wharf, and because of that, he tried to kill me. Because of you, my partner is sitting in a hospital bed. You've done a lot of bad things, and nothing that you could do can really make up for that, but you can at least do the right thing now and tell us where Thea Brody is."

"I don't know where she is. I didn't do any of this, I swear." Zeb was starting to look panicky. One of his eyes was twitching, his fingers were drumming on the table, and his voice had risen.

"Is she still alive, Zeb?"

"I don't know. I didn't kidnap her. I didn't kidnap *anyone.* You know me, Sapphire. You know that I would never do anything like this."

Zeb sounded desperate now. He wanted an ally, but Sapphire was the last place he was going to find one.

Sapphire stood. "I will find her, Zeb, and I will make sure that you pay for what you did. You are under arrest for three counts of murder and two counts of attempted murder of a police officer. You can expect more charges to come. You're going to spend the rest of your life in prison."

That wouldn't bring back the people who had lost their lives, nor would it undo the trauma caused to those who had survived, but at least it would stop Zeb from hurting anyone else.

~

7:39 P.M.

"It's after seven thirty. I think that's time to call it a day."

Sapphire heard the voice but not the words. "Hmm?"

"It's after seven thirty. I think it's time to call it a night and go home."

"Home?" she echoed, her mind still firmly stuck on work.

A hand grasped her chin and forcibly turned her head away from the computer screen. "It's seven thirty. You were in the hospital this time yesterday. I think you should go home, eat some dinner, and get some rest."

"It's too early to go home. It's not even dinnertime," she protested. She had at least a couple more hours to go before she would consider heading home.

Gideon laughed. "You didn't hear a word I said, did you?"

"I listened," she said defensively.

"You did not," he said, smiling tenderly at her. "I told you it was after seven thirty; that's later than I eat dinner most days. Come on, I'll drive you home."

"You can go if you want, I can take a cab," she said. She didn't want to put Gideon out, and if she'd had her car it wouldn't be an issue, but she didn't because he'd picked her up this morning, their agreement being he'd take her home at the end of the day. But she wasn't ready to go yet. She didn't want to leave this building until she had enough evidence to keep Zeb in prison for the rest of his life.

"No," Gideon said firmly. "Despite the fact that you seem to think you're superwoman, your body needs time to rest and recuperate; otherwise, it's going to take longer to heal. It's time to go home."

Although his tone was one of those no-nonsense, don't-argue-with-me ones, she couldn't help herself. "Just one more hour?"

"No," he chuckled, reaching for her hand. "No more hours. It's time to go. You aren't going to get what you want tonight. All you're going to do is wear yourself out."

He was right on one point.

She wasn't going to get what she wanted tonight.

What she wanted was to have enough evidence piled up that any jury in the country would find Zeb guilty. But that wasn't possible. Right now, all they had was the pen, and although Zeb was safely tucked away in a jail cell, he wasn't going to stay there. A lawyer would no doubt come up with an excuse as to how the pen got there, and this case might never even make it to court.

She couldn't let that happen.

Zeb had shot her. He'd nearly killed her partner. He'd killed an innocent couple right in front of her and another four women. He had let them think that Mason Wharf was the killer, nearly getting her raped and killed because of it.

Someone that dangerous couldn't be allowed to walk the streets.

If they couldn't find enough to keep him in jail, Zeb was only going to keep killing until he died.

There was no doubt about that.

"Does your brain ever turn off?" Gideon asked affectionately, reaching over to turn off the computer.

"Not really," she admitted. She didn't usually answer personal questions, but this was Gideon, so ...

So, she guessed that made a difference.

She wasn't really sure why, but at the moment, she didn't want to overanalyze it. It just was what it was.

"No wonder you're a workaholic."

"My job is pretty much all I have in my life." She shrugged. She didn't mind being a workaholic; she loved her job, and no matter how hard she worked at it, there would always be more people that needed saving.

"It doesn't have to be that way," Gideon told her.

She knew that, of course. She wasn't stupid. She knew that most people had more than just their job that was important in their lives. But she wasn't like most people.

What she didn't know was what angle Gideon was aiming at with that comment.

Was it just a casual reminder that she should be a more well-rounded individual?

Was it a calculated comment with a hidden agenda?

Was he trying to tell her that he wanted to be the something else in her life?

"Stop doing that." Gideon pulled her to her feet and took her face between his hands. Sapphire couldn't bring herself to meet his gaze because she was afraid of what she would find there. She was afraid of seeing that he liked her, and she was afraid of seeing that he didn't.

"Doing what?"

"Thinking. Turn your brain off for a while and just feel." His thumbs brushed lightly across her cheekbones, and she shuddered at the physical contact. Not only was she not used to people touching her, but she definitely wasn't used to anyone touching her like this. This level of intimacy was new to her, and it was both exciting and terrifying.

"I don't know how to do that." For some, reason Gideon compelled her to be truthful. She wasn't sure exactly why that was. It wasn't like he actually forced her to do it. It was just when he asked a question, she answered it instead of deflecting like she would with anyone else.

"You can learn. Sapphire, look at me," he said, and because it was Gideon, she complied. "You can learn if you want to."

She didn't know what to say, so she just nodded.

Gideon made it sound so easy, but it wasn't.

Nothing about her life was easy.

Because she was feeling overwhelmed now, she gently pulled backward, out of Gideon's grip. She expected him to look upset or hurt, but he looked neither. He just smiled his usual chirpy smile at her and started to gather up her belongings.

He was really something else.

It was like nothing she did got to him.

That had been one of her fears about getting involved with someone, especially romantically. How could she ask another person to take on her ridiculously heavy emotional baggage when she herself had to struggle every day to carry it?

Simple answer was, she couldn't.

Which was why she stayed single.

Single was safe, she had always thought.

"Come on, let's go," he said, taking her hand again. The guy was really big on hand-holding. She hadn't held hands with anyone since she was a little girl, but it was kind of nice.

Sapphire hesitated as they waited at the elevator. How could she go home when there was so much work to do? It didn't feel right; it felt like she was reneging on her responsibilities. Thea Brody was still out there somewhere, possibly hurt, definitely alone, and no doubt hungry and thirsty, maybe cold. How could she go home to her nice, warm, comfortable house knowing that?

"Gideon—" she started.

"It's okay to take time for yourself," he said before she could even express what she was thinking. "You are not letting anyone down; you are not being lazy; you are not doing anything wrong by going home at a semi-reasonable hour to recover from being beaten twenty-four hours ago."

"Part of my brain agrees with you, but Zeb and I worked together, and I didn't see that he was the man we were looking for. That means that some of the responsibility for everything Zeb did falls on me."

"No."

The ferocity in his voice and the loud volume startled her and she shrank away from him. She wasn't used to Gideon acting like that.

"I'm sorry," he said, calmer now and reaching to take her hand, which she had snatched back when he had raised his voice.

She withdrew, the safe place he was starting to create for her shattered in that one second. "It's fine."

"Don't do that. Not when I'm starting to get through to you. I didn't mean to yell at you. It's just so frustrating to see someone so smart, so compassionate, so hardworking, someone who would literally give her own life or anything she owned to help someone who needed help, blame herself for something that she has absolutely zero control over. Do you hear me?" He grabbed her shoulders and shook her gently. "You are not responsible for what he did. All of it—and I mean *all* of it —is on Zeb Tuck."

Sapphire felt herself soften. She didn't believe what Gideon had said, but it was nice of him to say it nonetheless. "All right. Let's go home."

"Finally," he said, his teasing smile back in place. "I didn't think I'd be able to make a dent in that thick head of yours."

That coaxed a smile out of her, and she even held her hand out before Gideon reached for it, not even caring that there were other detectives here still working who would see them holding hands.

She still didn't know where things with Gideon were headed, or if they were headed anywhere at all, but even if this was all she ever had, Gideon making her feel like she was important, just for a few days, was something she would treasure for the rest of her life.

~

11:14 P.M.

He wanted to kiss her so badly, it was all he could think about.

The only reason Gideon hadn't kissed Sapphire already was because he cared enough about her to not do anything that was going to hurt her.

Although he knew that she did like him, and that she wanted to kiss him every bit as much as he wanted to kiss her, he still couldn't get a read on her as to what she wanted long-term.

Dealing with someone who had been through something so life altering—so personal identity alternating—as Sapphire had, meant he had to proceed with caution. Not because he thought she was going to break; he knew that she wasn't. She was too strong, and she had too good of a grip on her emotions, but she still had scars.

Deep scars.

Scars that hadn't just marred her but had irrevocably changed her. Changed her in ways that he didn't think she was even aware of.

That meant that he had to be careful. He had to make sure that he was certain of what he wanted and what he was prepared to do to get it. There were many things standing in the way of him and Sapphire starting a relationship, practical things that had nothing to do with her scars and his desire to help people.

Was he prepared to give up the job he loved to be around for her?

Right now, he traveled the country regularly working cases, with only his dog for company. He had an apartment, but he rarely spent more than a couple of weeks at a time living in it. If he and Sapphire were together, it wouldn't be fair to her for him to spend more time away from home than at it.

Was he prepared to settle down at this stage of his life?

He was thirty, and he wanted to get married and have kids one day, but just as Sapphire's job was important to her, his job was important to him, and he couldn't imagine giving it up to move here and settle down.

Was he prepared to take on Sapphire's baggage?

He was a psychiatrist, trained to help people, trained to understand them, but doing his job was different than being someone's partner. If he and Sapphire were a couple, then he needed to set aside his training and just be her husband, and his job was so ingrained in him, he wasn't sure how he would be able to do that. It wasn't that he was daunted by the prospect, he just wasn't sure that he could set his Mr. Fix It hat aside and just be Mr. Supportive.

There was so much to consider, and trying to figure out what he was and wasn't prepared to do was difficult without knowing exactly where Sapphire stood. He wanted to talk to her about it, but he was worried about overloading her when she already had so much to deal with.

Finding out that the serial killer she'd been hunting was a colleague of hers, and one she knew well, was hitting her hard. She'd spent the whole day trying to find enough proof to convince a jury to keep him locked up in prison for the rest of his life, but he could tell that what she really wanted was proof that this was all one great big mistake. She wanted Zeb to be innocent because she didn't want to be betrayed by another person that she trusted. Knowing that they had been looking for a cop was a very different thing than knowing which cop it was.

Betrayal was what had hurt Sapphire the most.

She had been sold to human traffickers; she'd been tied up and taken away from the only home she had ever known. She had been kept in a barn like an animal, then made to run for her life as people hunted her, and she had no doubt been sexually assaulted, although there was no mention of that in any of the case files he had read. But what had hurt her the most was the betrayal of her parents.

If he and Sapphire were to start dating, he was going to have to be extremely aware of that and make sure that he never did anything that she could construe as a betrayal.

Gideon wished there was something he could do to ease her suffering, to erase a little bit of it and give her something good to take its place. When he had driven her home tonight, he'd wanted to ask her out to dinner. He was sure if he could just get her alone for a bit—away from work—that he could help her see how nice it was to relax.

She was addicted to her job because it was the only thing that helped her mask the pain of what she had been through. Saving others made up for her not being able to save herself. But the problem with relying on that was that there was an infinite number of people in the world who needed to be saved. She was trying to save them all, but all she was doing was spinning in a wheel that there was no way off.

Sapphire needed some balance in her life.

But she kept herself locked away from anyone that might encourage her to take time out from work and do something just for fun. She didn't date, and she didn't really have friends. She had her sisters, but only spending time with them when she wasn't at work was like being in a codependent circle that both helped and hurt all four of them.

If he hadn't known that she needed good, solid rest, he probably would've asked her to dinner. But sleep was what she needed tonight, and he hoped that she was getting some.

He, on the other hand, was not.

With a restless sigh, he shoved back the covers and climbed out of bed. Luna lifted her head and shot him a perplexed look but lay back down and promptly dozed back off.

After he'd dropped Sapphire off, he'd picked up dinner at the hotel's restaurant, then came up to his room and eaten. He'd walked his dog, done a little work, then gone down to the gym to work out a little of his frustration on the treadmill before coming back up here to shower and go to bed.

That was an hour ago.

For the last hour, he had tossed and turned and thought of nothing but Sapphire and how he could help her.

So far, he hadn't been able to come up with much.

What they both really needed was to sit down and talk honestly and openly about where they were and where they wanted to be. Although he didn't like to keep putting it off, Gideon felt like he should probably wait until they had this case wrapped up.

Yes, they had Zeb in custody, so in essence, his job was done, and he could probably go home and wait for a call to come and consult with another police department on another case. But he couldn't do that. Zeb might be in prison for now, but if they didn't find something else to keep him there, then he suspected Zeb would soon be out on bail, and he wouldn't leave Sapphire to work alone on finding evidence to keep him in prison.

He was here until they had an ironclad case that no defense lawyer could tear to shreds.

And that was how he would help her.

Right now, that was what she needed him to do. She needed him to help tie up this case so she could find a way to move forward, to finally start healing from the betrayal that had almost claimed her life.

Grabbing clothes from the closet, he threw them on. He was going to go back to the precinct, see if he could find something that Sapphire had missed. It was late, but he was sure there were a few detectives about, should he need access to anything. He'd love to be able to go and pick Sapphire up for work in the morning and be able to give her good news.

Feeling reinvigorated, Gideon headed out of his hotel room. He would do anything to help Sapphire at this point, and giving up a night of sleep was easy. If he could make her smile, that was worth more than a million hours of sleep. She was so beautiful when she let herself relax and smile, and knowing that he was the one to coax one out of her made him feel proud.

His feelings for her were unexplainable.

A couple of days weren't enough to have developed such strong feelings for another person. Although he didn't believe in love at first sight, from the very first moment he had laid eyes on Sapphire, he'd felt a pull toward her. The universe was obviously trying to tell him something. The attraction, the protectiveness, the desire to help her and make her happy, those things could be the basis of a lifelong partnership.

Who was he to argue with the universe?

11:28 P.M.

Sapphire rolled over on to her left side.

Almost immediately, she rolled back over to her right.

She couldn't get comfortable.

Her arm where Zeb had shot her was itching like crazy, almost to the point where she wanted to rip the bandage off and pull out the stitches just so that it would hurt instead of itch. Her ribs and stomach where Mason Wharf had kicked her were hurting worse today than they had yesterday.

She felt stiff and achy all over.

All day she'd barely even noticed the pain and discomfort. Finding out that Zeb had been the one who shot her and Elijah had pushed any other thoughts out of her head. She wanted so badly to have found enough evidence today to be able to mark this case as closed and move on.

But she hadn't.

And now she was lying here in bed, all uncomfortable and on edge, thinking about what a failure she was for not having stopped Zeb earlier nor having found enough evidence to seal his fate, and wishing that

Gideon had asked her out to dinner. And just because she didn't have enough on her mind, she was also *glad* that Gideon hadn't asked her out to dinner, and was thus debating it on a loop.

"That's it." Sapphire threw back her covers and got up. She couldn't lie here torturing herself any longer.

She appreciated his words, telling her that she didn't have to blame herself for what others did, nor did she have to devote her entire life to saving as many people as she could, but she didn't agree with him. She was saved; she *had* to save others. To her, it was as simple as that.

Sapphire didn't even have to think twice about what she was going to do.

Work.

She had to go back to work.

Maybe after she put in a couple more hours, she might be able to wear herself out enough that she could convince herself that she had earned a few hours of sleep.

After Gideon had dropped her off, she'd done a load of laundry before grabbing some dinner and going to bed, so her favorite sweater wasn't in her room. Since she only lived with her sisters, she dropped the oversized sweatshirt she slept in into the hamper and wore just her jeans and a bra as she walked through the house and headed down to the laundry room.

Her favorite sweater was still warm from the drier and felt all snugly when she pulled it over her head. If she had to go out at almost midnight on a cold winter's night, at least she was heading out all warm and cozy. The house was quiet. Amethyst was working tonight, and Diamond was no doubt in bed already. Ruby would either be sleeping or in her library, and either way Sapphire didn't want to disturb her.

Her coat hung on a hook by the front door and her bag and keys sat beside them. She'd brought her cell phone downstairs with her, so she collected her things, shrugged into her coat, and slipped out into the night.

Although she often worked nights and regularly worked until way after dark, Sapphire didn't particularly like being outside once the sun set and the moon came out. It didn't take a rocket scientist to figure out why. It triggered memories from being forced to run for her life through the woods. Whenever she was outside at night, she was always hypervigilant, always waiting for someone to jump out at her from behind any tree or building or wall that she passed.

When she got into her car and closed and locked the door, she relaxed a little. It was only about ten minutes from her house to the precinct, and at this time of night, traffic was virtually nonexistent, and she made it there in seven.

The station was never empty, but it was quieter at midnight than it was at midday, and she walked through the mostly empty halls and took the elevator up to the homicide floor. She nodded to two colleagues who were at their desks, deep in talk as they worked whichever case was top of their list right now.

"Oh." She stopped in her tracks when she opened the door to the conference room where they were working Zeb's case. "What are you doing here?"

"I could ask you the same thing," Gideon replied, shooting her one of his trademark grins. She couldn't remember ever having known anyone who smiled as much as he did. It was nice. Every time a smile lit his face it was like a tiny ray of sunshine broke into her dark little world.

"Couldn't sleep," she said, sliding into the seat beside him.

"Neither could I. I wanted to come here, try to find something that would help you keep Zeb in jail."

"Thank you." That was thoughtful of him. He was a thoughtful guy. Sapphire supposed it went with being a shrink. "You didn't have to do that, though."

"I know. I wanted to."

That was a good enough answer for her. "Did you find anything?"

"No, nothing that will help."

"Are you sure that we're right about this?" she asked. "Are you positive that Zeb is the killer?"

"Positive."

"We thought it was Mason, and we were wrong."

"*You* all thought that it was Mason; I had doubts. I thought he was capable of violence but not of the complex measures this serial killer was working."

"But this time you don't have doubts, right?"

Gideon hesitated.

Which immediately raised her anxiety levels.

There was something that was making him hold back on committing to the idea that Zeb was the killer.

"You *do* have doubts," she said, a little accusatorially.

"Some," he acknowledged.

"Why?"

"Because of you."

"Me?" she asked, confused. Why was she making Gideon doubt that they had their man?

"Yes, you." He gave her an affectionate smile. "You were shot by this man, and because of that, I'm not sure that I can be as objective as I'd usually be."

"Huh," she said, stunned, not really sure how to respond to that. She could be offended, but she knew without him having to say it that he didn't mean it in a negative way.

"Knowing that someone shot you makes me so angry I almost can't think straight. When I even think that it could be Zeb, I want to hit him until I feel this pressure in my chest ease. I keep thinking, what if I'm wrong? We were wrong once, and you paid the price for that. What will happen if we're wrong again?"

Sapphire didn't have an answer to that.

Besides the obvious that if they were wrong, Thea Brody and more teenage girls would die.

Beyond that, anything else could happen.

"I'm sorry, Sapphire. I'm not sure that I'm going to be much help to you as far as this case goes. I've lost my objectivity."

Her heart stopped.

Was Gideon trying to tell her that he was leaving?

It wasn't like she didn't know that when this case was over, he was going to go back to his life, but she didn't think she was ready for that yet.

"Are you leaving?" she asked tightly.

"What? No." He sounded as horrified by the possibility as she felt. "I would never leave you to deal with this case on your own. I just don't know how much help I'm actually going to be. You and I ... we're in this together until we nail this guy to the wall."

His words invigorated her and reassured her, and yet hovering over them was the "until." What would come after that? Nothing? Or would they find a way to make a long-distance relationship work? They needed to talk, find answers to some of those questions, but she had no idea how to go about initiating such a conversation.

Look a killer in the eye, she could do without flinching, but ask her to have a discussion with a prospective boyfriend and she was so out of her element she couldn't even fathom how to find her way back.

"Let's go sit on the floor," Gideon announced.

"The floor?" She arched a brow.

"I like sitting on the floor."

"Okay," she said with a smirk.

They gathered the laptop and the iPad and took them to a corner of the room. Gideon brought their coats and spread them over their laps when they sat down.

Sapphire wanted to ask what Gideon wanted. She wanted to ask if he wanted to ask her out on a date. She wanted to ask if he wanted to try a relationship. She wanted to ask if he saw a future with her. She wanted to ask if he was willing to make a go at a long-distance relationship and if she was worth the effort of all that went with that.

But she didn't.

Instead, she opened the laptop and just enjoyed sitting beside him while they worked side by side in silence.

CHAPTER
Ten

January 8th
6:47 A.M.

The sound of a door opening disturbed her.

Was she asleep?

Sapphire opened her eyes and groggily looked around.

It took her still half-asleep brain a moment to realize that she wasn't at home in bed. Instead, she was at work, in the conference room, sitting on the floor, her back against the wall, her head on Gideon's shoulder. He was still asleep, his head tilted back against the wall, his arm draped around her shoulders.

Had they really fallen asleep like this?

She didn't remember going to sleep. The last thing she remembered was discussing a possible incident from Zeb's past that could be the catalyst for the person he had become and the abductions and murders.

Apparently, when he was seventeen, Zeb had been out with his parents and his girlfriend. They'd been celebrating her sixteenth birthday, going to dinner and a movie, when they'd been mugged at the movie theatre. What could have been a simple robbery, turned deadly when the teenage boy had been spooked by a passing ambulance and fired his gun, killing both Zeb's father and girlfriend.

That was enough to warp a person.

She knew.

She knew what it was like to watch someone die right in front of you, and she had only known Tasha a couple of days. For Zeb to watch the father he loved and the girl he loved die right in front of him, he would never forget that. The feelings of helplessness, as he no doubt did everything he could to save them, would leave lifelong scars.

They had been excited by the discovery and had moved on to searching for any connections to a deserted country road.

Now that they had a name, it was much easier to look into his past, and they were able to find out that his mother had been badly injured in a car accident. A hit-and-run on a deserted country road.

Neither of those revelations were going to help them keep Zeb in prison, and searching into his past hadn't been what she wanted to focus on. She wanted evidence that would convince a jury of his guilt, but Gideon had suggested focusing on finding information that might compel Zeb to incriminate himself.

After admitting to Gideon that perhaps he'd been right in focusing on Zeb's past instead of the case as she'd been doing all day, she must have closed her eyes and drifted off to sleep.

"Sergeant Langsworth," Sapphire said, catching sight of the woman watching them with an amused smile. It must have been the sergeant opening the door that woke her up.

"You two look pretty cozy. I'm glad you got some sleep," Sergeant Langsworth said.

Sapphire felt her cheeks heat up. She liked to keep her private life just that—private. Falling asleep here at the precinct, all cozied up to Gideon, was not the way to go about doing that.

"Gideon ..." She jabbed him in the ribs.

"Hmm?" he replied, sleepily.

"Sergeant Langsworth is here."

That snapped him awake. "Did something happen with the case?" he asked.

"We have a witness who saw Thea Brody being carried out of her house."

Hearing that washed away the last of the sleepy cobwebs in her head. "Do we have an address?"

"She's here. She came straight in as soon as she heard what happened."

"That's great." Sapphire felt that usual rush of adrenaline and excitement that she got when a case was finally starting to move forward. She needed this case to be closed perhaps more than any other case she had ever worked. It wasn't that she had been shot by Zeb or beaten by Mason Wharf, it was that her partner had nearly been killed. That was unacceptable. Elijah was a good guy, and he didn't deserve to be sitting in a hospital bed right now. He should be here, working with her. She might not consider Elijah a friend, exactly—or maybe she did but had never really thought about it before—but they worked well together, bouncing ideas off each other, and she knew that he trusted her opinion and her gut.

"Who is she?" Gideon asked, standing and holding out a hand to her, pulling her to her feet beside him when she took it.

"Her name is Rena Shabow. She's the daughter of the couple that live across the street from the Brodys. Her parents are away on a cruise in the Mediterranean and she's been popping in every couple of days just to make sure that everything is okay and to take in the mail and the trash cans. She was there the day of the abduction, then again today, she met one of the other neighbors leaving as she was arriving and heard what happened. She realized she had seen something that we needed to know so she came right here," Sergeant Langsworth explained.

"We'll go speak with her immediately." Sapphire picked up the laptop and iPad and put them on the table. "Where is she?"

"She's waiting for you at your desk. You can use interview room one if you want."

"Let's go," she said to Gideon, already heading for the door. He had only been here a few days, but she was already accustomed to him being there. He didn't really say anything while she was interviewing someone, but she liked knowing he was there, watching and listening to everything the suspect said and evaluating it in a different way than she would. Maybe having a shrink here to give opinions on the case wasn't such a bad thing after all. Her mind worked like a cop, and Gideon's as a psychiatrist, and the two complemented each other.

"Good luck," Sergeant Langsworth called after them.

"Mrs. Shabow?" she said as she approached her desk.

"Yes," a woman with a full head of gray hair who appeared to be in her late thirties turned to face them.

"I'm Detective Hatcher and this is Dr. Barlow. We understand you witnessed something at the Brody house two days ago."

"I did." The woman nodded vigorously.

"Why don't we come and sit in here," she said, leading Rena Shabow to a small room they often used to interview victims and witnesses. It was quieter and easier to focus in here, but it was bigger and nicer than the interview rooms they used with suspects. "You were taking care of your parents' house while they were on vacation, is that right?" she asked once they were all seated.

"Yes. I'm an only child, and my parents are both retired. They like to travel, and I always take care of their home while they're away."

"What time do you usually go?" she asked. She'd been there early this morning, and Thea Brody wasn't abducted until around eight thirty. They knew that based on Mrs. Brody's statement and the fact that Zeb and Gray had been at the crime scene where Amelia Lexis's body had been found, then had gone their separate ways because Zeb had to take care of something. It wasn't until around ten thirty that they both showed up at the station. That left a window of about two hours where the abduction had taken place, and Rena's statement could help them narrow that down.

"I usually go early before work. My husband does the school and daycare drop-offs and I do the pickups. But that day I went later. My youngest was sick, so she wasn't in daycare. I had her with me, and we went after I dropped the older two off at school."

"What did you see when you drove up?"

"There was a cop at the Brodys' door," she answered immediately.

"How did you know it was a cop?"

"He was wearing a uniform."

That was odd. Zeb was a detective; he wasn't in uniform anymore.

Why would he be dressed like that? Was it a deliberate action meant to mislead them? Maybe he wanted to make them think the cop they were looking for was a uniform so they wouldn't be looking in his direction. It made as much sense as anything else.

"I didn't think any more of it, and I took my daughter inside, then realized I left her blankie in the car. She can't go without that thing for more than a couple of minutes without having a meltdown, so I went to get it and I saw the cop carrying Thea out of the house. I thought it was a little odd, but I don't really know many of my parents' neighbors. I assumed it was a boyfriend or a relative or even a friend."

"Did it look like she was unconscious?" Sapphire asked.

Rena Shabow paused and thought about that for a moment. "At the time, I didn't think so. She wasn't over his shoulder or anything, she was just hanging in his arms, like he was cradling her. Now that I think back, I believe her arms were hanging limply at her sides and not curled around his shoulders like I used to do when I was younger and my husband used to hold me in his arms and carry me up to bed sometimes."

"What did he do with her?"

"I don't know. I'd gotten the blankie by then and was already heading back inside because I'd left my daughter in there."

If Sapphire had to guess where Zeb had put the body, it would be the back seat, at least until he got somewhere quiet where he could transfer her into the trunk. How long had Thea been in there? Had he driven her somewhere before he came to the station? If he had, then that would narrow down their search area. If he hadn't, Thea could have been lying in there for hours right here in the parking garage of the precinct.

They needed a warrant for Zeb's car.

5:40 P.M.

"We got it."

Gideon looked up as Sapphire came rushing into the room. There was a huge grin on her face, and she was practically vibrating with excitement. That she loved her job was evident. She didn't know how to be anything but a cop. It gave her life a purpose, and it helped to heal the wounds her parents had inflicted on her.

As much as he was happy that she had it in her life, and that it helped her so much, he wished that she could see that there was nothing wrong with making room for other things as well.

"We got the warrant?" he asked.

"We did." She beamed. Gosh, she was stunning when she smiled. It was like her entire face was transformed. The worry lines in her forehead disappeared, the serious way she kept her lips in a thin line eased, the careful barriers she kept in her eyes to hide what went on inside her head lifted. She looked happy.

"You want to go straight and check out the car now?" he asked. They had been waiting all day to get a warrant. After Rena Shabow gave them her statement, they had asked the DA to get one, but Zeb's lawyer had argued that since Mrs. Shabow could not identify the car she had seen parked outside the Brody house that there was no proof it was Zeb's. After a lot of back and forth, it seemed like they had finally caught a break and got the warrant. If they could find Thea's DNA in the car, then they might have enough to keep Zeb where he was.

Which would mean this case would be closed.

Which meant it would be time for him to leave.

Which meant he had to make his move with Sapphire now or he might never get a chance.

And he knew that walking away without finding out if there could be something between them was not an option.

"Of course," she said like it was obvious. "The car is down in the parking garage. It's been torture knowing it's been here for the last twenty-four hours, and I haven't been able to touch it. But I don't want to do anything that would jeopardize this case when it goes to court."

"You would never do that," he said seriously. He respected that about her. That was what had sparked his attraction to her in the first place. He respected so many things about her. That she had not only survived what would crush most people, but had gone on to not only live a productive life but to excel at life, made her someone he admired very much.

"Nope," she agreed cheerfully. "Come on." She hurried him up, already at the door, hovering from foot to foot as she waited for him to join her. A big change from a few days ago where she would barely acknowledge him.

He walked a step behind her as they walked to the elevator. He liked watching her, especially when she was all full of energy like this. Her muscular legs practically bounced as she walked, her green sweater clung to her body, highlighting every curve, and accenting her gorgeous eyes. Gideon thought he could watch her forever.

Forever.

Things had been moving so quickly that he hadn't really thought any further ahead than the next day, but his mind had just solved that problem for him. It knew what he wanted without having to think about it and analyze it.

Sapphire suddenly froze as the elevator doors opened, and he bumped into her.

"Sorry," he was just saying as he saw the reason for her sudden halting. "Gray, hi." They hadn't seen Zeb's partner since they had taken Zeb off to interview and arrest yesterday morning.

The other man stood and glared at them, then slowly his face softened, and sadness took its place. "I'm sorry, Sapphire. I was angry with you yesterday, and that isn't fair. You were just doing your job, going where the evidence took you, I should have been too, but ..."

"But Zeb is your friend and your partner and you couldn't deal with what the evidence was saying. I get it; it's fine," Sapphire assured him.

That was always her response when someone did something that upset her. Gideon just couldn't figure out if it was because she was truly able to be rational and brush those things off or because she didn't feel worthy of being upset by the way someone treated her.

"We're going down to search his car. Do you want to come?" Sapphire asked.

Gray hesitated, but then gave one sharp nod. "Yes."

"You don't have to," Gideon said. It didn't take a psychiatrist to read that the cop's body language screamed that he would rather be anywhere other than examining his partner's car.

"No, I should be there," he said firmly.

He and Sapphire joined Gray in the elevator and the three of them stood in silence while they travelled down to the basement parking garage. When the doors opened, they saw that a couple of crime scene techs were there waiting for them.

"This way," Sapphire said, leading their small group off to the right then stopping beside a large sedan. "This is his car. We need you to go through the whole thing, looking for any blood or fingerprints or hairs —anything that would prove that Thea Brody was in this car. Can you pop the trunk?" She directed the question to one of the crime scene techs who nodded, opened the front door, reached inside, and pulled the lever.

The trunk popped open and immediately any doubts that his feelings for Sapphire had clouded his judgment and made him miss cues that pointed to Zeb being innocent vanished.

"It's a uniform," Sapphire said. "Rena Shabow said that the man she saw was wearing one."

Although they had shown the woman an array of pictures, Zeb's among them, she had not been able to pick him out as the man she had seen. But that the detective had an officer's uniform in the trunk was proof enough for him.

"There's something else," one of the CSU techs said as she reached over and with a gloved hand picked up the uniform. Underneath there was a scrunched-up cloth. Even from here, he could smell the faint sweet odor.

"Chloroform," he and Sapphire said simultaneously.

"That's how he got Thea Brody out of the house without her fighting him," Sapphire added.

"I can't do this," Gray announced, turning and stalking back toward the elevator.

Sapphire looked from the car to her colleague and back again, obviously debating what she should do.

"You can go with him if you want," he told her.

"It'll take us a while to go through the car, then we have to take anything we find back up to the lab and compare it to the samples we have from the Brody house," one of the crime scene techs added.

"We may as well go upstairs," he said.

"Yeah, okay," Sapphire agreed. Part of her looked like she wanted to stay, but right now there was nothing she could do here. It was time to temporarily hand things over to the experts and wait to see what they found.

"Sapphire?" he asked as they waited for the elevator.

"Hmm?" She sounded distracted.

He wasn't usually shy and bashful when he asked girls out, but this was different. This could really go somewhere. "Do you want to have dinner with me tonight?"

That got her attention. "Like a date?"

"Yes."

"I ..." *Want to* her eyes said. But instead, she said, "Aren't you going to be going back home soon? We have proof now that Zeb did this, so you'll be leaving soon."

He knew what she needed.

She needed to hear him say that he would stay.

But he couldn't do that.

Not yet.

They hadn't even been on one date. He couldn't give up his job and his life if he didn't know that there was a new life waiting for him here.

If he knew for sure that this would work, he'd move here in an instant.

Right now, it was too early.

"I will be leaving soon," he reluctantly acknowledged.

"Oh." The light left her eyes, but like she always did, she quickly pulled her mask back into place. "Maybe dinner isn't the best idea."

He was disappointed.

Not that he could argue with her answer.

He was asking her to take the biggest leap of faith of her life, and yet he had basically told her that it was pointless because he would be walking away anyway.

What exactly was so important about his job that he couldn't transfer to work here? Sure, he would miss the travelling and working with different people, but maybe he could get a job consulting here instead.

Waking up every day with Sapphire at his side would definitely make up for it.

But he couldn't make any promises to her until he had everything sorted out. He wouldn't get her hopes up for nothing if things didn't work out.

Once he had things sorted out, he wasn't going to stop until he had convinced her to give them a chance.

~

6:54 P.M.

"You're quiet tonight."

"I guess," Sapphire agreed distractedly, pushing food around on her plate without really eating any of it. She wasn't used to being home this early. She never usually left work before eight, and today she'd left at six thirty, arriving at home in time to join Diamond and Ruby for dinner.

"Is it your case?" Diamond asked. "Finding out that it was Zeb who shot you has to be hard to deal with."

The good thing about all of them having been through the same experience was that she didn't have to explain how it felt to be betrayed by the two people who were supposed to be there for you without question, who were supposed to nurture you and love you. Most people could imagine what that would feel like, but they couldn't truly understand. It wasn't like she wished they did. She wouldn't wish what had happened to her on anyone, but it was nice to be around people who got it, who had lived it.

While it was usually her cases that she obsessed over, lost sleep over, forgot to eat over, dedicated every second of her thoughts too, it wasn't a case that she was preoccupied with today.

It was Gideon.

Specifically, his invitation to dinner.

She'd wanted to say yes so badly, but how could she let herself get attached to him when by his own admission he would soon be leaving?

"It's not a case," she admitted. "I am shocked and hurt about Zeb, but that's not what I've been thinking about."

"You've been thinking about the shrink, the one you claimed you couldn't stand," Ruby said.

There was no point in denying it, and besides, she didn't lie to her sisters. "I have been."

"You're not pretending you still don't like him, are you?" Diamond asked.

A small, rueful smile curled the corner of her mouth up. "No."

"Good, because it was as obvious as the nose on your face," Ruby teased.

"I think I might like him, and we almost kissed, but ..." She trailed off, uncomfortable having this conversation with her sisters. They might always be honest with one another but that didn't mean that they discussed every aspect of their lives. And she hadn't even had a dating aspect of her life since she was sixteen. All of this was new to her, and she felt embarrassed talking about it because she still felt as naïve as a sixteen-year-old when it came to matters of the heart.

"But what?" Ruby asked. "If you like him, then why would you hold back? Isn't this what you wanted when we were sold and we thought we would never have a future like everyone else? I know it's what I thought. I thought that I was going to die and I'd never get to fall in love and get married and have kids of my own. If you have a chance to have that, why would you not grab it with both hands?"

"Because it's not that simple," she said. She *had* had those same thoughts. She *had* felt the loss of the future she had assumed she would always have. She *had* thought that if by some miracle she was saved she would go back to a normal life. And here they were, no normal life in sight. She was stuck between wanting that future and being terrified of it.

"It can be though," Diamond said gently. "I know what we lived through was horrific, and I know it left scars. I know that those scars can make seeking a partner scary, but I don't want to see you shut the world out and obsess over your job. You're so good at being a cop, and I know that you feel it gives your life meaning because you're saving people like you were saved, but maybe you need Gideon Barlow to save you in a different way. Maybe you need him to show you that it's okay to be happy, it's okay to have fun, it's okay to love, because not everyone is going to hurt you."

"Do you think that he would every betray you like mom and dad did?" Ruby asked.

"No," she answered immediately. She was positive that he wouldn't. She knew that he was a good guy even if he did have a knack for getting on her nerves.

"Do you think he could make you happy?" Ruby asked.

She hesitated for a moment, more because she was about to take a leap of faith than because she had to debate the answer. "Yes."

"Then go for it," Ruby said.

"He doesn't live here. Any day now he's going to be leaving. What would be the point in seeing if there really is anything between us?" Sapphire wasn't sure whether this issue was actually what was giving her doubts or if it was just an excuse her brain had come up with to give her an out.

"If it's meant to be, you two will find a way to make it work. And distance is just that—distance. It doesn't mean that you won't find a way to make it work, and all relationships are work. But bottom line is you like him. I can see you do in the way your eyes light up when you talk about him and the tone of your voice. We're happy for you. We want you to be happy, and if he makes you happy, then go for it," Diamond said, giving her that big sister smile that she remembered from their childhood.

"He asked me to go to dinner with him tonight. A date," she added, as though that wasn't obvious.

"Then why are you here?" Ruby asked.

"Because I said no. The whole 'he's about to leave' thing," she elaborated.

"You have to go over there right now." Diamond said, pushing back from the table and standing up.

"Now? I could probably just talk to him tomorrow," she said, the idea of going to Gideon's hotel room tonight terrified her. She needed to take baby steps, and turning up at his hotel room unannounced after she had turned him down when he asked her out was more like a huge oversized adult step.

"Not tomorrow. Tonight. Now," Ruby echoed their older sister's sentiment.

"You need to do this, Sapphire," Diamond added.

Maybe they were right.

Maybe she *did* need to do this.

Maybe she had spent the last ten years trapped in a prison of her own making.

She had been saved, but in a way, she hadn't. In a way, part of her had never been saved. Part of her was still a prisoner, unable to live a normal life.

"Okay," she said slowly, trying to gather her courage. For most people, this was no big deal. You dated, you moved in and out of relationships until you found the one, but for her, this was a major milestone that she had been convinced she would never make. It might seem silly to others, but just the simple act of going to a potential boyfriend's place to accept an invitation to dinner was enough to make her break out in hives.

"I'm so proud of you," Diamond encouraged.

With shaking hands and trembling legs, she stood up and collected her bag and coat. It never even occurred to her to obsess over her outfit or go and do her hair or put on makeup. What she thought she might be able to have with Gideon was nothing to do with putting on a mask. She spent enough time as it was wearing masks, and that was exactly what she liked about Gideon. When she was around him, she felt like it was okay to let that mask slip.

"Good luck," Ruby said, kissing her cheek.

"You'll do fine. You got this." Diamond gave her a hug.

If she didn't have her sisters to keep her accountable, she might have backed out, but since they were standing in the doorway watching her, she walked to her car, got in, and drove off into the night.

At least a dozen times in the fifteen minutes it took her to drive to Gideon's hotel, she very nearly pulled over to the side of the road and gave into the anxiety that was steadily building inside her.

But she didn't.

She forged on.

If she didn't do this now, she was going to lock herself away forever, and she didn't want to be an old lady, unable to work any longer, and look back at her life and realize that she didn't have any reason to keep living.

Sapphire parked her car in the hotel's parking lot and then paused at the door.

It was time.

As terrifying as it was, it was time to go inside, find Gideon's room, and finally remove her mask and lay bare everything she kept so carefully hidden away.

~

7:37 P.M.

Gideon was just about to change and head downstairs to the hotel's gym when there was a knock at the door. He hadn't ordered room service or anything from housekeeping, and he didn't have any friends here, so he didn't know who to expect when he opened the door.

Who he found there was the last person he expected.

"Sapphire." He couldn't help but smile when he saw her standing there. She might have been the last person he expected to see, but she was also the person he wanted to see the most. "What are you doing here?"

"Yes," she blurted out. Her face was anxious, and she was fidgeting nervously.

"Yes, what?" he asked, confused.

"Yes to dinner." She relaxed a little as she said what she had obviously come here to say.

Surprised, but pleased by her change of heart, he held the door open farther. "Come in."

She hesitated for a moment, but then drew in a deep breath and stepped into his room. He understood what a big step she had just taken. Her trust and her view of humanity had been shattered by what her parents had done. Trusting anyone, especially someone she had only known for a few days, was a huge leap of faith, and he was so proud of her for finding the courage to take it.

Curious about their visitor, Luna wandered over and sniffed Sapphire's hand. "You have a dog in here? Are you even allowed to have pets in a hotel?"

"Luna goes everywhere with me. I only stay at hotels that allow pets." Travelling could be lonely, and he appreciated Luna's companionship.

"Does she stay in here all day?" Sapphire asked, crouching down to pat the dog.

"I pay a few of the employees to take her out for walks on their breaks."

"What's her name?"

"Luna, and she's nearly four years old."

"She's beautiful."

"She is," he agreed, thinking that the dog wasn't the only beautiful one in the room. He still couldn't believe that Sapphire was here, but he was glad she was. "I don't have anything to eat, but we can go out, or I can order room service," he suggested as he closed the door.

"Actually, I'm not really hungry," Sapphire said sheepishly. "I know I came here to accept your dinner invitation, but ..." she trailed off and appeared unsure how to proceed or what she should say or do.

"Let's sit," he said, hoping to put her at ease. He knew this was a big deal to her, and he wished that he knew what she needed him to do to help her feel comfortable.

"Okay," she agreed. She came and perched on the sofa, looking stiff and unsure. It was clear she had things on her mind but didn't know how to say them.

"Do you want to talk?" he asked, sitting beside her, while Luna went and jumped back up onto the bed. Being a psychiatrist meant he was good at reading people, predicting their behavior and needs, and acting accordingly, but he wasn't a mind reader, and Sapphire had had a decade to perfect the mask she wore each day.

She shrugged fitfully. If he was reading her correctly, she *did* want to talk, but she somehow viewed that as a weakness. Perhaps because of the experience she had with the therapist she worked with after she was rescued or maybe because of her job. Maybe it was him and his constant pushing to get her to open up.

Perhaps he could make things easier by asking her questions that she could answer rather than a big open-ended discussion that was no doubt overwhelming for her.

"You were the first of your sisters to be rescued, right?" He knew this was the case, but he thought it was a good lead-in to the hard stuff.

"Yes." She gave a sharp nod. Something about that bothered her.

"You were gone for three days."

"More like two. We were taken at night. I was kept at this huge mansion overnight, then the next day I woke up at the barn."

Something about that was untrue. It wasn't the days and times because according to the case files he'd read that was correct. So, it had to be the time between the mansion and the barn. She hadn't just woken up at the barn. Something had happened before that.

Once again, he felt like he was walking a tightrope between getting her to talk because he knew that she needed to, but not pushing her too hard and causing her to shut down.

Because of the protectiveness he felt toward her, it was harder to push her than it would be with any other victim. He didn't want to hurt her or cause her pain, and he knew that talking about the worst time in her life would do just that.

Gideon had to remind himself that *she* had come to *him* tonight. She had known that coming here, that agreeing to a date meant that they could be at the start of a new relationship, and she knew that as such, she was going to have to be open and honest about her past and the effect it still had on her.

"Something happened at the mansion, before you woke up at the barn," he confronted her.

"You're good," she muttered, but she didn't seem particularly upset that he had seen through her lie of omission.

"Remember that, missy," he joked, then sobered and took her hands. "You're safe here with me. This is a place that you can say whatever you want to, even things you've never told anyone else. I will never judge you. I will never think less of you. I only want to help, and no, not because of my job, but because I care about you."

"You're *really* good." She offered him a weak smile. "You know how the blindfold kind of freaked me out the other night?"

"Yes."

"Well, it's because they put a blindfold on me that night."

He felt his gut tighten as he prepared himself to hear what came next. He wanted her to talk to him, to open up, because she had spent far too long locking these emotions away, but that didn't mean it was easy to hear. "Did they rape you?"

"No. Well, not really ... there was no penetration, so sexual assault." Her tone had gone clinical like she was talking about someone else and not herself, and he didn't—couldn't—ask her to change that. She was doing what she had to do to survive. "They were human traffickers. They sold girls like me every day. I didn't mean anything to them beyond the bag of cash they were going to get when they sold me. They got more money if we were virgins, so since they couldn't have sex with me, they performed oral sex instead. It was a game to them. They won money off each other if they could get me to orgasm." Her cheeks burned as she said the words, and he knew that some of them had been able to make her come. The betrayal of her own body coupled with the betrayal of her parents had no doubt made it doubly traumatic.

"I'm so sorry," he said, because he didn't know what else to say. If it were possible, he'd rip those psychopaths' throats out with his bare hands, but he couldn't. All he could do was sit here and say things that sounded wildly inadequate.

Sapphire nodded like that was the response she expected and he wished he could do so much more. He hated feeling helpless like this. It was the same way he felt with his own family's trauma. There was nothing he could do to take away that pain. All he could do for his father and grandparents was just show them that he was there, and that was all he could offer Sapphire.

"I'm sure you've been told before that anything that happened wasn't your fault, and that the human body is designed a certain way. The fact that your body responded the way it did doesn't diminish what happened to you or mean that you wanted it to happen, but I'm repeating those things because they're true. Have you been able to have sexual intercourse since it happened?"

"Right after I went back to school. I wasn't sure I would be able to. I was so terrified that I would freak out, but I wanted to prove to myself that I could do it, and that what had happened to me hadn't changed me, but I was wrong. It did change me."

"Things didn't go well that first time?"

"They were okay; awkward, like I suppose everyone's first time is. But I didn't freak out; I just didn't like it."

Which was perfectly normal. She'd just been sold and sexually assaulted. Enjoying sex at that time in her life was pretty much impossible. "Have there been others since then?" He wanted to know exactly where she was coming from so when their first time came, he knew how to proceed.

"A few. Just one-night stands, or I guess more like three- or four-night stands, if there is such a thing. But it never goes anywhere." She paused and seemed to be trying to gather courage for what she wanted to say next. "Nothing every goes anywhere because of me. Because I'm too cold and too hard. What happened to me changed me too much."

"No," he said a little more vehemently than he had intended, but he didn't like to hear her put herself down. "Your compassion and empathy for the victims in the cases you work every single day say differently. A cold, hard person doesn't behave that way. You have a big, warm heart. You're just angry, and you have every right to be."

"Gee, thanks for the permission." She rolled her eyes at him.

"Okay, you're right, that did sound a little condescending, but I didn't mean to patronize you. I mean that. Anyone would be angry after going through what you did. You were betrayed in the worst way a person can be. Being angry after that is completely normal."

"I'm mostly angry at myself," she admitted in a small voice.

"At yourself? Why?" She squirmed and wouldn't look at him, so he gently grasped her chin and tilted her face up. "Why are you angry at yourself?"

"Because I was saved so quickly. Ruby was with those monsters for four years. What's three days compared to that? Because I had to be saved. Because I kept trying to escape and to get away, but in the end, I couldn't, I had to be rescued," she replied quietly. It was plain from the look in her eyes that she was upset about this, despite the fact that *no one* would have been able to escape if they had been in the same situation she was.

"They were human traffickers, Sapphire. They knew what they were doing. There is *no* way you could have escaped from them. And survivor's guilt is perfectly normal in situations like yours. But three days or three thousand days, it doesn't change anything. You were hurt, and that matters." This was why he'd gotten that feeling earlier that something was bothering her when he'd asked her about being the first to be rescued.

She lifted one shoulder like she disagreed. "I feel so guilty that I was rescued so quickly, and I hate that I couldn't save myself, both of those things make me feel ..." She paused, searching for the word she wanted. "It makes me feel unworthy. Like if I couldn't save myself, then I don't deserve to have anyone love me. Maybe it doesn't make any sense to you, but it's how I feel."

If there was one thing he had learned in his years as a psychiatrist, it was that oftentimes emotions and feelings didn't make sense. "There is no right or wrong way to feel. You feel how you feel, but let me tell you that you are not unworthy of love. You are a gorgeous woman." He released her chin and brushed the back of his knuckles across her soft cheek. "You're smart and kind and dedicated to your job, you care about people who are hurt and suffering, and like I told you earlier, you deserve to be happy and to focus on yourself for a change instead of everyone around you. You are not responsible for stopping all the evil in the world. You are important. You're important to me." His eyes found hers, seeking permission, and when he found it, he dipped his head and feathered his lips across hers.

"I'm scared," she whispered. "Telling you all of this was hard, some of these things I've never even told my sisters, but I ... I ... I like you, and I ... trust you, and I want to see if we could be together, but you're leaving soon." Her eyes searched his, looking for the same reassurances she had needed earlier this evening. He hadn't given them to her then. He didn't want to let her down again, but, at the same time, he didn't want to give her false hope.

"I don't know what the future holds," he told her. "No one does. All I can give you in this moment, is to tell you that I like you too, and that hearing you say you trust me means so much to me, and that I want to see if we could be together too. You have to decide if that's enough for you right now. If it's not, that's okay. You can go home or we can just eat dinner, or we can just be friends. It's up to you. What do you want?"

~

7:59 P.M.

What do you want?

Sapphire couldn't remember the last time she had been asked that.

The question was so simple, and yet, there was such a mass of emotions and fears and insecurities that they brought up. Answering was like jumping out of an airplane without a parachute.

No, it was more like jumping out of an airplane *unsure* of whether she had a parachute or not.

If Gideon wanted the same things she did, then her parachute would appear and she would float safely down to earth. But if he didn't, she was about to endure a world of pain that she would probably never recover from.

You're overthinking, she told herself. He had already told her that he liked her and that he wanted to see if the two of them could have a future. It was just that she needed to hear him say he wasn't going to leave. She understood why he wasn't telling her what she wanted to hear. He was worried about hurting her, and he didn't want to commit to something as big as moving his entire life before he even knew whether the two of them worked as a couple. And, add to that, that her past was a lot to take on, even for a psychiatrist, and he probably wanted to make sure that she was capable of having a normal relationship before he made any commitment.

"I want you," she finally answered.

Like he had been metaphorically holding his breath as he awaited her answer, the second she gave it, his entire being relaxed and his mouth descended on hers. The kiss was passionate enough to feel like he was claiming her as his own, and yet not pushy, like he wanted to let her be the one in the driver's seat.

Fire burned in her stomach, and Gideon was the only thing that could quench it.

Since she knew he wasn't going to do anything she didn't give him permission to do, she ran her hands up under his sweater, tracing her fingertips along the hard muscles of his abs.

He groaned into her mouth as he continued to kiss her, and knowing that she was doing things right, encouraged her. She might be twenty-six, but she didn't know anything about pleasing a man sexually or about being pleased herself.

Her fingers dipped lower, brushing along his waist and stopping at the buckle of his jeans. She didn't need to wonder if she wanted this; she already knew that she did. She'd spent the last four days sexually frustrated as she battled her attraction to Gideon with the genuine feelings he stirred up inside her.

She wanted this so badly.

She wanted to feel loved and cared about and special.

She wanted to know that someone wanted her, that they understood her, and that they could see past her scars and love her anyway.

Gideon made her feel all those things.

Sapphire undid the buckle and slid her hand inside.

Gideon groaned again and grabbed her hands, stilling them before she could touch him. "Are you sure?"

"Do you think I ever do anything that I'm unsure of?" she asked.

"No." He chuckled. "Okay, but this is about you. I want this to be amazing for you."

"It's about both of us," she corrected. She didn't want a man in her life who was going to add to her feelings of frustration and helplessness over being unable to save herself. She wanted someone who would see her as the strong and independent woman she was. Yes, she had a lot of psychological scars and associated issues, but she was living her life the best way she could and she wanted someone who would make her life better, not put her on a shelf and treat her as though she were too fragile to be touched.

"You are something else, you know that?" His large hands spanned her waist and he lifted her up and placed her on her feet in front of him. "Strip."

"Excuse me?" she asked, excited but nervous about what was coming next.

"You heard me." He winked. "You want to do this, then let's do this."

With shaking fingers, she quickly pulled her sweater over her head and tossed it on the floor, then shoved her jeans down her legs and stepped out of them.

"Underwear too," Gideon said.

She had never been completely naked in front of a man before, and definitely not in the light like this. In her previous sexual encounters, she usually left her bra and top on, and always insisted that the lights remained off.

But it was different with Gideon.

She wasn't ashamed of her body, and she wasn't ashamed for him to see it, just anxiously excited. The good kind of anxious, though. The kind that made her skin extra sensitive, and her pulse echo in her ears. The kind of anxious that made her want everything to happen quickly because she wanted it so badly, but also made her want to savor every single second.

Complying with his request, she shimmied out of her panties, and unclipped her bra, letting both join the growing pile of clothes on the floor.

Gideon gave her a long once-over, then whistled his appreciation. Her cheeks pinked. She'd never had a guy whistle like that at her before, and although she would find it offensive from anyone else, from him, it just made that fire in her belly grow.

"Come here," he ordered.

She took a step closer, and he wrapped his hands around her bottom and pulled her closer. He put his nose to the v where her legs met, and breathed in, moaning as he did, then trailed a line of kisses up her stomach, between her breasts, along her neck, before his lips found hers again.

Without stopping the kiss, he guided her to straddle his legs, and curled one hand around the back of her neck as his other went between her legs. He stroked her slowly, teasing her, working her higher, making her squirm, and shiver delightfully.

Then one of his fingers pressed its way inside her.

She tensed at first. She was tight; it had been nearly two years since she'd last been with a man, and that first intrusion hurt.

He slowed things down, stroking her some more, before slowly edging back in, giving her body time to adjust. It wasn't long before that pain evaporated, and he was driving her wild, adding another finger, stroking, rubbing, making her feel like she was possessed.

She was going to come at any second, but she didn't want to, not like this, she wanted him inside her when she had her very first proper orgasm.

"Wait," she said, reaching down to grab his hand. For a second, it looked like he thought she didn't want to go through with it, but she was already climbing off his lap and dragging him toward the bed, making it clear what she needed.

"Hold on." He stopped her, then scooped her up into his arms and carried her the rest of the way to the bed. He shooed the dog away and laid her down, then stared at her like she was some sort of precious stone. "You really are gorgeous," he said, running a hand lightly up and down her body.

"Hurry up," she urged, as just the feel of his fingers on her skin pushed her closer to coming.

Gideon just chuckled and took his time shedding his sweater, jeans, and boxers. Seeing him naked for the first time, she gave him her own appreciative once-over. He was pretty gorgeous himself. The muscles in his arms and legs were perfectly defined, his six-pack looked like chiseled stone, and he was pretty well endowed in the man department.

He grabbed a condom and slid it on, then stretched out above her, his mouth taking hers again, and he balanced his weight with one hand so his other could take a little tour of her body. It circled her breasts, teasing her nipples, then would dip down between her legs to touch the spot that was screaming out for him, then his hand would come back up to claim one of her breasts again.

If he was going to torture her, then she was just going to do the same to him.

She reached between his legs and grabbed ahold of him, squeezing firmly and making him moan into her mouth.

"No fair." He tore his lips away from hers long enough to pout playfully.

"I never said I played fair." She winked, squeezing him again.

"Okay, okay," he laughed, grasping her hand and uncurling her fingers.

Then, finally, he was sliding inside her. It took a moment for her to adjust to the size of him, but then the two of them were moving, kissing, touching, rocking, and then exploding into a different universe as pleasure consumed them.

Sapphire fell slowly back to earth, and by the time her ability to think returned, Gideon had already pulled out of her, disposed of the condom, and was cradling her against his chest.

Somehow being held like this was even better than what she had just experienced.

Sex was something you could have with anyone, but only someone who truly cared about you held you in their arms like this.

CHAPTER
Eleven

January 9th
5:55 A.M.

Sapphire woke slowly, stretching contentedly like a cat, the feel of Gideon's warm body tucked tightly against hers was the first conscious thing she registered.

Just like the night before, she didn't remember falling asleep last night. She remembered talking with Gideon about their pasts—the good and the bad—and their hopes for the future. She remembered lying in his arms, her head on his chest, the steady beating of his heart relaxing her. Then the next thing she knew, she was waking up.

Careful not to disturb Gideon, who was still fast asleep, she carefully eased out from under his arm and rolled over to reach her phone, which sat on the nightstand. It was almost six. The last time she remembered seeing last night was ten. That meant she'd slept for almost eight hours, the amount of sleep normal people got most nights.

Not wanting to wake Gideon, she had a feeling he hadn't gotten much more sleep the last few nights than she had, she climbed out of the bed and padded toward the bathroom. She still wasn't wearing any clothes, but she didn't feel self-conscious. She was comfortable around Gideon. She wasn't sure how he had done that, how he had managed to break through barriers she thought were impenetrable, but he had.

He really had.

It still didn't feel real.

How had she managed to get to a place where she wanted to have a future that included something beyond just work?

How had she managed to find someone whom she wanted to share that future with?

Sapphire felt incredibly lucky.

It wasn't like all of her problems and anxieties and insecurities had magically disappeared. They were still there. They would *always* be there, but for the first time in a decade, she felt like all of her issues were things that she could learn to manage in a more productive way than she presently did.

She finished up in the bathroom, deciding to wait to take a shower. Gideon's scent was still on her skin, and she wasn't ready to wash it away just yet. Maybe once he woke up, they could take a shower together. Making love in the shower had always seemed so romantic to her when she was a teenager. She'd even had a fantasy about how that would be her first time.

Things hadn't worked out that way, and she had been in a bad place for so long, that it finally felt like a weight had been lifted from her shoulders, the light had come back into her life.

It felt so good.

She just wanted to smile and laugh and even dance about like a kid, just spinning in circles and expressing the joy in her heart.

Since she didn't want to disturb Gideon, she sat down on the sofa, tucked her legs up underneath her and tucked a blanket over her lap so she didn't get cold. Then she grabbed his laptop from the coffee table. She didn't think he would mind her checking her email and looking up a couple of things before they headed into work.

Although her desire to check the computer had been completely innocent, as soon as she opened the lid, her name caught her attention. Sapphire knew she shouldn't look. She knew she shouldn't pry; it was probably just notes on her case, and she already knew that he had known about what happened to her before they had talked about it last night.

Despite that, her eyes automatically focused in on her name.

And what she found was not what she had expected.

Just like that, her good mood evaporated, and she suddenly felt icy cold.

She'd thought that Gideon would never be able to do anything to hurt her, and yet, what she was reading, was cutting through her heart as effectively as any knife could.

"Morning," Gideon's sleep-laden voice floated behind her, and a moment later she heard him get out of the bed and walk toward her. The look on her face must have worried him because he quickened his pace and crouched in front of her. "Sapphire? What's wrong?"

What's wrong?

She had opened herself up to the possibility of falling in love. She had taken the biggest leap of faith of her life and allowed herself to be vulnerable to this man.

That was what was wrong.

"You're scaring me. What's going on?" He reached out to touch her, and she jerked away from him, sending the laptop wobbling. Gideon reached for it to steady it, and saw what she had seen. "That's not what it looks like," he said quickly.

Of course, it was what it looked like.

What else could it be?

It wasn't like she was stupid, and what he'd written was in plain English. She could read it, so she knew exactly what it was.

"I didn't intend to pry," she said, her tone emotionless. "I just wanted to let you sleep so I thought I'd check my email. I didn't think you'd mind."

"I don't," he said, taking the laptop and closing the lid, setting it down on the table.

"You knew it was a cop all along," she said. She meant it as an accusation, but it came out sounding empty.

"Sergeant Langsworth suspected it was someone at the precinct. The way the killer was so careful to leave the bodies clean and not leave any of himself behind. The way the abductions were so smooth, she thought it might have been a cop pulling the girls over and abducting them. That was why she called me in. She thought since I didn't know any of you that I might stand a better chance at figuring out who it was."

"You lied to us." Her whole world was spinning wildly around her, making her feel sick.

"I was doing my job. If I told you that we already thought it was a cop and that I was there to figure out which one, you would have just shut me out, and I wouldn't have been able to do what I was brought in to do."

She didn't want to hear excuses.

She had trusted him, but it had all been a lie.

From the very first day they met, he'd been playing her.

"I don't think that you're the killer, Sapphire. I believe that we have the right man in custody."

She wished she could believe that.

But she didn't.

"You did think it could be me," she said softly, the first hint of emotion creeping back into her voice.

"I looked into everyone, including you," he corrected. "That's not the same thing. You and Elijah were the lead detectives on the case. I looked into both of you first. With your past, I would have had to look into you."

That cut her deep, and she physically winced at the words.

She had opened up to him about what being sold to human traffickers by her parents had done to her, and he was using it against her.

She thought he had understood, but he didn't.

"I passed my psych exam," she reminded him.

"I know you did, and I know that you don't possess the ability to hurt anyone, but I had to look into it. I didn't even know you then. We'd never met. Sergeant Langsworth called me just before you and Elijah were attacked. You both gave identical accounts of what had happened that night, and since we didn't think we were looking for a killing pair, that meant both of you were out as suspects."

He said that like it would be reassuring, but it only hurt her worse.

He hadn't discounted her as the killer because he didn't believe she was the killer; he had discounted her because she'd been shot.

That took her heart and shattered it into a million pieces.

She was an idiot to believe that she could be happy. She couldn't be happy. She could never be happy. Happiness had been ripped out of her life the day her parents had sold her.

This room, which just ten minutes ago had made her feel safe and full of joy now made her feel dirty and used.

Without a word, she stood, covering herself with the blanket, no longer feeling okay with him seeing her naked, and began to gather her clothes.

"Sapphire." Gideon stood and reached for her, only stopping from touching her because she recoiled. "I didn't do this to hurt you. I didn't even know you then. You were just a name on a piece of paper. I didn't know that I was going to fall for you."

She didn't want to hear this.

She didn't even want to be in the same room as him.

"We have Zeb in custody. There's no reason for you to stay here any longer," she said as she walked into the bathroom, closing and locking the door behind her. She quickly put on her clothes, fighting to keep back her tears. She wasn't going to cry in front of this man; he wasn't worth it.

Without taking another look at him, she grabbed her bag and walked out of the hotel room. Her one chance at having a normal future ended as she closed the door.

~

6:31 A.M.

So far, so good.

She had almost made it.

Sapphire was only two streets away from home. As soon as she made it inside and up to her room, she was going to go straight into the shower, turn the water on, and then under the cover of the streaming water she would let herself cry.

It was the only place she ever cried.

Because no one could hear her.

She had been so stupid to think she could escape her past. She could never outrun it no matter how hard she tried. It would always be there, taunting her, reminding her that she could never be normal. It didn't matter how good she was at her job, how many people she saved, or how many criminals she put behind bars. She was always going to be judged by the fact that she had been sold to human traffickers.

Some days she wondered if her life would have been better if she had never been rescued.

If the cops hadn't been there that night to raid and bring down the ring, she would have been sold to whoever managed to catch her. She would have been taken and locked away—raped and tortured—there was no doubt about that. She probably would have died long before she reached twenty-six, but at least she wouldn't have had to try to build a real life.

That was the hardest part of being a victim.

Rebuilding a life.

It was a struggle every single day to try to put the past far enough in the past to keep it there.

And it never worked.

Well, she was done trying. She was done trying to build a future. It was stupid anyway. No matter what she did and what she had in her life, she *did* have a future. It just wasn't going to look like the future she'd thought she would have when she was a kid. Her future wouldn't have a husband and children. It wouldn't have family nights and board games and vacations to the beach. It wouldn't have birthday parties and Christmas mornings around the tree.

Her future would be filled with criminals and victims, but that was okay. She was making a difference. However small, she was making the world a better place.

Sapphire pulled into the driveway. She was here; she was home. She'd made it without shedding a tear. Now all she had to do was get upstairs. Hopefully, her sisters were still asleep, she couldn't deal with them right now.

She slid the key into the lock, and made it all the way to the bottom of the staircase before she heard voices.

Of course, her sisters were up.

Could her luck get any worse?

"Morning, Sapphire," Ruby sang out. "Stayed out all night, huh? I guess I don't have to ask how things went with Gideon."

That was it.

She couldn't hold her tears in any longer.

They trickled out, that trickle quickly becoming a stream, and she sank down to sit on the bottom step, pulling her knees up to her chest and burying her face in her arms.

"Sapphire? What's wrong?" Diamond asked, sitting beside her and wrapping an arm around her shoulders.

"I was only teasing." Ruby sat on her other side. "I didn't mean to upset you."

That only made her cry harder. She loved her sisters so much, she didn't need a husband and kids to have a family. She already had one that she adored. As unlucky as she felt sometimes, she knew that she had a lot to be grateful for. She had been saved; she had a chance to live her life even if it wasn't the life she had envisioned, and she had a family that she loved to pieces and would gladly die for.

"Did you go to Gideon's hotel?" Ruby asked.

She nodded.

"Did you speak to him?"

Another nod.

"Did you work something out?"

She nodded again.

"Then why are you crying?" Diamond asked, perplexed.

She didn't want to tell them. She felt embarrassed and stupid and like such a fool for believing him when all along he had been wondering if she was a serial killer. But if she didn't tell them, they were only going to worry more and pester her until she coughed up answers.

"Honey, what's going on?" Ruby asked.

"H-he lied to me," she managed to get out through her tears.

"What did he lie about?" Diamond asked.

"He investigated me, before he even came. The whole time he didn't really care about me. He just wanted to see if I was the killer." Although her head believed that was true, her heart wanted to contradict it. Her heart wanted to say she wouldn't have felt safe to open up to Gideon if she really believed he was the kind of person who would do that.

"Are you sure?" Ruby asked. "That doesn't sound like the man you told us about."

"Do you think I'm lying?" She lifted her head and looked at her sisters through her watery eyes.

"Of course not." Diamond reached over and brushed a lock of hair off her wet cheek. "I can see that you're hurting—we both can—but I don't think you would have gone to his hotel room last night—and stayed all night—if you really believed that he thought you were a killer."

"Trust me, I won't be staying out all night ever again," she said, wearily resting her head on her oldest sister's shoulder.

"Don't say that," Ruby said, with more heat than she'd heard her sister use in a long time. "Don't give up on your chance at happiness. You're the first one of us to have a real chance at moving on, of being happy—really and truly happy. You can't throw that away. If you give up, then what hope do the rest of us have?"

Sapphire didn't want the burden of having to worry about her sisters on her shoulders right now. She just wanted to wallow in her own misery for a while. She wanted to think only about herself, just for a few minutes, and not have to think about anything else.

"It's okay to feel sad for a while," Ruby told her. "But only for a little while. We've all been through so much, you maybe more than all of us. Don't give up on your future."

She knew Ruby was only being nice. Of all of them, she had suffered the least in their ordeal. She was the lucky one. She was the one who had been rescued after only a few days. She was the one who shouldn't be complaining. She was the one who should be able to move on.

If Gideon were here, he would tell her not to minimize her feelings. That it wasn't a competition. They had all suffered. It was nothing to compare against one another, but she had always felt like she had to set aside what she was feeling because someone else was feeling worse.

Gideon would tell her that it was okay to think about herself, that she was important too, and that it was okay to dedicate some of her life and her time to having something outside her job and her family.

Why did what Gideon would think still mean something to her?

She was such a glutton for punishment.

It was time to suck it up.

Gideon had hurt her feelings—made her feel like she had been used —but she could recover from that. It wasn't like she had known him for months. She hadn't even known him a week, and he had given her one very special night.

She'd be okay.

In the end, when it came down to it, she always found a way to be okay.

Sapphire wiped her cheeks. She was done with wallowing. She still had a job to do. Thea Brody was out there somewhere. Zeb wouldn't tell them where she was, so it was up to her to find the girl before it was too late.

"You okay?" Diamond asked. Both she and Ruby were watching her carefully.

"Yeah." She dragged in a breath and calmed herself, finding her center again. "I'll be okay."

"Are you going to give Gideon another chance?" Ruby asked.

That was a question she couldn't answer right now.

She didn't know.

When she'd left, she'd told him to leave, and since he hadn't even been able to commit to staying or moving here when there was a chance for them, she didn't think he would stay now.

"Right now, I just want to focus on keeping Zeb behind bars and finding his last victim who might still be alive," she said. It was the best she could do right now. She might act tough. She might even try to convince herself that she was tough, but inside she was a lot more vulnerable than she liked to believe she was, and she was worried that she had reached the end of her rope. That even if Gideon didn't leave town, she would never be able to trust him—or anyone else—ever again.

~

8:14 A.M.

Gideon sat on the edge of the bed, his phone in his hands. He opened the contacts and tapped on Sapphire's name, his finger hovered above her phone number, but he didn't touch the screen.

He wanted to call her, but he didn't think she was ready to hear from him yet.

Or ever.

Sapphire had been pretty upset when she'd left, and he couldn't say that he blamed her. When Sergeant Langsworth had contacted him to say she believed someone in the precinct was the serial killer two of her detectives were hunting, the logical first step had been to look into those two detectives. Especially since one of them had such a traumatic history.

Had he ever really looked at Sapphire as a viable suspect?

No.

Had he taken a cursory look into her to make sure he could discount her as a suspect?

Yes.

But that was as far as things had gone.

Back then, Sapphire had just been a name on a file. He'd felt bad for her when he read about what she'd been through. From what he'd read he thought she was a good cop, but it wasn't until he met her that he got the feeling that said she was someone special.

As soon as she and Elijah had been shot, both of them had been positively discounted as suspects, but even before then, he'd known she wasn't a murderer.

After what she had endured, she could have turned to drugs or alcohol. She could have suffered from depression or post-traumatic stress disorder. She could have turned down a bad path, but she didn't do any of those things. Instead, she focused her life on saving others who, like her, had been thrown headlong into a nightmare that they couldn't escape on their own.

Like he'd told her last night, Sapphire was a good person. More than that, her resilience amazed him. He just didn't know how to convince her of that. Maybe it had been naïve of him to think that one night of intimacy was enough to convince her that her past wasn't an issue for him. Maybe it had also been naïve to think that her past wasn't an issue for her.

No, not naïve.

He'd been deluding himself because he wanted things to work between them.

He liked her and he thought that despite the rocky start they could actually have a really wonderful future. He had brushed away everything else because he wanted to focus only on what he viewed as most important, which was the two of them. But for Sapphire, her past was obviously going to be a stumbling block—probably for the rest of her life. He should have known that; he was a psychiatrist. It was his job to know those kinds of things.

It would take time, but they had time.

They didn't have to rush anything. They could go slow. They could date for as long as she needed to, letting her slowly learn to trust the idea that he didn't care about her past. He cared about it only in the sense that he hated it had happened to her and would erase it if he could, but it wasn't something he ever envisioned coming between them. She just had to get used to that idea. If she thought he was just going to pack up and leave quietly, she was absolutely one hundred percent mistaken.

Gideon almost dropped the phone when it started to ring in his hand.

For a second he hoped it was Sapphire. Now that she'd had a little time and space to calm down she might have realized that he didn't judge her for her past, and her past didn't affect how he saw her. He'd just been doing his job.

When he looked at the screen, it wasn't Sapphire's name he saw. It was Gray Yul's. Surprised to see the detective calling him since he had been primarily working with Sapphire, his first thought was that something must have happened to her. Had she been in an accident? Zeb Tuck was in prison, but he knew Sapphire must be working half a dozen other cases. What if one of the killers in one of those cases had decided to target her?

"Just answer the phone and you'll know what's going on," he ordered himself. Pushing answer, he said, "Hey, Gray, what's going on?"

"We got a body. Looks like it could be Thea Brody."

Although he was happy it was nothing to do with Sapphire, his heart dropped hearing that. He'd thought the girl was still alive. Zeb was smart and he valued his time with his victims. He also believed he was never going to get caught. It didn't make sense that he would kill her while he still believed that.

"Gideon? You still there?"

"Yes, sorry, I was just thinking that doesn't make sense. Zeb has been in jail since we found the pen. Before that, he wouldn't have thought that we would ever pin the crimes on him, so why would he have killed Thea?"

"I have no idea. To be honest, I'm still just struggling to believe that Zeb did all of this, but the evidence all seems to be pointing to him. Right now, we don't know for sure that this is Thea. The body is, uh ... pretty beaten up."

He sighed. The poor girl had probably said or done something to make Zeb angry, and he'd lost it, beating her to death. "Okay, I'll be right there. Can you text me the address?"

"Sure thing. See you soon."

"About thirty minutes," he said before he disconnected the call. It seemed Sapphire was going to have to work with him a little longer whether she liked the idea or not.

His plan to start the day in the shower with Sapphire was clearly ruined, so he took a quick two-minute shower on his own, threw on some clean clothes, made the bed—because he could never leave the house, or hotel, if he hadn't—fed the dog, and headed down to his rental car. Upon entering the car, he popped the address into the GPS and drove out into the street. It was snowing lightly, and while he usually enjoyed the snow, today it only served to remind him what a mess he had left things with Sapphire.

Maybe he should have followed her this morning, not let her leave until they'd had a chance to talk things through. Everything had happened so quickly that he hadn't really had a chance to properly process it until she was already out the door. By the time he came to his senses, put clothes on, and went out into the hall, it was already too late. She was gone.

As soon as they finished up here, he was going to sit her down and make her listen to him. Despite her fears of people taking her past and using it to make assumptions about her, she was smart and logical. When she set her emotions aside and just listened to him, he was sure he could explain everything.

Gideon parked his car behind another movie theater and looked around. He must be the first one here. Should he call Sapphire, make sure she was on her way here? No. It was probably better that either Gray or Sergeant Langsworth called her to tell her about the body. That was the smart thing, except he knew how hard she would take it and he wanted to be able to help her through the feelings of helplessness and self-recrimination that he knew she would be dealing with.

Deciding it was best to wait to talk to her until they could talk face-to-face, he turned the engine off and got out of the car. Immediately a cold gust of wind passed straight through him, chilling him to the bone. He wished he was back in the hotel, in bed, snuggled under the blankets, with Sapphire tucked against his chest, his arms keeping her close against him. He wanted to watch her while she slept, her face peaceful with all traces of the stress and anxiety and the weight of her perceived responsibilities gone.

If he was lucky, they would spend tonight together.

If he could convince her to listen to him.

As he walked toward the dumpsters, assuming that was where the body would have been dumped, he started to feel like something wasn't right. There should be a police cruiser here, officers taping off the area, other detectives, a crime scene van, the witness who found the body. But there was no one, not even Gray. Had he accidentally texted him the wrong address?

Deciding that he should trust his gut, he turned and headed back to the car to call Sergeant Langsworth to find out what was going on. He was halfway there when he noticed a flash of movement to his right.

Gideon turned to see what it was, but something slammed into the back of his head, sending him crashing to the ground.

The world swirled around him, and he tried to reach for his phone to call for help but he couldn't control his movements.

He tried to get up, staggered, and fell back down.

His vision dulled.

A rushing sound filled his ears.

Pain pounded around inside his skull.

Then, despite his best efforts to remain conscious, he plunged into the darkness.

~

9:43 A.M.

"Thanks for coming with me," Sapphire said as she and Diamond walked through the hospital halls. She hadn't felt like being alone today, nor did she feel like going straight into work, so she had showered, dressed, and asked if Diamond wanted to go with her to visit Elijah before she steeled herself and went into the station.

"No problem," Diamond said. Her sister had been *very* willing to come with her, and Sapphire had to wonder if it was just because she was being the big sister or because she really wanted to see Elijah.

"You like him, don't you?" The idea of one of her sisters and her partner getting together left her feeling really unsettled. Those two parts of her life should stay separate. Her sisters had been through enough, and she didn't want them exposed to the darker side of life ever again. She did this job because she had to. She needed to do it to function. But the others weren't like that. They had all lived different experiences and had come out of it different people who coped in different ways.

If Diamond and Elijah became a couple, that delicate balance that she struggled to maintain between the two halves of her life, would be gone.

She wouldn't be able to leave work and come home and have that safety of not having to keep her mask quite so firmly in place. Elijah would be there hanging out with Diamond—with all of them. She would always have to make sure that she was careful about everything she said and did. The very thought of that was exhausting.

If that was what Diamond wanted, though, she would do it.

She would never do *anything* to stand in the way of her sister's happiness.

If there was anything that she had learned from her very brief affair with Gideon was that there was always going to be an excuse to stop yourself from being happy. She was full of excuses, and they were probably going to prevent her from ever finding lasting happiness, but she didn't want that for her sisters.

"Diamond?" she prodded when her sister didn't answer. "Do you like my partner?"

"I think he's nice," Diamond reluctantly admitted. "But I don't really know him well enough to know whether or not I like him. And I would never do anything to make you uncomfortable, and I know anything happening with Elijah and me would make you uncomfortable."

While it was nice to be that important in someone's life that they would sacrifice their own happiness for yours, she didn't want her sister to do that. She could suck it up and find a way to make it work if it was what Diamond and Elijah both wanted.

"If you think that Elijah can give you the life you deserve, I don't want you to give that up for me. I'll be okay no matter what you do. I love you, Diamond, and just like you said to me this morning that you don't want me to give up on life, I don't want you to either." In a very uncharacteristic move, she stopped walking and wrapped her arms around her sister's neck, hugging her hard.

"I love you," Diamond said, returning the hug and holding on just as tightly. They were all each other had in the world, and that made them closer than they would have been if their parents had never sold them.

"Love you too." She held on for a moment longer, not caring that there were nurses and doctors and patients and their families in the halls watching. She loved her sister, and she wanted Diamond to know it.

"Isn't this sweet."

They both spun around at the voice, and she rolled her eyes at her partner when she saw him standing behind them. "You're out of bed; that's great."

"Hoping to go home tomorrow. Doctors seem pleased with how I'm healing," Elijah told them.

"I'm so happy for you," Diamond said softly. Her sister was always so soft-spoken. Even before they were sold, Diamond was the quiet one, the shy one, the one who was usually hovering in the background.

"I just want to get back to work as quickly as I can, help keep Zeb in jail where he belongs." Fire flashed through Elijah's brown eyes, followed by helpless frustration at being kept on the sidelines while one of their own was found to be a killer. "And you obviously need me there to keep an eye on you," he said, deliberately pushing his annoyance away and winking at her. "I turn my back on you for a couple of days and you get yourself beaten up. You okay?"

Barely resisting the urge to poke her tongue out at him, she nodded. "I'm fine. A little banged up, but better than you."

"Touché." Elijah grinned.

He was looking like he was starting to hurt, so she said, "Why don't we go back to your room, and I can fill you in on what we have against Zeb so far."

"I still can't believe that he was who we've been looking for these last few months," Elijah said as they all started walking.

"You and me both," she said. Sapphire wasn't sure that she was ever going to get over that betrayal. It was another little chink in her armor, and although she worked hard to keep her armor on and strong, she wasn't infallible, and Zeb's betrayal hurt. It was probably why finding out that Gideon thought she could have been a killer had cut so deep.

"So, what do you guys have on him?" Elijah asked as they reached his room and he shuffled back into the bed.

"There was a pen with his fingerprint on it found at the scene where we were shot. The pen was under the body of the girl he used as a human shield. That was what we used to arrest him. Then after, we got a witness who saw the latest victim abducted by someone dressed as a cop and put into a car. We got a warrant for Zeb's car, and we found a uniform and a scrunched-up cloth with chloroform on it in the trunk," she explained.

"Has he confessed?"

"No. He's adamantly denying that he did anything." She hated that criminals made excuses for their crimes and pretended that they hadn't committed them like everyone else was stupid. Her parents had insisted up to the day of their sentencing that they hadn't sold her and her sisters and that they'd been abducted by people who broke into the house that night. They had insisted on sticking to that story, despite the fact that they knew that she and her sisters knew differently. Zeb was doing the same thing. They had proof he had killed those girls and abducted Thea Brody, so why couldn't he at least admit it?

"I wish I could be there," Elijah said again. She could feel his frustration. If she was stuck in a hospital bed right now, she would be feeling the same way.

She was about to tell him that, while she missed him, he was where he needed to be right now when her phone rang. She kind of hoped it was Gideon. Maybe it was wrong, but it could be in order for her to trust him, she needed him to fight for her, to show her that she was worth the effort. It was probably messed up, but she was too tired to argue with herself about it.

"It's Sergeant Langsworth," she told Elijah and Diamond. "Maybe it's a break in the case." The break in the case she was hoping for was that Zeb had given up Thea Brody's location or that the girl had managed to get free and been found.

"Hopefully it is," Elijah said.

"Hello?" she said as she pressed answer.

"Sapphire, I'm afraid I have bad news," Sergeant Langsworth said.

She hoped it wasn't about Thea. "Has Thea Brody been found?"

"No, it's Gideon."

Gideon?

She froze.

What had happened to him?

Had he been hurt?

If how she had left things with him this morning was the last time she ever got to talk to him, she was never going to forgive herself.

"What happened?" she asked tightly.

"I don't know exactly. His car was found about fifteen minutes ago. It was behind a movie theater. His keys and wallet were found on the ground about twenty feet away, his cell phone was beside it. Someone had smashed the phone."

The news sank in slowly.

Gideon was missing.

Abducted.

If he was at a movie theater, then the logical conclusion was that whoever had him was the killer they'd been looking for, but they already had Zeb in custody.

"What was he doing there?" she asked. None of this made any sense.

"I don't know."

"I'll be right there."

"I'll text you the address. Sapphire, whatever you need to find him and bring him safely home, you let me know," Sergeant Langsworth told her, and by the tone of her boss's voice, she knew that the sergeant knew that there was something between her and Gideon.

At least, there had been.

Until she had ruined it.

"I have to go," she told Diamond and Elijah when she hung up. "Gideon is missing. Diamond, are you okay to wait here until Amethyst or Ruby can come and pick you up?" she asked, already hurrying toward the door.

"Of course. I'm praying you find him."

"Thanks," she mumbled as she took off down the corridor at a quick pace. Gideon had to be okay. He had to be. Because she didn't know what she would do if he wasn't.

10:10 A.M.

He had a vicious headache.

He never had headaches.

In his entire life, Gideon had only had one headache. When he was fourteen, he had been riding his skateboard, slipped in a puddle, lost control and crashed into a tree, knocking himself out and ending up with a concussion.

After that, he had suffered with headaches for almost a week, but then they were gone, and he hadn't had another in sixteen years.

Until now.

It was so bad, he couldn't think of anything else.

It was so bad, he could barely breathe, and he wished he could fall back into unconsciousness.

But then, he heard a frightened whimper.

Somehow, he managed to shove aside the pain and crack his eyes open.

That was a big mistake, and immediately he retched, rolling over quickly so he didn't throw up all over himself.

Just the act of vomiting was enough to wear himself out to the point that all he wanted to do was lie down and go to sleep. Preferably for a really long time, and when he woke up, the headache would be gone.

Knowing that someone else was here with him—wherever here was —was the only thing that spurred him into fighting through the sluggish fog that blanketed him.

This time he was prepared for the onslaught of pain and nausea, and he steeled himself before attempting to open his eyes again.

Because he was more prepared, he was able to get his eyes open and taking in his surroundings helped him to wake up a little. He was in a small wooden shack. There was a bench and a table. He was propped up in a corner. His ankles were bound with rope, as were his wrists, and a third rope connected his tied wrists to a metal hook in the ground.

If he had enough time, and he was able to pull it together and ignore the headache, he might be able to get free. The metal hook looked like it had been hastily screwed into the wooden floor. There was already a small crack around it, and if he worked hard enough, he could probably work it free. The rope that had been used to tie him up was thin, and if he pulled it back and forth against the metal ring, he could probably break through it.

Knowing that strengthened and encouraged him a little, and he found himself able to push away the symptoms of the concussion he no doubt had because he'd been hit over the head. Getting him out to the movie theater had been a ruse. He'd been lured there by the killer, and since he didn't believe they were looking for a killing pair, it meant that they'd been wrong about Zeb.

The phone call he'd received had been from Gray, but there were plenty of apps that allowed it to look like you were calling from another number, which meant there was no way to know that the call really had come from Gray.

Was Gray the killer?

Was it Zeb and a partner?

Was it Mason Wharf?

Was it someone who wasn't even on their radar yet?

That he didn't have any concrete answers left him feeling both frustrated and unsettled. His gift was talking, but if he didn't know who he was going to be trying to get through to, then it meant he was going to have to wing it when the killer came back. The problem with winging it meant there were too many variables, too many things that could go wrong, and too many things he couldn't control. He needed something that would help him come up with a plan.

He smelled fish.

Sapphire had smelled fish the night she'd been shot.

That meant that he was definitely in the hands of the serial killer; he just wasn't positive who that was.

Sapphire.

When she found out that he was missing, she was going to freak out. She might have been hurt and angry this morning, but she cared about him, probably deeper than she realized. She would do whatever it took to find him, which meant he just had to stay alive until she got here.

Which reminded him he wasn't alone.

Lifting his head, he saw a face staring back at him.

Thea Brody was tied to the table in the middle of the room. She was dirty, her face was streaked with tears, and her eyes were terrified, but she appeared to be physically unharmed.

Pasting on a reassuring smile he certainly didn't feel, he said, "Hi, Thea, my name is Gideon. I'm a criminal psychiatrist who's been working with the cops to catch the man who brought us both here. Are you okay?"

"I'm okay," came the sniffed reply.

"Has he hurt you?"

"He hasn't hit me or beaten me or anything," Thea answered.

"Has he done anything else to you?" Gideon asked the question but he already knew the answer, he knew what this killer did to his victims before he killed them, and he knew it was possible that those things had already been done to Thea.

"He raped me," she said dully.

That was all he needed to know. He would do whatever he could to make sure that didn't happen again, but he was tied up, and he had a head injury. He wasn't really in a position to be protecting Thea. "Has he talked to you about why he's doing this? About what he hopes to achieve?"

"He said that he lost someone that he cares about. They died when he was a teenager. He wants to find out what's on the other side of this life, where you go when you die. I think he thinks that if he looks into my eyes when he kills me that he will somehow find the answers that he wants."

That was interesting, and possibly something that he could use to his advantage. He knew about the death of a loved one, although not firsthand. The death of the uncle he'd never known had affected his entire family, including him. Perhaps if he got the man talking, he would be able to stall long enough for Sapphire and the others to find him. Gideon knew that he would never be able to talk the man into letting him and Thea go and turning himself in. He had gone too far for that, but stalling was definitely an option.

"We need to come up with a plan," he told her.

"I can't get free," Thea said immediately.

"Are you sure? How has he restrained you? Did he use rope?" While he knew they were looking at a cop, whoever had tied him up hadn't done that great a job. If they had done the same with Thea, maybe she could get herself free. If he could get her out of here, he would stand a much better chance at distracting the killer. It was the girls who were the killer's focus. He was just collateral damage.

"Rope, but it's no good. I won't be able to get free."

Thea started to cry. She was hovering on the precipice between holding it together and falling apart. As much as he wanted to grab her and shake her and make her listen to him because both of their lives depended on it, he had to remember that she had been here for seventy-two hours. She had been abducted; she'd been left alone here for days. By the smells of things, she hadn't been taken anywhere to go to the bathroom and had had to go right where she was, and she'd been raped.

Which made him think of something.

"Thea, honey, try to hang in there with me, okay?"

"Okay," she sniffed, trying bravely to fight back her tears.

"When he raped you, did he untie you first?"

"Yes, he would untie the ropes and take me over there." She nodded to a corner of the room where he could see a sink and a bucket. "He would fill up the bucket with water and throw it all over me to clean me off."

That was exactly what he wanted to hear.

Sooner or later, the killer was going to come back here, and when he did, he was going to be anxious to spend a little time with Thea. Gideon didn't think that having an audience was going to make this guy shy, so he would do what he had done before. That meant that, for a little while at least, Thea would be free. There was definitely a way that they could take advantage of.

"Thea, between the two of us I am sure that we can work out a plan so that we both make it out of here alive, but to do that you need to stay with me, okay? Can you do that for me?"

∽

10:38 A.M.

She was losing patience.

She'd had enough.

Sapphire was at the end of her rope and she *was* going to get some answers.

Now.

Right now.

She stormed into the interview room at the jail and waited impatiently for Zeb to be brought in to talk to her.

"Finally," Zeb said when the door opened, and he was led in by a guard.

That was not the greeting she had expected. Who knows? Maybe he was finally ready to talk. The guard sat him down and attached his cuffs to the table then left them to talk.

"I've been waiting to talk to you. What took you so long to come back?" Zeb demanded.

After getting the warrant yesterday to search Zeb's car and finding more evidence inside, she had tried to do her best to calm Gray down before heading home. So far this morning she had been too preoccupied to come see him, not that she had even known he wanted to see her. Or maybe he was just trying to mess with her head and play some sort of game.

Well, she wasn't in the mood for games.

"Do you have a partner?" she demanded.

"You mean Gray?" He looked confused. Actually, he looked genuinely confused, and she was starting to wonder if he was putting on an act, he was mentally impaired in some way, or he honestly was innocent.

"No, not Gray. I mean a partner, a killing partner."

"I told you, I didn't kill anyone," he insisted.

"We found a pen with your fingerprint on it. We found a cop uniform and a chloroform-soaked rag in your car. We know you killed those girls, and you must not have done it alone because now Gideon is missing, and we know you didn't do it because you're stuck in here. So, who is he?"

"Gideon is missing?" Zeb looked shocked and horrified.

"Stop messing with me. I am *not* in the mood," she snapped. She wanted answers. She wanted Gideon safe. She didn't know yet where the two of them stood or what the future held for them, but he was a good guy even if he had hurt her feelings and she wanted him to be okay.

"I'm not messing with you, Sapphire. You know me, you *know* me. I wouldn't do this," he said earnestly.

She wanted to believe that.

She really did.

She didn't want to think that another person she had trusted had betrayed her, but what else could she think?

"My lawyer told me everything that you have on me, that's why I wanted to talk to you. Sapphire, I think I know who it is," he said seriously. "I think it's Gray."

"Oh, you do, do you?" She laughed, not a real laugh, more of a skeptical bark. "Well, isn't that convenient. You didn't commit the murders, but your partner did. Maybe the two of you are in on it together. You were both MIA the morning that Thea Brody went missing."

"Because *Gray* said that he needed an hour to take care of something," Zeb protested.

"Then let's bring him here and ask him about it," she challenged.

"Fine," he said, calling her bluff. "Bring him here. I thought he was my friend, but he's setting me up, and I'm not going to sit here and take it."

"Setting you up?" she asked dubiously. That sounded so cliché. Oh, I'm innocent and being set up. Wasn't that what every criminal said at some point? Nothing was ever their fault. They were just poor innocent bystanders, and the world and everyone in it was against them.

"You found a pen with my fingerprint on it, right? Underneath the body of the woman that the man who shot you and Elijah used as a human shield."

"Right," she agreed.

"Gray takes my pens all the time. Just because it has my fingerprint on it doesn't mean that I'm the one who dropped it."

"Okay," she agreed somewhat reluctantly.

"And the hypothesis was that whoever abducted Thea Brody was someone who the girl knew, you think it's me because my mom lives on that street, but Gray has been there before too. He's met the Brodys. I bet he never told you that, and I bet he made sure that he was someplace else when you interviewed them."

Actually, both of those things were true.

Gray *hadn't* told them that he had met the Brodys before, nor had he been there when they interviewed them.

Zeb must have read that in her face because he seemed to relax a little, like he finally felt like he was being heard.

"So, you have an excuse for the pen and that Thea was taken by someone that she knew, how do you explain the cop uniform and the chloroform?" she challenged.

"I can't explain the chloroform other than to say that Gray must have put it in my car to frame me. But the uniform is my old one. I wore it last Halloween, remember? To the costume party. You were there, too. You saw me. I just never got around to taking it out of my car."

Again, that was true.

She had—very reluctantly and only because she felt pressured into it —gone to the precinct's Halloween party, and Zeb had gone in his old uniform.

Slowly, she nodded. Everything that Zeb had said *could* be true. It didn't mean that it was, but it was a possibility.

"All right, let's say you're right. Let's say that you're innocent and that Gray is the killer and setting you up. What's his motive?"

"What's *my* motive?" he shot back.

"I know about your past, Zeb. What happened that led to you being adopted by your aunt and uncle.

"Which is the reason I would *never* do this," he said.

"Or the reason you *would* have a reason to do this. When you were a teenager your girlfriend and adopted father were shot and killed in a robbery gone bad. It happened at a movie theater, and your adopted mother was badly injured in a hit-and-run on a deserted country road. She was in a coma for six months before she finally passed away."

"I loved my father, and at the time, I thought that my girlfriend was going to be the woman I would marry, but their deaths didn't turn me into a killer, and neither did my mom's accident."

"We'll see," she said, determined to remain unconvinced until she had more information. "So, what's your theory on Gray?"

"Did you know that his wife recently kicked him out?"

"No," she answered honestly. She'd had no idea that Gray was having marital problems. She wasn't friends with any of her colleagues and didn't discuss their personal lives with them.

"It was over some problems with their oldest daughter. She's fifteen and started staying out until all hours of the night, then her mom walked in on her and a boy in her bed. She blamed Gray, said that he was never around and that she just wanted some male attention and would get it any way she had to. Gray lost it. I don't know exactly what happened, but whatever it was, it was enough for his wife to ask him to leave."

"When was this?"

"Around six months ago."

"And how do you know all of this?"

"I know he moved out because sometimes I pick him up. The rest I picked up from overhearing phone calls. I wasn't listening in on purpose, but Gray would get phone calls from his wife sometimes, usually about problems their oldest daughter was having in school, behavioral things, fights with other kids, and disrespecting teachers. He would get loud, tell his wife she told him to move out, so what did she expect would happen."

"If you knew all of this, if you knew that Gray was potentially violent, why didn't you say something?" When someone knew that someone else was dangerous and didn't do anything to stop them from hurting another person, in her mind, they were complicit in the acts the other person committed because they never spoke up.

"What was I going to say? That I heard Gray on the phone and he'd be yelling at his wife, and she kicked him out. No one would have taken me seriously. They would have thought I was trying to stir up trouble. If I had known that he was this violent, this dangerous, then, of course I would have said something."

As much as she hated to admit it, she guessed she couldn't argue with his logic. If he'd said something, no one would have cared, because without facts there really wasn't anything to care about.

"Do you believe me?" Zeb asked, his eyes searching hers, seeking reassurance.

If he was trying to play her, he was doing a really good job. Everything he said was plausible, and if his lawyer presented it all at court then there was a good chance that he would be found not guilty.

But was it enough to convince her that Gray—and not Zeb—was the killer?

Sapphire wasn't sure.

The idea that the two were working together was still on the table as far as she was concerned.

"I don't know," she answered honestly. "But you've given me enough doubt that I'm going to check Gray out."

"Thank you." He breathed a sigh of relief. "Be careful, okay? Gray is dangerous. If he's killed all those girls, shot you and Elijah, set me up, and now kidnapped Gideon, there is nothing he won't do to try to keep himself safe. Watch your back, and don't underestimate him."

"Don't worry about me. I know how to take care of myself. You be careful in here. And if you are innocent, I'm sorry, Zeb, about all of this."

"You were just doing your job."

His words didn't make her feel better. If he was innocent, he had been sitting in a jail cell for days while the real killer walked free, hurting more people. She was going to make this right.

She was going to make *all* of this right.

11:11 A.M.

Sapphire had no idea how she was going to fix this.

Although she knew that Gideon would tell her that she was taking responsibility for other people's actions, which were things she had zero control over, she couldn't help but feel like at least part of this was her fault.

She had allowed herself to develop feelings for Gideon. Feelings that had gotten in the way of her doing her job. If she hadn't been distracted, maybe she would have seen that there was more to Gray than there appeared to be. Maybe she would have seen that Zeb was innocent.

The more she thought about it, the more she knew that Zeb was not the serial killer. There was a sincerity in his eyes and his voice that she had only seen in innocent people. And Gray ...

Well, there had always been something that didn't sit well with her about him.

She couldn't put her finger on it, and it was nothing more than a feeling, but she remembered the first time she'd met him, she'd gotten that hairs standing on edge feeling when she shook his hand. She had convinced herself it was nothing. He was a detective. He wouldn't have gotten where he was if he was evil, and she had trusted the other people in the department.

Maybe if she had trusted her instincts, then, this wouldn't be happening.

If she hadn't freaked out on Gideon this morning, she knew for a fact he wouldn't be missing right now, so she was most definitely to blame for that.

What was happening to him right now?

Had he been hurt?

That was a stupid question. Of course, he'd been hurt. She'd been to the scene of his abduction, and she'd seen his blood on the concrete. He had most likely been hit over the head to incapacitate him enough to be taken somewhere else.

Probably to wherever Thea Brody was.

But why take him?

Why bother to kidnap Gideon instead of just killing him?

Surely it was more hassle to have another hostage than it was just to kill him if you wanted him out of the way.

So, what was the endgame?

If Zeb was right and Gray was the killer, then what did he hope to gain by abducting Gideon?

Having him wasn't going to be the same as holding a young teenage girl hostage. Gideon was bigger, stronger, and the fact that he was a psychiatrist meant he would no doubt find a way to get the guy talking, which might just end up saving his life.

Sapphire prayed it did.

She didn't think she could cope if he died, not when there was so much that she wanted to say to him.

Top of that list was to tell him she was sorry.

The way she had acted this morning was wrong. She'd let her emotions get the best of her. That was the problem with constantly keeping your feelings locked away. Sometimes that meant they came bursting out at the wrong times. She knew that Gideon had every right to look into the possibility that she was the killer. With her past, he'd have been crazy not to. He was only doing his job, and they hadn't even met at that point. She was just a name in a file—nothing more.

Up ahead of her, Gray turned the corner, heading toward his house, so she turned and followed him. If he was the killer, could he really be keeping his victims at his house? That was plausible, depending on how long he had been planning this. He could have soundproofed a room, or it was possible that he was either keeping his victims gagged or drugged.

Gray turned again, and now she was sure he was heading home. She'd been to his house once before—a Christmas party the year before last. She usually avoided any kind of social gathering. She just wasn't comfortable making small talk with people she saw only as colleagues, but sometimes she was pressured into attending. When she was, she'd go for just an hour or so before sneaking away.

Why was Gray going to his house if he'd been kicked out?

Sapphire was sure that Zeb had been telling the truth when he'd said that Gray and his wife were having marriage problems, so she believed that Gray had moved out. So why did it look like he was going home?

She got her answer less than a minute later.

Instead of turning down the street he lived in, he passed it by and continued down the road.

Where were they going?

She had a bad feeling in her stomach and she hoped it wasn't because Gideon was already dead. She wasn't ready to accept that possibility yet. Seeing the look on her sister's face when Diamond looked at Elijah had made her think. Did she look at Gideon like that? She was always so careful to monitor what she projected to the world, but Gideon had messed with that. He'd messed with all of her. It was almost like he'd found the key to unlock the person she was before she was sold, and bit by bit, that person was creeping back out.

It was disconcerting, and yet, it was also a little exciting.

Other than when she was about to arrest a criminal, or they had just saved someone's life, she didn't really get excited about things anymore. She hadn't even realized she missed the feeling until Gideon started bringing it out of her.

Gray made a left turn, and keeping her distance, she did too. She had to wait for some traffic to pass, and by the time she turned the corner, she saw that Gray had pulled in about halfway down the block and was already out of his car and heading toward a small townhouse.

This did *not* look like the kind of place you could keep someone hostage. The house was too small, and there were other houses right on either side. Keeping someone quiet would be too difficult.

Just as she was parking her car, she saw Gray return to his. This must have just been a pit stop. Where were they going next? She was going to be annoyed with herself if it turned out that she was wasting her time. The whole point of following him was to see if he would lead her to Gideon and Thea.

Sapphire waited until Gray was in his car and driving up the road before she pulled out. They drove through the city, and next time they stopped, it was in front of an old abandoned apartment complex.

She remembered this place. There was a fire here around seven months ago. There had been bad structural damage, and several of the former occupants had filed lawsuits against the company who had built it when it was found that they had cut corners, making the building unsafe—even before the fire.

The place was now empty, which would make it the perfect place to keep someone prisoner. Gray could keep the girls here and do what he wanted with them, and no one would ever be any the wiser.

Gray disappeared inside the building, and she quickly jumped out of her car and hurried across the street. Her hand was on the butt of her gun. Zeb had warned her to be careful and not to underestimate Gray, and there was no way she would. She knew how dangerous an animal backed into a corner could be, and she was going to make sure that she, Gideon, and Thea all walked out of this alive. She hoped that Gray saw that the best option was to surrender, but if he didn't and she was left with no choice, she would shoot to kill.

It was quiet inside the building, and there were way too many floors and apartments for her to check every one, so she went to the elevator and pressed the button. When the doors opened, she carefully looked at the buttons. There were fifteen floors, and a layer of dust coated all the buttons but one. Assuming that meant that the only button that looked recently used was the one where Gray had been staying, she pushed it and the doors closed.

Sapphire pulled out her gun. Gray could know she was here by now —he hadn't been far ahead of her and he could have heard the sound of the elevator when she touched the buttons.

On high alert, when the doors opened, she carefully scanned the corridor. It was empty.

The halls went off to the left and around a corner, and off to the right and around a corner.

"Eenie, meenie, miney, moe," she whispered to herself. "Off to the right we go."

She took off down that way, trying each door as she went. None of them were locked, which wasn't surprising since no one lived here anymore, and each door she opened she found an empty apartment.

Sapphire had just gone around the corner when she heard the ding of the elevator doors opening.

Gray.

Quickly, she backtracked and made it back to the main hall just as the doors closed.

Now she had to decide. Take the stairs, or wait for the elevator to come back, and try to catch Gray, or see if Gideon and Thea were here somewhere.

It took her only a second to make her decision.

Gideon.

If he was here, she couldn't leave. She had to find him, make sure he was okay. Once she had him and Thea safe, then she could put out an APB on Gray, and they should have him in custody fairly quickly.

Heading down the left corridor, she did the same as she'd done before, trying each door as she went.

The fifth one yielded a result.

The apartment was empty, just like all the others had been, but over in one corner, the wall and the floor looked like something had been ripped off them. There was no sign of either Gideon or Thea, but someone had been doing something in this room.

Walking over to the corner, she wondered what had been here. Had Gray made his own little cell to keep the girls in? She crouched down right in the middle of the triangle area that was different than the rest of the carpeted floor. There was a large hole on either side of which were two smaller holes, it looked like something had been screwed in here.

She was sure Gray had used this place to hold the girls at some point, but was he still using it? Sapphire knew she was going to have to call in backup. If Gray had set up in another apartment, it would take her too long to find which one, and Gideon and Thea might not have that long.

Putting her gun back in its holster she pulled out her phone as she walked back out of the apartment, heading for the elevator. She reacted too slowly as the first door she passed was flung open and something connected with her head hard enough for her to hear a crack before the world spiraled into a vortex of pain and she collapsed.

~

11:36 A.M.

"Are you making any progress?" Gideon asked, giving a frustrated yank on the ropes around his wrists. He was making progress getting through the ropes, and the metal ring was coming loose, but it was taking too long. The killer was going to be back at any moment, and he wanted them both gone by then.

"Maybe," Thea said. "My right wrist is getting loose, but I don't think I'm going to be able to get my hand out any time soon."

"You know what we do if we can't get free, right?"

"Yes. If he comes, you're going to try to get him to talk, and I'm just supposed to lie here and try not to draw attention to myself."

It wasn't much of a plan, but it was the best they could do for now.

What he really wanted was to get them both out of here, or at the least, get Thea out of here. If he had a chance to run, he wasn't sure that he would take it.

If he and Thea both left, sure they'd both be alive, but if the killer came back here and found the fishing shack empty, he would know it was all over. He would know that Thea knew who he was and that she'd probably told him, so he would know that there was no way he was going to get away with what he had done. The only logical thing for him to do would be to pack up and run. If he did that, they would probably never find him, and he would continue to kill until either he was eventually caught on other charges or he died.

"Remember: if he unties you, you kick him or punch him or hit him in the groin and run." Like any man, he couldn't say that without wincing, imagining himself on the receiving end of the strike. "Don't worry about me; don't look back. Just hit him and run, and don't stop until you get somewhere safe," he reminded Thea. That was the other half of their plan, and he hoped that if Thea was in a position to put it into action that she did. If she didn't hit the killer with enough strength, she would miss her chance to run.

But thinking of what ifs wasn't helpful right now.

He had to believe that everything would work out.

There was no way he was going to die here without having a chance to find out if he could fall in love with Sapphire.

Who was he kidding?

He was already falling in love with her.

It seemed like it was too early, but what he felt for her wasn't like anything he had felt for any other woman he had dated. He felt a connection to her—a deep connection—and he wanted the chance to explore that.

"Gideon," Thea's excited voice broke through his thoughts. "I almost have my arm free."

"That's great. Keep—" He broke off when they both heard the rev of an engine.

He was back.

They had been so close. If they'd had just another hour or so, Thea probably would have gotten her hand free. Once she had one hand free, it would have been much easier for her to free her other hand and legs, and then him. But any hope of getting the teenager safely out of harm's way was gone now.

"Close your eyes," he instructed. "Just lie there and don't say anything; don't look at him. Try not to even listen to him. If you think you can keep working on freeing your hand without being noticed, then go for it," he added. It couldn't hurt to have Thea partially free if an opportunity to get the jump on the killer presented itself.

Just as he finished giving his orders, the door swung open, and his heart practically shot right out of his chest.

Gray Yul wasn't alone.

He had a limp Sapphire slung over his shoulder.

Anger consumed him.

How dare Gray hurt Sapphire.

"What did you do to her?" he growled, the ferocity in his voice startling even himself. He hadn't realized he was capable of caring about someone so deeply this quickly. Yes, he adored his parents and his brother and the rest of his family, but this ... this was something else.

"She'll be fine," Gray said, dumping Sapphire on the ground. Her body bounced as she hit the floor, but she didn't flinch. She was definitely out cold, and he could see blood on the side of her face. Gray had probably knocked her out just like he had knocked him out. "For now," Gray added with a smirk. He was loving this.

For now.

Gray thought he was so clever, but he was underestimating Gideon.

"Why bring us here?" he asked. "Why not just kill us? Zeb is in prison, the cops think they have their man, now they know that they don't."

"So they'll think my partner has a partner." Gray shrugged. Apparently, he was confident that Sapphire wouldn't be waking up any time soon because he didn't bother to restrain her. That terrified him because he didn't know just how badly she was hurt, but he had to push through that fear if he was going to get them all out of here alive.

"And who do you think they're going to think it is?"

"They have no reason to think it's me. The only ones who might have figured it out were you two, and I don't think you're going to be talking to anyone." He winked.

So, if Gray thought that they could figure out it was him, then they obviously knew something important and just didn't know it. "Again, though, why not just kill us? Make sure we stay silent forever?"

"Simple. I need to know exactly what you know and who you might have told. Once I know that, then I'll kill you." He said it so matter-of-factly, like taking a human life meant nothing to him. "Or I might have a little fun with Sapphire first. She's hot, but with her prickly personality, no one is getting near that thing."

Gideon knew that Gray only said that to provoke him, and even with all of their lives at stake, there was nothing he could do to stop the sharp rage that cut through him. He growled again and yanked on the ropes. If they weren't there, Gray would be dead right now.

He was going to have to pull it together.

This was all on him.

Sapphire was unconscious and Thea was just a kid. He was the only one who stood a chance at getting them out of here.

Losing it again couldn't be an option.

"Who did you lose?" he asked. Get him talking—that was all he had to focus on—block everything else out.

Gray looked at him and cocked his head, no doubt trying to figure out his angle. Apparently, he decided he had nothing to lose because he started to talk. "A friend, and I sometimes used to rob people. It was no big deal. Neither of us had a lot of cash. We both came from poor families, and sometimes we pickpocketed, and sometimes we mugged them. It was no big deal," he said again, although obviously it was because it had brought them here, to this point.

"Someone died?"

"One night we were in the park. There was this girl. I didn't know he was going to do it, but my friend shot her. We grabbed her bag and we ran. The park was quiet. No one else was there; no one saw us. We got into his car, and we drove off. Everything would have been fine, only as we were driving back to his house, he lost control of the car and we hit a tree. I thought he was dead, so I ran. As I got out of the car and started toward the trees, I heard him calling out. Headlights were approaching, so I didn't stop. He died." The last was said with a hint of recrimination and Gideon assumed that was the obsession with finding out what lay beyond this life. He wanted to find out where his friend was and whether he was angry about the betrayal.

"No one ever knew you were involved."

"The gun and the woman's bag were in the car. The cops assumed that they had their man."

"So why leave the bodies at the movie theaters?" He couldn't see the connection yet.

"Because I knew about Zeb's past, and I thought it would give Sapphire and Elijah something to focus on if they realized they were looking for a cop."

That was devious. He had planned all along to set up his partner.

Gray had the ability to remain mostly in control of his actions. He was devoid of empathy, and he knew how to evade the authorities. He was basically a well-oiled killing machine.

"So how does this end?" Gideon asked. Right now, he wasn't seeing any way to talk Gray into doing the sensible thing. If he couldn't figure something out, all of them were going to die here.

~

12:02 P.M.

Voices roused her.

She had no idea who the voices belonged to. All she knew was that they were cutting their way through her brain like scissors, tearing and ripping at everything along the way, leaving a trail of agony in their wake.

Sapphire almost succumbed to the pain and let it send her flying back into the abyss when she realized who one of the voices was.

It was Gideon.

He was alive.

Relief washed over her, and she passed out again.

She didn't know how long she was out this time, but when she surfaced next, the voices were still jabbering away.

She tried to focus on them. She had to figure out what was going on so she knew how she could be most effective.

Although she tried to focus on the words, she couldn't seem to make any of them out. They were just unintelligible sounds floating around her like clouds. She could see them, feel them almost, but she couldn't make out any definition.

Giving up on that for the moment, Sapphire turned her attention to herself. Pushing away the pain in her head, she tried to figure out if she was hurt anywhere else. Nothing stood out to her, and she didn't think that Gray would have hurt her. He just knocked her out so he could bring her here, to wherever he was holding Gideon and probably Thea too.

It didn't feel like she was tied up in any way. She didn't feel anything around her wrists or her ankles. The only thing she felt was a hard wooden floor beneath her. Gray probably thought she was still unconscious and hadn't bothered to give her any more thought than that.

The pressure in her head said moving wasn't an option yet, so she tried once again to listen to what Gideon and Gray were talking about.

"Because I knew about Zeb's past, and I thought it would give Sapphire and Elijah something to focus on if they realized they were looking for a cop," Gray said.

So, Zeb was right.

His partner had tried to set him up, and very successfully.

It was probably why he'd dressed in the uniform when he abducted Thea because he knew that Zeb had the uniform in his car. It was probably why he picked Thea to begin with; he knew the girl lived on the same street as Zeb's mother and that that would have them pointed in Zeb's direction.

"So how does this end?" Gideon asked. Hearing his voice was such a relief. She had been conjuring up so many ideas of what might have happened to him, and to know that he was okay strengthened her.

"It ends exactly how you think it does. I kill you, Sapphire, and the kid, and then I walk out of here a hero," Gray replied.

"A hero?" Gideon asked.

"Sapphire and I managed to track down where Zeb's partner was hiding the victims. Unfortunately, she didn't survive, but I killed the partner, thus closing this case for good."

"Who are you going to frame as the partner?"

"There's a cop in VICE I used to work with a few years back I didn't care for. I thought he would make the perfect partner for Zeb."

"What's the connection between this cop and Zeb? How will you convince everyone that the two of them were partners?"

"It doesn't matter if there is any proof they're partners or not. He'll be dead, and Zeb is in prison with enough evidence against him to keep him there for life. No one is going to look any deeper than that. Especially since I was tragically injured while taking out the serial killer who was tormenting the teenage girls of the city."

From the sounds of things, Gray had thought of everything.

He'd set Zeb up and got him locked up. They *did* have enough evidence against him to keep him there for life, especially with her and Gideon and Thea—the only ones who knew the truth—all dead.

After he killed them all, his next step was no doubt to go and abduct that cop, bring him out here and kill him, then shoot himself so he could look like the hero in the situation.

If they were going to stop him, she needed to start getting her bearings and getting prepared to make her move.

Very slowly, she lifted her eyelids. As if her eyes had a direct link to her nose, the first thing she smelled was fish. So, she'd been right when she'd smelled it that night and known that it had something important to do with the killer. Gray must have kept the women in the abandoned apartment building but brought them here to kill them.

Without moving her head—afraid that if she did her concussion would have her throwing up—she roamed the shack with her eyes. The walls were made of wood, just like the floor. There was a table near her head. She couldn't see what was on it but she would guess fishing gear since this was obviously a fishing shack. In the middle of the room was a large bench. She could see someone on it; it was probably Thea.

Then she saw Gideon.

He was in the opposite corner of the room to where she was, the table with fishing gear on it between them.

He looked okay.

He was sitting on the floor. His wrists and ankles were bound, but he didn't look badly injured.

Sapphire was so thankful of that that she very nearly forgot about everything else but running to him—or crawling if she had to—and throwing her arms around his neck, kissing him until she convinced herself that she hadn't gotten him killed.

She resisted the urge and forced her body to remain still—not that it was all that hard. She felt like lead had replaced blood in her body. Every limb felt heavy, and her head screamed at her to sleep.

But she couldn't.

Gray stood between her and Gideon, a gun in his hand.

One wrong move, and they would all be dead.

"That's never going to work, Gray," Gideon was saying. "You brought us all here in your car. You hit me over the head. Sapphire too. Our blood is going to be in there. When you come up with this story, you don't think they're going to check into it?"

"Why would they?" Gray was so cocky, he honestly thought he had this in the bag.

"Why wouldn't they?" Gideon shot back. "You think that Zeb's not going to be shouting his innocence from the rooftops?"

"I made sure that no one's going to believe a word he says. Evidence speaks louder than proclamations of innocence."

"You won't get away with this."

Gray just laughed at that like it was the funniest thing he had ever heard.

"I mean it, Gray. Laugh it up now while everything seems to be going your way because it's not going to last. If you think that it is, then you're even more delusional than I think you are."

"What did you say?" Just like that, Gray's voice went from cocky and amused to angry and menacing.

Don't repeat that, she silently screamed to Gideon, wishing that telepathy was a real thing.

"You heard me," Gideon challenged. What was he doing? Why was he deliberately antagonizing a man who was clearly evil and who clearly had the advantage in this situation? Gideon was tied up, Thea was tied up, and she could barely think, let alone move. Not only was Gray free, but it looked like he had a gun in his hand that he would gladly use. Sapphire was sure that Gideon had a plan, but right now it didn't seem like a good one.

"You think you're so smart, don't you?" Gray took a step toward Gideon, and in one smooth move, slammed the gun into his head.

Sapphire winced, but Gideon seemed unconcerned.

"I'm not the one who thinks that he can get away with multiple counts of rape and murder and pin it all on someone else. You tell me which one of us is the smart one and which isn't?"

Gray slammed his foot into Gideon's side, and the gun into his head again. Gideon grunted in pain, but the look on his face didn't waver.

Stop goading him, Gideon, Sapphire begged.

"You won't think you're so smug when you watch me take your girl-friend right in front of you."

The darkness that flashed across Gideon's face made her shudder. She was his weakness, and Gray not only knew it but was prepared to use it to his advantage.

So far, Gray hadn't seemed to give her a second thought beyond using her to taunt Gideon. That wasn't going to last indefinitely, so she was going to have to take advantage of it while it was still on the table.

It was time to make her move.

∼

12:14 P.M.

Gray wasn't worried about things going wrong.

Why would they?

He had worked out this plan down to the very smallest detail. He had paid attention to everything; he had thought of everything; he had made sure that there was no way that this could ever be traced back to him.

As far as he was concerned, he was already home free.

Sure, there were a few things to deal with still. He had to kill these three, after taking a bit of time to have some fun with Sapphire. He'd thought she was gorgeous yet unattainable since they'd met. He had initially planned on sweet talking her into bed but quickly realized that was out of the question. Her prickly personality and refusal to let anyone get close meant it was never going to happen.

But now, he didn't need her permission.

She was his prisoner. She wasn't even conscious, so she wouldn't know what he was doing, and even if she did, he didn't care.

He was sick of caring about other people.

Where had that ever gotten him as a kid?

It hadn't stopped his baby sister from dying of SIDS. It hadn't stopped his grief-stricken father from turning to alcohol and losing his job, sending them into poverty. It hadn't stopped his mother from killing herself. It hadn't stopped anything.

It hadn't mattered how hard he had tried to be the perfect son. He'd done everything he was asked, and he never complained. He never begged or whined for toys or candy. He did his chores and then some. He tried to be enough to help his parents through their grief; he tried to be enough to help his mother through her depression; he tried to be enough to stop his dad drinking, but he wasn't.

He wasn't enough.

Once he had finally learned that lesson, he changed.

He became the person he was today.

The relief of letting go of the heavy burden of trying to please everyone around him, trying to be what he thought they needed him to be, was the most freeing experience of his life.

Why shouldn't he have what he wanted?

It seemed like everyone else got what they wanted, so why should he be the only one missing out?

Mugging people meant he had money to buy the things that all the other kids at school had. It meant he didn't feel so left out anymore. He and his father usually didn't have money for food, let alone for video games and a car.

If his friend hadn't shot that woman and then crashed the car, killing himself, then his life wouldn't have ended up this way.

Becoming a cop wasn't some way for him to atone for the sins in his past. It was a way to learn how to do what he wanted with immunity.

"Leave Sapphire out of this," Gideon Barlow growled at him.

The man's protectiveness amused him. What did he think he was going to achieve tied up?

"Think of your daughters, Gray," Gideon said. "Is this how you want them to remember you?"

"What part of, 'I'm not going down for this' did you miss?" he drawled. He was enjoying this, but he needed to get moving. If he wanted sex with Sapphire and Thea Brody before he killed them, he didn't have a lot of time. People would soon start to notice that Sapphire and Gideon were missing, so he had to kill them, then go and find the man he planned to frame as Zeb's partner.

Did he feel remorse for framing his partner?

Nope.

Not one iota.

He didn't dislike Zeb on a personal level. He just didn't mind sending him to prison for his crimes. The alternative was to go to prison himself, and that obviously wasn't going to happen.

"My daughters are my business, not yours," he reminded the shrink. Shrinks were always so darn nosy. It was the therapist his wife saw after a battle with stage four cancer, she hadn't been supposed to survive, who had changed her from the woman he had groomed to be his subservient wife into the woman who had kicked him out after she lost control of their daughter. "You should worry more about what I'm going to do to your little girlfriend over there. Have you had her yet? Was she as cold in bed as she is out of it?"

"I'm going to kill you," Gideon said through clenched teeth.

Gray couldn't do anything but laugh at that. "You got it backward. I'm going to do your girlfriend right in front of you, and then I'm going to make you watch me kill her. Then I might make you watch me do the kid as well. Then, when you've sat there and watched them both die, it's your—"

Something slammed into him from behind, sending him stumbling forward, almost losing his grip on the gun.

He was just turning around when Sapphire came at him a second time. He'd thought the woman was out cold from the blow to the head he'd given her back at the apartment block, and from the looks of her, she should be. She was wobbling on her feet, she looked queasy, and from the shadows in her eyes, she was clearly in pain. None of that seemed to stop her though, and she reached for the knife on the table that he used to gut fish.

So, he wasn't going to get to do her before he killed her. That was a disappointment, but ultimately no big deal.

Without a second thought, he lifted the gun and fired.

Sapphire dropped immediately.

Before he even had a chance to shoot a witty retort at Gideon, he heard a primal roar, and once again, he was slammed into from behind.

Thankfully, he had the presence of mind to keep a hold on the gun as they both hit the ground hard. He had no idea how Gideon had gotten free, but he *did* know that the man wasn't going to ruin this for him. He had put too much time and effort into this to lose it now. There was no way he was going to spend the rest of his life behind bars. He'd rather die.

Swinging the gun at the other man, he got a sense of satisfaction when he heard the smack of the metal connecting with bone. Gideon grunted but didn't back off. It was like the man was possessed. Maybe, he didn't just have the hots for Sapphire; maybe, he actually loved her.

Gray knew what it was like to love someone, and if he were a better person, he probably would have felt some measure of compassion for the man who was only fighting for the life of the woman he loved. He might even have had enough empathy to let them both go, let them see if they could find the happy ending that had always evaded him.

But he wasn't that man.

Compassion and empathy had been pushed out of him and all that was left was self-preservation.

To that end, he slammed the gun into the man's ribs and finally managed to keep him down.

He lifted the gun.

Aimed it at the shrink's head.

"Looks like you won't have to watch what I do to your girl, but know that if she's still alive, I'm going to make her wish she wasn't before I finally put a merciful bullet through her head."

Just as he was about to fire the gun, the door to the shack burst open, and a wave of cops flooded inside.

Gideon darted sideways, flinging his body protectively over Sapphire's. It was kind of sweet in a pathetic and highly annoying way.

"Put the gun down, Gray."

Surprised, he spun in the direction of the voice.

It was Zeb.

What was his partner doing here?

He thought he had left enough evidence pointing to Zeb to have the man rotting in a jail cell for the rest of his life.

"It's over, Gray. We know it was you. We know what you did to your wife. We know that you were beating her, raping her. We know that while she was sick you turned your attentions onto your oldest daughter, and that's why she started acting out. She told us everything. We know that you were the one who abducted and killed those girls. You tried to set me up, but it didn't work. When Sapphire left to follow you today, she told the sergeant where she was going. She had a tracking device on her, we followed it right here, and here you are. This is where you killed them, isn't it?" Zeb asked.

He'd already played the twenty questions game with Gideon, and he wasn't in the mood for round two.

It was time to make a decision.

It looked like Zeb was right. It *was* over.

Which meant he had to decide how he wanted to go out.

He could put the gun down, let them cuff him, get carted off to jail, plead guilty or await trial, and then go to prison.

Or he could do what he had spent most of his life doing and write his own destiny.

"Don't do it, Gray," Zeb warned.

It wasn't any surprise that his life was going to end this way.

Gray turned, winked at Zeb, then aimed the gun at Thea Brody.

Ten bullets hit his body simultaneously.

He was dead before he hit the floor.

~

12:28 P.M.

Flying bullets filled the air, and Gideon pressed his body down on Sapphire's, doing his best to act like a human shield and protect her from the gunfire.

He didn't know if there was any point to it.

She had already been shot, and he had no idea the extent of her injuries because he'd been too busy trying to kill Gray Yul.

Kill.

Not subdue and wait for the man to be arrested.

Gray had been going to rape Sapphire, and then he'd shot her.

He wanted him dead.

From the sounds of things, he'd probably just gotten his wish.

When he heard the sound of a body hitting the ground, he finally lifted himself a fraction of an inch off Sapphire and looked behind them.

Gray lay there, his empty eyes staring at the ceiling.

He was gone.

Sapphire was safe.

If she was still alive.

"You're heavy," came a muffled voice from beneath him, and at the sound of it, his entire body and soul relaxed.

"Better than being shot," he retorted with a grin. Gideon lifted himself the rest of the way off Sapphire and looked down at her. She looked back at him, their eyes locked, and he leaned down and touched his lips to hers. She was alive, he was alive, and in this moment nothing else mattered.

"I was so scared you were dead," Sapphire said when he ended the kiss.

"Nah, takes more than a deluded serial killer with illusions of grandeur to take me out," he joked, shaky now that everything was over. She might have thought he was dead but seeing that bullet fly into her had scared the life out of him.

He hadn't even known she was conscious until she had launched herself at Gray. Then the bullet had sliced into her and rage had somehow strengthened him because the next thing he knew he was launching himself at Gray.

It had come down to seconds.

If he had been just seconds faster at getting free then Gray would already have shot him before the cavalry arrived.

He might have been saved, but Sapphire had still been shot.

His eyes scanned her body. At first, they zeroed in on the blood on her head. Was it from Gray hitting her, or was that where the bullet had hit?

"Your head—" he started.

"Gray hit me," Sapphire interrupted.

Gideon nodded and continued his search of her body.

Her chest.

Her sweater was soaked in blood.

Had the bullet pierced her chest?

Was she bleeding out?

Had her heart been nicked?

If the bullet had passed through her lung it could collapse.

Frantically, he began to shove the hem of her sweater up. He had to stop the bleeding. He wasn't going to lose her; he couldn't.

"Gideon. Gideon." He heard her voice but didn't stop. He had to know how bad it was. He had to prepare himself if she was about to die.

"It's okay. I won't let you die," he said, managing to get her sweater out of the way so he could see the wound.

"I'm not going to die," Sapphire said matter-of-factly. "The bullet just bounced off my ribs. I'm fine." To prove her point, she tried to sit up.

He put his hand on her shoulder and held her down.

She wasn't moving until he was positive she was all right.

The wound was on her left side about halfway between her breast and the bottom of her ribs. The gash was deep, but it looked like Sapphire was right, the bullet hadn't plowed through her. It had bounced off her ribs, leaving a bloody cut but nothing that was life-threatening.

"You're okay," he whispered in relief.

"Told you." She smirked.

If she was feeling well enough to banter with him, she definitely wasn't at death's door.

"Can I get up now?" she asked.

"No way," he said, yanking off his shirt and pressing it to the wound on her side. The bullet might not have gone through her body but she was still bleeding pretty badly.

"But I'm okay."

"You don't have a bullet inside you, but you were unconscious when he brought you here, and your pupils are still dilated. You have a concussion."

"Well, you have blood on your head too," she shot back. "And Gray hit you at least three times that I saw."

"You're still recovering from being shot by him before, *and* Mason Wharf beating you up."

"Not that you two arguing about who's hurt worse isn't adorable, but paramedics are here," Zeb said, crouching beside them.

"If you say you don't need a medic, I'll shoot you myself," he warned, anticipating Sapphire's next comment.

Zeb laughed. "I'll go grab them and bring them in. You two be good."

Once they were alone again, Sapphire's emerald eyes clouded over. "This was my fault," she said softly. "If I hadn't lost it this morning because of what I found on your computer then Gray would never have gotten you. I'm so sorry."

"Honey, that is not your fault, and you know it. If Gray was determined to kill us, he would have just waited for a different opportunity."

"But—"

"No, no buts. We're both alive—a little banged up, but alive—and so is Thea."

"You make it all sound so simple, but I can't just forget that I nearly got you killed."

He knew how to make her forget.

Gently, he eased an arm under her shoulders and lifted her until she was partially sitting, then propped her up against his knee. Brushing a lock of hair off her cheek, he gathered her close and dipped his head and kissed her. He intended to keep it chaste given the fact that paramedics were coming in to treat her and take her to the hospital, but Sapphire immediately lifted her hands and threaded her fingers through his hair, kissing him fervently. All of her pent-up fear and regret and what she felt for him, but was too scared to say out loud, all came out in that kiss.

It was that exact moment that he knew that he already loved Sapphire.

Not in the same way that his parents loved each other after decades together, after building a life together, but it was the kind of love that said he knew for sure that they had a future. They had time to build that life together—a life that lasted.

"Sir, ma'am?"

Gideon ended the kiss, and was all ready to hand Sapphire over to be checked out, he wasn't getting looked at until he knew for sure that she was all right.

"Wait," Sapphire said.

"No." He frowned at her. "You need to be looked over."

"And I will be, but I need a moment, please," she added.

With a sigh, he gave in. "Can we have one second?" he asked the paramedics.

Neither of them looked pleased but both nodded and moved a respectful distance away.

With an entire two steps between them and the rest of the dozen or so people in the shack, he turned his eyes to Sapphire. As far as he was concerned, it may as well just be the two of them.

"I know you're just going to say that what happened isn't my fault, but I need to tell you why I was so upset this morning."

She looked so earnest, so he didn't interrupt. If she had things she needed to say, he wasn't going to take that away from her.

"Most of the time I push everyone away. I don't have friends, and I never date. It's because I'm scared," she admitted, and he knew without her having to tell him that this was the biggest admission she had ever made. "Not just scared because of what they did to me and knowing that there isn't anything stopping it from happening again because there are evil people everywhere. But I get scared that what happened to me will make me a bad person, like the people who hurt me."

"Why would you think that? Why would what they did made you evil too?"

"I don't know." She shrugged fitfully. "I'm not saying it makes sense. I just know that it's how I feel. What if their evil rubbed off on me? What if one day I hurt you? What if one day we had kids and I hurt them? I guess when I saw this morning that you thought—even for a second—that I could be a killer, that it made me think that all those years I'd thought that I'd been right, because what you think of me matters to me, because I like you," she finished shyly.

Underneath the calm, cool, always-in-control exterior was a sweet, vulnerable woman who was more afraid than she liked to believe. He loved the different sides to her. It made her complex, and complex made life interesting.

Taking her face between his hands, he made sure she was looking him straight in the eye. "You listen to me. Evil doesn't rub off on people. It's either inside them, or it's not. Sometimes circumstances bring it out, but only if it was already there. You don't have an evil bone in your body. You know how I know that? Because I like you too."

She smiled, and he knew that his words were slowly starting to penetrate. One day, she would believe him.

"Kiss me," she said.

"Can't say no to that."

Ignoring the cops and medics, he kissed her again—slowly, sweetly —like he had the rest of his life to get his fill of the taste of her. And he did.

CHAPTER
Twelve

January 10th
12:47 A.M.

Twelve hours.

It had been twelve hours since she'd last seen Gideon.

She was having withdrawals.

Was that even a thing?

Sapphire had no idea, but she was definitely feeling the effects of not having seen him for so long. She couldn't concentrate on anything, and her attention kept darting to the door at the slightest sound or movement. She was alternating between wringing her hands together and nervously fiddling with anything that was within her reach, and even though she was lying on the hospital bed, her legs kept bouncing anxiously up and down to the point where all three of her sisters had already mentioned it.

After the paramedics had started treating them, they'd been split up, transported to the hospital in separate ambulances, then kept apart as they each gave their statements about Gray and what had happened at the shack.

She knew that he was okay. She had pestered the nurses until they went and got an update for her. They both had concussions, she had a line of stitches along the side of her chest closing the bullet wound, and Gideon had some bruising from Gray beating him, but their relatively minor injuries were a small price to pay to know that it was all over. Gray was dead. He would never hurt his wife, his daughters, or anyone else ever again.

Knowing that gave her a small sense of peace that she knew from experience wasn't going to last because after her mandated couple of days off to recover, she would return to work and a whole new pile of cases.

For now, though, she just wanted to be grateful that everything had turned out the way it had.

"Do you want to try eating something?" Amethyst asked, striding back into the room in that purposeful way she always moved.

She curled her nose up at the idea. "Not yet, I'm still nauseous."

"Water then?"

Even the idea of putting liquid in her stomach was enough to make it churn. "No, thanks."

"Why don't you lie down and try to get a little sleep. You're spending the night here anyway, so you may as well get comfortable and stop sitting there all twitchy," Amethyst snapped.

Sapphire couldn't help but laugh.

She wasn't a twitchy person, and she'd been sitting here twitching away for the last few hours.

There wasn't really any end in sight until Gideon finally got here.

What was taking him so long?

She'd wanted to go looking for him after she gave her statement but her legs weren't quite steady enough yet to go searching the hospital, and when she'd asked her sisters, they had said no to getting a wheelchair and taking her around.

Because she was supposed to be resting.

But how could she rest when her body was screaming out for Gideon?

"If you go get a wheelchair, and we go find Gideon's room, I'll stop twitching," she told Amethyst.

"Nice try, little sister," Amethyst said. "But I don't think that's going to happen. You heard the doctor. You're supposed to stay in bed and rest so you can go home in the morning."

She sighed dramatically.

As exhausted as her body was, and it *was* completely wiped out—like every single drop of energy had been drained out of her—but as tired as she was, her brain was wired, and sleep wasn't going to happen right now.

"So, are you going to go for it with Gideon?" Ruby asked.

"There's still a lot we need to talk about. We had one kind of date before I got upset, and then I spent the day worrying that he was dead. There is so much we have to sort out, and I don't know where his head is. He doesn't live here, and that's going to affect things. I don't know if he plans to move, or if we're going to try a long-distance relationship." She was rambling, and she knew it, but she was afraid to commit to an answer because, despite their proclamations that they liked each other, she and Gideon hadn't had a chance to talk, so she really didn't know where they went from here.

"Is that the long way of saying yes?" Diamond asked.

Sapphire drew in a long breath.

She had already taken so many risks when it came to Gideon. She had admitted so many things—some things she hadn't even realized until she'd said them. Surely, she could take one more risk and admit out loud that she was willing to do whatever it took to make things with him work.

Admitting it out loud wasn't going to jinx anything.

It wasn't going to change anything.

She couldn't be afraid to live her life because something else bad might happen to her.

What kind of life would that be?

That was something she didn't have to wonder about. She knew what it was like to live your life too afraid that you could get hurt again, so you eliminated all possibilities of being hurt because that was how she had lived her life for the last ten years.

"Yes, I'm going to go for it with Gideon," she said, and immediately felt relief instead of the panic she'd thought she'd feel once she finally said those words.

"I'm so proud of you." Diamond hugged her.

"Me too," Ruby said, coming to sit on the bed beside her.

"Me three," Amethyst said with a smile. Amethyst never smiled. If she could be prickly, then her sister was a porcupine. That her sister was happy for her meant the world to her. That *all* of her sisters were happy meant the world to her.

It was hard being the first to find her way again because it felt like she was leaving her sisters behind. She loved them so much, and moving away from here was the only thing she couldn't do to be with Gideon. Her sisters were too important to her to be far away from them.

Even though she wouldn't leave the city, if she and Gideon worked out and their relationship developed, she'd eventually move in with him. It would be weird not living with her sisters. She was so used to them being there—so used to their comforting presence—and not having them around every day would take a lot of adjusting.

"Maybe one day we'll all be married and have kids of our own," Sapphire said. Now that she had finally found someone that she thought she could love and spend the rest of her life with, she wanted all of her sisters to have this feeling.

"Maybe," Diamond agreed, a wistful look in her green eyes, and Sapphire knew she was thinking about Elijah. Even though it still left her feeling uncomfortable to have her sister date her partner, there was no way she would get in the way of her sister feeling the same way that she did right now.

All of them had been through so much, and it was surreal that she finally had a chance to have the life she would have had if her parents had never sold her.

No.

Not the same life she would have had.

A *better* life.

Because as much as she hated what had happened to her, she wouldn't be the person she was today if she hadn't lived through it. And if she wasn't the same person she was now, then maybe there would be a few more criminals on the street and a few more families grieving the loss of the people they loved.

She knew what grieving was like.

Her own family was still missing a piece.

"Do you think one day Emmy might be here with us?" she asked. Whenever she thought of her little sister, she remembered the night they'd been taken. In their bedroom she had tried so hard to escape and take Emerald with her, but she'd failed. Maybe if she had been able to get out of the bedroom, none of this would have ever happened.

Gideon would tell her that it wasn't her fault. She was a sixteen-year-old kid outnumbered by half a dozen well trained men. She supposed he was right, but still, she couldn't help but wonder how things would have turned out if she *had* gotten away that night.

"Even if we don't ever find her," Ruby said, "she'll still always be here with us, because we love her, and we won't ever forget her or stop believing that one day she'll come home."

While she was sure that the thought lingered at the backs of all of their minds, they never discussed the possibility that Emerald was already dead.

Sometimes hope—even if it was false hope—was all that kept you going.

"At least we have each other," she said, putting an arm around Ruby and Diamond's shoulders, as Amethyst came to sit on the bed with them.

"Always," Diamond said.

She was pretty lucky. She had three sisters who were always there for her, and a guy who cared about her enough to look past the trauma that had shaped her and just see *her*.

1:13 A.M.

She hadn't seen him yet.

Sapphire was sitting on her hospital bed. Her sisters were with her.

Gideon had never met them, but the brunette with the green eyes who looked just like Sapphire had to be her oldest sister, Diamond, and the two blondes were the twins, Amethyst and Ruby. He knew there was a fifth sister, the youngest, Emerald, who had never been found.

Although she hadn't realized he was here yet, he knew that she'd been waiting for him. He had been able to feel her anxiety as she waited, and the burning need to see him that had consumed her.

It was odd. He didn't believe in telepathy, but he couldn't deny the fact that he could feel her emotions just as strongly as though they were his own. He'd been able to feel her fear when Gray had abducted him and held him prisoner and she hadn't known if he was dead or alive. He had been able to feel her pain when the bullet cut through her flesh and bounced off her ribs, and he'd been able to feel how badly she needed him to come.

Well, he was here now, and he wasn't leaving her ever again.

Like she could read his own emotions just like he could read hers, Sapphire turned her head and spotted him in the doorway. Her eyes were watery, her cheeks wet, and yet the second their eyes met, her face immediately brightened, and she shot him a huge smile. She may still be learning about getting in touch with her feelings again and that it was okay to express them, but that just the sight of him could turn her mood around definitely stroked his ego a little.

"How are you doing?" he asked.

"Okay. Sore, but fine," she replied. "You?"

"Same."

He wasn't sure how much her sisters knew about the two of them, or how much Sapphire wanted them to know, so he didn't want to do anything to make her feel uncomfortable. He was intending just to stand near the bed and ask her how she was, but Sapphire held her hand out to him.

Taking that as his cue, he walked over and took it, kissed her cheek, and when one of her sisters—the twins were identical and he couldn't tell them apart—moved off the bed, he sat beside her.

"I missed you," he said as she immediately leaned into him.

"I missed you, too. What took you so long?"

"I had a couple of things to take care of," he answered vaguely. He wanted to wait until they were alone before they had that conversation.

"Well, I'm glad you're here now. This is Gideon," she told her sisters, "and this is Diamond ..." She pointed to the brunette. "... Ruby ..." She pointed to the sister who had been sitting on the bed and moved to make room for him, "... and Amethyst."

"Nice to meet you," Diamond said with a smile.

"Sapphire's told us a bit about you." Ruby also smiled.

Amethyst just glared.

If he'd thought that Sapphire had an attitude that kept people at a distance, then Amethyst's was ten times that strong.

It wasn't until Ruby jabbed her in the ribs that she finally said, "Yeah, nice to meet you."

Her tone and her face clearly conveyed her message. *Hurt my little sister and suffer the consequences.* She didn't have to worry. He would never do anything that he didn't one hundred percent believe was in Sapphire's best interests. He couldn't guarantee that she would always be thrilled with everything he said and did, because he was human and he made mistakes, and sometimes he would push her to do things that made her uncomfortable, but he would never knowingly cause her pain.

"You don't need to worry," he told Amethyst. "Your sister is safe with me. I would never maliciously hurt her."

"So, you can stop giving him the evil eye," Sapphire added.

Amethyst surprised him by relaxing and even giving him a small, one-sided smile. "I like that you added maliciously in there, because chances are that if you two are together, sooner or later you will hurt her. But to know that you know that and are acknowledging it, makes me feel better."

He had just passed the first family test. He was sure there would be more, and he was sure that if he ever did hurt Sapphire, Amethyst would gladly make him pay, but he knew that would never happen.

Although he would never ask her sisters to leave, he wanted some time alone with Sapphire. They still had a lot to talk about and there were some things he didn't want to wait to tell her.

Thankfully, Diamond leaned over and kissed her sister's cheek. "We'll get going, let you get some rest." She shot him a pointed stare.

"And come back and see you in the morning. Well, later this morning," she added.

"Thanks for hanging out here with me," Sapphire said.

"Any time, although don't make a habit of it," Ruby said, giving her a hug.

"Night." Amethyst patted her sister on the shoulder then shot him a fierce glare. "Remember, I'm watching you."

"Sorry about Amethyst," Sapphire said once they were alone.

"Don't be. I think it's great that you have sisters who love you so much they'd threaten anyone who might hurt you."

"For a long time, we've been all each other had," Sapphire said, and he caught the underling meaning to what she was saying. She was telling him that her moving away from them was not an option.

"I'm glad that you weren't alone," he said as he settled back against the mattress and settled Sapphire at his side. "And you don't have to worry, I would never ask you to leave your sisters. I know how much they mean to you."

"Then where does that leave us?" she asked, allowing the fear she felt to seep into her voice. She might not even realize it, but in the last few days, she had changed a lot. It was like after taking the first step, everything else had started to follow suit.

"The reason I didn't come straight to your room after I gave my statement and finished getting checked out was because I called my boss and told him that I was quitting."

"You quit your job?" She bolted upright, then winced as it obviously hurt her head.

"I also called my real estate agent and left a message telling her that I wanted to put my house on the marker."

"You're selling your house?"

"I won't need it when I move here."

"You decided to move just like that? Why would you do that? How can you just give up your life?"

"Because my life isn't there anymore. It's here, because you're here."

"Are you sure you should be making huge, life-changing decisions with a concussion?"

He laughed at that. It was so hard for her to believe that she was enough to make him move here, but she would soon learn just how special and amazing and deserving of love that she was, because he would make sure of it. "It's not the concussion, silly girl." He took hold of her shoulders and pulled her back down so she was snuggled at his side. "I had already decided to move after the other night in my hotel room."

"But then I kind of freaked out," she reminded him. "Doesn't that make you want to rethink things? I'll probably do that again—lots of times. Just because, for the first time I really want to leave my past in the past and move on doesn't mean that it won't always follow me. Doesn't that scare you?"

"No," he answered simply. "We all have a past that follows us. Yours is just darker than most. Nothing would make me rethink moving here because I see a real future with you. A future that will have bumps in the road like all futures do, but it will also be one filled with happiness and fun and laughter, and one day marriage and babies."

"You really think that we can have that? That *I* can have that?" She anxiously searched his eyes to see if he was telling the truth.

"You're already reaching for it," he reminded her, hooking a finger under her chin and tilting her face up so he could kiss her. "Want to break out of here? Go back to my hotel room?"

"Yes," she said, and her face went from needing his reassurance to sexy in a second and he couldn't help but laugh.

"You do know we both have concussions and a myriad of others cuts and bumps and enough bruises to look like patchwork quilts."

"I'm no weakling." She arched a challenging brow.

"You're going to be the death of me, you know that?" he groaned, delighted to hear her laugh ring out. He lifted her over so she was in front of him, perched on his lap, and kissed her long and hard.

She was one amazing woman. She made him feel protective like no one else could. She also turned him on like no one else could. She was strong and tough and resilient, and at the same time, she was vulnerable and desperately in need of someone to love her and show her that she mattered, and teach her how good life could be.

She was his.

~

1:42 A.M.

She couldn't stop staring at him.

Had she turned into some sort of creepy stalker type of woman who worshipped the man she loved?

That should repulse her more than it did.

Sapphire didn't worship Gideon, but she trusted him, she admired him, and she respected him. She might even be on the verge of loving him.

Okay, that was a bald-faced lie.

She wasn't on the verge of loving him. She had already stepped off the precipice and was plummeting quickly toward love.

It still felt very surreal.

It had been a long time since she had resigned herself to the fact that she would be spending her life alone. It wasn't that what had happened to her had made her afraid of men. She knew there were just as many good ones in the world as there were bad ones, but it had made her afraid to trust anyone.

When she was sixteen, it had never occurred to her that her parents would sell her and her sisters to human traffickers just for cash. She wasn't beaten or locked in a closet or neglected. She lived in a clean home with plenty of food to eat and clothes to wear and most of the other things she asked for. She wasn't verbally abused—neither was she emotionally or psychologically abused. Her parents were distant and detached, but other than that, her life was the same as all her friends. It was like one day she had been a normal teen living a normal life, and the next, she'd had her world crash down around her.

That kind of trauma didn't just rock the boat. It took the boat, smashed it to tiny pieces, and left you floating alone in the ocean in the midst of wild waves and wind and rain.

There weren't enough pieces of the boat left to build a new one, so you had to find a way to adapt.

Her way had been to emotionally shut herself down and just avoid any scenario where she was likely to get hurt, which basically meant no friendships and no relationships.

Then Gideon had come along, and while he didn't possess the ability to help her rebuild her boat—no one did, not even herself—he had a new boat, and he'd pulled her up out of the sea and set her down on his boat.

Now she had a safe place to stand while she built a new boat. It would be different than the one she'd had before—shakier, smaller, not as strong—but in a way, it would be better because she'd had to fight so hard to build it.

She had so much to be grateful for. She had a life again. She could learn how to let go and not always be so rigidly in control. She could learn to have fun, to laugh, to enjoy the little things in life.

He might have driven her crazy when she first met him, but maybe that was because instinct had told her that he had the ability to change her life, and sometimes change could be such a scary thing, even if it was change for the better.

"You know staring at me like that is doing terrible things to my ego. You keep it up, and it's going to grow so big there won't be enough room in here for the three of us," Gideon said, taking his eyes off the road to grin at her.

Sapphire giggled like she was fifteen again. "I don't think we have to worry about that. You don't have a big ego, and besides, you deserve all the praise I've been thinking." She reached across and put her hand over the one he had resting on his thigh, lacing their fingers together.

"Don't give me the credit for any of that. The changes you're making are all you." He lifted their joined hands and pressed a kiss to the back of hers.

"Do you get credit for looking ridiculously sexy in those hospital scrubs, or is that all me, too?" she teased. What had happened to her hadn't made her afraid of sex, but it had made her disinterested in it. She did it because she wanted to prove to herself that she could, but before Gideon she would never have imagined metaphorically counting down the seconds until she could rip his clothes off and make wild passionate love, and then sweet tender love.

"No, that's me." He winked.

"You really do have an ego, don't you?" She didn't mind that. It was one of the things she liked most about Gideon. He didn't try to hide who he was. He was just himself, and that was what had allowed her to open up to him. If he'd tried to coddle her or been fake with her in any way, she would never have taken the chance of trusting him with the feelings she kept buried away.

"I choose not to answer that on the grounds that I might further incriminate myself," he said as he turned the car into the driveway of the hotel. "You should probably text your sisters and let them know where you are while I give the keys to the valet."

"No way. If they knew I was here, you could expect Amethyst to be breaking down your door in the next ten minutes. I want a little time just the two of us. I'll text them later, after I have my way with you." She deliberately brushed her body seductively against his as he opened the car door for her and she climbed out. Then she gave him a wink of her own and walked on ahead, sashaying her hips as she went, leaving him to deal with the valet.

He caught up to her just as the elevator doors were sliding open, and immediately scooped her up into his arms. "You think you get to tease me like that and walk off?" he asked, then crushed his mouth to hers, kissing her until her chest was bursting.

"I thought your ego could do with a little taking down a notch." She smiled sweetly.

"Oh, you did, did you?" He smirked, then began to trail a line of impossibly light kisses down her neck, immediately making her hungry for more. She tried to find his mouth again to kiss him, anything to ease the pressure that was winding itself up inside her, but the doors to the elevator opened again and he just grinned at her and started walking.

"You're enjoying this, aren't you?" she mock growled.

"Yep," he agreed cheerfully.

"Just remember, I give as good as I get."

"Oh, I bet you do."

Without putting her down, Gideon juggled the key out of his pocket and let them into his room. He went straight for the bed, but she stopped him. "Shower," she murmured. That was the only word she could get out. Her whole body was on fire now. It needed Gideon like it needed air.

He detoured straight to the bathroom and set her on her feet, pulling off the hospital scrubs a nurse had given her to wear before she even had a chance to blink. He shed his own and turned the water on, waiting until it was steaming before hooking an arm around her waist, lifting her feet off the floor and stepped them both into the shower.

That he was every bit as hungry for her as she was for him encouraged her and only made her wish he would hurry up and make love to her.

"Patience, patience," he murmured as he grabbed the shampoo and squeezed some into his palm. "I want to touch every inch of you before I come inside you."

"You want to drive me crazy," she huffed.

He gave a husky laugh. "Mmhmm."

Gideon turned her around and began to soap up her hair. His fingers felt so good kneading her scalp, and he carefully avoided the lump from where Gray had knocked her out. When he had her hair good and soapy, he moved her so she was under the water's spray and then began to scrub her body. Starting with her neck, he worked his way down her arms, then went back up and washed her chest and stomach, and then her back, his strong fingers massaging every place they touched.

He moved down one of her legs, then started up the other. Finally, he was touching her where every desire in her body was focused. He teased her relentlessly, touching her lightly, then slowly increasing the pressure, then just when he had her legs shaking so badly and barely coherent pleas falling from her lips, he would go back to the feather light touches. Gideon repeated this process several times until she couldn't take it anymore.

Standing on tiptoes, she started to kiss him, then while one hand was tangled in his dark hair, her other reached between his legs until her fingers touched the part of him that she could use to drive him crazy. He tried to push her hand away, but she wasn't to be dissuaded. She used his own form of torture against him, and touched him lightly, then increased the pressure until she had him groaning into her mouth, then promptly eased right off, brushing her fingers softly up and down his hard length.

"You do give as good as you get," he whispered against her lips.

"You better get inside me now," she whispered back, dizzy with need and desire.

"Can't say no to a lady."

Finally, he pushed inside her, making her moan in pleasure, and the two of them began to move together like they had been doing this all their lives.

It took less than a minute and then a rainbow appeared before her closed eyes, bursting into a mess of sparkling glitter as she came so hard her body trembled with aftershocks for several minutes. Then, spent, she slumped against him, letting him take her weight.

"That was unbelievable," Gideon said, moving them so the spray rained down on both of them.

"We are pretty good at that," she agreed sleepily, resting her head against his strong chest and enjoying the way his heart beat beneath her.

"Not so good that we don't need plenty of practice," he teased.

"Can't argue with that."

She was done arguing with life as well. She wasn't going to fight against it anymore. She wasn't going to fight happiness. She wasn't going to give in to fear, and she wasn't going to let the past rule her.

She was just going to be happy.

With Gideon.

Because he made her happy.

He made her feel special. He made her know that she was loved and cared about. He made her feel like a real person and not just a victim. He made her believe in happiness and goodness and soul mates. He made her believe in love.

He gave her something to hold onto when life was unpredictable and scary.

Sapphire wrapped her arms around his waist and held on to the best thing she'd ever found. What was better was that he held her, one arm around her waist, his other hand tenderly stroking the length of her spine, his cheek resting on the top of her head, holding her like she was the best thing *he* had ever found.

For the last decade she had felt like one of the unluckiest people on the planet.

Now she felt like one of the luckiest.

As teenagers they were sold to human traffickers, now the Hatcher sisters have to rebuild their lives. To find out what happened to Ruby Hatcher continue with book two in this gripping romantic suspense series now!

Crushed Ruby (Broken Gems #2)

Also by Jane Blythe

CRUSHED RUBY

FRACTURED DIAMOND

SHATTERED AMETHYST

SPLINTERED EMERALD

SALVAGING MARIGOLD

River's End Rescues Series

COCKY SAVIOR

SOME REGRETS ARE FOREVER

SOME FEARS CAN CONTROL YOU

SOME LIES WILL HAUNT YOU

SOME QUESTIONS HAVE NO ANSWERS

SOME TRUTH CAN BE DISTORTED

SOME TRUST CAN BE REBUILT

SOME MISTAKES ARE UNFORGIVABLE

Candella Sisters' Heroes Series

LITTLE DOLLS

LITTLE HEARTS

LITTLE BALLERINA

Storybook Murders Series

NURSERY RHYME KILLER

FAIRYTALE KILLER

FABLE KILLER

Saving SEALs Series

SAVING RYDER

SAVING ERIC

SAVING OWEN

SAVING LOGAN

SAVING GRAYSON

SAVING CHARLIE

Prey Security Series

PROTECTING EAGLE

PROTECTING RAVEN

PROTECTING FALCON

PROTECTING SPARROW

PROTECTING HAWK

PROTECTING DOVE

Prey Security: Alpha Team Series

DEADLY RISK

LETHAL RISK

EXTREME RISK

FATAL RISK

COVERT RISK

SAVAGE RISK

Prey Security: Artemis Team Series

IVORY'S FIGHT

PEARL'S FIGHT

LACEY'S FIGHT

OPAL'S FIGHT

Prey Security: Bravo Team Series

VICIOUS SCARS

RUTHLESS SCARS

Christmas Romantic Suspense Series

CHRISTMAS HOSTAGE

CHRISTMAS CAPTIVE

CHRISTMAS VICTIM

YULETIDE PROTECTOR

YULETIDE GUARD

YULETIDE HERO

HOLIDAY GRIEF

Conquering Fear Series (Co-written with Amanda Siegrist)

DROWNING IN YOU

OUT OF THE DARKNESS

CLOSING IN

About the Author

USA Today bestselling author Jane Blythe writes action-packed romantic suspense and military romance featuring protective heroes and heroines who are survivors. One of Jane's most popular series includes Prey Security, part of Susan Stoker's OPERATION ALPHA world! Writing in that world alongside authors such as Janie Crouch and Riley Edwards has been a blast, and she looks forward to bringing more books to this genre, both within and outside of Stoker's world. When Jane isn't binge-reading she's counting down to Christmas and adding to her 200+ teddy bear collection!

To connect and keep up to date please visit any of the following

www.ingramcontent.com/pod-product-compliance
Lightning Source LLC
Chambersburg PA
CBHW031612240626
47153CB00002B/723

Dear Dad

Letters to Our Fathers

compiled by:

Vanessa Canteberry

Table of Contents

Dedication

This book is dedicated to fathers who find themselves not truly understanding the importance of their presence, regardless of the relationship they have with the other parent. Too many fathers have the potential to have an amazing relationship with their children, but for some reason, life lessons take over, and the child is placed on pause in the process.

So many fathers don't get recognized for their dedication and determination to be an amazing dad to their children. Too often they are overlooked and/or pushed to the side due to the lack of representation of men who walked out. It's not fair that he has to pay the consequences for their shortcomings.

For the fathers who constantly have taken a backseat, who stepped in when others stepped away, for being consistent no matter what, we honor you. You are appreciated.

We need your time and your presence so we will see the world through your eyes. Show us the way, regardless of what transpired in your upbringing or relationship with your parents.

We need you more than you may ever understand. We will always be your little girl, no matter how old we get or even when we have a family of our own. Can you take time to focus on us and build our everlasting bond?

Love always,
Your Child

Introduction

Too often men don't understand their value in a child's life due to their own life experience of their parent(s) walking away, thus leaving the child to question themselves along the way.

When life gets too tough, men break down in silence and close other people out so they can figure it out themselves. At the same time, when you have figured it out, the children have built a wall up because they are unsure if and when you will walk away again. Then there are parents who use the child as a pawn because they have built up anger and resentment to have to raise a child alone, so the child suffers yet again.

Then there are the fathers who are willing to put up a fight to stay the course of instilling love, affection, and life tools into their child(ren), no matter what. Creating memories to look back on and share with others. Understanding it will not always be easy, and there will be challenges; you will go to battle and stand your ground. Providing a way when it seems as if there is no way, yet persevering through it all.

Linking arms with you may feel like a task we are willing to fight together in order to win the war of not becoming what others want us to become, which is an absentee father, abuser, womanizer, and the list goes on and on. For you to take a stand to beat the odds of what society labels you is a bold and courageous step to prove them wrong.

You are the hero we look up to, who comes in to save the day, even if it means having to teach us tough love when we made a bad decision. We need you to continue to be the road map to navigate us through life lessons, even if we have to learn them together.

It will be a challenge, but we rather for you to stay and resolve the puzzle in full view than do it alone. There will be times when it seems unbearable, but I want to stand by your side, rooting you on, just as you have been rooting me on to be great in this world. Seeing you from the sidelines of one of my many activities makes me scream with excitement knowing you did not forget me.

Then there is a moment when I prayed for you to attend one of my activities, and you left me disappointed again and with no other choice than to keep smiling as if nothing is wrong. Giving you the benefit of the doubt that you will at least call to say you are on the way or we will celebrate my latest accomplishments.

Either way, dads, we need you to remember we are part of you. We need to know the other half of us. The story cannot be complete if there's no knowing how the story will end, if you are not willing to play your part.

There's a mixture of untold stories some good, bad and even the ones that left you feeling unwilling to share but it can help someone else, so we decided to come together and share our stories.

I hope you enjoy the letters from these amazing ladies who had a variety of experience with their dad.

The Angels That Carry Me

By:
Laura Jones

Dear Dad,

First, I want to thank you for meeting my mom in order to create me. She never had anything bad to say about you, so I'm assuming the two of you parted on good terms. I'm not sure if you knew you had a daughter, but I'm here. I'll give you the benefit of doubt that you had no clue I ever existed.

However, if you were aware of my existence, then I have so much I would like to share with you.

I entered into this world on June 9, 1969, at Queen's General Hospital in New York City. I roughly weighed maybe about six pounds. My mom had a hard time delivering me. I wish you were there to comfort her through her fear and pain. In case you didn't know, Dad, Mom was a trooper. God decided to keep her in your absence.

I'm sure it was hard on her to raise my brothers and me. However, she made it work.

Dad, I am a product of my mother's strength. I began to watch my mom handle everything by herself, and she handled it with dignity and grace. Her most important daily commitment was to make sure I wanted for nothing. Even in your absence, she prevailed. When I thought I could not do something, she encouraged me to conquer anything and everything that was placed in front of me.

Growing up as a little girl, I always wondered what part of you was of me. Was it my facial features? My height? Or my personality? Dad, I will never know because your mere presence never existed. I wish you were there on those days that I just couldn't figure things out. Even though I was strong, growing up was a process. It was a process of figuring out just where I actually fit in with this thing called 'life.'

I remember, as a little girl, I would find my 'safe place.' My first memorable 'safe place' was a field at my grandparents' house. This field would have a patch of flowers that I loved visiting. I would go out there every day and pretend that was my home. I was in a world of my own and so comfortable.

You see, Dad, I was working on filling that void. There were times I would sit there and envision you coming across the field to check on me to see what I was up to. I would picture you picking me up, holding me and spinning me around. I wish I had memories of some sort of contact. Everything that I wished for that a father and daughter should share was just a figment of my imagination.

I wanted to walk across the field with you while holding your hand and believing that we were untouchable. I wanted to be able to hear your voice and see the look in your eyes whenever you saw me.

There were times I would just think about all of the conversations that we would have about whatever was on my mind. However, there was complete silence; it was just my thoughts and dreams.

I figured one day everything that I wished for would come true. I remember a man that my mom had dated and that I had sat on his lap, but it was not you. He was a nice man, but I still felt empty but accepted. That void existed in me, and I was destined to fulfill it.

There was a time in my life where that void I felt was filled. It all started when I was living with my grandparents in Prospect, Virginia. At first, adjusting to a different area was a bit confusing from being only with my mother and then transitioning to a totally different state to live with my grandparents.

As grandparents do, they welcomed my brothers and me with open and loving arms. I learned firsthand at an early age how to work hard and enjoy life all at the same time.

My grandfather was my greatest inspiration. He treated me with the utmost respect and portrayed the love and protection that I would expect from my real father. I have memories of going to work with him when I did not have a sitter. My grandfather worked in the logging business and formerly worked for the railroad. I remember going into the woods with him while he worked. The motion of the truck as my grandfather drove was an experience. As the truck rolled on top of the tree stumps, I would feel the big truck go side to side.

There were times that my grandfather would carry me on his shoulders when he was looking for good lumber to cut. Once he found it, he would take me back to the truck and instruct me to just sit there and wait until he returned. He didn't go far because he wanted to have me in his eyesight, and I in his. I would hear that chainsaw consistently running and then, all of a sudden, a thump. That tree had fallen and then the chainsaw continued. My fear was, whenever that chainsaw was running, that a tree would fall on him. However, my grandfather was so skilled, and that never happened. He was a strong man because it took strength to cut down all those trees and load the truck up by himself. That, to me as a little girl, was amazing to see someone do all that work by himself and remain humble. When it was time for lunch, he would come back to the truck and have lunch with me and discuss whatever came to mind. Those times were very precious to me.

For me, the feeling of feeling safe and feeling that I can be myself around him was priceless. My grandfather showed me how a man can go out and work hard for his family and be compassionate when it's necessarily needed. I feel the love that my grandfather portrayed in my life exceeded everything that I could have received from my own father. He created a foundation that I could build on that taught me how a father should perform in a little girl's life.

When my grandfather became ill from cancer, I watched the strongest man I knew waste away. Even though his body was fragile, his mind remained strong. Sitting by his side and never wanting to leave.

When I lost my grandfather to cancer years ago, my world became dark. I felt that everything positive that I built up within me came crashing down in front of me. The memories of him came to a halt, and the feeling of starting all over again, of having a father-like figure in my life, ceased. That was a turning point in my life. However, I held onto the memories that I could gather of the love that he had shown me all those years.

I became a loner within myself, and I was happy with that decision. It's not that I don't care for people to be around; it's just that when they decide to leave, I would be okay or at least pretend to be okay. Dad, I wish you were there to just take the pain away.

In my adolescent years, I was a little comfortable with who I was; however, still wondering why my biological dad was not around to watch me grow. It's true that I had several male mentors in my life growing up, but it was not the same. That feeling of security and protection from an unknown world. My father was not there to teach me about the dangers I may face, the heartaches I may encounter, or the lessons to be learned growing up as a child.

When I became a teenager, his presence was greatly needed, as I was entering into a world and trying to become more secure in who I was. I was steadily building a character that I was comfortable with portraying. I was looking for that father figure in whomever I could find it from. That constant connection with someone to make me feel that everything was going to be okay. I needed guidance and a sense of direction which I feel only my father could have provided.

I wondered if people would place me in a category of being 'a fatherless child.' It is true that I have my mother's strength, but that child in me that yearns for her father still lingers. I began noticing other families that had the love of both their mother and their father. It appeared to me that their lives were so perfect and that I constantly was in a state of confusion and trying to pretend that everything was all right within me.

Inside, I was a wreck, feeling lost, conquered and worthless. My emotions were all over the place. I did mention I was a 'teenager'; that within itself is quite a struggle, and being without a father really started to become full circle.

When I got my first job, I had questions and concerns about interacting with people from a father's point of view. I remember my first date, which in turn was my first heartache. I thank God for my brother who was there for me when I experienced it and comforted me. I don't think my mother knew, but a mother can always feel what her daughter was going through.

I missed my dad at my graduation from high school, which was a huge milestone. To see me walking across the stage to receive my diploma would have been such a joy if he would have taken that walk with me. I am not saying that my family was not there to support me, but I needed my dad to complete this process with me.

Now the world awaits me, and what lies ahead is unknown. So I ventured out on my own. I was still searching for that security and protection anywhere I could find it. There were times I ended up searching for it in all the wrong places and experiencing continued heartbreaks and disappointments.

I began living a life with a hidden pain. I would smile and interact with others, but deep inside, the void existed. On August 14, 1992, and September 9, 2004, I became a mother of two handsome sons. Again, the cycle repeated itself, as I myself birthed two 'fatherless children.' At this point, I had to provide my sons with the love they needed, being that their father was not there to actively participate in their lives. I constantly thought about what their world would be like with a father. As they grew older, I always wondered if they would develop this feeling that I felt all those years.

I tried to play the mother and the father for the longest time. If I began dating again, I only dated someone with father-like qualities and had children of their own. I wanted their world to be complete. I had to come to the realization how could I try to portray someone I never had in my own life?

Throughout the course of my life, I've tried on several occasions searching for my father. Being that I was informed that he was in the military, I searched the area in which he was stationed for duty. It was a difficult process because his name was George Gray, which is a very common name. I used to look through the phone directory, and I started calling every George Grays in the New York City area. I became desperate and then eventually losing hope.

I wished that my father had put in the effort in finding me as I was for him. I felt that if he missed the majority of my life, then I could find him so that he can be with me now. I wanted him to come accustomed to my world.

I envisioned the day that I would finally meet him. I created in my mind how he would look and how we would react once we've found each other. I pictured having long talks with him, telling him every event that took place in my life. You never give up hope because you know that in some state, he exists. You get to the point that you feel his presence surround you but not in person.

I know if I ever met my father, I would give him the biggest hug and let him know that even in his absence, he was loved. I'm sure that he would look at me in a strange way and wonder why his daughter that he never met loved him so dearly.

I will let him know that even though he was not there, I never was truly angry; I was just unsure as to why he never stayed. I had more questions rather than resentment. That chapter in my life that can never be fulfilled until I had more answers.

As I became older and more mature in my life, I gave up looking for my father. I came to the conclusion that even though he was not in my life, I became that fearless individual who loves life and her children. Life for me was not easy at all, but it takes commitment. There were so many responsibilities added to my plate.

Everything I wanted in life, I worked for it. I became that woman who always believed that just because you did not have a father in your life does not define who you are. As a matter of fact, having no father created in me a powerful spirit. I learned to fight for what I believe in, never giving up on my responsibilities. I became a warrior against all obstacles. I fought hard for my children in order to make sure their lives were not affected by not having a father.

You begin to accept the fact that it was not your fault for not having a father in your life. You appreciate everyone that God has placed in your path throughout the years mentoring and praying for you. All of life's obstacles and setbacks were just a test for you to grow into a stronger person.

Once you create within yourself who you are and whom you've become, life becomes easy to live and to love without restrictions. Throughout life, in his absence, I finished high school, attended and graduated from college with my associates in legal studies and raised two wonderful young men.

I've learned that no matter who you are, the absence of your father should never decrease your self-worth in life. How you determine the outcome of your life is based on your experiences and how you handled them. I had to learn that the father I never knew was always a part of me that I had to find within myself.

My outlook on life at this very moment is beautiful. When you finally have made peace within yourself, you realize that a loss is actually a gain. Someone's absence never determines your growth.

ABOUT THE AUTHOR

 Laura Jones was born in Jamaica Queens, New York, and at an early age transitioned and raised in Virginia. Her main goal in life is to become an individual with a purpose to ensure that not only her dreams come true but that she also assists others in achieving their goal by mentoring them. Laura worked in many different careers in her life, including restaurant, medical, mental health and is currently working as a paralegal at a law firm (for over twelve years now). She works part-time as a rideshare driver, which enables her to interact with many individuals and hear their stories. She believes everybody has a story and a solution. She is a single mother of two boys; she teaches them consistently about life and maintaining their self-worth throughout their course in life and to be purpose-driven.

As she matured in her legal field, she began to venture out into other areas of her life and follow her passion. She believes that everyone should have a voice in what they truly believe in. She strives for excellence in not only herself but the lives of others. She's hoping that her story will reach others who had gone through life without a father so they realize that the pain within does not have to determine the outcome of their future.

Feel free to stay connected with Laura Jones via email at Lauraej991@gmail.com

My Daddy

By:
Pam Murray

Dear Daddy,

There 'they' are again. Ever since I decided to become part of this anthology, it seems like everywhere I look, I see fathers and daughters. It is like when I was having surgery, and I was told not to eat after midnight. It seems like the food was everywhere. The McDonald's sign was bigger and more yellow, and I wanted everything. I could not get the thought of food out of my head. I thought about dropping out of this project so many times. I was feeling like "why should I bother and why did it matter?" I felt as if I was drowning in my own pain and despair, and I did not have the patience or energy to even begin to express how I feel about you. I am just so tired and frustrated that I did not want to try. But there 'they' are again. Another 'Father and daughter duo' right in my face. Again, a reminder of what I need to do. I have to push all of my madness aside and do this.

"For you"... That sounds funny. It seems like you have always done for me. And you did. And still do. I find that as I begin to think about what I want to say to you, I find you everywhere. I think of you often. I heard in a class that life is broken up into a series of events. An event is when your life can be broken up into a 'before' and an 'after' like when Nana died or when I fell and had to have surgery and was out of work. When I look back over these 'events,' I find that you were the thread that stitched things back together. When there was no heat or the car broke down or whatever happened, you were always the one who came up with the answer even though sometimes I did not understand. But now, you are having 'events.' You do your best to shield me from it, but I still see. I can't visit as much as I would like to, but I still see.

As we both get older, I am faced with the concept of losing you. It is inevitable. Just this past week, a nurse at my job received a phone call at work that her father had just passed away. I was stunned. I felt for her. It felt like there was no oxygen in the room, and I could not breathe. All I thought of was you. What if it was me getting that call? What would I do? Who would I call? There would have been so many things that would have been left unsaid. I want you to know that I am proud of you. I admire your strength. I know you did not tell me things because you did not want me to worry. You are a survivor, and now you are faced with another health challenge. I want you to know that you have done an excellent job. You did the best you could with what you had.

You may not have had the best example of a father, but you were always there for me even now. You taught me. You did it. You have raised a daughter who can fight with the intensity of a man but is also compassionate and kind-hearted. You have raised a daughter who can see possibilities that not even you can see. You have raised a daughter who can find within herself whatever is needed to bring to whatever situation that she is presented with. She brings strength, hope, and faith. You talk about my 'pie in the sky' religion, but you don't realize that I got that from you. Faith is not about words. Faith is about action, and you always took action. Whatever problem, you did something about it. Whether it was right or was wrong, you did something or tried to.

It was after work. I was on the number 3 train going to Penn Station. Sitting next to me was a young father and his two little girls. The older girl reached over and removed her father's hat and put it on her head. She smiled proudly as if to say, "I'm wearing my daddy's hat," and he smiled back at her. That hat looked ridiculous - obviously too big. The hat just engulfed her small head. But her smile was so big and so bright, and when he smiled back, he showed all of his 32 teeth, and his smile was even bigger than hers. I noticed the lady sitting across from us. She was looking and smiling too. I could not help being happy and smiling, but I had to wipe a tear away from my eyes. I thought of you, Daddy.

Looking back, not through the eyes of a playful child or an emotional wreck of a teen-aged girl or a rebellious and stubborn young woman but through the eyes of a 53-year-old Registered Nurse who has witnessed both the best and the worst of what life has to offer, I can truly say that these are my fondest memories of you, Daddy. You were my first playmate. I remember, as a young child, Mommy would pick me up from Nana's house. We would sing, and she would cuddle me and make me laugh and feed me and bathe me and put me in my pajamas and put me to bed. But when you came home it did not matter what she did or how many hours it took her to do it (sorry, Mom) it was 'Play Time!' I would get up and run around all of a sudden rejuvenated and energized just because Daddy was home. Everything my mom spent hours doing was undone in a few seconds. I remember my poor mother saying, almost pleading, "I just fed her!" or "I just put her in bed!" I remember deciding, as a young girl, that I never wanted 'Mommy-Role.' No, sir, not me. It was too much work. I want 'Daddy-Role' when I came home, it was 'Play Time,' and nothing else mattered.

'Play Time' whether we went to the shooting range, or we were playing Knock Hockey in the living room or listening to music and you were teaching me how to dance or playing badminton in the backyard constitutes my fondest memories of you. I remember you telling the story of when you heard a noise and went to check on me and found me (or so you say) sitting in the middle of the floor ripping up newspaper, or me wanting to have long hair so bad that I walked around with a towel on my head or when something in the house was broken, and you asked me who broke it, and I said, "Batman did."

I remember playing one day at Nana's house. I was running towards you, trying to catch you. That was our little game, and on this particular day, you side-stepped me, and I kept running. You extended your hand to catch me right before I fell into the bushes. And you have been extending your hand and keeping me from falling into the bushes ever since. I remember getting up early in the morning and driving to New York with you and Mommy every day. I would wake up in the back seat, and Mommy would be sleeping, and you would be driving. You would drive Mommy to work, and then we would take the trip to Nana's house on 159th Street and 8th Avenue. The walk from the car to Nana's house was our time. We would play, and I would try to catch you. And you would say that you were so fast sometimes you were. Nana would take me to school. Mommy would pick me up after she got off work. We would drive to the entrance of the Lincoln tunnel where you would be waiting. You would get in the car, and we would be on our way home.

Over the years, our relationship has been stressed and strained, but somehow, you could always make me laugh. Even when I thought you were being unfair or I thought you did not love me, we have always shared that special bond. I am so thankful that God has prolonged both of our lives long enough so that I have the opportunity to tell you exactly how I feel. It is a rare gift to be over 50 years of age and have my father still alive. I can't imagine going through life without a father, even though many women do. This is a blessing denied to many, and most people, both male and female, would love to be in my shoes.

Sometimes we have to grow out of the playfulness of childhood, the stubbornness of the teenage years and the rebelliousness of young adulthood to truly appreciate what has always been present. You have always told me the truth. You always kept it 100% about everything, from how much things costs to the truth about people. You taught me how to plan something and stick with it until something better comes along. You have been my greatest supporter. You are the only reason I got my BSN degree. I was injured a month after I started the program, and I told you I was going to quit. You said that I was going to go to school, and you and Mommy moved in and took me to school and to Physical Therapy, even though you had your own health problems at the time.

I never told you but I knew long before you said anything to me. You show your love through your actions. I heard someone say that a father's role is three things protection, provision, and presence. Now that I am older, I can take the necessary steps to protect myself. I have an education so I can provide for myself, but your presence is yours alone, and people can't provide it for me. And that is what I miss most your presence.

As I sit on the train, and I look at the two young girls interacting with their father, I wonder, *Does a father's presence make life easier? Does it guarantee a good life? Does it make for a good home, a loving spouse, and adorable children?* No. Sadly, it does not. What it does provide is a safe place to retreat when things are not good. I find that when I'm here, I just think of you sometimes of funny things that happened, sometimes of conversations we had, sometimes of me talking about life in general and you saying, "I don't know, Pam." The memories of the fun we had are precious to me, especially now. When I am down, I look back and remember us. Not the difficult years, but 'Play Time.' You are my first playmate and my best friend. Sometimes when we are together and even sometimes over the phone, I still catch glimpses of when I was wearing a towel on my head or you catching me before I fall into the bushes. I look forward to our conversations about my day that I remember and cherish. This is what made me me who I am. Just me and you. Me and my daddy. I love you.

ABOUT THE AUTHOR

 Pam Murray was born in New York and moved to New Jersey at the age of 5 years. She received a Bachelor of Arts degree from New York University, a Bachelor of Science degree from College of Saint Elizabeth and a Masters degree in Public Administration.

She hopes to return to NYU to complete the Nurse Practitioner program. She works as a Unit Manager at a Nursing Home in New York.

She enjoys crochet, dancing and going on boat rides.

Feel free to stay connected with Pam Murray at at SistahPam@gmail.com.

Because of You, I Found ME

By:
Basheba Maiden

Dear Dad,

I have had so much that I have wanted to tell you for so many years. So much that I wish you knew about me. So, I take this time now to let you know how your absence and your existence has made me the woman that I am today.

As a young girl, I remember you sporadically being in me and my siblings' lives. I remember being very quiet, timid, with no sense of my identity; a little girl that did not smile much. In elementary school, I was the class clown. That is the way I received attention because I could not verbalize how I felt inside, so I expressed it outwardly. I was the little girl who was defiant by fighting and being a bully. Not having you around really impacted my life. Those were the years that I needed your love. I needed to hear that I was special. I needed to hear that I was beautiful. I needed to hear that I was the apple of your eyes. Those few times that you came to

24

pick us up to spend time with you meant the world to me.

My love for horses was because of you letting us ride the horses, as you trained them at the racetrack. Those were the times, times when life felt great. I didn't have a worry in the world because, for that moment, everything felt right. I was spending time with my daddy. We enjoyed ourselves when spending time with you in New Orleans. Those times were so fun; you made us laugh you were so funny, and you gave us whatever we wanted. I'm smiling because those were the times. You drank, and we laughed because you would fall down and need our help picking you up, but we didn't care because we were with you. But then those times became short-lived and then non-existent. When you stopped coming around, it made me question a lot about myself, creating a lot of inadequacies within such as low-self-esteem, fear, abandonment. This little girl desired a relationship with her father.

As I continued to grow up without you, I continued to fight. I continued to be defiant. I continued to bully people. These were all things I did to deal with the little girl who was hurt, rejected … I wasn't happy when my mama remarried at first because I did not want anyone to take your place. You were supposed to be with us, but the thing about it is, he stepped up and treated us like his own. We were never his stepchildren; we were his children. In my heart, I longed for you to fulfill your role as Dad, but it didn't happen. Your visits were sporadic and few and far in between. I didn't get any calls from you wishing me a Happy Birthday. I didn't get any calls from you wishing me a Merry Christmas nor did I receive any gifts from you. The thing that I know, though, is that you were a good man, a hard worker, very independent, despite your disability, and one of the funniest men I know, but you lacked in the fathering department.

I grew up looking for your love, your acceptance. I knew that my sister was your favorite. She could treat you any kind of way, and you still gave her anything that she asked you if you had it. I knew that my brother was my mama's favorite, and y'all, too, had a bond. I did not feel like I had a place; I did not feel like I was anyone's favorite. Your cruel words and remarks confirmed that. Those times that I acted out again, it was because I wanted some attention too.

It was your job and my mama's job as parents to show me love. I grew up not knowing what love was. I started to get the attention of boys. That attention, to me, made me feel special and wanted and I navigated towards that. This soon led to a life of promiscuity. Not for the enjoyment, but for that moment, it met my emotional need to feel loved. The love I desperately needed at that time … I was headed down a downward spiral of self-destruction. I struggled within myself throughout life, trying to find meaning for my existence. I drank, did drugs, tried to fit in, people-pleased, etc., nothing filled the void. I struggled to finish high school. I just did not

26

believe that I would amount to anything in life. The reason why I didn't quit was because I did not want to disappoint my brother. My brother has been my protector, my role model since I can remember. When I was scared, he let me sleep with him or on the floor in his room. He protected me when my sister tried to bully me. He was there for every monumental occasion in my life. My brother, at that time, was the dad I never had. Dad, you missed my high school graduation.

I went to college with the intention of becoming a Nurse. Two years into my collegiate studies, I changed my major to Rehabilitation Services. I wanted to help people … One of my college professors encouraged me to complete an internship at the Baton Rouge Detox Center due to my love for people. Little did she know this internship would change my life. As long as I can remember, you had addiction to alcohol, and I do not ever know a time that I saw you sober. I felt like this internship would provide me the means to help you get sober one day. I graduated from college, but again, you were not there. Another accomplishment without you.

I got married at 24 years old to a man who was old enough to be my father. He loved me. He took care of me. I realize now that he was the father figure I still desired in you. He had an addiction too, to alcohol and drugs. He was a mean drunk. He got physical with me when he would go on alcohol and drug binges. That was short-lived. I left him the morning of Hurricane Katrina after he attempted to killed me.

You were affected by Hurricane Katrina. You had to be rescued from the flood and evacuated to Texas. Then you decided to come and live with my mom's sister. The thing that I am most grateful for is that I chose to forgive you for not being an active part of my life and chose to foster a relationship with you. You were my dad. I still wanted you to be a part of my life. We were able to share laughs, create memories. Then, in February 2006, a day I will never forget, I get a call, saying you are not breathing, and the paramedics are working on you. I knew then you were gone; without warning, without notice you were gone. Some may say you died of a heart attack, but alcoholism was the cause. When I think of you or share your story with others struggling with addiction, the thing that I hate the most is that alcoholism killed you because you did not recognize that you had a problem.

Since then, I have received a master's degree, remarried, bought a house and have created a great career for myself. I have since assisted thousands of men and women on their road to recovery, and I dedicate it to you. I imagine that everyone I help is you if you ever acknowledged that you had a problem. Your life and your memory live on through me.

Dad, I want you to know that I truly have forgiven you, and I love you. I believe that you did your best with what you had. I am happy for the memories that we did create. My life, my story still has a purpose, and despite everything that I have been through, I am happy. I do not have children of my own, but I make sure that I am a vital part of my nieces', nephews', great-nieces' and great-nephews' lives. Through me, they will know what love and support looks like.

Dad, I have your work ethics and humor. That you gave me for free. I longed to hear "You're beautiful," "You're special," "I love you." Maybe I wouldn't have made so many bad relationship choices.

I am thankful that I found Jesus. He became what you couldn't be. Every empty, broken place in my life has been filled with His Love. This is the BEST decision I have ever made in my life.

Your presence and the lack of has played a significant role in my life. I have made mistakes but had an opportunity to learn. I battled with figuring out who I was and why I was allowed to be born, but I had an opportunity to find my purpose. I battled with my worth but had the opportunity to find the jewel within myself.

I realize that I belong here, that you were instrumental in me becoming who I am today. So, thank you, Dad. I appreciate you as a person.

Words of Advice

Dads, you are needed. You are a vital part of your child(ren)'s life. You are one of the first people to show and teach your child what love looks like and feels like. Children are entrusted into your care. Materialistic gifts cannot take the place of your time. Your child(ren) could avoid a lot of mistakes by having you around. Children don't care what areas you lack in; they just want you and need you around. Spending time with your child(ren) is free. Your child(ren)'s love is without judgment and is pure.

ABOUT THE AUTHOR

 Basheba Maiden is a multi-faceted individual, from ministry to relationship strategist to addiction professional; a downright fun-loving individual. Through the word of God and the power of the Holy Spirit, she breaks down walls of brokenness, insecurity, and rejection. In relationships and/or marriages, she equips men and women with a spiritual and natural action plan to not only restore relationships but to foster a relationship that thrives. As an addiction professional, she provides knowledge and real-life, no-nonsense techniques to catapult patients with addiction on the road to recovery. Lastly, as an individual, Basheba is witty, compassionate, and makes everybody feel special.

Basheba Maiden has overcome many obstacles in life, including rejection, brokenness, promiscuity, divorce, low self-esteem and self-worth, and destructive behavior patterns. She has conquered them all through the power of Christ and His agents on earth.

God has utilized her pain to promote her to her purpose. Basheba utilizes the same premise with the clients she serves. There is purpose in pain, happiness after bitterness, and victory in all situations.

Basheba Maiden is a native of Lafayette, Louisiana, but currently resides in Denham Springs, LA. She is a graduate of Southern University, Baton Rouge Campus, with a Bachelor's Degree in Rehabilitation Services, a Master's Degree in Rehabilitation Counseling, an Associate's Degree of Divinity Christian Education from the Don Bradford Bible College, Baton Rouge Campus. Basheba is a licensed and ordained minister, relationship strategist, addiction professional and self-proclaimed comedian.

In her spare time, Basheba loves to spend time studying the word of God, spending time with family and friends, especially with her host of nieces and nephews, serving as an example and mentor for them. She loves to travel, read books, and enjoys lots of self-care.

Feel free to stay connected with Basheba Maiden on Social Media at

www.Facebook.com/BashebaMaiden
www.Instagram.com/IamBasheba
www.Twitter.com/IamBasheba

Broken Wings

By
Trica Pringle

Dear Dad,

I apologize for not being who you wanted me to be in the beginning of my life. I didn't ask to be here; you brought me into this world. Instead of having my first love be my father, it was a heartbreak that I just can't get over. There I was, a little girl craving your love as a father, friend and mentor

I will never understand why you left your little girl. I don't even know when you left me. I grew up with my mom and her parents and that side of the family, and your mom and her family that lived in that house. Never met anyone from your side of the family; if I did meet anyone, I don't remember. Why is that? Did they even know about me, or was I one of those secrets that you don't talk about? Did your wives even know about me? Did you ever think of me while you were gone? I thought of you all the time; I would even daydream about things, about you as a father to me.

I remember when I first saw you. You came to my grandma's

house and knocked on the door, and why this stands out to me is the fact that you had to bend to get in the house, and my mom was like, "Your dad here," and I was scared. You were so tall, and I didn't know you, had not seen you before. I went with you, and we went to get ice cream, and then we went to your mother's house. And after the visit there, I didn't see you again for a while.

There's another time I remember when I went to your mom, and you were there, and I didn't even know you were in there. You were sitting at the table, drinking a beer, and you were shocked to see me. It seemed that you didn't even want me to know that you were there. You played it off well; I felt the tension, and I didn't truly understand it. When I got older and was trying to figure things out, I got the idea that you didn't want me, and it finally sunk in. I never gave up hope that you would love me as a father should.

There was this one time that I guess the army called and said that you were missing, that they found your car on the side of the road, and you were nowhere to be found. Everyone was worried, and they called to tell me, and I was numb, not knowing how to really feel about the whole thing. I admit that I was scared that I wouldn't see you again when I learned that you didn't stay in the states. You were overseas and married to someone else. You left me in a space wondering why you never told me about my stepmom, or did she even know about me?

Also, there was a time that I couldn't go outside because there was a rumor going around that you were trying to kidnap me. As for me, that rumor made me smile. I even packed a bag and had it at a friend's house, and I used to sneak out of the house so you wouldn't find me. Yes, I was ready to go away from all this. All I knew was that Daddy wanted me finally, he wanted me to come to him. I found out later that this happened while I was in elementary school

In high school years, I started to fight and run away a lot. I didn't feel like I belonged to that family anymore. I just wanted to leave and stay gone. I was still looking for someone to feel that void, and I finally thought I had found it in a guy a city away from mine. He was so amazing to me, and I would always run away to see him. Then one day he got shot. I was so sad, so I made plans to go visit him. So, of course, I ran away again and saw him in the hospital. I stayed for a couple of days before I was caught and brought home, and when I got back, I went to a juvenile. My mom wanted to send me to job corp; I didn't care anymore. Something happened that I couldn't go, so I was stuck once again with someone who didn't want me. I always felt like I didn't belong; I felt unwanted.

I got pregnant at the age of 15, and you came to see me, but not for what I thought you came for. You picked me up, and we drove around talking until you hit me with the question, "Can I have your unborn child?" I was so shocked by that question I didn't know what to say. How could you want my unborn child and not me? Were you trying to fix a mistake that was sitting next to you, or was it that it was a boy I was carrying?

So, after I had the baby, my mom made us get married. She held jail over his head and threatened to send him away over me, but that same night, my mom kicked me and my son out in the rain while my grandma just sat there. That night, I learned what domestic violence was. I stayed for my child and me; I had nowhere to go. Living in a small town where everyone knew everything, it was hard to hide, even though I tried my best. I keep having children by him in between the fights. Later, I learned the reason why he was like that towards me.

Why did I stay? I have so many reasons for staying. The one that sticks out to me is, I didn't want my kids to grow up like me without both parents, plus where was I going? I was left alone to figure it out. Broken wings with a broken spirit; family not talking to me; trying to find help in a place that didn't want me.

When I did finally get the courage to leave him and raise my children on my own, after a few weeks, I had a change of heart and let him back in, still not wanting my kids to be raised by one parent. Yet it didn't work out. We did keep trying till I just gave up and left my children with their family and let someone raise them. I was more like you at the moment that it sent me into a tailspin that I did not think I would recover from, but by His grace, I have recovered.

Now, everything wasn't bad in my world. I had a set of triplet boys that are fifteen right now, and I keep reminding myself that they are a gift from my higher power. I have finally decided to forgive you so I can move on. I'm also going for my dreams that I thought I couldn't achieve. I have changed that little girl growing up into that woman that you would be proud of one day.

My children talk to each other; yes, they have siblings' disagreement, and that's OK with me. I talk to my boys every now and then. I know they're still upset with me; I'm just glad they let me in their life even if through Facebook. I'll take any means necessary. I did them the same way you did me, and I'm hoping that one day, they forgive me. I didn't mean to be like you. Hey, I ended up being like you after all. What more can I say? We are more alike than we know, even if we never spent time together. I am my father's child; your blood run inside of me, and you will always be a part of me. My children and I still wonder to this day: *Did you even try? Did they do something or say something wrong? What was the reason that you never fought for me? Or why was it just a couple of phone calls and a couple of visits?* I never asked you these questions.

I don't know if you're alive or deceased since I don't talk to your family. I don't even know how to get hold of them. Even if I wanted to, it's been so long that the only person I remember is your mother and the house location; everything else is so blurry. Some of my memory is gone for good; that's another story.

Wishing you were part of my life at the beginning. Maybe you were thinking that if you weren't there, you couldn't mess it up anyway. The universe had other ideas when it came to us, and this time, I want to apologize for not being what you wanted. I have learned from all my lifetime lessons that I'm enough, and that's what matters most.

In ending this letter, I learned that my broken wings have survived being broken and that they can heal and fly again. As for us, I will always have the spirit of fight. I understand that I will always stay and fight. I love you for what you taught me in your absence. And even though I will never know the real reason, I forgave you and me so I can grow in my life.

Love you wherever you are,
Trica Pringle

ABOUT THE AUTHOR

Trica Pringle was born and raised in Warren, Ohio, and resides in Las Vegas, Nevada. She's a stay-at-home mom who loves writing poetry and spending time with her family and friends. Trica is dedicated to making a change by sharing her journey with other women, letting them know they have the strength to survive anything once they put their mind to it.

Trica is ready to branch out sharing her story in hopes of making an imprint to other women fighting to overcome what broke them.

Feel free to stay connected with Trica Pringle on Social Media at:

www.Facebook.com/tricapringle
www.Instgram.com/tricapringle702

Release From Guilt

By
Ira Warren

Dear Dad,

Dad do you know how I feel?

I'm sitting here at my computer, typing this letter to you, and the tears will not subside. It's been three years since we last talked over the phone. The last thing you said to me was that you loved me, and you never want to have anything else to do with me. (*pause tears*) I do miss you sometimes. Some of the things I miss about you dad were your jokes, your encouraging words, your laughter, and you telling me everything was going to be ok when the struggles of life got hard for me to bear. In my mind, I thought our daddy-daughter relationship took a turn for the better. Once again, I was robbed of a relationship with you. I cried for 5 days straight, Daddy. I was depressed. I thought you were in full support of me sharing my truth. Weren't you the one that told my husband I needed to share my story? I beat myself up for opening my mouth to the world about being molested by you.

It just hurts that you made the decision to never speak to me again. I thought you were in full support of me sharing our story. Yes, Daddy, our story. It was time to pull the secrets from under the rug. The little girl, your daughter on the inside of me, just wanted you to love her unconditionally. She wanted you to protect and keep her safe. Yet you were the one she feared the most. Even in the midst of all the abuse, I still appreciate the things you did do right. I'm grateful to God that I even had a dad in the home. I'm grateful that you provided for me. But Dad, you must understand that as a child, I felt I had to satisfy your needs to feel worthy of love. For many years, I blame myself for your sickness. You told me I had to obey and do everything I was told to do. Daddy, in all honesty, when I couldn't live up to your expectations, I gave up fighting you to give you what you wanted.

At the age of 4, I was intuitive enough to know what you were doing and saying to me was wrong. You told me that it was Daddy's duty to teach their daughters about sex. You convinced me I was your special daughter, and no one could take my place. It was hard to believe those words when I knew what you were doing to me was wrong. I tried to end my life at ten years old, Daddy. (Pause, crying.) I would literally blame myself for your actions. I get it now! It was about control and power with you and the ability to humiliate me. I'm not trying to condemn you, Daddy. I just want you to know how I felt. I now understand hurt people hurt people. I was powerless and without a voice.

Dad, you know what really blew my mind? When I was told that I was no longer your daughter! I couldn't believe it when I heard through the grapevine I was now dead to you. Ouch! You're entitled to feel the way you want to feel. What did I do for you to want to delete me from your life?

So now you're playing the victim? Wait a minute! Did I take away your innocence? What did I do wrong to you, Dad? If I did do something wrong to you, why can't you forgive me like I forgave you? What did I do other than be your daughter?

Dad, how could I truly honor and obey you under these circumstances?

"No one loses their innocence. It is either taken or given away willingly." –Tiffany Madison

I didn't give my innocence away.

I no longer blame

Dad, listen, I'm no longer in the mindset of living in shame or guilt. It just kept me stuck in the problem. Giving this issue power was killing me inside. I want us both to rise above all that has happened and move on with living our lives. I understand the past we cannot change.

In the words of William Shakespeare, "Things without all remedy Should be without regard: what's done, is done and Give me your hand." Dad, what's done is done and can't be undone. The little girl on the inside of me hated your existence. She wants you to know she no longer looks at you as a monster that took her innocence. She no longer sees you as an offender but a victim that was also robbed of your innocence some way shape or form. You demonstrated to me a learned behavior that possibly happened in your own life. I don't know your full story, Dad. I just know you played a big part in my story. I do know when you were asked by the family therapist, "Were you ever molested?" you said, "No." You also lied to mom when she asked you if were molesting me, you said, "No."

I simply never imagined that I would be in the position of having to defend myself. Dad, you were free in your behavior with me. I was sure you would confess what you were doing to me. I knew you needed help, yet, you turned the tables on me, calling me a liar. Just as I never dreamed I would need a defense, it crushed me when my mother took your side and believed your lies. I kept your sick secret for 12 years. But what you didn't understand was, I didn't need the blaming. Name-calling and crafting of an airtight defense against me were all unnecessary. I did not want an admission. I did not want your lies. I was shattered from the inside out. I was forced to live with the hurt and the pain. Through the grace of God, He showed me how to love and to forgive. I must admit I was holding on to the past hurts like jewelry around my neck. Daddy, do you know how long I waited to have a pure relationship? I mean, I forgave you for the molestation and the beatings.

Poem

Control and Manipulation was your first and last name

Yet I carried the hurt and the shame

When the truth came out - I was the one that people blamed

My mom didn't even believe me

I felt you both deceived me

You lifted me from my bed night after night

You knew in your heart it wasn't right

You would whisper the words in my ear "I will never do it again"

Dad – your flesh enjoyed the pleasures of this sin (molestation)

I begged and pleaded for you to stop

My words just got chopped

By the whisper, I love you" in my ear

Dad - you cared nothing about my tears

Your actions were unwanted and forced

You continued without remorse

I was not emotionally, physically and mentally prepared

I was confused and scared

With my innocence you played truth or dare

By Ira Warren

Removing the Veil

"Nobody can go back and start a new beginning, but anyone can start today and make a new ending." ~Maria Robinson

I now know I had to gain acceptance to be able to move on. I was letting the abuse destroy me. I didn't know how to live in the skin I was in. I didn't know the true meaning of love. So, I gave my body to men because I thought that's how one showed love. Dad, your actions robbed us of having an authentic daddy-daughter relationship. The pain was weighing my soul down like iron weights. I was operating in guilt, shame, and fear; therefore, I was powerless. I was a black hole without form or substance. I had to face the reality of my past and go through the process. It didn't happen quickly. The first thing I had to do was confront you, Dad. All the lies and the secrets you spoke to me had to be exposed. Dad, do you know how dirty I felt? I hated that I was even born. I would scrub my vagina area with copper brillo pads, shave off all my hair off my head because I hated the person I saw in the mirror. My spirit was broken. I wanted to die.

Second, I had to understand the abuse wasn't my fault. Do you know how bad it hurt me when you kept denying what you had done? Do you know how bad it felt for me to be telling the truth, and no one believed me? You were clever enough to convince Mom, your parents, and others around you that you were innocent. People looking at me as if I was the villain. Dad, deep down inside, you were guilty. (Pause, tears.) I couldn't compete with you. You know what's crazy? I had to stop caring about the abuse. I just wanted you to get the help you needed, we needed, so we could heal. I promise you I'm not trying to condemn you. I'm just letting you know where I am now in this situation.

Third, me talking about the abuse is therapy for me. Talking about it has given me the freedom to turn pain into purpose. The abuse happened to me, Dad, but it was not for me. Do you know how many people could receive healing and deliverance from our story?

Dad, I don't hate you!

Typing this letter to you has given me clarity on how abuse has shaped my life I now realize the abuse has bruised many relationships throughout my life. I attracted men that saw all my insecurities and vulnerabilities to crush me even the more. I couldn't turn to you to be my safety net. I stayed in dysfunctional relationships because I came from dysfunction. Dad staying with my abusive high school boyfriend almost cost me my life. He was a true narcissist. He was in love with himself. He thought the sun rises and sat on his behind. He would beat me and say it was my fault. He was very manipulative and controlling. He loved to tear me down with name-calling and beating me with belts, his fist and burning me with lit cigarettes. He would always say if I left him, he would find me and kill me. Some of the characteristic I saw in you, I also saw in him.

He was very controlling and aggressive just like you. Mark would lies to manipulate people to get what he wanted just like you. He would put his hands on me just like you, Dad. He also used to belittle me with name-calling and telling me I will never amount to anything just like you used to do Mom. Dad, "It has been said, 'time heals all wounds. 'I do not agree. The wounds remain. In time, the mind, protecting its sanity, covers them with scar tissue and the pain lessens. But it is never gone." ~Rose Kennedy

Protector

Dad, there was an episode in my life I do remember. You came to my rescue on a gut feeling that my children and I were in danger. What you felt was correct ...

Mark had kicked in the door to my house, demanding my FDC check and food stamps that I received the first of every month. I refused to give it to him, so he beat me nearly to death until I gave him the check and food stamps. I was screaming and begging him for my life. He repeatedly punched me in my face. I was covered in blood. Both my eyes were black and swollen and sealed shut, making it difficult for me to see. He kicked me in my stomach and ribs. Dad, the pain was unbearable. However, I managed to drag myself to the living room. I struggled but was finally able to push the couch up to the door to secure it. My children were crying and screaming for two days. Mark took the rent and food stamps and left. They drank spoilt baby milk. They had on soiled, dirty diapers.

(Pause, crying.) Dad, you came to me and my children's rescue that night. I remember you screaming out my name through the kicked in door. I could see the flashing of a light through the living room window. The next thing I knew, the front door was being shoved open. Dad, you called out my name a second time and flashed the light in the direction of my voice, only to find me a bloody mess. I was holding my boys on each side of me. You were astounded at what you witnessed. "Baby, what the hell happened to you? Where is Mark? Did he do this to you?" The concern in your voice completed me at that moment. You held me in your arms and comfort me, rocking me back and forth. I could feel your tears fall on the top of my head. That was the first time I ever saw you cry. Dad, I felt a release in my heart, my mind, and my soul. It was a healing moment for the both of us. You went out of your way to make sure me and my kids were safe. I was now receiving that unconditional love that I always wanted from you. For the first time, I saw you as a father who cared. I felt protected. You went a step further that night to help me pack me and my children's clothes and gather our important documents.

I was so afraid when Mark returned to the house in the middle of us leaving. I knew he was high from shooting heroin. The money and the food stamps must have run dry.

He was back to his controlling ways. When he tried to grab my children out the car, Dad, you punched him so hard he stumbled backward and hit the ground. I didn't think you were going to hit him, but that was the risk you took to protect me and my children; heck, even yourself.

I know you didn't want me to be with Mark. I kept going back to him because I felt he would change or at least I could change him. Boy was I wrong. I was no longer a victim of Mark's abuse. I became a volunteer because I kept going back. Dad, your mantra was always: "Think about your impact on the next person. Show consideration. Consider the consequences before you act." Dad, these were very powerful words coming from you. All my life, I have sought to take the most ethical approach to life.

"Children obey your parents in everything, for this pleases the Lord." (Colossians 3:20)

(My thoughts.) All my life, I've strived to not do the things you've done but do the things you say. All my life, I've tried very hard to not simply be reactive but honor, obey you, Dad. All my life, I've strived to have self-control in all areas of my life. Dad, you have given me the gift of how to think about my own life. Whether your actions were good or bad, I have learned from them. Dad, when it's all said and done, I know you love me. A destructive love that got mixed up with passed-down generational curses you nor your own parents knew how to deal with. All that has happened to me in my life has created purpose for me. I had to let go of hating you in order to face the pain.

Healing and deliverance from abuse is an on-going process. I will continue to share my truth without anyone's authorization to do so. I'm not saying this to be disrespectful or out of anger. Dad, I just know sharing my truth is therapy for me. I know you have made up your mind not to talk to me anymore, and I'm fine with that. If you have peace with your decision concerning me, Dad, I respect that. We both will never be able to take away the fact that I have your DNA. We both can't take away the fact that you're my dad and I'm your daughter. I will continue to pay it forward by helping others to overcome child abuse and move on to be what God intended them to be. God knows I totally forgive you. If the abuse didn't happen, I wouldn't be the woman I am today.

Typing this letter to you, Dad, has allowed me to dig deeper into the crevices of my heart. Typing this letter has helped me to let go of any hidden grudges or bitterness. Dad, I wish you no harm. God has vindicated me. God has healed and restored me. Forgiveness is not a feeling for me, Dad, but a decision to do what is right in the eyes of God. It's important for me to rest in the freedom of forgiveness. Well, Dad, I'm not going to preach any longer. Just know that I will always love you. Ernest Hemingway once wrote, "The most painful thing is losing yourself in the process of loving someone too much and forgetting that you are special too."

Dad, I am worthy because God said so. I am loved unconditionally. All that has happened to me was for someone else to see how God can turn pain into purpose. God gets the glory and will continue to get the glory.

Though my father and mother forsake me, the Lord will receive me (Psalm 27:10).

P.S.: I'm glad God chose you to be my dad.

Love your daughter,

Ira Warren

ABOUT THE AUTHOR

 Ira Warren was born in Gary, Indiana. She is a mother of 6 boys and 1 girl. She's a mentor, wife, poet, singer, motivational speaker, actress and author. She is also an ordained minister with a BA in Religious Studies. She's been through a lot in her life. Ira has been a victim of rape, incest, molestation as well as other forms of physical and mental abuse. She has been able to stand strong through the trying times and is now reaching back to help others. Throughout the years, Ira has worked with troubled youth in a number of capacities. She started 911 Ministries in 1996, reaching over 300 youth in Houston, Texas.

She worked as a Youth Minister Coordinator for Fort Sam Houston Military Base in San Antonio, TX. Ira Warren recently started a Television Talk show with her husband on Christian Vision Entertainment called "As 1" hosted by Divine and Ira Warren. They discuss aspects of life, relationships, love as well as marriages. Their goal is to reach and help as many people as possible who may be going through adversities in their relationships as well as life in general. Their vision for the future is to start an organization called Divine Minds. This organization will be an outlet to help inspire and motivate children to overcome hardships and adversity they may have been through in their lives.

Ira is not afraid to tell people her story. Being a survivor of abuse herself, she feels that it is her purpose to use her voice to help break the epidemic of rape, molestation as well as other forms of abuse. She's been told that her story has inspired others to "Overcome to Become."

Feel free to stay connected with Ira Warren on Social Media at:

www.facebook.com/IraWarren
www.instagram.com/irawarren
irawarren1@gmail.com

Why Do You Drink?

By
Tinesha Boswell

Dear Dad,

As I started thinking about my childhood and some of the issues I had, I contemplated on participating in the book. It took me a few weeks after seeing the original post to decide on what I was going to do after praying to God and talking to my husband about it. My husband thought this would be a great way to heal from the internal wounds I kept inside or had forgotten about because it was too painful. I've learned that 'pain' is not inclusive and can mean different things to different people.

As I thought about the title *Dear Dad*, I started to fear the memories that I had left behind because it doesn't always feel good to remember. I prayed on this and waited, and God spoke to me and said it needs to be done.

I had a ton of mixed emotions because I didn't want to re-live some of the things that I went through as a child. However, we must all take the bad with the good; right, he is my dad.

Our parents can only teach us what they learned, whether it is good, bad, or indifferent behaviors. Hindsight being 20/20, it wasn't as bad as I wanted to remember.

Hey, Dad, as I am sitting here, taking a trip down memory lane, I realize that you and Mommy have been married for over 42 years and together much longer than that. I remember you guys telling me that you met Mom when she was in her teenage years, and my grandma loved your personality, but you were 5 years older than Mom, which is funny because my first boyfriend was 5 years older than me, and you guys had a problem with that. Weird, but since I am now mature, I do understand the difference. I've learned that when you are mature, it doesn't seem to make much difference, depending on the age. You have always supported Mom and have been doing so ever since she was 16 years old. I think it was a cute story you and Mom told us about you getting Mom her first apartment after she graduated from high school. What an amazing graduation gift for anyone to receive! That was the start of your loving relationship until this day.

I know Mommy was happy that she didn't have to work because you took care of all the bills although she did work a few jobs because she liked her cigarettes and wanted a house phone, which she paid because you didn't think a phone was necessary. To this day, you still don't own a cell phone, which I think is crazy, but I do understand it.

The one thing I have always loved about you is your work ethic. I remember us talking about you being a truck driver with a company for over 20 years and were paid in cash, which created a lot of issues with money. You didn't believe in bank accounts and paid everything in cash, which I thought was weird, but that was your way of handling things. The one great thing that I can say about you is that no matter what happened, you made sure the bills were paid first, and it's still that way today. It was crazy learning how much you did not know about saving money, writing checks and paying rent with a money order and bills at the check cashing place. I don't think you really understood that until the company you worked for went bankrupt. While that was a traumatic experience for the family, it turned out to be the best thing that happened to you. It was such a blessing that your old boss made sure he got you a job, which is where you are today and have been working for over 20 years. I can appreciate this job for you because it taught you how to budget, save money; you started writing checks and learning what it meant to have a 401k plan. More importantly, it helped you become more responsible.

I remember when you and Mommy were both working, you would drop me off at either my grandmother's or Dee mamma's house first thing in the morning. I remember thinking, *Wow, this is a big ole truck that my dad is driving.* I really had fun when you pretend like I was driving, and that made me want to learn how to drive a stick shift vehicle. I bought a stick shift as my first car because I wanted to learn to drive like you.

All I could think about when I was younger was a man. *I would love to have someone who loves to work and who takes care of me.* When I saw that you were handling business, and Mommy was a homemaker, I used to think to myself, *This is the right thing to do as a man.* You are truly a hard worker and hate taking time off work.

I must say that I learned a lot from you. I can appreciate how you taught me and Shawn how to run, walk; we had tea time. You taught me how to jump double dutch, play jacks, ride my bike, skate (skate backward), fry chicken and cook eggs. You weren't a cook at all, but you sure did know how to fry some chicken.

I remember being very young, maybe 4 or 5, and you would say, "Let's go," and I would be ready in no time because I was going outside with my dad. You used to make fun of me because I would just get dressed without washing up. Man were you fast, and I had to run to keep up with you. Well, I must say that me running to keep up helped me to become a great runner in school. So, I guess it wasn't too bad. Anyway, I remember us going to a bar not far from where we lived, and I would sit in the corner eating chips, soda, or eating those nasty peanuts that are left on the table. Of course, I didn't know they were nasty back then, but thinking about it now, I'm just glad I didn't get sick from folk's nasty behind hands.

I used to love going out with you, especially after I learned how to ride my bike. You and Mr. Eric would walk to the playground to play ball, and Shawn and I would ride our bikes with you. I always had a great time when we were out.

As Shawn and I started to get older, our interest changed. I was running track, played softball; Shawn wanted to play football with the guys in the neighborhood. Eventually, she was playing music, playing softball and track. I went to Logan Drill Team for a few years until I got pregnant at 16 years old. I remember you helping me learn drill team steps when I was stuck. You used to show your moves too, and they loved you coming around. Now, you might be reading the top half of the text, saying to yourself, *Wow! Now that sounds like I was a great guy and dad.* Please don't get me wrong; you were a great dad in all of the ways I talked about above. However, you were a totally different person when you were drinking.

Growing up, when you think of your dad, you think of him as being your hero or you think to yourself that you may want to marry someone like your dad when you grew up. Well, that's not how I felt. To a degree, you weren't the nicest person, and your best friend was Seagram's Gin. Mommy used to say, "I don't have to worry about him cheating with another woman, but I do find myself competing with Mrs. Gin." I realized at a young age that while you were great, you were also a butt hole all in the same breath. I felt like you were prejudiced against everyone it wasn't about race or color and thought you were mean and hateful and didn't care what came out of your mouth. I remember you getting mad at Mom, and you would act like a child and start turning off the TVs, lights, and sometimes the heat when you got angry. I don't think you realized how much that hurt to see a person who should be taking care of things being childish.

I remember one day you would say how it was my grandmother's fault for getting you started with drinking at the age of 25, which I thought was a weird statement since your dad and brothers were drinkers too. In fact, all of you guys were alcoholics but didn't want to believe you were. So, honestly, it came naturally to you without you even realizing it. It wasn't Grandma's fault; it was your upbringing and your surroundings.

The one thing I didn't appreciate about you was how you spoke to me. When I would fall off my bike or skating and skinned my leg, you would always say, "You are going to have a hard time finding a man because your legs are so ugly, being marked up from falling all the time." I'm sure you thought you were helping me from being so clumsy, but it did nothing; rather, it hurt my feelings and made me very self-conscious. I'm pretty sure you would totally disagree with me, but you guys weren't always the most encouraging parents as one would think the ideal parents should be. You didn't realize that your words were considered abusive to my sister and me, but to your defense, most people are usually a product of their environment, and you both had issues with your parents growing up. We can't teach what we don't know!

I can remember growing up, and you loved going out to eat for breakfast and would ask us if we wanted to go. Most times when you wanted to go, Shawn was asleep. She would sometimes get upset that she couldn't go, but you were an early bird, and if you wanted to eat, you had to be up and ready way before 8 a.m. You knew Shawn loved sleeping, so she would miss out on a lot of things that we would do together. I don't understand why you just wouldn't wake up her to go because I'm pretty sure she felt left out. Things such as these made me dislike you and Mommy at times because I felt like you really didn't care, and that you were just mean, sometimes selfish and hateful. While my sister never really complained, she wanted your love and attention more than I did.

You are a fun person to be around because you loved to dance and sing but can be extremely annoying when drinking because you didn't always know when to stop. Even today, I must remind you that you're not 25 anymore and can't be doing the James Brown split in your 60s. I guess to your defense, all your friends have passed away, and you would never admit this, but I am positive you felt lonely. You've always used drinking at the bar as an excuse to be around other people who drank, who were just as loud as you many of them loved to sing and dance just so you didn't have to remember that all of your friends were gone.

When you would come home drunk, I would ask myself, *Why does Dad drink?* It's not something I could ever answer, but I thought about it all the time. One time I did ask, "Why do you drink?" and you said it's because you like to have fun. You would never admit that you were an alcoholic, but you were, and although you drink less now, you are still an alcoholic. It's no fun having a dad who would drink a lot because all you would hear are excuses.

I remember, as a child, having adult conversations with my dad before an important event. Because my dad would drink and didn't always care he drank. For example, for my 8th-grade graduation, I had to sing a solo. He helped me to practice and learn the words so I didn't embarrass myself, so I would have to sit him down and say, "Dad, please don't drink the day of my graduation. Please make sure that you shower, put on clean clothes and brush your teeth." He would respond and say, "I will do my best because I want you to be proud of me being your dad." Those words meant a lot to me, but it angered me every time I had an event that I wanted him to attend. I shouldn't have had to have these conversations as a child or teenager.

As I write this letter, I realize I had unanswered questions because I always wanted an answer to the question: "Why do you drink?"

Dad, you've always bragged about my sister and I and how proud you were of us, but it didn't always come off with love. I always loved how you taught us to be strong but would like to know, "Why do you drink?" Were we not good enough to keep you sober and do more things with you such as going skating more or even to the movies? Why did you drink? Was it because you didn't know how to have fun without alcohol? Why did you drink? Was it because my grandmother and most of your friends drank, and you were struggling to be the true leader that you are? Why did you drink? Was it because you didn't know any better and just wanted to fit in with the crowd. Why did you drink? Was it because you had no other way of showing your emotions and to get rid of your past hurts from your upbringing? Why did you drink? Do you even care how it affected my sister and I growing up? Why did you drink? Do you even realize that your actions damaged how I thought of me? Why did you drink? Do you even realize that I tried my best to not date anyone that has any resemblance to you? Why did you drink? Do you know that I had an issue with a man taking care of me because of how you treated Mom at times? Why did you drink? Your drinking made me so angry growing up that I would try and hurt others because of it. Why did you drink? All I could say to myself is, *I don't ever want to have a marriage like my parents. I don't want any man to think that they can control who I am or anything I can do* because I saw how it hurt Mom. Why did you drink? Do you even realize how bad you hurt me when you found out I was pregnant at 17 and tried to beat the child out of me? I lost my child because of you. That hurt me.

You don't realize that your actions made me a mean and depressed person growing up. I was so good at hiding my depression that you guys never even cared to notice. You just thought I was being disobedient, a smart mouth or a hoe. I didn't want to be around others because most people drank, but for a while, I, too, became an alcoholic until one day I looked in the mirror and said, *I am not my parents*, and I started to change. I remember you saying, "Even when I am doing bad, I am doing good." Which is a phrase that I use today.

Although my letter to you may hurt your feelings, it is how I was feeling. Fast forward to today, I know that you did your best with what you had. I know that you love us and truly wanted the best for us, just didn't know how to put it into words. You would always say that when I became an adult, to find someone who loves me for being me, who is not an alcoholic; someone to help me grow. I am sure you wanted these qualities for me and my sister because, deep down, you wish some things were different.

Now that my sister and I are adults, both married and have a family, you and Mommy always show up when we need you. You make sure that we spend holidays together as much as we can. You attend important events without us giving you a speech about drinking. You do everything you can to show us how much you love us. I can tell you that Shawn and I appreciate everything you have done for us growing up because you made sure we were safe, had food on the table and clothes on our backs. For that, I am grateful.

I never want to hurt your feelings but do need you to understand mine.

I love you with all of my heart. Nesha!

ABOUT THE AUTHOR

Tinesha Boswell was born and raised in Philadelphia, PA, and she is a wife, mother, motivational speaker, wellness coach, an aspiring author.

Tinesha has a Bachelor of Science in Business Management degree from the University of Phoenix. She is also a Certified Wellness Coach, Certified Life Coach, Marriage Mentor Coach and is currently studying Nutrition and Aromatherapy.

Tinesha is also the founder of i.P.U.S.H Wellness Coaching and Consulting, LLC. She was led to create i.P.U.S.H is due to her multiple chronic illnesses, which are asthma, high blood pressure, high cholesterol, type II diabetes, and fibromyalgia. Its purpose is to help you become at peace with your illness by learning how best to deal with your chronic illness.

i.P.U.S.H Wellness' mission is to help women PUSH past their pause by teaching them how to balance their mind through personal development, their body with fitness and nutrition, and by creating peace and tranquility in their lives.

Feel free to stay connected with Tinesha Boswell on Social Media at:

www.facebook.com/Tinesha.iPushWellness/

www.instagram.com/TineshaBoswell

www.twitter.com/BoswellTinesha

Expectation

By
Dr. Aikyna Finch

Dear Dad,

Let me start by saying thank you for giving me life. Without you, I wouldn't be the person I am today. I know our situation was not ideal, but it was our situation. I had no expectations of you because I didn't know you existed. It was my mother's decision not to tell me about you; it was my grandmother's decision to tell me about you.

You can imagine being 8 years old, finding out that the father that you've known all your life is actually your step-father, and your real father is in Texas, living his life without you. When I went to ask my mother about you, she turned ghostly white, and I knew that it was true. I don't know the situation between the two of you, but for her not to tell me about you means that you had your own situation.

At 12 years old, I met you for the first time. I looked exactly like you, and I had many of your quirks. I was excited to meet you and to find out that I had three older siblings and one younger sibling. As an only child for 12 years, it was amazing to say I had brothers and a sister. You took me around your cab and introduced me to the family your brothers and your sister and my brothers and my sister. I even came home with a Gameboy. Of course, my mother wasn't too happy about that; she was more focused on me having a pair of glasses. It was super cool to be a part of a family that looked like me.

The next year, I came to stay with you for a week or two. I got to hang out with my little brother and your wife. Your wife proceeded to tell me about how she was dealing with the fact that I existed. This was the first time that I realized that I was a problem for the rest of the family. I thought that I was just going to come in and be a part, but being that my sister was 17 years older than me and my brother was 9 years younger than me, I definitely stuck out in the mix. I realized that I was not really wanted in the family, and that hurt. Then, of course, I'm sure you were getting a lot of grief from the family members as well that I existed. It is amazing how bad rejection feels from people that look just like you. Filled with the same blood you're filled with, it's fascinating, to say the least. Later that year, you came for Thanksgiving, and that was the last time I saw you until I was 26 years old. You said that it was causing too much drama in your household to have me in your life. You chose your wife over me. I opened my heart to you, and you left me. Now I have an expectation of you ... Rolling Stone!

By the time we met again, I definitely felt some kind of way about you. All the things that had transpired had made me bitter. I just did not understand how you could just throw me away and everyone else in the process. Why did you do this? Why did you leave? I was going to find the answers in a way I didn't expect. I was getting ready to graduate from college, and I decided I wanted you to come to the graduation. I sent a letter to the last address I had on file and hoped for the best. I received the email a week later from your ex-wife stating that you did not live there anymore and that the only person that talked to you was my sister. She said that she told my sister about the letter, and she would reach out to me further. I thanked her for answering me and reaching out to my sister.

I received an email from my sister asking for time to chat. She called me to screen me before she would give me your number to talk to you. I found it amazing that I had to go through interrogation to speak to my father, but that's the way it had to go. After the call, I received an email with your contact information in it, and I called you. You picked up the phone, and you sounded so old. But at this point, you were 67 years old and in a new realm in life. I knew that I had a decision to make, to build my life with you in it or sever all ties. I chose to build a life with you, but I didn't choose not to be angry at you. I was determined that I was going to have the answers that I needed.

I moved to Colorado with you and October of 2003 for what I thought was going to be a year. Seven years later, when I left in 2010, my life would never be the same. In that seven years, I learned so much about myself why I thought the way I did, why I did the things I did. It was such a revelation to finally know where I belonged; to learn history about my family was priceless. Now I can't say that the journey was smooth, but it was necessary.

In 2013, you moved to Texas after my sister found you at 124 pounds. We eventually found out you had stage 4 cancer after you spent a month in the hospital. During this time, my sister put you in a nursing home and then an assisted living home. I think this was the first time in your life that you weren't in control, and you learned a lot about how you have treated others in the past. When you were able to break free, you came to stay with me for two months. You had to bring everything you owned because your home closed, and none of your children would store your stuff while you were gone.

While you were there, my sister informed you that she was not going to help you find a new home in Dallas, and it was my turn to take care of you. That was the blow that made you see what your actions had done over the years. You reached out to your Mormon brothers, and they found you a place to stay before you returned back to Texas. When you got off the plane, you headed to the doctor to find out that after two years, you were in remission and good to go. In your style, you decided not to tell the family for about a year later.

At this point, we have a good relationship, and I love you. I enjoy talking to you and listening to your stories and opinions. I get a better understanding of myself and how I think each time that we speak. I am glad you are my father because I am stronger because of all I went through with you. I am not the most affectionate person, and my guard is always up, but your rejection did not stop me from reaching greatness. It was just a stepping stone to my next level.

ABOUT THE AUTHOR

 Dr. Aikyna Finch is a Podcaster, Social Media Coach and Speaker. She is also a Forbes Coaches Council Member. She coaches in the areas of Empowerment, Life, and Social Media at the individual and groups levels from Finch and Associates. She co-hosts the Motivate Social Podcast by Changing Minds Online. She speaks about Motivation, Education, and Social Media.

Dr. Aikyna Finch is an Educator and Author. She received a Doctorate in Management, MBA in Technology Management and Executive MBA from Colorado Technical University. She has a Masters of Management in Marketing Management from Strayer University and Bachelors in Aeronautical Technology in Industrial Electronics from the School of Engineering of Tennessee State University. Her teaching disciplines include business, leadership, marketing, social media, and information systems at the graduate and undergraduate levels.

She is the Co-Author of six books and launched her first solo project, Motivation Ignited, in November of 2016. She is a Contributor to the Huffington Post, Goalcast, Forbes and Thrive

Global. She has been interviewed and featured on Huffington Post, Hello Beautiful, Women Speakers Association, and many others. Dr. Aikyna Finch has spoken on many platforms, including the Periscope Summit, Women In Leadership Summit, The Boldly Empowering Entrepreneurs Conference, The Business Vlog Summit, and many more!

Feel free to stay connected with Dr. Aikyna Finch on Social Media at:

www.Facebook.com/Dr.A.D.Finch
www.Instgram.com/DrADFinch
www.Twitter.com/DrADFinch
www.Linkedin.com/in/DrADFinch
www.aikynafinch.com

What About ME?

by
Andrea Hamilton

Dear Dad,

I hope this letter touches your heart. This letter includes the many expressions from my childhood until now that I haven't been able to tell you because we just haven't had the time to sit down and talk. I hope that this letter opens your heart, and through this letter, I hope that you get to know and understand me a little more. Dad, first, I want you to know that I am considerate of the fact that you may have had it rough in your past being an African American male. I understand this because I have had it rough coming up being an African American girl/ woman. I have faced many obstacles alone, with no one to trust for advice. Because of this, now I am determined to change my future and not let my past hinder me from moving forward in my life. I want you to know that you are forgiven for not being a part of my upbringing. I commend you for stepping up when I reached out to find you.

Growing up without you was rough. I always wondered where my features came from and what your side of the family looked like. I really give thanks to God for my little sisters. Even though we were not raised together, they are loving and caring and remind me in certain ways about myself. I hope that my relationship with them flourishes and that I can teach them a couple of things. There is a lesson in this. The lesson is that no matter how old a father or daughter gets, a bond and a relationship can still be established. I want this to be the reminder that there could be a happy ending. Finding you was one of my long-term lifetime goals that I set for myself when I was a child. I thank God every day that I accomplished that particular goal not only for myself but also for my children.

My children get super excited when they talk about their granddad, so you are really important to them as well. I was very happy to know that you're still alive and well when I found you because I was never able to meet my mom's dad because he passed away when I was just a baby. Having your last name and not spending time with you and getting to know who you are was really difficult. I felt at times I did not belong in my family. I was always reminded that I was a Hamilton; that was not a good feeling only because I did not know anyone with my last name, and I and you were not in contact. I was able to meet my grandmother and great-grandmother but never able to meet my grandfather, so my children being able to meet theirs brings my heart great joy. The first time that I got a chance to see you, and you had to leave, I cried like a big baby. My age did not matter. I did not feel like I was too old. The tears flowed out naturally.

Growing up, I wondered if you loved me, if you thought about me. I wondered, did you go off and have children and forget about me? At times I wondered, was something wrong with me? I did not choose the right relationships when I decided to start dating because I was not sure of how a man should treat me. I made some bad choices but learned from them. I wished that I had guidance from you. Maybe I would have made better choices. Even though I talk real fast and rush you off the phone when you're getting on my case, I still hear every word that you say. I'm never too old for your advice. Some of my emotions come up from childhood trauma, which causes me to go into a depression and mentally shut down. I'm working to overcome these feelings. I also deal with my feelings.

Knowing that you have Sickle Cell Disease saddens me because we've missed so many years already, and I couldn't prepare myself for saying goodbye to you. For now, I want us to continue working on our relationship because, no matter how many years pass us by, knowing and hearing you, my father, say those three words 'I LOVE YOU' brings joy to my heart. I know that I have gotten angry and said things that I did not mean, but forgive me and know that I am truly sorry. I'm approaching 30, and even now, I want my parents to be proud to call me their daughter. Getting compliments from my parents really build up my confidence.

Growing up my, self- esteem was really low; I know that if we would have connected sooner than now, my life may have gone in a completely different direction. Dad, I still need your love and guidance. I hope and pray that our relationship gets better with time and you and your grandchildren get to establish a great bond. I know that you can teach your grandsons some stuff that they will remember. Dad, I look forward to many more family gatherings and visits with you. I want to share my victories and the kids with you. I want your support and encouragement so that I can move forward and overcome these things that weighed me down. I want a healthy relationship with you, my father, and all of the advice that you can give to me while I await my soulmate. I want a wedding with all my family there one day. I know I'm not the only child, and I am not selfish. I want the same thing for my siblings.

Our situation is what we make it. I want us to make it the best that it can be, making up for lost times and building memories together. Without you around, I have been through and overcome so many different trials, from abuse growing up to abuse while living in the foster care system. I did not feel as if I belonged anywhere not knowing nothing about where I came from. We can turn this family situation around and have a fresh start with one another. I hope that this letter touches you and other families so that they can reconnect with their past and move forward, having a healthy family life. Anything is possible with God.

ABOUT THE AUTHOR

 Andrea Hamilton is currently a college student, a single parent of four children. She was born and raised in Texas and relocated to Pittsburgh to get a fresh start. Taking a leap of faith to rebuild herself and seek a peace of mind for her children, Andrea was able to find a new residence and employment fairly quick.

Even though it was challenging, she was willing to give it her all. She's determined to make a difference, and she knew it must start with her. Coming from a background of being a youth in the foster system can leave you psychologically damaged. Andrea is determined to educate others on how they, too, can break the cycle of remaining broken due to the system tactics.

Andrea is pursuing her Masters in Law and working in the judicial system to provide better opportunities to foster children. She is also a co-author of the best-selling book *Cries Of A Broken Man and Screams Of A Broken Woman*.

Feel free to stay connected with Andrea Hamilton on Social Media at:

www.Facebook.com/andreahamilton

www.Instgram.com/andreahamilton1336

A Silent Whisper in the Dark

By
Karyn Quick

Dear Dad,

As I sat by the window, watching the birds play on the porch, waiting to be picked up for my usual long ride to your home for my summer visit, I often wondered what it would be like to have the presence of a full-time dad in my life. The summer visits were always fun, and I truly enjoyed every moment that I spent with you and the family, but the visits seemed to go by faster than they would come, and it was back to a reality that was surreal. The dad that was supposed to provide daily protection, support and love would be a silent whisper until the next summer visit.

Growing up as a little girl, I lacked what most little girls yearn for, and that is the presence of a full-time, emotionally available dad. Although I had my mother with me full-time, who did an excellent job raising me, her compassion, love, and support could not fill the void where I longed for the acceptance, validation, and support of a present dad. In my life, your presence was like a silent whisper in the dark. I knew you existed; we talked from time to time, and the summer visits helped, but this interaction just scratched the surface of what I would have deemed fair to a little girl trying to find her way. I will always appreciate and cherish the moments we spent together, this time only puts patches on the hole left imprinted in my heart which needed a more permanent seal.

I often wondered: Was I good enough? Did he really want a little girl? Just some of the many questions that go through a childs head when a parent is not present. Then another barrage of questions bombarded my mind when I thought about the times you must be spending with my sister in the home you both shared. Then other questions hit me like a ton of bricks. I thought, how was it OK for you to build a relationship with another little girl while seeing your biological daughter in the summer or a drop-in visit to my aunt's house? How was it OK for you to protect her and ensure no harm came here way? How was it OK for you to read her bedtime stories while I lay wondering if you were going to head my way? How was it OK for you to teach her the ABCs and 123s while I lay and wept in dismay? These amongst other questions left me broken and bruised to the core.

There were missed birthdays, special moments of recognition, daddy/daughter dances and those times that create lasting memories and build strong relationships. These special times where memories are built and engrained in a child's memory for the most part just isn't there. Due to the minimum amount of time we had together, it just didn't lend itself to being able to invest the necessary time needed to build the type of relationship that would set the stage for how I should be treated and loved by a man. Today, I am single, and I do believe not having a full-time father readily available has led me to not having a lot of faith and trust in men; therefore, I end up sabotaging most of my relationships because I go in with the expectancy that he will not be faithful, reliable, trustworthy and all the other qualities a woman would want in her husband.

Forgiveness Refreshes the Spirit

Time has passed, and with lots of prayers and tears, I have healed and forgiven you for the distance that was created and the lost memories that will never be shared. I tried putting myself in your shoes and became empathetic when I thought we both had similar experiences in that we both did not have our dad on a full-time basis. I am sure you must have dealt with some of the same struggles and feelings of abandonment that I had to deal with growing up.

I had to work hard on my feelings and myself so that I could see the blessing in what I thought as a little girl was a curse. As a grown woman, Dad, I understand now how your attention was divided due to working a full-time job, moonlighting on a business and trying to provide for your immediate family. What you couldn't provide for me as a little girl that undivided attention and emotional connection, you did invest time in teaching me life skills that have aided in me being the strong, humble, caring woman I am today. If I could sum them up, they would fall into these 5 categories:

1. Entrepreneurial Spirit
2. Sense of Adventure
3. Foundation for my Future
4. Resilience
5. Perseverance

Entrepreneurial Spirit

Dad, growing up, you totally blew my mind, and I stand in awe to how a young man who started off making .25 cents an hour with no college degree could retire himself early so that he can fulfill his dream of owning his own businesses. I remember us having the conversation where you told me all of the skills you had learned along the way by just asking the right questions from the right people who knew how to do what you wanted to learn how to do.

In my mind, there was nothing you didn't know how to do, and I truly admired you for that. If the cars needed an oil change or mechanical work, you knew how to do that; you knew how to build homes; you were an entrepreneur, building your farming business and renting out land to farmers; you served in the military for your country. This was truly the spirit of a hard worker and the will to win which every entrepreneur must have in order to be successful.

I was looking, listening and learning even when you may have thought I was not paying attention. I remember hearing you making the business phone calls, inquiring from other businessmen how to do certain tasks or make certain deals. I drew from those conversations and learnt that you have not because you ask not; the art of asking so that you learn and grow in your skills or craft. I also learned that in business, you cannot make it alone and that everybody needs somebody, and not just somebody, but the right person that can sow into your dream. I have run multiple businesses as well as worked full-time jobs due to watching how you worked over the many years and still today. When people knew I was working full-time in IT, running a Mary Kay business and selling Real Estates, they would ask me if I was Jamaican, and I would say, "No, just the daughter of a dad who is a very hard-working man, and this is one of the characteristics that was passed down through his DNA."

Sense of Adventure

I looked forward to my summer trips because I knew it meant traveling and seeing the world, even if it was taking the scenic route versus the highway. I used to dread taking the scenic route, but as I think back as an adult, it allowed me to see and appreciate a part of life I probably would have never seen. I was able to enjoy the beauty of seeing farm animals walk the land, beautiful homes, beauty of nature and stopping to check out peculiar things like the water well that was out in the middle of nowhere, and you tried the water and then tried to warn me, but of course I was curious and wanted to try it and was sadly surprised with how awful the water tasted coming from the well. These moments heightened my sense of adventure and further broadened my perspective on how I saw the world, and it inspired me that there was truly life outside the hood I grew up in. The love I have for traveling today was derived from the experiences I received on the many trips I experienced with you as a kid.

The financial support you provided that enabled me to travel and be a part of the International track and field team will never be discounted or forgotten. This trip was the first time I had a chance to experience flying and traveling to a country outside the United States of America. Having the opportunity to travel to Germany intrigued me in such a way that I gained an appreciation for other cultures and how they lived. The one thing I learned in Germany is how the people take life very slow and actually enjoy every moment of life, where we in the USA are so used to the hustle and bustle that we don't spend time enjoying the day; we just rush the day away. I was able to truly see and experience what it feels like to not only live my life but enjoy the life I am living and actually fill alive. Today, I love traveling and experiencing other cultures so much that I have visited 4 of the 7 continents and have visited some places most people dream of visiting.

Foundation for my Future

Dad, as you know, I love to shop, travel, eat and everything that requires me to spend lots of money. One thing, Dad, that always rings true in my head that grounds me when I want to overindulge is what you told me many years ago, and that is, "Karyn, it is not what you make but what you keep." Sometimes the smallest things have the biggest impact, and this statement is what keeps me grounded when I want to splurge and act a complete fool in the shopping malls. The impact of this statement has stayed with me, and although I may not always do right by my spending, you can rest assure that I do a whole lot better when this rings in my ear, and this was one of the best advice a father could gift his daughter. This statement is why I was able to purchase my first and now second home because I kept more of what I was making; I didn't act reckless with credit cards, and I protected my credit so that I positioned myself to even qualify for a mortgage.

While in college, a lot of my classmates had issues with their cars, from burning out their engines to running their cars hot and all the issues that come with a car because they were not keeping up on the maintenance for the car, and that was due mainly to them not knowing how to maintain the car. You prepared me for moments like this by showing me how to check my oil, radiation fluid, power steering fluid and just how to maintain my car so that I would be prepared so I didn't experience any of these hardships my classmates experienced with my car.

The ultimate impact that you had on my life was redirecting my career decision while I was in college. I remember the conversation like it was yesterday when you called me and asked me what I was majoring in, and I told you communication. You asked me what I was going to do with that degree, and I said I wanted to be an anchorwoman on the news. Being the researcher and fact finder that you are, you told me there were not many jobs in the communications field and that you saw a lot of jobs in computers and that I should consider that field. You ended the conversation by telling me to get a paper so I could do the research and see for myself the computer jobs and the starting salaries. I followed your suggestion the very next day where I did see the jobs in the paper and what they were paying. The very next semester, I changed my field from Communications to Computer Science, and the rest was history. Today I have been working in IT for over 20 years and have been successful in developing and growing my career in this field. I am very grateful you took the time to share your research and to impart this wisdom on me that would have a profound effect on how my life would thrive.

Resilience

Dad, in the midst of you wearing many hats, you made it a priority to ensure all of your children could see each other and spend time together over the summer. I remember the moments shared with my sister and brothers; us having fun, playing games, doing chores and having talks, getting to know each other. We didn't know there would come a time where one of us would be gone so soon. When I received the call while in my dorm room studying that my brother Cameron had passed due to a seizure, I was devastated and broken.

As I drove down to Anniston Alabama, what I reflected on that brought me joy was knowing the efforts you put forth to bring us together as children to get to know each other. I had the opportunity to spend time with him and get to know him, even if for a short time. If you had not made the time to bring us together a priority, I would not have those moments to reflect on and cherish now that he is gone. I still miss laughing and seeing my brother today, but even through this difficult time, I learned from you that weeping endures for the night, but joy comes in the morning. You showed me the strength and faith you have in God, even in losing a child; where I am sure you had your moments and was sad, you continued to push forward with trusting and believing God would give you the strength to continue on. I gained strength in watching how you handled grief; that inspired me to believe that although he is gone from this earth, I would see him again in heaven.

Perseverance

At this moment in my life, I hope I have made you a proud father. The accomplishments that I have made in my life, I do attribute some of my successes to the many lessons I learned from you. I have obtained several degrees; a Bachelor of Science in Computer Science and a Master's in Business Administration. In High School class of 1990, I was named athlete of the year. I have built a very successful career working in IT for over 20 plus years and have worked my way up from entry-level to a Global Tech Leader for a very large Pharmaceutical company. I have built multiple businesses and have been able to experience what some people only dream about in that I have had the awesome opportunity to travel, visit and work in 4 of the 7 continents in the world. I am very grateful for my life and have no regrets; as that little girl, I had moments where I doubted if I even mattered and had a divine purpose in this life, and today I know I mattered, and there is a reason why I still stand and can share my story.

According to the US Census Bureau, children in father-absent homes are four times more likely to be poor. In 2011, 12 percent of children in married-couple families were living in poverty compared to 44 percent of children in mother-only families.

Due to perseverance, I beat these odds, and I hope my story inspires some little girl or boy to continue on, despite the challenges they may face due to having an absentee parent or parents and to not use that as a crutch but a catalyst to stand tall and play big in this world. I hope this story also inspires some young man who is struggling with being that good father to his children, knowing it does make a difference and the connection that is built through the relationship is priceless.

Thanks, Dad, for showing your love the best way you knew how. I have great joy in knowing we will continue to spend our lives building our relationship and friendship.

Love Always,
Karyn Quick

ABOUT THE AUTHOR

 Karyn is a Global Technology Leader with over 20 plus years' experience in Information Technology. She has extensive experience in mentoring and coaching global leaders. She has worked in 4 of the 7 continents in the world. She is irrationally passionate about helping career women get unstuck and get the raise or promotion they deserve. From just starting out to mid-career, she will give you the quick steps you need to jumpstart or reignite your career. She does this leveraging her proven system called 'The Quick 6.'

Karyn has been speaking for the last 10 years and delivers an energetic, fun, informational and thought-provoking experience that moves her audience to take massive action in their lives. She has spoken for many organizations, to name a few—Zeta Phi Beta Sorority, Inc., Black Data Processing Association (BDPA), Chocolate Chips Association of Lake County, IL., College of Lake County, Women Expo's and Leadership Conferences—on the topics of Leadership, Networking, Career Development, Team Work, Fear, Adversity, Resilience, Technology and Communication.

Karyn is the author of *Cubeonomics: How smart women get beyond their cube, build strategic relationships and boost their brand* and a contributing author in the *Dear Dad* anthology.

Karyn is a philanthropist and enjoys giving back and supporting the residents in her local communities. In her spare time, you will find her feeding the homeless, serving on non-profit boards, participating in local walks to support a cause, mentoring youth and women.

Feel free to stay connected with Karyn Quick on Social Media at:

www.Facebook.com/KarynQuick
www.Instgram.com/Karyn2Inspire
www.Twitter.com/KarynQuick
www.Linkedin.com/KarynQuick
www.Quick6Wins.com

Daddy's Girl

By
Eve Gomez

Dear Dad,

I am writing this letter to let you know of the things that I never said or thought I could say to you while you were alive.

When I was born, I didn't see your face, didn't hear your voice. You were nowhere to be found. Mom did not know where you were and had not heard from you. All I know is that you were in America trying to work to give us a better life. I don't hold that against you, Dad. I know that it was the American dream that you were after.

I'd like to start out by saying that I am blessed to have had you as my father. I remember when I was 3 years old, and little Jimmy (name changed) was born; you were not there for that either. I saw Mom walking with Nina and the baby to our house. I didn't understand why you were not there, even though I didn't put much thought to it. After all, what kid at 3 years of age thinks about those things? Did I ever tell you that I tried to carry Jaimito, and I was so gentle and proud of that moment? Yeah, Dad, I loved my little brother.

I remember the times when you would come and visit us back home (Mexico). I was always excited to see what you would bring me and that very special aroma that you had on your clothes. It was a scent that let me know that you had been in *El Norte* (The North). Gee, Dad, I never thought that just in reminiscing these moments, it would make me cry. You know I am the strong one of the family. The child that loves talking to everyone. I can still see those moments when you would open up your suitcase, and we would all surround you and smell that aroma in all your clothes and in the things you brought us. I wish I still had those moments now.

Papi, do you remember those moments when we were little? So, now I am going to fast forward. When I was in *parbolito* (kindergarten), I was a leader in the classroom. You would have been so proud of me. I was the flag girl. These were moments that Mamá would share with you and show you the pictures. Oh, by the way, did you know that while being in school in Mexico, the nurse would come and give us our shots, and that one day, I ran home and got in trouble for not waiting? Mamá wanted us to get our immunization shots, and I was scared. It's funny now thinking about, but it sure was scary then. So, guess what? Mami still had to take us to the clinic to get the shots. They were painful. Heck, I remember Coco the nurse and Ana from the <u>Botica</u> (pharmacy) would be the ones to inject us, especially when we were sick. Those were scary big needles. I don't think you were even there.

I wonder how you would have coped with us during those moments. Would you have been upset too? Actually, you know Mom didn't really get upset about things; I think maybe you would have. As time went on, I got to know you a little bit more. While we were in Mexico, you did what you could to support us, but did you really know how much Mom had to do for us while you were looking for work in the U.S.? Did you know that she had to make food, sow clothes to make a living for us? I don't hold that against you either. I just wondered sometimes if you actually knew what Mom had to go through to take care of all eight of us. She was one strong woman with endurance and perseverance.

In 1974, I remember you coming home (Mexico) to get all our documents and apply for legal residency to move to the USA. We all went to Mexico City to get our passport. We took a family photo, which I still hold dear and close to my heart. That was the beginning of a new life for us all. I never really shared with you how I truly felt about our move. I was sad and excited at the same time to move to a foreign country. We left everyone else behind aunts, uncles, cousins, grandparents, and friends; that kind of hurt, Dad. I sometimes think about how things would have been had we not moved to the US.

I remember when you met us at the border in Texas. You did what you had to make sure we all made it to our new home in Gary, Indiana! It was so weird but at the same time interesting to me. I know that you had to work hard and long hours at US Steel Mill. I hardly saw you. I missed you, Dad, even though I never really told you until you got older and fell sick. Papi, did you really love me? You know I think you did—but in your own way. Now that I am much older, I know that you did, that you did what you only knew. You helped Mom raise us as best as you could. You provided us however way you could.

As a teenager, I did not spend much time with you. I know that you meant well, up until I turned 15 or 16 years of age. I sometimes wondered if you ever really knew what happened to me at the age of 5–8, I believe. Did you know that I was molested by your kids and other family members? I was never taught the right touch or the bad touch. It was a topic that was never talked about. It was something that was kept a secret from you and Mom. Does that make you a bad dad for not protecting me? Should I even think that you did not protect me?

At some point in time, I actually felt that I had to protect myself from you too, Dad. Do you remember when you wanted to get closer to me? How you intended on doing that? Whether you meant it for the good or not, I actually forgave you.

So many things went through my mind. I did not want to come home; you cried, you felt bad, but all I wanted to do was stay away from you. Mom was out of town during that time. The following year, something happened to me, and you made a choice for me. I got pregnant, and you took me to a hidden clinic. I was distraught. I was the shame of you and Mom. I gave you a bad name. I cried, DAD. Did you even really care about how I felt, what I actually went through? I know we had an estranged relationship with you, even though I respected you and loved you through it all. It was something that I had to live with for the rest of my life. Dad, I know you meant well. That was the best thing to do according to your thoughts and feelings. It's okay, Dad. Many years have gone by, and I have been okay. I forgave myself and learned from it.

I wish I could just tell you so much more, Papi. But I know that time will tell. I know that everything happens for a reason. I have become a very strong woman. So much has happened in my upbringing. Mom was always the loving, caring, giving woman of God that showed me unconditional love, and you, Dad, you showed me work ethics, to work hard and support the children. You showed me to work without a complaint, to always bring home the bacon. I thank you for that, Dad. I appreciate everything you did for me, even through our storms. You see, Dad, after all these years, I have learned to always, love, honor and respect you.

I cherish every good moment we had. Even though through my young adult years, I didn't feel like being home anymore I felt that I needed room to breathe.

I believe that it was because of how you raised me. I could not do much with friends. You know I was not the normal or regular teenager/young adult. You were very strict. When I wanted to go shopping or to the movies with friends, you would say no; thank God for the friends I had on our block. You would at least let me hang out with them. Once I got to go to college, I felt like I could breathe, Dad. No offense, but sometimes when you hold a child too tight, they become slightly rebellious. I was not the perfect kid that you would have wanted to have. I know I made you angry.

Fast forward, after having my own children, I saw what it took to take care of them. I am blessed that God gave me you as my dad. Even though it wasn't the greatest, but it certainly wasn't the worst. I remember, when I got married, you had a problem with the man I married; then later, I got divorced, and any boyfriend I had, you had a problem with them too. I know that you were somewhat racist, but you also didn't like anyone for me. Was it that, in your eyes, they were not good enough for me? Or was it that you felt jealous? I will never know.

You might be asking why am I telling you all of this. Well, Papi, I believe that in writing this letter, it helps and lets you know that you were not a bad father after all. Although, years later, many young adults in their early thirties came into my life, and I in theirs. It's like having the child that I would have had, but never did. As I mentioned to you, things happen for a reason. God gave me many spiritual kids. I am humbled and blessed by that and to be called 'Mama Eve' or 'Mom.' Most children would have held a grudge against their father or not love them, but I, on the contrary, love you unconditionally. Forgiveness is huge. It brings peace, Dad. Remember how many times I had to tell you to calm down and not to let things get to you? As you got older and sicker, the Lord showed me that it would be me to be there for you.

I also know that with your language barrier, I had to help you through it all. I know that the Lord chose me to help take care of you and Mom. I had to learn to be patient when it came to you. I know that you didn't see the errors that you committed by talking about your kids to your kids in a negative way. I paid no mind to it; otherwise, we would always be bickering and fighting. I now know that it was not you; it was a spirit inside you. When I started going to a non-denominational church, you criticized me. You spoke badly about it, but you know what Dad? I know that you did not know you spoke out of ignorance. You see, Dad, I did not allow it to hurt me. After all these years, the negative things you said to me and about me only gave me a reason to show the opposite. It gave me courage and strength.

Mi Niño (my little boy), I showed you that I loved you, even though I didn't tell you often. I didn't make it about me. Through the years, I had only grown to love you more and more each day. I prayed for you, for God to heal you, to bring you peace in your heart. I know that not everyone was nice to you. I know that you were sometimes a handful. As some would say, you were an ornery man, but I preferred to make you laugh instead. You were not always truthful either. My spiritual gift of discernment helped me realize when you were fibbing or not because of slight dementia you had. All I wanted was for you to have peace with everyone, for all of us to get along. Somehow it seemed to be that I was the only one that could deal with you and knew how to handle you. In your last months of life, I know that not everyone understood you, Papi. I know that we did not always show you love and appreciation. You were not a loving father like how Mom was with us, even though I am sure you loved us.

Looking back as to how you were raised, it can only explain the way you were. You took after your father. You were cold at times and controlling, but that's all you knew. It was how you were raised. So, I understood how and why you were the way you were. You don't know what you don't know. I can't say that about everyone else, though. I just wished that they saw what I did. You were a man needing love, compassion, empathy, and understanding.

You know, Dad, I am so forever grateful that I had a habit of taking pictures and recording videos. Who would have thought that two years after Mom's death, you would make your transition? Thank you for all the great memories that we had together. Some of those memories were shared among your children. I sometimes come across them on social media.

The videos of you dancing in the van, shopping at Walmart and Carson's and at other stores. The many times we went to the doctor, out to eat, watched your *Telenovelas* (soap operas).

No más un recuerdo queda (only a memory is left), as mom would say. Memories are better when they are good; although, what was meant for evil, God used it for good. Through the good, the bad, and the ugly, you will always be *Mi Niño*. I have something to hold on to. Oh, by the way, you know, I got the clothes you had when you were rushed to the hospital, your shoes, jacket, socks, shirt, and pants. Memories that I will hold dear to my heart and will forever cherish. Now that you are with Mom, I bet that you are now happier than ever, you are no longer seeing Mom suffer, and you can breathe right and are able to feel no more pain. You are having the best life ever.

I am so thankful that it was I that spent the last days with you at Methodist hospital. I can honestly say that God was in control. Thank you for allowing me to anoint your head with oil and pray over you. It was such a relief to hear you ask the Lord to forgive you and that you forgave your children and family. To hear those last words coming from your lips 'Oh God,' God is so good, Papi. I will always speak of you with much respect and honor. Thank you for helping me financially and picking up the kids from school when they were little. Thank you for all the help you provided us with. Thank you for being you.

I know that at times, Teresa, Maria Elena and not sure if it was Eddie or Roger that felt like there was more to our relationship because you helped me, but the Lord knew the truth, and so did Mom. You only helped me because you saw that I sacrificed a fulltime job to be there for you and Mom.

You are now looking from above, giving the okay. Smiling down on us. Emily and Omar will always remember you and love you. You know they were the closest to you. They are still trying to get over your death, Dad. It was very hard for them and still is for Omar 'Omarcito.' So many times they spent with you and Mom. They will remember the times we spent in the hospital and at your home with you. We will always remember the times that we all ate together at the restaurants. Every time we go to the Wheel, we remember what you had to eat, Mom's favorite meal baby back ribs. It was the last time you ate out and the last week you lived here on earth. In fact, we have a picture of you, Em, and me eating lunch there that day.

Wow, Papi, I am so at peace knowing that you are in a better place. I know that we will be together one day, no time soon, I hope. There is never a moment that I don't think about you. May you forever rest in peace.

While I am still growing and learning about life, I will always be your daughter that did all she could do with what she had for you. I may have been your youngest daughter, but I was never a 'daddy's girl,' and I think I know why. As you used to say, "Is okay." All is well with my soul. You will forever live in my heart. I love you with all my heart and soul. God bless you, Papi. Until we meet again only this time, it will be much better.

ABOUT THE AUTHOR

Eve Gómez, is a successful business leader, public figure, media personality, motivational speaker and advocate for the youth, the elderly and a social activist. She is the owner of EG Spanish Interpreting & Consulting, LLC, which provides Spanish translations and interpretation services. Eve also consults agencies and companies on ways to reach the Latino market, offering over 30 years in Customer Service/ Sales experience of those, 12 years as a mortgage consultant. She is also launching a media company this summer, Ethereal Lifestyle. She is a graduate of Leadership Northwest Indiana and an Elder at her church.

Throughout her life, she's has followed her passion by helping people and being a community advocate, especially for the elderly and the youth. For 7 years, she was a talk radio host of "Sound Off with E.V.E." She covered a gamut of global community issues. Eve has been able to make a difference in people's lives. She has also been a Co-Host of "Nuestra Comunidad NWI" since 2008.

She is the Board President of The Crossing School of Business and Entrepreneurship (East Chicago Campus), an alternative school that serves children that are struggling and do not quite fit the traditional school; Secretary of Thea Bowman Leadership Academy, Junior Achievement, to name a few.

As part of what she does, she has been recognized for all her public and humanitarian services. She has received the Distinguished Service Award, Humanitarian Award, Community Service Award, among others. Her heart has won many people's love.

She mentors and empowers groups of individuals, organizations, students and her radio listeners. E.V.E. is working on publishing her first book.

Feel free to stay connected with Eve Gomez on Social Media at:

https://www.facebook.com/eve.gomez.378
www.Instgram.com/officialevegomez
www.twitter.com/officialeveg
www.LinkedIn.com/Evegomez

Forgiving You Has Freed Me

By
Tyrena Richardson

Dear Dad:

I am so relieved to have the opportunity to address some of the issues that have troubled me all of my life, and although you are deceased. I need the closure and to potentially help another young lady who is dealing with the same issues.

My earliest remembrances of you were when my mom would make me come over your mom's house on the 53rd and Thompson Street on the weekends that she had to work, thinking that the time spent with you would be mutually beneficial. I can remember carrying that blue suitcase trimmed in red on the 11 trolley and 52 bus on Friday evening when Mom was off work and begging her to not leave me. I remember her waiting until I had to go to the bathroom and slipping out of the house, only for me to begin hysterically crying at the front door because the one constant in my life (Mom) decided to leave me in a place where I didn't feel welcomed. It was so traumatizing standing at the screen door with my face pressed up against it screaming for my mom to come back for me.

I didn't understand why I was being ignored and didn't have a say. *Why am I being subjected to remain here when I just want to be at home in my safe place with my friends nearby? Why doesn't anyone listen to me?* I remember Aunt Fannie and Uncle Jimmy bringing little Robin (cousin) over so that I would have company and not cry the entire weekend, and then there were times when they would take me to their house to play with her. I never remember you talking to me or wanting to get to know me, but I do remember you trying to discipline me because my quick wit was simply a 'smart mouth' in your eyes. Back then, I didn't understand why there was such a disconnect, especially since you were my biological father. All of my friends either had a relationship with their father because he lived in the home with them, or their daddy took time to develop a special bond by taking them to the park, to the mall to shop or out to eat. It was during this phase in my life that I knew that I was different, and that was not a good thing. Why wasn't I good enough for my dad to love me? Why doesn't he come see me in his truck? What kind of baby must I have been for you to lose interest and walk away from a part of yourself?

As time went on, and I was still dragging and kicking on those Friday evenings, my mom told me that I had to attend child support court with her to tell the judge how I felt about what was happening. And though the sacrifices that she was making were great, she needed help in buying my clothes and shoes, keeping my hair done and the basic essentials that any kid needed in my age group. I remember going inside the courtroom, and your boss from the fireproofing company was there to show your proof of wages, but you were not present. Even at that young age, I felt abandoned emotionally by you, and my thoughts of ever being accepted and cherished by you were shattered. I remember the judge ruling that you had to pay a mere $25.00 weekly (I guess that was a respectable rate for whatever your wages were in the early 1980s), but I also remember that you never made 1 payment. Was it not worth $100.00 a month to ease the burden on my mom? Was it not worth it to ensure that I was taken care of? What could I have possibly done to deserve such treatment that you never looked back to see the scars that appeared?

Looking back now, I can see that I began to build a wall around my heart and my emotions and the mechanism that I used was sarcasm, just enough to keep people from getting close to me. After all, if the person who helped to create my life didn't want to be bothered, how would I know who was genuinely interested and who would stay around because, obviously, I wasn't a nice kid, right? My dad vacated the premises of my heart before I graduated from elementary school, and emotionally, a part of me remained in that stagnant place for years to come. It never dawned on me that one encounter in those formative years of development would eventually shape my opinion of men and my interaction with them. I never fathomed that I would harbor jealousy in my heart for the little girls in my life that would share stories of what they did with their dad. I never thought that I would miss buying cards and gifts for birthdays and father's day, but the little girl in me cried each time those days rolled around. I saw a picture of when I was 3 or 4 years old in an album, and the caption said that you came to visit me on Christmas day and bought me a desk and chair set. Was that the last gift that you ever bought me? Why did you stop?

Mom always reminded me of your birthday on an annual basis. I truly believe that she wanted me to find peace with what had impacted me and move beyond it, a task that seemed impossible to me; after all, the hurt and feelings of abandonment were now part of me, and I clung to them for life as my companions. As I reached the age of 17, Mom and I had a 'tough season,' and she convinced me to put the time behind me and to give you a chance, as I was older.

I reached out to ask if I could come and stay with you for a few months. I can remember moving my bed and a small number of clothes to your house, and since I was finishing high school, which was in walking distance from your house, I hoped to make the best of it. During this time, your daughter Robin was dealing with some of the impediments of life, and we were not getting along, and during one of our altercations, you immediately came to her defense when I was the one who was attacked. I never understood how a parent can choose without hearing the full story or speaking with both children, but it happened, and that was my defining moment to leave the situation that was created by my decision to give you a chance. I withdrew even more and was angry with myself for making myself vulnerable to more hurt. Why couldn't you side with me just once? Why be partial at all since we both carry your blood in our veins?

As I grew into a young woman, I was scared and very afraid to allow myself to date or even consider that a young man would be interested in me. I had heard over the years that one of the amazing blessings that a father gives to his daughter in life is affirmation, and if the relationship with Dad is a positive one, the young lady grows with a strong sense of self as she interacts with male counterparts, she should be very comfortable in her conversations and what she can contribute to a relationship, etc. When I was dropped emotionally, my outer shell became shattered from the impact, and my insides were 'all over the place,' and every now and again, feelings of anger, resentment, and bitterness would emerge. I became sarcastic to a fault, but with so many years of perfecting the protection of my inner shell, the biting words would slip from my tongue as easy as if they were a part of reciting the alphabet.

I grew up physically normal, but the emotional component was so abnormal that I didn't comprehend a young man being flirtatious or 'showing interest' in me, and I placed the one young man who is arguably my 'forever lovebug' in a friend zone because I was clueless by the signals that he exhibited. Just once, Dad, I wish you could have shown me the difference in body language between a man and a woman. I wish you could've told me that I was an AMAZING prize and that any young man would be blessed to have me in their life.

One of my last memories of you was when Mom was in a crisis situation, and I reached out to you because she wanted you to come and see her. I remember to this day calling from the hospital and telling you what was happening and that she was asking to see you. You told me in no uncertain terms that you would not come to see her, and that was that. Your words have never rung louder in my head because that was the last time that I would ever allow you to deny any requests that I made. That was the last time that I would watch you turn your back on me and my mom. I was too young to remember what transpired between the both of you, but I know that it was unfair to make a child pay for the mistakes of the parents. How do you rationalize always saying no? Was there ever a time that you wished that you made a different decision? Were you ever curious to know how you would feel when you made me smile?

On the day that Mom died, I remember some of your siblings asking what they should say to you about her passing. I remember their concern for your feelings, saying that you were on oxygen and that your health was failing, and they didn't want to upset you. I can also recall the anger surging through me in those tense conversations because I had just lost my mom, the only constant in my life, the one who provided for me and sacrificed her basic needs so that I could have. Why would anyone turn it to be about you?

You were the one who rejected us time after time, so why would I care? I made it known that you were not welcome at her service and that any disruption that you may cause would be dealt with. That day went off without a hitch, as I lovingly honored my mom, but your sisters and your beloved daughter Robin were there to support me and to honor Mom's memory. It was eerily strange that just 3 months later, I received the call that you had passed away. I never asked what you passed away from. I never asked if you suffered.

I remember over the years, people would tell me that I would be filled with regret if you passed away without us making amends of our 'relationship,' and yet that did not happen. I remember going to my supervisor and telling him that I needed to use bereavement time because 'the donor' passed away, and I may as well get the paid time off. So, I went to your service, and I sat on the last row in the funeral home, not to pay my last respects but to get the paperwork needed to submit to my job and to support Robin, as she was grieving the loss of her dad.

She shared with me how you guys would do lunch to celebrate birthdays. You attended her graduations and had relationships with her children and grandchildren. I sat on the last row and heard the minister speak about the legacy that you left to your girl(s), and I snickered and commented on how people don't know what to say sometimes at final remarks or the eulogy. I never knew your favorite color. I never knew your favorite song or artist. I only knew that you liked to play golf, and that was a big part of your life. Your passing didn't give me closure, only more questions. This year will be the 5th anniversary, and I have made the decision to push past it all, all of the hurt, pain, disappointment, anger, etc. Your life is over, but I have the opportunity to improve mine and positively impact others.

The great thing that has happened in my life is that although I was raised in the church, it wasn't until my late teen years that I rededicated my life to God, and HE has opened my eyes to many things. He has placed people in my life to see what a loving father-daughter relationship looks like. He has allowed me to see love lived out in successful marriages and that loving gestures of hand-holding and small pecks of kisses in public settings are possible. While spending time with my Heavenly Father, HE is making all things new in my life, and He has shown me that **I must forgive you.**

I no longer desire to embrace those old feelings which cheat me of happiness and the potential of having a man in my life who loves me as he loves Christ. I have endless possibilities before me to learn a new way of thinking. Daily, I am watching what I say and attempting to believe the best of people and that some are coming into my life to genuinely love me, and they show me that I am worthy to receive that love. The 'yoke' inside my hard shell that served as a wall of defense is softening up. My shattered insides are moving into their proper place in my life, and my heart is ready to receive. I wish you were still alive so that you could see that the young lady that you encountered is slowly disappearing, and in her place emerges a strong confident woman full of wonder and intrigue. This new Tyrena laughs more, and she apologizes when she hurts others' feelings. She even believes that she is beautiful.

All of the things that pained me through the years are the same things that I look forward to experiencing, celebrating the men in my life for their accomplishments and some days … just because. I am taking my time to learn the differences in adult men and women, and I seek opportunities to help little girls to never feel as I did. I have been pushing some dads and even some pop-pops to step up in the lives of their daughters and granddaughters to affirm them and show them their worth at a young age so that when a young man comes around, she can decide if she wants to be bothered based on what she knows she will and should accept. It is empowering, it is inspiring, it is liberating on all levels. I watch Dads with their daughters and how they handle them lovingly, and some days I cry for the young me that never experienced any of that. Other days, I sit in wonder of doors that God still has to open in my life. All days, I give thanks that there is strength on the inside of me that pushes me to reach my potential because some of the hardest days that I had to face are behind me.

I can finally say thank you for being the person that God selected to participate in creating my life. I believe that someday, I may be able to speak your name without having to explain the complexities of the relationship. At some point in my life, I will refer to Robert B. as my dad, nothing more, and nothing less. I am on the journey and look forward to that day because I have just made a major stride, I am learning that although the process was to forgive you, it is healing me.

ABOUT THE AUTHOR

Tyrena B. Richardson was born and raised in Philadelphia, PA, and graduated from the Philadelphia Public School system. After attending a few colleges, Tyrena found her niche in Human Resources at Peirce College and has experienced a fulfilling path through the dual role of being a results-driven professional and having various experiences in directly touching lives. Tyrena is currently a solo practitioner as the Human Resources Manager.

Tyrena loves to help others and is also an entrepreneur and the founder of Diversified Consulting Group, LLC, a human resources consulting organization created to meet the need of ensuring compliance and regulatory issues, talent acquisition, and employee relations to companies and small businesses in need. In 2002, she also founded Simple Sentiments, LLC, a specialty gifts company designed to suit the personal or business gift giving needs of individuals, small businesses, and the corporate structure.

Tyrena spends her quality time reading, writing, trying new things and re-engaging in travel. She enjoys having hearty laughs with great friends and the solace found in a spa day.

Tyrena hopes in the future to increase her entrepreneurship by expanding her company Simple Sentiments, LLC, from a home-based business to a boutique. She also dreams of writing her own autobiography in order to inspire and motivate others by showing that them no matter how many or how big the obstacles in your life, you can and will succeed if you keep pushing and striving. Tyrena is presently weighing options to serve on a board of directors to engage, encourage and empower other single women on their journey to self-love.

Feel free to stay connected with Tyrena Richardson on Social Media at:

www.Facebook.com/Tyrena B. Richardson

The Power Of A Father's Faith

By
Cornetta Murray

Dear Dad,

For as long as I can remember, you have always been my rock. I am not saying that Mommy was not good to me, but we had a very special connection. You were the person who thought outside the box. I would never think in a million years that I would be able to live without you after we reconnected in my late teens. I do, however, thank God every day for the years and opportunity he allotted me to spend those precious years together and even give you the opportunity to spend some valuable time with your grandchildren, especially your grandson. I remember as if it was yesterday the night before my departure from you.

"Maureen, come bathe so you can go to bed early" (in a strong Jamaican accent), my adopted sister said. I was excited as I usually was; she would let me play in the bath water and then massage me after she gave me a bath. After my bath, she

116

brought me into the room, and she started telling me that I was going to travel and that I was going to become something big in life. I wondered what she was speaking about. See, my parents never told me they were sending me away because they did not want me to tell anyone at school. I found out the same week I was leaving.

I had my usual rubdown with Vaseline and was given my bedtime tea, which was milo, before being sent off to bed. It is now about 8 p.m. It is pitch-dark outside, and the kerosene lamp was burning bright in the room that I shared with my cousin who I called my sister. I had two adopted sisters, both of them my father's nieces. The house had four bedrooms, my parents stayed in one, my sister in one with her daughter, and the other was locked because that room belonged to my aunt the one that I was supposed to live with in NY. The date still stands out in my head as if it was yesterday. It was December 7th, 1978. My mom and dad woke up super early to take me to a family house because this was the place that I would meet the lady that would take me to the promised land the United States of America (aka 'Foreign'). So, I had to wake up at 2 a.m. so my parents could walk me to this home in Manchester.

We walked about what seemed like 20 miles that morning because we had no transportation, and there was none running at that time. As we walked down, it was pitch-dark at 4 a.m., nothing on the road but scary animals. My dad walking with a flashlight, and my mother holding my hand, walking with me. I swear I saw a man appear in front of me while we were walking in the dark and just disappear. When I asked my parents if they saw the man, they both said no. We just continued on our way; it was about 5 a.m. now, and it was still dark out; my dad always speed-walked, and we had to keep up.

My dad had my little bag that they packed for me. I was happy that I was taking my favorite things with me. At about 5:30 a.m., my heart started feeling really heavy. I started realizing that I was not going to ever have a chance to be with both of my parents ever again as a child. This moment was scary for me. I began to get scared, but I did not say a word.

When we got to our destination at about 5:40 in the morning, the lady who was responsible to take me abroad was already up, making breakfast. She was a very heavy set, light-skinned, beautiful woman with long dark hair. My dad drank a cup of coffee, his favorite thing, and my mother had her tea; they then both said their goodbyes to me and went back on their way up the hill. I was terrified; I could not understand why my little stomach had such a knot in it, but I was excited at the same time to be given the opportunity to travel and become famous. I just knew I was going to be an actress, a lawyer, or a nurse just someone great.

For years, while I was struggling to understand why my parents sent me away, I blamed my parents for the suffering that I endured at the hands of my adopted mother. When I became a mother at the age of fifteen, I then understood the sacrifice my parents had to make. My mother thinking that I blamed her for my life made me aware that it was my father who insisted on sending me away, as he did not want me to suffer. They did not realize that I had to go through what I went through as a child to appreciate what they did for me (as a child). I truly believe that our lives are given to us just the way it was designed; what happens in between depends on the actions we take as we go through the experience that we encounter.

I thank my parents every day for the faith in God they had to have had, to have their only child and sacrifice her for the good of others. For this reason, I feel the need to pay homage to the man who sacrificed everything he had to save his little girl. Dad, I love you "world without end" as you would often tell me when I spoke to you daily. I often told you that I would prefer God take me before you, and you would say to me that I was "speaking foolishness" because that is not how God created life to be. Please accept this as part of the strength that you have given me to live because it has taken a lot of courage to write these words to you.

Dad, if I was sitting in front of you today, I would say I am sorry. I am sorry I did not see the vision for me the way you saw the vision. All I could think of was that I was alone. I never realized that in life, to get anything good, sacrifices have to be made. I could not understand why my parents would send me away and then raised so many other children. It took you years to even conceive me; you were almost fifty years old when I was born. You see, I now know how powerful of a man you were. It is only a strong man that would send his only child, the one he loved and cherished, away because your faith was so strong. You had the faith of a mustard seed; I am proof that you did. You always told me that I could become anything in life that I wanted to become. You told me that you had faith that I would become anything I wanted to be. I am so sorry that I did not trust you enough to do the work that you knew I needed to do before your spirit departed from your body. Gone too soon, long before I got a chance to show you that your sacrifice was not in vain.

I remember like it was yesterday, you made kites for me and flew them high in the sky. I remember you working the ground where you planted your crops with my mother so happily together. On days when I did not go to school, I would follow you and watch you and the men you had working on the field. When returning from the field, you would search for Guava for me to eat, as you knew I loved fruits. During what Jamaicans would call mango season, you would get the best mangoes for me. I would eat so much that I would get sick to my stomach. I got anything I wanted; you would plant ground provisions just for me. Wow!! Unbelievable! I was without want.

On days when we would walk home together either from my primary school or your farm, you would stop and cut off leaves from a certain plant and make a windmill out of it for me. You would make bird traps for me in trees, and we would lay on our backs, waiting on the birds to enter the cages. You would then bring them closer to us so that we could take a closer look at the many birds such as robins, sparrows, hummingbirds, to name a couple, and then you would let them fly away. You then would tell me that we should never keep anything trapped. These moments are priceless, and it brings tears to my eyes, as I wish I could just relive these moments over for just one day. I lived my best life yet with my dad.

As a child growing up in Jamaica, farmer as parents, in a poor community, I never knew that I was poor. I felt privileged. I was not even allowed to walk barefooted something other children did because shoes would only be worn for church and special occasions. I never wanted for anything, Daddy. You provided me with everything I could possibly want, and yet you thought that wasn't enough. You wanted to make sure I received what you did not get in life an education. You saw for me what not even my mother could fathom. You were a man ahead of his time. You always hated when anyone yelled at me. You were my rock, my light and my salvation.

On many occasions, I would sit and reminisce how loving and forgiving you were not only to family but to strangers. You were the counselor to many, and yet they did not know that you could not even sign your name. Because of you, I know that education does not make an individual have substance; one has to be born with it. You taught me that no matter what, I must always respect myself, I am the first to teach someone how to treat me. I must treat everyone with respect even when they do not do the same.

Dad, I want to say thank you; thank you for the memories money can never buy. You gave me unconditional love, a love that burns so deep in my soul. You taught me how to love unconditionally, and in turn, I love my children and everyone's child unconditionally. The love you taught me kept me alive when my spirit should have left my body a million times over since I left your home at eight years old. Because of your unconditional love, I was able to survive sexual abuse, physical abuse, and mental abuse. The love you showed me gave me the strength to strengthen others even when I felt weak. Whenever I found myself in a dark place, that love you gave me pulls me out. I just want to say I love you and thank you for your many lessons.

Thank you for teaching me forgiveness because if it wasn't for the power of forgiveness, I would not be alive today. I was able to forgive the very uncle that molested me. I was able to forgive my cousin for taking advantage of me. I was able to forgive my cousin for having a relationship with my then-boyfriend while she was living in my home. I was able to forgive my adopted mother for the years of physical and emotional pain that she inflicted on me. See, I knew she wanted to break me down the way she was broken down. However, she didn't know that I was protected by my parents' love, no matter where I was on the planet.

After years of not seeing you, I finally reconnected with you after eight long years. I now had a child of my own and had to make a very difficult decision. You did not think twice about helping me with anything; it was as if I never left, and I was still your little girl. You once again became the rock I needed; you did not judge me for any of my past. You just wanted to find out how you could help me.

Dad, you loved me, despite being a disappointment at least I thought I was because I became a teen mother. You never once said why didn't you finish school. You just showed me love and showed your granddaughter love. You and mommy kept my daughter for eight months without criticism or judgment when I had to get myself together. You never made me feel bad about myself. Wow! That is love.

When I was able to bring you to the United States to visit me, we would sit and have long conversations about how I should be treated by any man. I was still your little girl with now three children of my own. You made me aware of what love should feel like from a man and that it is not about making babies or sex. You explained to me that a man should always respect, protect and provide for his woman, even if she doesn't have a child for him. Those conversations were priceless. Because of your guidance, I now will not accept nothing but the best in my life. I love unconditionally because you told me that it is the only way to love.

The conversations that we had and the quotes that you would quote made me believe you had your doctorate. One of your favorite quotes was from the Bible, John 3:16 "For God so loved the world, that he gave his only begotten son, that whosoever believeth in him should have everlasting life and not perish." Can you imagine how surprised I was when I found out that you could not even sign your name? Yet your genius was of Einstein.

You made me realize that education does not make a person; what they possess in their heart and mind is what really matters. Dad, because of your guidance, my children are being raised better than I would have ever thought in a million years. I am most grateful that you had the opportunity to spend some valuable years with my son, your grandson, and he found out how great of a person you were. He really cherishes those moments he spent with you. In his word, he stated that those times was 'priceless.'

I cannot explain the gaping hole I feel in my stomach every time I speak to Mommy and want to speak to you just to realize that you are not around. It is unexplainable. Memorial weekend is really a weekend for me to reminisce about your love, as that was when you left me. Father's Day will never be the same, as I had to lay you down at your final resting place. Just like how you planned and calculated everything in life, I believe you planned and calculated your going home dates. I appreciate you for your thoughtfulness. I will never forget you, as memorial weekend is a weekend I will always celebrate your life, and Father's Day, I will always remember how great of a father you were.

Dad or Papa, whichever one you would like me to call you these days, I will honor you and pay homage to you by building a school in your memory. I will honor you by continuing your mission of serving and giving unconditionally to as many as possible. The day that I laid you to rest, I submitted my capstone for my Master's in Social Work. I now have two master's degrees and am currently working on my doctorate. I do know that education does not make a person, but I do know that it was your dream for me to acquire what you did not get the opportunity to acquire because you spent your youth taking care of your mother and siblings. I thank you for giving me the opportunity to accomplish all that I did. The strength that you gave me allowed me to survive on my own for over three years when I ran away from my home in New York, when I was only fifteen, until I was able to connect with you.

Dad, you had a vision like no one had. I now know that through your faith, I can achieve anything in life. Dad, you have raised many children, and they all speak very highly of you. Whenever I speak to one of your nieces or nephews, they say that you were a great uncle, and friends would say that you were a great man.

I would like to ask all and any man who wishes to become a father to be an example of what you would like your child to be. My father was a farmer with no education, yet the abundance that he gave me by giving of himself could not be bought. Do not ever think that you need money to spend time with your children; time lost cannot be replaced. The time that we are living in, our children need their father in their lives. Please talk to your children, love them unconditionally, no judgment. Guide them, protect them, and they will be exactly what you pray for them to be without you even telling them. Be the example of how you want them to be. Action speaks louder than words.

Dad, no one can never fill that void that I felt after losing you. To the world, you were just a man, but to me, you were my world. I know you protect me daily. At times, I feel your presence, and when I feel confused or weak, I just ask myself, What would daddy do? I get the answer that I seek. I miss your warm smile, your hugs, and your caring demeanor. I love you world without end, to infinity and beyond until we meet again.

ABOUT THE AUTHOR

 Cornetta Murray born (Cornetta Thompson) in Jamaica, West Indies, as the only child of her parents. At age seven, they decided to send her to the United States to live with relatives to further her education.

Ms. Murray is the mother of four children and the founder of TOBBFuture, an empowerment program located in Far Rockaway, Queens, New York. She currently works as a school social worker and has been an Army reservist for the last seventeen years. She has a Master's in Social Work and a Master's in Education. She is currently working on her first book, *The Faith of a father*, scheduled to be released on January 26, 2019. She is also a master facilitator, conducting workshops on empowering your child. Her future plans is to continue writing books about her journey and to build the first charter school in Jamaica, W.I.

Feel free to stay connected with Cornetta Murray on Social Media at:

www.Facebook.com/TOBBFuture
www.Instgram.com/TobbFuture
https://twitter.com/TobbFuture
https://www.linkedin.com/in/cornetta-murray-643a97101/
www.Tobbfuture.com

Inner Peace

By
Vanessa Canteberry

Dear Dad,

There are times when I wonder what the definitions of a dad and father are because I really didn't get a chance to know you like my brothers had a chance to know you.

It was painful to see that on a consistent basis, you would come to the house and pick up my brothers and spend time with them on the weekend but didn't pick me up, or you would make promises to do things with all of us together but rarely showed up. I always wondered, did you ever want a daughter? Did I do something wrong? Was I not pretty enough? Did I not look like you well enough or have any of your traits?

I resented both of my parents because, for many reasons, with the ongoing issues you two displayed, Dad, you forgot one of the most important things was sitting right in front of you. I never got a chance to form that relationship, that bond with you, let alone to get to know your birthday or your favorite color. Do you have a favorite color?

I remember when I was a little girl, and something was going on, where I had to go live with my teachers for an entire year, and I didn't see you at all. I had to stay with my teachers who showed me love. I had a warm place to stay, had food on the table and never had to worry about where I was going to lay my head. I never heard from either one of my parents and thought I would never see you again, even though I didn't see you much.

The moments that I was surprised at school with both of my parents coming to see me was the day that I had to move back home with my mom. I remember you giving me a couple of dollars, and I thought to myself, *We are back on track.* When you surprised me at school, you hugged me and told me that you loved me, but then you disappeared again. For years, I struggled with this habit you created in me.

Now that I am older and have children, I never want my children to feel the pain of having their grandfather treat them and do them the same way I was treated. I remember sitting down with you and having a conversation just to get a better understanding of you. I expressed how important it is for you to be involved in your grandchildren's life so they could be able to get to know and love you better than I got a chance to love you, even though I'm open to getting to know you, and you agreed. I thought our slate was clean.

I remember coming to your house with the children, and it

was your birthday. All I remember is, it was March, and we sat down and had a deep conversation, and then I saw how you interacted with my children. It was the happiest day of my life, just seeing my children smile and giggle with their grandfather but it was short-lived

I have to take some time out to do some soul-searching to find out why you are distant. Are you distant with me alone, or are you just the distant person? Why are you like this? Sometimes I blame myself because I can't seem to really understand it. With me being the first daughter, yet I don't get it. I still sometimes I ask myself the same question, did you ever want me? Because, before me, there were two boys, and they knew you, spent time with you, but I didn't spend as much time with you as they did.

But then once I learned more about my grandparents and got to learn a little bit more about the history of their relationship, I started to understand a little bit more why you are so distant and why you didn't spend some quality time with me.

Becoming a teen mom, I needed you. Being in an abusive relationship, I needed you. In making better decisions in relationships, I needed you. When I needed the advice of a man, I needed it from you.

I understand both my parents were young when they got together, and they both come from broken homes. They had children early on in the marriage and didn't have the opportunity to truly work on themselves; therefore, you all had to roll with us but at the same time left us. You left us with the pain that you were afraid of facing the questions that went unanswered. We were left to feel that way, at least I did feel that way.

Those moments actually made me understand the broken homes of my parents, their dysfunctional relationship with my grandparents. Dad, I understand that what transpired in your life is as a result of the foundation it was laid upon, which made it appear as though it was OK to go through such.

You taught me more about men in ways you were never thought, and I had to unravel what you taught me. Now I can show my children the best way I know a woman can get her brokenness mended. I also don't have to see my children the way I saw you. The greatest thing I did for myself was to forgive my parents because I came to understand that they were not strong enough to overcome the turmoil that broke them.

Dad, the last time I saw you was at my brother's funeral, and prior to that, we hadn't seen you for 4 to 5 years, and now, years later, I still have not seen you, but I'm already used to the disappearing acts, thank you. I thank you for allowing me to be able to see the world much clearer through your eyes, which made me understand that the storm doesn't last always and that with hope and faith, I am able to accomplish a lot of things. Now I am able to pass something different and even better to my children and my grandchildren. I understand that I have to go and make a name for myself and build a legacy that my children will be proud to look back at and see that their mother broke the generational curse. Being an adult, I look at things differently, and I had to let a lot of pain and questions go so it can no longer consume me.

Men, show up, no matter how much you have in your pocket, no matter your attire or means of transportation. Go see your children. Show up, no matter the relationship that you have with the child's mother, no matter where your headspace is. Show up, even if it's just for a hug, because time is something that you cannot get back.

I understand that I needed to accept the cards that were dealt, but at the same time, it caused so much confusion in my life to the point that dead-end situations continued to be present in my life. I had to make bold decisions that others couldn't understand in order for me to get through the wall that seemed to have surrounded me due to the poor choices I was making.

Maybe you felt you were protecting me, Dad, but instead, sometimes I wish I was educated. Still, in all, I've grown to accept you for who you are; your capabilities to be a stand-up dad was null and void.

With that being said, it boils down to the question, "What do I really call you? Dad or Father?" I prefer calling you your first name because I truly never really got a fair chance to get to know what to call you either.

I'm proud of the inner peace I have found, accepting circumstances for what they are. We tend to point at others but truly never check the fingers pointing back at us. I had to check the fingers so I can make better decisions what I need to hold onto and those things I need to let go of. I'm proud to say that it's no longer in my hands, as I have turned it over to my Heavenly Father above.

In retrospect, I must say I was honored with the privilege of having the presence of a dad, and even though it was for a short moment, he instilled so much that I continue to be grateful for. He made me understand how a dad protects their children through his actions. He taught me how to be responsible and to appreciate family. Even though things did not work out with my mom and him, he always made sure he checked in and let me know about the power of prayer. I will be always grateful and honored to call him my dad.

ABOUT THE COMPILER

 Vanessa Canteberry is the Founder and CEO of InspiredByVanessa. She was born and raised in Chicago, Illinois. She's determined to continue to break the cycle of poverty, negligence, and unnecessary hardship. Vanessa worked in Corporate America for 20 years as a Secretary. After being laid off in 2011, she knew something needed to change, knowing she was a single parent of three. Vanessa was not able to obtain employment, and the mere thought of being unable to support her son attending high school and two daughters attending college was unbearable.

For that reason, Vanessa challenged herself. She took a stand of faith and changed her mindset. She's on a mission to educate individuals on the importance of transformation of the W2 mindset in life and business. Now, she is a business owner, speaker, mindset coach, co-host on Motivate Social Podcast, and best-selling author working from the comfort of her home. She is also committed to teaching individuals how they, too, can become a business owner and overcome obstacles in their lives.

Your past does not determine your destiny; make what seems impossible possible. InspiredByVanessa stands on FAITH and refuses to allow FEAR to void VISIONS that need to be seen and heard on so many platforms. She teaches you that you are more than a W2.

Vanessa is the Best Selling Author of *Shifting Your Mindset* and *Breaking the Cycle of Brokenness*, co-author of *I Am More Than, Do I Not Matter* and the Compiler of the anthology *Cries of a Broken Man and Screams of a Broken Woman*.

Feel free to stay connected with Vanessa Canteberry on Social Media at:

www.Facebook.com/InspireVanessa
www.Instagram.com/InspiredByVanessa
www.Twitter.com/InspireVanessa
www.LinkedIn.com/in/VanessaCanteberry
http://www.InspiredByVanessa.com

Acknowledgment

To all the authors, from the bottom of my heart, I say thank you. Thank you for sharing your transparent stories of your dads. Some may have been easier than others, but still, in all, we are helping somebody else with our stories.

Thank you for trusting the vision of this collaboration God has given me. I will be forever grateful.

Much respect,
Vanessa Canteberry

www.ingramcontent.com/pod-product-compliance
Lightning Source LLC
Chambersburg PA
CBHW051305250626
47155CB00009B/3438